This book is dedicated to
Robert Clay Glancy
1927–2003

My Friend
Promoted and transferred Home
Resting in Peace

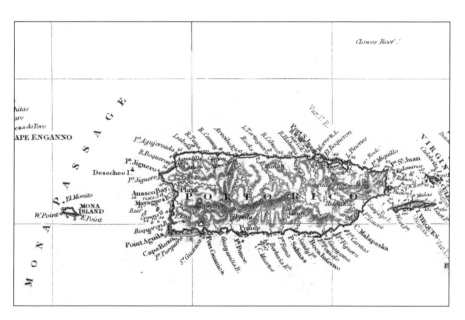

Puerto Rico, Spanish Empire
—from an original 1860 chart

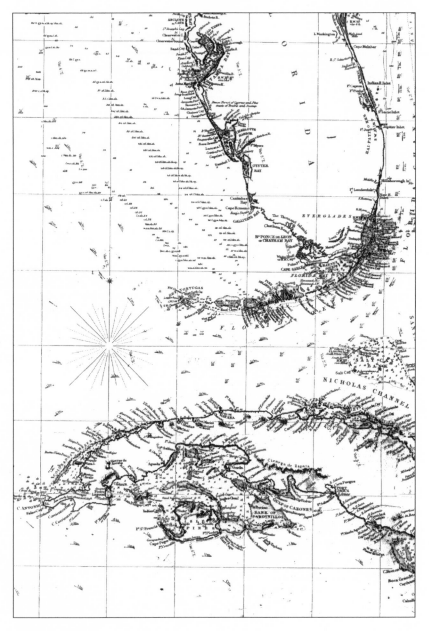

The Lower Florida and Western Cuba area of operations for the
U.S.N.'s East Gulf Blockading Squadron
—*from an original 1860 chart*

HONORABLE MENTION

the continuing exploits of
Lt. Peter Wake
United States Navy

Robert N. Macomber

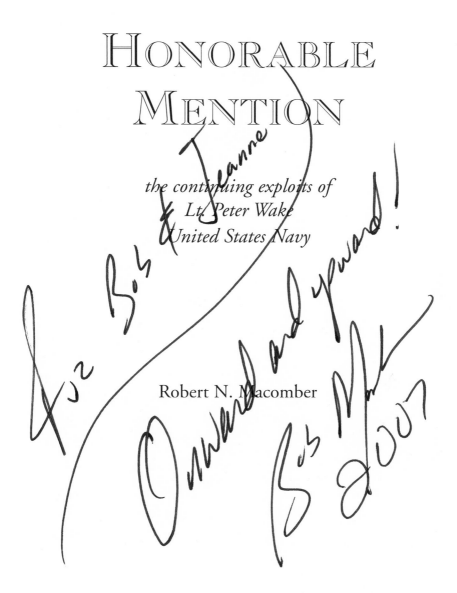

Pineapple Press, Inc.
Sarasota, Florida

Inquiries should be addressed to:
Pineapple Press, Inc.
P.O. Box 3889
Sarasota, Florida 34230
www.pineapplepress.com

Library of Congress Cataloging-in-Publication Data

Macomber, Robert N., 1953–
  Honorable mention / by Robert N. Macomber.
    p. cm.
  ISBN 1-56164-311-4 (alk. paper)
1. Wake, Peter (Fictitious character)—Fiction. 2. United States—History,
Naval—19th century—Fiction. 3. Florida—History—Civil War, 1861–1865—
Fiction. 4. United States. Navy —Officers—Fiction. 5. Americans—Bahamas—
Fiction. 6. Americans—Cuba—Fiction. 7. Bahamas—Fiction. 8. Cuba—Fiction.
I. Title.
  PS3613.A28H66 2004
  813'.6—dc22
                                                            2004004542

First Edition
10 9 8 7 6 5 4 3 2 1

Design by Shé Heaton Composition by Ramonda Talkie
Printed in the United States of America

Preface

It is October of 1864, and Lieutenant Peter Wake has been in the United States Navy for eighteen months since he reluctantly volunteered and was immediately assigned to the East Gulf Blockading Squadron based in Key West, Florida. In that time, Wake, a third generation New England schoonerman, has learned about leading men in combat and the consequences of wartime decisions. At first commanding the small armed sloop *Rosalie*, and subsequently the schooner *St. James*, Wake has spent most of his duty along the coast of Florida, in the dirty and frustrating work of close inshore patrol, where the difference between friend and foe in a civil war can be elusive.

Since this squadron operates in such close proximity to the empires of Spain, Great Britain, and France, Wake has also experienced some international intrigue. Demonstrating a flair for initiative that came to the attention of the squadron's admiral, Wake has been given the unusual and difficult tasks of gathering intelligence in Cuba and the Bahamas about the blockade runners and their organizations—missions completed with his customary thoroughness.

But Peter Wake's experiences in this tropical site of the war have embraced more than conflict and intrigue with the Confederate enemy. Inadvertently, he found the love of his life in Linda Donahue, daughter of a staunch pro-Confederate family in Key West. Ostracized by both sides of the war, they have nevertheless boldly married, with Linda now living in an isolated pro-Union refugee camp at Useppa Island up on the southwest coast of the peninsula.

In spite of all these problems, both personal and professional, Peter Wake is not content to merely do his duty and wait for events to unfold. Wake is the type that makes his own luck. This translates to victories which gain Wake a reputation for action within the squadron and the notice of certain quarters in

Washington. His experiences also persuade him that the life of a naval officer is his natural calling, and he makes the fateful decision to make the U.S. Navy his life's profession. Success translates into a tangible reward when Wake, originally a volunteer for the duration of the war with a temporary officer's commission, receives the rare compliment of a regular commission in the United States Navy. He knows that his career won't be easy, since, unlike most of the regular junior officers around him, he did not graduate from the naval academy. But Wake also knows that results outweigh pedigrees, and he is a born leader of sailors who can get the job done.

Eventful as the past eighteen months have been, the next fifteen promise to bring even more action, intrigue, challenges, and victories. Lieutenant Wake has been given command of an armed ocean steam tug, the U.S.S. *Hunt*, which will require this lifelong canvas sailor to learn and master the new technology that is transforming the navy.

Wake's love for Linda, his anchor of normalcy, deepens with their marriage and the inevitable responsibilities that come with it. He is no longer a man alone in the world, and his every decision now affects more than the lives of the men of the *Hunt*.

Wake will encounter war in ways he has not previously seen or even imagined—from the chaos of a defeated society falling into anarchy, to the depths of an inhuman hell that some men inflict savagely upon others. And then, just when the seemingly endless war appears to be drawing to an end, the ultimate battle nightmare begins to come true for the unprepared squadron. Lieutenant Peter Wake, U.S.N., will need all his skill and strength to overcome what is dead ahead.

Stand to. It's time to steam into harm's way with Peter Wake once again.

—Bob Macomber
Off the coast of Florida
15 June 2004

1

Exigencies of War

Lieutenant Peter Wake, newly appointed commanding officer of the United States Navy armed steam tug *Hunt*, could sense the tension in the humid October air around him. As he passed the young Marine sentry at the front doorway to the Naval Headquarters he could see the fear in the eyes of the men and hear it in their strained voices. They could stop the Rebel threat, but they were powerless against sickness and storm, and it scared them. Wake understood that completely. It scared him too.

The squadron, devastated by yellow fever for the previous two months, had many ships dangerously shorthanded. Washington's demands to keep the blockade tight and also assist the army in its coastal raids had become absurd. Many ships' crews were too sick even to weigh anchor, much less enforce a blockade, and weathering a hurricane was not even a question if the crew was too weak to work the ship. But Wake knew that the national election was pressuring Secretary of the Navy Welles to provide more victories like Farragut's at Mobile Bay, for 1864 looked to be the crucial year to determine the political will of the Union. Lincoln was campaigning for the total defeat of the

Confederate states and needed to show the weary people of the North it could come soon. The fevers and storms of Florida were not considered valid excuses for failure.

Wake made his way through the outer rooms and into the moldy warren of the squadron's clerical staff. Exhausted, uniform soaked with sweat, he felt unprepared as he walked toward the insignificant-looking den of one of the most powerful men in the squadron. Wake would have preferred to face a Rebel cannon than fight the bureaucratic battle of wills he was about to enter. He slowed his gait and considered the factors.

The situation of Wake's ship was desperate, and therefore, *he* was desperate, or he wouldn't have come to this office. Instead of raw courage, this battle would take the skill of a poker player, he counseled himself as he stopped short of his destination. He heard heated words within. They confirmed his worst fears, and he covertly looked around the corner at the confrontation inside. "Kindly do not confuse your rank . . . with my *authority*, sir. The answer is still no, sir. You cannot get those men for your ship. They are allocated for another."

The yeoman's words were weighted with fatigue, even though it was but one o'clock in the afternoon. From his vantage point in the doorway, Wake saw the effect this statement had on the lieutenant standing in front of the chief yeoman's desk.

But Wake could see that it was more than just the senior enlisted man's words to the officer. Delacroix Yves DeTar, chief yeoman on the admiral's staff of the United States Navy's East Gulf Blockading Squadron in Key West, had not even looked up from his ledger when he made his comment, which aggravated the message. The scene was even more incongruous with DeTar sitting down in his shirt-sleeves behind his battered and paper-covered desk, while the lieutenant was in full uniform. The final spice to the statement came with DeTar's softly drawled Virginia tidewater accent, an aspect slightly unsettling to some in the Union Navy—but DeTar was a veteran of twenty years of naval service and loyal to the Stars and Stripes, a point he had proven to a number of men in barrooms over these last three years of civil war.

The officer, a man Wake knew only as the commander of a newly arrived large schooner in the squadron, reacted to DeTar's words as if he were having some sort of seizure, for a moment the commander looked as if he might reach across the desk to strangle the petty officer sitting there who made such a statement to a commissioned officer—not to mention the captain of a naval vessel. The lieutenant's face contorted and turned a dark hue of red, while his eyes opened widely and glared at DeTar.

"Confound it all, man! Did I just hear gross insubordination to a superior officer, Yeoman? Aside from the manning issue that I am here to solve, *kindly* tell me why I should not have you brought up on charges immediately! Or perhaps a little sea time on a working, fighting, schooner would be more appropriate, especially since we are so short of *experienced* men such as yourself?"

Wake observed that the chief petty officer didn't flinch at hearing such dire threats. DeTar looked bored as he put down his pencil and ledger and stood up to face his accuser, slightly nodding in Wake's direction to acknowledge his arrival in the doorway. DeTar was not a large man, but when he stood to speak the room appeared to diminish in volume, an illusionary effect, Wake was sure, that came from his bearing and not his size.

"Lieutenant Martin . . . I am under personal orders from the *admiral* commanding the East Gulf Blockading Squadron himself, to prioritize assignments of personnel according to *his* wishes, and not to be induced or coerced by anyone, including lieutenants who refuse to understand the squadron-wide factors involved. Now, sir, if you would care to make that charge of insubordination, then the squadron chief of staff's office is in the next building. I can show you the way right now, sir, since you are so new to the squadron.

"However, Lieutenant Martin, I should add before we go there, that number one—I was simply explaining that my authority comes personally from the admiral and therefore your rank cannot override it. Number two—I did render the proper respect due your rank and say 'sir.' And number three—your making a complaint such as this would merely show the admiral that I am doing precisely as I have been ordered, and thus be beneficial for me. The effect for you, however, might not be so positive.

"And oh . . . *sir,* the admiral will not allow me to serve on a schooner, or any other ship on the blockade. He feels that I am needed right here, working for him, trying to solve the manning requirements of the many ships under his command."

Lieutenant Martin, recently of the blockading forces in the Chesapeake Bay region, was stunned. He backed a step away from the desk, his eyes continuing to stare at DeTar, his head shaking slowly as if to clear something from his mind. Martin's voice had lost its edge when he finally spoke. He sounded incredulous at being refused his request for more trained seamen.

"Well, I'll be damned, you've got me stammered, Yeoman. Damn your hide if you ain't taken my wind. No men to man the vessels—not a single one, you say! An inexcusable situation. Never heard of that kind of thing in my last squadron. In fact, in all my days in the Navy I have never seen or heard such a thing as that."

DeTar smiled pleasantly at the lieutenant, his next words coming out almost paternally, especially couched in his accent. "Lieutenant Martin, I'm sure you haven't seen anything like it here. I've been in this navy, man and boy, for over twenty years, and *I* haven't seen anything quite like it myself, sir. This squadron is at the tail end of everything, from supplies and equipment, to coal, to ships and men. Key West is the end of the world, Lieutenant, and you are now a thousand miles from that last squadron. Welcome to your new home."Martin didn't reply, so Chief Yeoman DeTar went on. "Now, how about you let me work on this manning problem with your schooner, sir? I'll send a messenger boy to you in a while with what information I can find. It won't be all you need, or very many at all, but maybe I can find you one or two if they become available in a few weeks."

Martin just shook his head again—not angrily but in wonderment. As he turned and left the Spartan room filled with boxes and filing cabinets, he cast a quizzical look at Wake, mumbled something, and walked down the hallway still talking to himself.

Wake stepped into the room and smiled as he greeted the petty officer. "Well, good morning, Chief Yeoman DeTar. I take it from what I just saw that you are having a particularly vexing day today."

"Aye, sir. No rest for the weary, and I'm feeling pretty weary already today. They always have the same complaints, and the same threats if they don't get their way. Makes one hope for at least a novel threat. No innovation anymore, sir. No interesting coercion that could stimulate a man's mind with the complexity of it. No, just the age-old blunt instrument of insubordination or sea duty. Boring, sir."

Wake laughed at the ridiculous notion of lamenting the lack of intriguing threats from superiors. DeTar was one of a kind, even in the arcane world of navy yeomen.

"You really are a renaissance man, Chief Yeoman DeTar. You need more Machiavellian challenges, don't you? A true gentleman, misassigned to this backwater of the navy. I cannot imagine what they were thinking in Washington. You could have had some very interesting challenges there. Why, I'd wager you could have been Gideon Welles' right-hand man. The secretary of the navy needs a man like you." DeTar nodded thoughtfully at that idea. "Captain Wake, I believe that I could do old Gideon a valuable service in Washington—the petty officer assignments at the Bureau of Navigation could certainly use some semblance of logic to them. In fact, at the beginning of this sad war I was at the navy yard there. Following that damnable affair at Sumter I immediately gave some wise but unappreciated suggestions to my section officer about which Southern officers to retain—and found myself gone the next day. Been stuck in this fever hole ever since. Ordered me to write my own orders, those crass naves did. They took some joy in that, I could tell. Obviously, they wanted to get this non-commissioned true gentleman—an oxymoron according to the navy—out of their sight. I believe that the location of my birth had more than a slightly prejudicial effect in the matter. But you are a busy man, sir, and must need my services for some weighty issue. How can I help you?"

Wondering for a brief moment what really had happened in Washington between the educated Southern-born petty officer and the entrenched naval leaders, Wake nodded his agreement that he was there for some assistance. He proceeded with his request, pulling out of his inside coat pocket a damp sheet of paper—authorization from the squadron chief of staff to draw any available men from the naval station.

"Same as every other ship captain, Chief Yeoman. I need men for the *Hunt*. I've been ordered to sea and have the authorization here from the chief of staff to draw some replacement men if any are available. Of course, now that I've been assigned to a steamer, I need some different kind of men than I usually ask for."

DeTar sat down and motioned Wake to the chair in front of his desk, his familiarity an apparent lack of respect, but actually quite the opposite. He liked Wake and his dry humor, and he respected Wake's considerable record so far in the war in Florida. Peter Wake had made a name for himself by being decisive and innovative. The whole squadron had heard of him. An experienced New England schooner mate, Wake had become a naval volunteer officer a year and a half earlier, in April of 1863. Since that time, Wake had shown himself to be a very capable small ship captain, and in January of this year had been given a rare promotion from volunteer master to a regular commission as a lieutenant. DeTar had personally written the admiral's recommendation to Secretary of the Navy Welles and knew the details, some of which were secret, of what Wake had accomplished. It included some intriguing missions to Cuba and the Bahamas that very few men in the navy knew about.

In addition to being the type of man who got things done against the enemy, Wake also was known as the type of ship commander who cared about his men, and one of the few who actually had men asking to serve under him. DeTar was glad that Wake got the regular commission and was going to make the navy his life's career—they could definitely use some decent officers. That Wake was respected by the senior petty officers of the squadron was a rare compliment. DeTar didn't know of many in that category.

"Captain, please sit down and let's see what we can do. What exactly do you need?"

"Well, Bosun Rork advises that for the deck we need six more ordinary seamen, two able seamen, and a landsman or two. Gunner Durlon requests two quarter gunners. My engineer officer needs three coal heavers and a fireman or boiler tender. And I need a yeoman clerk—the records and reports in this new command are twice what I had on the *St. James.*"

"I see, sir. You need quite a few men."

"The yellow fever that went through the *Hunt* before I got her absolutely ravaged the crew. We're very short on the assigned complement and I need far more than what I've said here this morning—but I know how short the squadron is, especially right now with the fever rampant, and there's no sense in requesting men who aren't there."

DeTar smiled and raised a thin finger slightly for emphasis in his acknowledgement. "Most correct, Captain. A realistic understanding of the situation that I wish more captains displayed, sir."

DeTar opened the desk drawer by his right knee and extracted three file folders marked "Deck," "Gunnery," and "Steam Mechanics." Spreading each open on top of his desk, he ran his finger down the lists of men written on the reports. The chief yeoman pursed his lips and sighed as he looked up from his lists of available manpower.

"Now we are very short, of course, because that yellow jack

hit this whole damned squadron in the last three months. Some of the ships are in worse condition than your *Hunt,* sir. Did you hear about the *Chambers?* Almost all of them dead or dying. Sent her up to Philadelphia."

Wake had heard all about the schooner *Chambers.* Two months over three quarters of her crew were sick, dying, or dead of yellow jack. "I heard about her. Have there been any drafts of new men from up North lately? I haven't heard of any."

"No, that rare blessed event hasn't happened lately. Last one was five months ago in May. Not a lot of folks volunteering to come down into the fever squadron, and Admiral Farragut's gotten the last two drafts of men since May that were originally headed here. Our admiral was not happy about that, I can tell you, but who can compete with Farragut? Man's got more newspaper correspondents with him than we have ships! 'Most famous sailor in the nation,' they call him. And us? We're famous for having that damned fever worse than any other squadron."

Wake was tiring of DeTar's rambling and couldn't care less about Farragut's newspaper image. This meeting wasn't successful at all so far, but perhaps the old veteran petty officer could find him some men somewhere. Wake knew that he had to be patient. There were a few men in the squadron with importance beyond their apparent rank or position, and DeTar was one of them. Suddenly the chief yeoman's brows furrowed and he looked at Wake with a nod.

"Yellow jack . . . hmm, let me peruse that sick list." He pulled another folder from the drawer. "Ah ha! I thought so. A hidden treasure trove just for you, sir. I *do* have some sailors coming out of the marine hospital who have recovered from the fever. Surgeons there have promised that these boys will live to fight and die for their country. Four seamen—ordinary seamen, I believe. Let that Irish pirate of a bosun, Rork, know he owes me one for sending him these four, sir."

DeTar paused a moment to revel in his triumph of finding seamen for Wake, then he plunged into a further reply to the request for more men. "No able seamen available for you though, sir, Captain Nickerson got the last of them. As for the gunners, I'm afraid that my old friend Durlon is out of luck—none unassigned in the squadron. We have three in the hospital but they're not on the surgeons' release list. I'll keep an eye on one of those just for the *Hunt,* though, sir, and let you know when he's available—if they live."

Wake nodded, thankful that he was getting at least a few men to help work the ship. "Thank you, Chief Yeoman. I'll certainly pass that along to Rork and remind him on the next shore liberty to look you up."

DeTar laughed and held both his hands up.

"Well, sir, please tell him to stop by *here* to find me. I am most definitely not going down to that poxy trollop-hole the squadron's bosuns languish in. Yeoman have standards, sir, and we do not frequent establishments of that sort."

Wake laughed too at the thought of a yeoman walking into the Anchor Inn and emerging unscathed. DeTar got back to the business at hand, frowning as he continued.

"And speaking of yeomen, sir, there aren't any of those available either. All are assigned to the larger ships. I don't even have enough here at the squadron offices to do our work. I am sorry, Captain Wake, I wish I could find you one."

Wake hadn't held much hope for obtaining a yeoman, and nodded his appreciation for DeTar's comment.

"About the steam mechanic people, sir. I do have a coal heaver named Chard who is six months past his enlistment and raising all Cain to be returned to his station of recruitment. Boston, of all places. Well, sir, the lad isn't going to Boston. He'll be lucky to get to a vessel bound for Charleston or Norfolk. He just might ship over for another enlistment if your engineer was to ask him and say it was your ship. His last captain put him ashore and he's doing duty at the station boiler shop by the wharf until he gets a transit north. Worth a try there, sir."

Wake pondered it all for a moment. He had authorization to

obtain replacements for open billets aboard his ship. Knowing that he could never get a full complement, he had asked for the minimum needed to work and fight the ship, as requested by his ship's subordinate leadership. That amounted to seventeen men—or a third of his allowed complement. He was receiving five. He set his jaw and looked at DeTar.

"Any hidden away, Chief Yeoman? You know I won't waste them. I've got a steamer now and suspect I'll be even a bit more busy than I have been in the past. Any man sent to me will be used well."

DeTar sighed again and smiled. He knew what was in Wake's mind. "Captain, I know that. I wish I could send you more, but I have thirty-three ships to man. I've got to keep some available for the others as well. All the captains are having to go short now, with the men doing double duty on the muster bills in order to work and fight the ships. The whole squadron is in the same situation, sir. I've heard the other squadrons have similar problems, but I think ours are the worst."

Wake knew it was time to take what he could and be thankful. He stood and offered his hand, which DeTar took while speaking in his slow soft manner. "Good luck, Captain. With Rork and Durlon aboard you're already well manned. I'm looking forward to hearing what endeavors you'll accomplish with that steamer."

"Thank you, Chief Yeoman DeTar. As always, a stimulating conversation and a productive visit. I appreciate that you were able to get me any men at all in these difficult times."

As Wake turned to leave he saw another officer in the hallway by the door. It was Lieutenant Jeff Nibarger, commander of the *Sullivan,* and he had the same worried mien that Wake had had when he had arrived at DeTar's office.

"Good luck, Jeff," said Wake to his friend as he strode down the hall and out the building, glad to be in the sunshine and fresh air after the damp, musty windowless room. Wake marveled that DeTar's office smelled just like below decks in a ship—even having the same navy-issue lanterns with their distinctive rancid-smelling oil.

The walk to the officers' landing was short, but long enough for him to think through his manning problems and realize that he needed to have a meeting with his officers and petty officers immediately upon returning to the ship. Wake would give them the grim news, and together they would find a way to ready the *Hunt* for sea, and work and fight with what they had.

The officers' harbor launch was already crowded, but they waited for Wake to clamber aboard. Today the steamer *Marigold* had the duty of providing the harbor launch. The sweating sailors strained at their oars with their eyes gazing aft at the water as the launch's coxswain steered to the various ships according to the seniority of the officers present. Wake, as a lieutenant, was taken to his ship before the two masters and the one ensign—but after the lieutenant commander of the gunboat *Sagamore* and a senior lieutenant from the steamer *Proteus.*

The sun was starting its descent when they turned toward the *Hunt,* anchored on the far side of the harbor, and headed for her. Wake surveyed her as they came closer. She was unlike any other vessel he had ever sailed in, much less commanded. Objectively as he could, he reviewed her characteristics as he examined the ship.

The *Hunt* was a screw steam tug, brought into naval service six months earlier at Philadelphia, where she had been built in '59. Because she had a draft of only six feet for her eighty-five-foot length, she was ideal for the shallow waters of Florida, and in a rare logical decision from Washington, she was actually sent to the squadron based there. Upon her arrival she was armed with two twelve-pounder howitzers that were placed on her foredeck and amidships, abaft her stack.

Wake thought about that stack. It was a tall stack and made her look ungainly, to his sailing man's eye. That stack produced a belching cloud of cinders and ash that befouled the deck and threatened to ignite the rigging of her two masts. Not a sail was bent to those masts, they were meant for signals and for hauling cargo aboard. The only sail on the ship was a steadying sail for dangerous weather. Wake hadn't been in that type of weather on her but could imagine the shallow hull rolling perilously without the balance of real sails. He wondered if the steadying sail really helped.

She was so different from what he was used to in his years at sea. Her reason for being was located within her hull—her steam engine. It took tons of filthy coal to feed that engine so it would make the steam to enable her to travel, and it took almost twenty officers and men just in that department of the ship to keep her steam engine running.

From the assistant engineer officer in charge of the operations of the steam machinery, to the firemen who tended the boilers, to the coal heavers who fed the monster, those men were all a completely different breed. They weren't like real sailors. They lived and worked below decks in the suffocatingly hot engine room and coal bunkers. They were constantly grimy and greasy— known as the "black gang" to regular sailors. Where the deck sailors lived in an outside world of orderly cleanliness, holystoning the decks everyday to a dazzling whiteness—the steam mechanics and coal heavers lived in the dark dirty world below and did not understand the anger that their soot and grease created when it coated the upper decks. Wake wondered if other steamship captains had to constantly calm each side of that dilemma—he suspected they all did.

And then there were the deckhouse and wheelhouse. Boxes really. No pretty lines like his schooner *St. James. Hunt* was a hull with a long box that had two signal sticks and a funnel standing out of it. She had none of the soul of a sailing vessel. On the *Hunt* there was no steering from aft—her helm was in a wheelhouse just twenty-five feet from her bow, atop a long deck house stretching aft to end before a large afterdeck. Used to steering from the stern and being able to look up and around at the trim of the sails, Wake felt unnaturally confined in the wheelhouse. He had always steered a ship out on a deck where he could feel the wind and watch the sails and gauge the seas.

The stern deck of the *Hunt* was taken up by a massive double sampson post towing bit, six feet across and four feet high, with a cable's length of thick hawser flaked down and ready to use. This was Rork's bailiwick—the seamanship required in managing a tow. *Hunt* could tow almost any ship by herself. The engine was powerful but the gear reductions to her five-foot wide propeller were such that she was designed for thrust, not speed. Her very fastest speed without a tow was nine knots and she usually moved at six or seven.

Yes, it was all so different from what he had known in his years at sea. Canvas was the motive equipment he was used to. Now it was a metal monster below deck, with a hole in the hull for a screw. Wake shook his head at the thought of it all.

The navy was changing, though, and he would have to also. Wake was determined to learn the ways of his steamer and use her well against the enemy. He knew that he was very lucky to get this command. Many other regular officers with more seniority would have jumped at it. The jealousy was unsaid but palpable at the squadron offices, for Wake was one of those few volunteers who had been given a regular commission. Though he was technically now one of them, he knew he would never be accepted as an equal by the officers who were naval academy graduates. He had even heard that some of his brother officers were speculating that Wake wouldn't be able to understand and command a steamship, and would be replaced within four months.

It was not only his regular commission that had them talking. His love affair with and marriage to Linda Donahue, a woman from one of the most vocal of the pro-Confederate Key West families, had had them talking for some time. Though she did not share her family's views, she was tainted with that stain. The two of them had been ostracized by both factions when the word went out that they had married—the navy didn't trust her and the Rebel islanders hated him as an occupier of their home.

But all the turmoil had just brought them even closer. Linda was the best thing that had happened to him in his life, and he missed her terribly. He pictured her up the coast on Useppa Island and wished he could be there.

The call of the stroke by the coxswain brought Wake back to the present—and the serious problem he faced of having such a shorthanded ship that was going to sea in the morning. *Hunt's* men were going to have to adapt to the situation—all of them, both deck and engineering. Wake had always taken the morale of his men into consideration in his previous commands, and had worked to improve their well-being. But this was different, and whatever morale problems the crew had before his arrival this week, they were secondary to accomplishing the mission given them by the squadron's chief of staff, Fleet Captain Morris.

The launch was still a hundred yards away when the coxswain called out "Hunt," the traditional warning to a crew that the captain of their ship was coming aboard. The scurry of activity among the sailors on watch on the quarterdeck reminded Wake of what had caused the morale problem.

Hunt had been in the squadron only a few weeks when yellow fever went through her unacclimated crew and decimated it to the point where the men could barely operate the ship. She lay at anchor for two weeks, with the sick and death toll rising each day. Sailors made morbid wagers as to who would get sick next, and whether they would die. They sat there, waiting and watching each other for signs of the sickness. The fever was gone now, but the men's malaise had lingered as they wondered if the sickness would return. Wake had seen what yellow fever could do to a man, and he understood the despair and the terror that seized even strong men. Some were never the same again, even if they did survive.

As he climbed up the side of the ship he was determined to replace the despondency with discipline and success. That would be the cure for fear, and the sooner the better. The bosun's mate's pipe called, and all hands on the side deck faced Wake as he returned the salute of Master Stephen Emerson, his executive officer. Wake got right to the point.

"Mr. Emerson, I want all of the officers and petty officers in my cabin in five minutes. We need to meet about the crew and the mission of this ship."

Emerson, the same age as Wake at twenty-six but with a little less sea time and one rank junior, snapped his lean frame to attention. "Aye, aye, sir."

"And Mr. Emerson, see if the steward can find any of that fruit juice for the meeting. I think that would go well this afternoon."

Emerson was pleased to hear the request—it meant the meeting was not about some sort of trouble or a failing by the crew. He was still getting used to the ways of Captain Wake, but had heard of his exploits and was glad to be serving under him, even if it was on just a lowly tug.

"Aye, aye, sir. Fruit juice for the meeting."

Moments later, as the officers and petty officers started to arrive in his cabin, Wake reflected on the best privilege of his new command. It was the cabin itself, which stretched across the beam of the deckhouse's after end. Unbelievably, it had standing headroom, a first for Wake. It was the most luxurious cabin he had ever occupied on any ship, naval or merchant. A real bed was built into the bulkhead, accompanied by a desk with chairs, and an actual table for meals and charts. It even had a skylight that opened for ventilation and sunlight. As large as it was though, it quickly grew crowded and stuffy with all of the *Hunt's* leaders jamming themselves into the cabin.

The officers were seated—Wake at the desk, with Emerson, Ensign Terrance Rhodes, and Third Assistant Engineer Albert Ginaldi in the chairs in front of the desk.

All three of his officers were volunteers in the navy for the duration of the war. None had indicated that they would make it a career when the fighting stopped. Rhodes was a young man of friendly deportment, a new volunteer officer who had served on

Ohio riverboats but never been to sea. Ginaldi was older, more worldly, and had been an engineer on a New York tug. Ginaldi was the only officer aboard *Hunt* with tug experience, but as an engineer he was junior to all line officers like Emerson and Rhodes. The officers were not the original ones that had arrived in Key West aboard *Hunt*—they were all dead or incapacitated by the yellow fever, a fact that was not lost on any of the men in the cabin.

The petty officers were standing in a tight semicircle around the seated officers, senior petty officers in front with their junior assistants in the back of the crowd, near the companionway. The bosun of the ship was Sean Rork, who had served under Wake on two other ships and was a man to be relied upon, with many years of experience. Two of his bosun's mates, Curtis and Jones, stood next to him. The third, Hamilton, was on watch out on the deck, keeping curious ears away from that skylight and the cabin ports.

The gunner, Mark Durlon, another former shipmate of Wake's first command, was there with his sole gunner's mate, Walker. The engineer petty officers, McKinney and Schnieders, wore their cleanest working overalls for this unusual occasion of being called out of their below decks lair up to the captain's cabin, and stood slightly apart from the others, looking nervous in such company.

Dirkus the steward made his way through the mass of men and laid a tray with a pewter pitcher and cups on the desk, then exited. Dirkus was a quiet man with an odd way about him that was slightly disconcerting, as if he were constantly evaluating whomever he was serving. Having evidently run off to the navy to avoid some financial and legal unpleasantness, Dirkus never gave reason for complaint, but did give the impression he wanted to be anywhere but in the navy. He was far from being a dimwitted servant though, and Wake decided to keep him as his steward. After Dirkus' departure Wake looked at Emerson and nodded.

"Mr. Emerson, would you be so kind as to pour me some of

that orange juice and then pass it around the cabin. Men, please have some of this juice, it tastes mighty good on a day like today. Of course, our British cousins say it keeps the scurvy away, but I suspect they view it as one more occasion to lace a liquid with some of their special issue."

His offer of the fruit juice to even the petty officers, and his joke about the Royal Navy's love of its rum had the desired effect of easing the tension in the cabin as several of the men chuckled. Wake had no reason to be angry with them and did not want them fearful, but he did have the deadly serious task of forming a cohesive crew, one way or another, that could overcome the incredible handicap of being short a third of their men. They would have to work together and learn each other's functions. The old boundaries could not stand. There would be no divisiveness in his ship.

Wake waited until he had their attention, then spoke in a quiet voice. "All right, now let's get to the matter at hand. In the week since I've been aboard, I've seen that we have some excellent leadership on the *Hunt*. The officers and senior petty officers have the skill and experience to accomplish anything that we are tasked with by the squadron.

"In addition to having the skills of running the ship, I have also seen that each of you has done a good job in attempting to elevate the spirits of the men in your divisions and get them past the devastation of the fever on this ship. I know the effect the yellow fever had upon them, and I know that it still haunts their minds. However, the time for sensitivity is over. It is the responsibility of the men now in this cabin to replace that fear with fortitude. Is that understood?"

A chorus of low "aye, sirs," came back to Wake from the men in the cabin.

"Good, because our situation is about to become more difficult. I have just come back from the squadron offices after getting our orders to go to sea, and also an authorization order for a replacement draft of men for those missing in *Hunt's* crew."

Wake paused for a moment as he saw that each of the men facing him was leaning forward to hear about how their division would fare with replacements.

"Knowing that there are few unassigned men left in the squadron I asked for only seventeen of the most badly needed positions. We are getting five—" Wake heard the collective intake of breath in the cabin and continued. "Four ordinary seamen from the hospital and a coal heaver, if he can be persuaded to reenlist. There are no other men available. The squadron is desperately short. This situation is perilous, but it is not just the *Hunt,* as you all know. All of the ships are short. We will have to make do. Simple as that. Any questions so far?"

Ginaldi raised a finger and an eyebrow. "Captain, would that coal heaver be named Chard by any chance?"

"Yes, that was his name. His enlistment ended six months ago. He was one of the 1861 men for three years. He may reenlist if asked properly."

Ginaldi did not seem pleased at the prospect.

"Captain, I've heard tell of him. The engineer on the *Proteus* had him and was glad to be rid of the man. Said the man was possessed of a manner that could make a saint a sinner, sir."

"Well, Mr. Ginaldi, then it would appear that your getting him to reenlist will be even more of an accomplishment, wouldn't it? You needed men to heave the coal. So go persuade him to come to us and heave coal."

Though the engineer petty officers did not laugh, the others in the cabin grinned. Ginaldi bowed in his chair to Wake and smiled. "Aye, aye, sir. This Chard's never met Italian charm before, I'd wager. I'll have him so proud to be aboard the *Hunt,* he may just *pay* me for the honor of it, sir!"

Wake grinned at Ginaldi's enthusiasm. He did not understand steam mechanics yet, but he understood spirit.

"Mr. Ginaldi, I believe the man won't have a chance against your considerable Italian charm. Now, men, I know you are wondering about how we are going to get this short crew to both work and fight the ship. It is simple—everyone will be trained in another's work, doing double duty if needed to get *Hunt's* mission accomplished. That means that deck seamen and gun crews will train and work in the engine room and that the black gang will have to train and help on the guns to fight the ship. Understood?"

No one spoke for a moment. Finally Emerson stood up and looked at Wake.

"Sir, we'll do whatever we must to get the *Hunt* ready for sea duty. How long till we weigh anchor?"

Wake knew this would be the worst part. It was one thing to tell them they would have to train men on tasks for which they had no experience and to ask them to do double duty if needed, it was another to do it all in an impossibly short time.

"We get underway tomorrow at sunrise with the ebb. Later, I will brief you on our assignment."

They were all stunned. Wake had been stunned also when the chief of staff had given him his orders earlier in the day, before the visit to DeTar. Emerson was about to reply when Rhodes spoke, most probably to himself but loud enough in his shock that all heard it. "We just can't do that."

Rhodes looked up and realized what he had just uttered was against regulations, and very much against the attitude an officer was expected to display.

"Ah um . . . sir. What I meant was that it's such a short time to get everything done, all the provisioning and supplies, and with a shorthanded crew and all."

Ginaldi nodded his head in agreement and added a comment. "Sir, it *is* a short time. We'll have to coal the ship too. We don't have but a half load in the bunkers right now."

Emerson tried to speak but Wake raised a hand and stopped him. All eyes were riveted on their captain as he addressed them.

"Gentlemen, and petty officers. Yes, you are right. It is not enough time to get the *Hunt* ready for sea in the accustomed fashion. That means we will have to get her ready for sea in an *un*accustomed fashion. There is no room for failure here, men. We are at war, and the exigencies of war do not stop because yellow fever has demoralized our crew and made us shorthanded. It is time to act and show what we are capable of, which is far more than you believe at the moment. Now, let us walk out of this cabin and get *Hunt* ready for sea, even if all hands—including every man here—have to work all night to accomplish that. Understood?"

This time there was no hesitation and the chorus of "Aye, ayes" was loud. Emerson immediately stood and started to give Rhodes, Ginaldi, Durlon, and Rork tasks. The drone of the petty officers conversing about what to do first had an excited air about it, and Wake was glad that the preliminary gloom was over. As the cabin cleared out Emerson came over to the desk with a serious look on his face.

"Sir, I am sorry about Rhodes' and Ginaldi's comments. They were out of line with those statements."

Wake saw that Emerson was genuinely upset and worried that his captain would find fault with him. Such was the life of an executive officer, but Wake was not going to dwell on it.

"Well, they spoke what first came into their heads, which was wrong. But it was a shock and a very difficult task, I realize. Don't worry, Mr. Emerson, I'm not angry—this time. But next time I expect leaders to lead, figure out how to overcome obstacles, and not whine."

"Yes, sir."

"And Mr. Emerson."

"Yes, sir?"

"If being shorthanded and short on time are our worst problems in the future, then this ship and crew will be very lucky indeed. Sooner or later we may have some real dilemmas to worry about—that are much bloodier."

Emerson had heard the stories about how fearlessly Wake had acted under enemy fire, but how afterward he had grieved for his men who were killed or wounded. Emerson also could see the scar by Wake's right ear, where a shot had nearly killed him in a river fight last year. The executive officer of the *Hunt* had not yet been under enemy fire himself, but he knew that the chances of that changing were pretty good with the famously aggressive Peter Wake commanding the ship, and what the captain said was not mere rhetoric. Emerson nodded as he replied.

"I understand, sir. We'll get her ready, and then handle what comes our way."

"Very well, Mr. Emerson. It's also time to tell you of the urgent assignment that has caused all of this turmoil. It won't be a pleasant one."

"Yes, sir?"

"We are headed to the Mosquito Inlet up on the east coast of the peninsula, where the schooner *Ramer* is lying with her crew dead or dying of yellow fever. The *Hunt* will help save the lives of all they can, and get that schooner back to Key West. There are rumors that the Rebels have heard of the sick crew and are planning on trying to take her. The men of the *Hunt* are going to have to overcome their fear and do their duty. And you and I and Ginaldi and young Rhodes are going to lead them."

"Yes, sir. I understand. When will you tell the others?"

"Once we're under way in the morning. I don't need speculation and fear hindering our preparations for sea—so keep that information to yourself and make sure all is completed quickly. There is no time to lose on this."

"Aye, aye, sir."

There was no disguising the concern in Emerson's eyes, but his voice had a confident tone. Well, that is all I could hope for right now, Wake thought, as he diverted the subject to the present.

"Now Mr. Emerson, I believe we should get over to the coaling dock first, then load ammunition off the ordnance ship. Do you concur?"

The two men then plunged into a conversation about priorities and procedures of ammunition resupply, reprovisioning, and coaling the ship as quickly as possible. They were soon engrossed in the effort, and no more was made of the issues of leading the *Hunt's* men back into another ship plagued with yellow jack.

All had been said that needed to be said. Now it was time to accomplish their orders.

2

The Enemy Within

When he heard no more bustle from the main deck, indicating that the *Hunt* was finally prepared to get under way, Wake needed no one to rouse him, for he hadn't slept in the short time he had been in his cabin. Earlier in the night he'd left the officers to their work, determined to not stand there watching over their shoulders. That would only show a lack of trust in them and in himself. So he had gone below to the privacy of his cabin.

There he had sat at his cluttered desk and, by the yellow light of a purser's lamp, reread the latest letter from his brother in Massachusetts. Luke was his oldest brother and a schooner captain on the family trading firm's sole remaining vessel—the others having been sold off due to the war slump in American shipping. The letter was melancholy. Their father was not well and getting worse. Luke wrote that it appeared the death of their brother James while on duty aboard a monitor on the Charleston coast had precipitated their father's decline. And just two months earlier, brother John also joined the navy, which made the old man even more morose. Their mother, a quiet strong woman who had raised her sons alone while their father was out at sea, told Luke that she was afraid her husband would die of heartbreak. Luke concluded the letter with the wish that Linda would make a good wife for his littlest brother, and the jest that he hoped Peter would not forget all the seamanship Luke had taken so long to teach him, now that he was a highfalutin' captain on some stinkbucket coal-eating steamer. Luke always ended his letters with a jest, but this one failed to produce a smile.

Wake gritted his jaw as he thought about being so far away from his father and mother. He wished he and Linda could be there. He wanted them to get to know his new wife, and see that their son was happy. He knew that his mother would love Linda, and felt that his father might regain his health and spirits by meeting his new daughter-in-law. They had only had boys, and Wake thought Linda could be like a daughter for them. And someday they would have their first grandchild to play with. But furloughs were not available, the *Hunt* had a mission that would start very shortly, and Linda was not here.

The thought of Linda set his heart aching, a hard, real pain inside his chest. He wanted to see her, hold her, touch that soft auburn hair, and look into those entrancing deep green eyes. But she was a hundred and forty-five miles away, living with pro-Union refugees at Useppa Island, by Boca Grande on the west coast of Florida. Though he would have given almost anything to be with her tonight in Key West, Wake knew she was probably much safer and certainly in good company where she was.

Word of their quiet marriage a few months earlier had spread throughout Key West and many people were upset, particularly with her. A Southern girl marrying an enemy Yankee sailor at a time when so many Southern boys were dying for their state—it just wasn't proper. It was one thing to be decent and hospitable to the Yankees, but quite another to marry one of them! Added to that, of course, was the fact that it wasn't even an official marriage in a real church by a recognized minister. A black Bahamian preacher had married them on the beach by the African cemetery on the south shore of Key West. Many Key Westers, especially the old-time Conchs who were set in their ways, felt that either Linda Donahue had completely lost her senses or that perfidious Yankee had done something downright evil to her mind.

In the months since then, Linda had survived an attack of yellow fever at Useppa and was nursed back to health by those good refugee people. Wake liked and trusted them, which is why he had sent his new wife there. Beyond the escape from Key West and the sickness though, Linda Wake had found a new home and friends at Useppa, and by her letters, was truly happy there, which alleviated the sadness of their separation somewhat.

For their part, the leadership in the squadron had ignored the marriage and treated Wake no differently. Not as much could be said for some of the officers, however. While he never heard them, Wake knew from others that they were talking about him in the officers' messes. He did not care and wasted not a moment on the issue. Those officers were like old women and gossiped about who was doing what with whom, and Wake knew nothing could stop them. Linda was safe from the tensions of Key West, which was the important thing.

He folded Luke's letter carefully and returned it to the drawer with the other family letters, which now included one a week written from Useppa. Wake had so much to do, to think about, to prepare for. Many things could happen over the next few days and he, as the captain, must have an idea of how he and the men of the *Hunt* would handle them. He snuffed out the lamp, savoring the darkness and privacy, and trying to think. Had he done all he could to get the ship and the men ready?

Mind whirling in a mix of navigational contingencies, watch bill assignments, supply orders, weekly status reports, and medical information from what the surgeon ashore told him to do on his arrival at the *Ramer,* Wake moved over to his berth and lay down. The constant rumbling of the engine could be felt all through the ship and usually could lull one to rest. He closed his eyes, but it was no use. Five minutes later he was moving through the companionway to the main deck.

The *Hunt* hadn't slept in the night either. Throughout the night the hissing of steam pipes, the thud of supply boxes and casks dropping on deck, and the loud giving and acknowledging of orders served to let all vessels in the naval wharf area of the harbor know that the U.S.S. *Hunt* was getting herself ready for sea in a hurry. Emerson and Rhodes were everywhere, their voices rising above the others, checking on the loading and stowing of the various equipment and supplies of a warship, those crucial items that keep her own crew alive and bring death to her enemies.

Hunt was coaled and had provisions for three weeks. All that was left to do was stow the supplies and get her ready for sea. They would leave shortly and take advantage of the ebb. In the loom of the lanterns placed safely to leeward of the men trudging up the gangway from the wharf, Wake saw Rork on the starboard waist directing a detail of sailors in the dangerous duty of bringing aboard the last of the shell ammunition from a cart on the wharf. Durlon's rasp could be heard below in the magazine, calling up that they were about to seal off the powder space and the shot locker was just about full.

Rork took his eyes off the sailors for a moment and nodded to Wake, then looked to the sky.

"No wind today, Captain."

"We'll make our own with this ship, Rork."

The bosun shook his head slightly, his eyes back on the men lowering the shells down the hatchway. "I hope we do, Captain. The lads could use a bit o' breeze with all the sweat they've worked up tonight. They're ready to fall, sir."

Wake looked at Rork. The man looked old and tired in the dim light, even though he was but thirty-three. Rork hadn't slept in two days, like most of the men on the ship.

"Rork, we'll be under way in a few minutes and then the men off watch can get some sleep. I know they're tired. You need to get some sleep too."

"Aye, aye, sir. I am tired, Captain. Ya have me there, sir. All this bloody coal dust reminds me of my packet days in the Irish Sea, when we'd go over to Wales an' see them ol' colliers wallowing like pigs in the sea, an' we'd sail by fast and clean. Used to feel sorry for the poor sods. Ships and men all as black as an African. Never thought someday I'd be covered with the stuff me ownself, though."

"Rork, I know what you mean. All this is new for me too. We're not alone, though. I do believe a lot of this navy's sailors' are going to get to know coal dust pretty well before this war ends. It's the way of the future. No stopping it."

"A filthy future it'll be then, sir. Filthy men and filthy ships."

Rhodes' voice came from forward, interrupting Wake as he pondered Rork's comment and wondered how his ship would look in the morning light. Rhodes' solid form materialized from the darkness as he stepped into the lantern light.

"Good morning, sir. We did it. We've completed the provisions and ammunition and are ready to get under way as soon as Bosun Rork here can get the hatches secured. Mr. Emerson was looking for you to make his report, sir. He's in the wheelhouse, I think, sir. Mr. Ginaldi's there too, sir."

Wake acknowledged the ensign's information, noting the positive tone in Rhodes' voice. Making his way forward and up the ladder to the small wheelhouse, Wake heard Rork and Rhodes conferring about which lines would be taken up in what sequence when they departed the wharf. It appeared that young Rhodes was feeling more confident, having accomplished far more than he'd originally thought, and his demeanor was showing it. Wake was glad to see the change.

The wheelhouse was dark, the binnacle giving the only light from its faint glow. Two forms stood by the wheel and straightened as Wake entered. One of them stepped forward into the light.

"Good morning, sir. Mr. Ginaldi and I were just getting ready to go to your cabin to make our reports to you."

"Good morning, gentlemen. Go ahead with your reports."

Emerson's weariness was apparent in his tone. "Sir, all authorized hands are aboard. We have water and provisions aboard for three weeks. Powder and ammunition spaces have been filled. Medical supplies were sent aboard with some extra clothing and hammock gear from the slop chest at the naval station. I thought we might have to burn the *Ramer* men's clothing, sir. I had the bosun lay out a towing hauser aft, and we have fenders ready for coming alongside. We also got another small boat from the carpenter's shop ashore. We're supposed to deliver it to the *San Jacinto* if we see her. It might come in handy if we need to transfer supplies in a sea to *Ramer*."

"Very good, anything else?"

"Ship is secured and the engine has steam, lines are manned, and she is currently being readied for departure."

"What about the men, Mr. Emerson?"

"The men? Yes, sir, they're tired out. I've sent half the sailors below and have half on deck standing by to get underway."

"And you, Mr. Ginaldi?"

"The bunkers are mostly full and stowed level. We have enough coal aboard for approximately fifteen hundred steaming miles at seven knots, sir. The steam machinery is up to pressure and the gears and shafts are ready. Condenser tubes have some corrosion buildup, but they'll last awhile. Oil pressure was down due to a leak, but McKinney says he's got it found and fixed, Captain."

"What about that man Chard? A coal heaver, if I remember correctly."

"Yes, sir. A coal heaver. McKinney and I persuaded him to join the crew. Told him we were heading north, which of course is completely true—just not as far north as he might like. He's below on duty right now with the other men."

"And your men—how are they?"

"Ready to drop, Captain. But they'll handle it. They have to. We're the ones that make this beast move."

Emerson darted a glance at the engineer in the gloom, starting to say something but then staying silent. Wake took note that Ginaldi did not make his comment with bravado or complaint. It was simply a fact. Exhaustion in the heat of the tropics was a normal state for the men in the engine room. Wake didn't know how they did it. He had only been in there while at anchor in the last few days, but it was too hot and claustrophobic for him even then. He was not looking forward to being in there when the engine was producing the heat needed for moving the ship, or the beast, as Ginaldi had called her.

Wake wasn't too sure about Ginaldi yet—he had no experience with engines or the engineers who made them run, and they seemed to be an odd type. Not at all like the deck sailors, the real sailors. More like passengers on a packet ship who knew the sailors disliked them, but without whom the sailors would have no ship. Wake was literally at Ginaldi's mercy as far as the ship's steam engine was concerned and would have to trust the man. There was no other choice.

"All right gentlemen, let's get her under way, then set the watches and allow the men to get some sleep. Mr. Emerson, you may stay here with me. Mr. Rhodes and the bosun can handle the lines.

"Mr. Ginaldi, I believe Schnieders and McKinney can handle the engine room. I would like you here to be a resource for me on how the engine will respond to commands. I know the commands and have read the book, but I want your opinion."

Ten minutes later, Wake and the two officers were standing on the starboard deck outside the wheelhouse, watching the men take in the mooring lines. Wake asked for suggestions and Ginaldi was the first to respond.

"Put the wheel midship, sir. Then back her by ringing astern slow. She'll back off into the stream of the ebb and be away from the wharf. With this ebb, I think we'd do better with astern slow, rather than dead slow. Need to get her away from the dock before the ebb gets ahold of her stern."

Wake nodded in understanding. In a schooner he would

have warped the vessel aft and kedged her out with an anchor. This was different—very different.

Emerson was looking at the area astern of the *Hunt.*

"I think he's right, sir. That should work. The tidal current'll catch us and help swing her around."

Wake took in a breath and smiled, then turned to the man stationed at the large bell outside the after bulkhead of the wheelhouse.

"Very well, ring for engine astern slow."

Three bells rapidly rang out as Wake leaned outboard and called to Rhodes forward, who had only the fore- and aftermost lines still holding the ship to the wharf.

"Take in the bow and stern lines, and stand by to fend off with spars. Stand by the anchor in case we need it fast."

"Aye, aye, sir," came the reply from somewhere at the bow as men along the starboard side of the *Hunt* pulled out the two extra spars kept aboard and held them in readiness.

And then Wake felt something very strange with the ship. At first he thought something had gone wrong and was about to ask Ginaldi, but that man showed no concern. Suddenly the source of the unusual tremble in the deck was obvious. Wake realized that it was logical when one thought about it, actually, and he stood there almost mesmerized by the sensation as the ship shuddered while the reversal gear was engaged. The wheelhouse started to shake, and the swashing sound of water could be heard as the propeller began to churn counterclockwise, pulling the *Hunt* away from the wharf and into the tidal current. Wake heard a high-pitched sigh come from above him and knew that the effort of the engine had sent a small black cloud from the smoke stack into the dark sky. The sight of the wharf gliding by next to them made Wake almost giddy, but he was brought back to his senses by the engineer.

"I believe that right about now I would ring for the engine to stop, sir. The stern is already swinging with the current. Then I would ring for ahead slow and put the helm over to port. That'll get her around."

"I agree with Mr. Ginaldi, sir," added Emerson, a trifle too quickly.

"Very well, make it so, Mr. Emerson," Wake said, and the engineer gave the proper orders.

The *Hunt* swung her bow around into and then across the current as she turned. The stern came toward the wharf but not close enough for the spars to be used. Then suddenly she was away, completing her circle and moving slowly with the ebb tide through the harbor as the eastern horizon showed a tinge of gray and the stars faded from view.

Wake moved back into the wheelhouse, followed by Emerson and Ginaldi. Dirkus appeared next to Wake and held out a mug of coffee without saying a word.

"Thank you, Dirkus. I think I will have some. You look as if you assisted in the loading too."

Dirkus looked down at his grimy shirt, then nodded without expression.

"Yes, sir."

Wake looked at his steward, gauging the man.

"Well, it was a job done well by all hands, Dirkus. See if you can conjure up a quick breakfast for the officers and me. Then get some sleep."

"It'll be ready in fifteen minutes, sir. I figured you'd want it once we got away from the channel and out to sea."

"Excellent, Dirkus. I'm very hungry this morning and looking forward to what you've got prepared."

The steward nodded again and walked away quickly in short gliding steps, delicately sidestepping Emerson, who was easily visible now in the growing light, watching the steward depart.

"He's an odd one, sir. But he does his job."

Ginaldi stopped on his way out of the wheelhouse.

"Mr. Emerson's made an understatement, Captain. Dirkus is beyond odd, he's eerie, if you ask me."

Wake felt the same way, but had only been aboard for a few

days and had no proof of anything.

"Gentlemen, he can be as odd and eerie as he wants, as long as the coffee's hot and the food is good. Thank you both for the assistance in getting away from the wharf. I've still some learning to do about the *Hunt*'s ways."

Ginaldi put a knuckle to his brow in a quick informal salute as he stood on the deck outside.

"You're learning fast, Captain. You'll pick it up in no time. By your leave, sir, I'm heading below to check on McKinney."

Emerson looked briefly at the engineer then moved to stand next to the helmsman, noting the bearing of Fort Taylor on the port bow.

"Fort Taylor bearing east s'east, sir. Channel mark for the turn is coming up. I'll ring for half ahead once we get to that leg of the channel. We'll be away from the anchorage then."

"Very well, Mr. Emerson. You have the deck. Take her out the channel to sea. Once we're beyond the ship channel, I want her at best speed heading nor'east along the Keys to the east coast. Use the lighthouses as references to keep her at least four miles off the reef, but keep her going fast. *Ramer* needs us there as soon as possible."

"Aye, aye, sir."

"And Mr. Emerson."

"Sir?"

"The decks are filthy, but they and the rest of the ship can wait for a cleaning until the men get some rest and some food. All duty watchstanders not being employed on something important should get some rest. I want the men still standing watch to have a good breakfast, and I want a good supper for all hands later in the day. When we arrive at Mosquito Inlet we'll need all our strength and our wits about us. Do not hesitate to notify me of any vessel sighting, weather change, or unusual occurrence."

Emerson stared at his captain, who had just spoken heresy in not keeping a naval vessel as spotless as possible at all times.

"Aye, aye, sir."

Wake looked around the wheelhouse as the gray on the horizon spread into pale blue, and colors aboard the *Hunt* became apparent. He watched as the helmsman gazed ahead, periodically glancing down at the binnacle to check his course. The messenger stood against the after bulkhead, arms folded behind him with eyes focused on the helmsman's head, and the lookouts on either side scanned the harbor and the sea beyond. None of those men had reacted in any obvious way to Wake's orders, but all of them had heard them and knew they were on a very different kind of ship than the one they had arrived in Key West aboard. It wouldn't be long before the whole crew would know what had been said in the wheelhouse.

The crew had heard the rumors about Wake. How he had a knack for finding action. How he made his own luck. They hoped that luck would hold, for the other rumors had them heading for a yellow jack death ship up on the east coast. They knew all about death ships. Their very own *Hunt* had been one.

As the sun moved west they moved east, counting off the lighthouses marking one of the most dangerous reefs in the country as they were passed—Sand Key, Sombrero Key, Carysfort Reef. These lighthouses were most unusual, since they were not built on land but on reefs offshore and had spindly frames that appeared quite frail. Wake pointed them out to Emerson as they slid by the *Hunt*'s beam.

"Interesting point of fact, Mr. Emerson. The famous General George Gordon Meade, who vanquished Lee at Gettysburg last year, was the man who designed and built those lighthouses for us a few years ago."

"They don't look that sturdy, sir. Been through any hurricanes?"

"Well, they have stood several storms so far. They're not that old. Mostly from the fifties, when Meade was a captain in the engineers. Screwpile design, where the iron is screwed down into the coral somehow. Amazing."

By sunrise the next day they were in the Gulf Stream's dark

blue water well north of Cape Florida's old brick lighthouse on Key Biscayne. The beaches of the Florida mainland were now visible far off to the west, mile after mile of them. Steaming northward through the undulating seas with an easy motion, and using that ocean river to make nine and a half miles good toward their destination each hour, *Hunt* was in her element. Not sleek and beautiful like the schooner *St. James,* but strong and purposeful. The ceaseless pounding of the pistons and cranks that drove the shaft around and turned the propeller reminded Wake of a beating heart. He was starting to feel that she was his. He just wished he understood her better.

In mid-afternoon they passed the new red lighthouse at Jupiter Inlet. Wake was peering at it on the far horizon when Emerson came up to him.

"Another of Meade's, sir?"

"Yes, his last one on this coast. Got it done in sixty. Navy hasn't repaired it since the Rebels sabotaged it in '61. It isn't worth it. We'd have to keep a garrison to protect it. Shame really. Brand new lighthouse and it's not even lit."

"Another casualty of the war, Captain. I guess the Rebels control the whole coast?"

"Yes, most of it. You never know where they will be, and so you have to always assume . . ."

Rhodes called out enthusiastically from the chartroom behind them. "Bearing on that distant lighthouse shows we are making good time over the bottom, sir. The Stream is helping considerably. I estimate we should be at Mosquito Inlet in approximately eleven hours at this speed. Possibly twelve."

Wake smiled at the report. These officers were new to Florida and the Gulf Stream. The Stream was a fascinating force of nature, but it couldn't help them all the way to their destination.

"Mr. Rhodes, thank you. Let me show you something."

Walking back into the tiny chartroom annexed to the rear of the wheelhouse, he put his finger on their present position.

Emerson followed, and watched as Wake began.

"We must always be very careful when around the Stream. It behaves very unpredictably. Today it has helped us, but we can't count on that. We also won't be in the Stream for much longer, because we won't be steering due northerly anymore. Sighting Jupiter was the sign to turn n'nor'west. That will do several things, gentlemen.

"First, it will allow us to follow the trend of the coast in that direction, but stay offshore enough to clear Cape Canaveral tonight. The Cape's light won't be lit—same Rebel sabotage problem—but soundings should be a good enough warning. Secondly, it will diminish our speed to around seven and a half knots. Thirdly, it will change our estimated transit time to about seventeen and a half hours. That will put us there just after sunrise tomorrow. Questions?"

Emerson looked at the chart and shook his head, Rhodes looked up at Wake, with a concerned mien.

"Sorry for the wrong estimate, sir."

"Not a problem. I am learning this ship, you newer officers are learning Florida."

Wake turned and departed the wheelhouse spaces, descending to the main deck and walking aft. At the number two gun, Durlon was teaching the gun's crew the loading and firing drill of the twelve-pounder howitzer, and Wake paused to listen for a moment.

"This darlin' will save your life, and the ship's life, if used properly. I remember a time when me and the captain were up a river on the west coast of this vermin-ridden state, surrounded by them dirty Rebs by the dozen. Thought they had us paid and done, but then the bastards knew they was sadly mistaken when they felt the hot touch of a navy twelve come their way. She was served by a gun crew much like yourselves, boys who knew what to do." Durlon looked up and saw Wake watching. "Do you remember that one, Captain?"

"Aye, gunner. That I do. You and your iron daughter did

good work that day. Saved our lives for certain, Durlon. You men listen to this man. He knows his guns."

Nods and grins all around rewarded Wake, who walked further aft as Durlon went through the numbers of the loading drill, calling them out and having the men repeat them.

Wake was seeing something he had hoped for—men were smiling and looking rested. They were laughing and complaining and cajoling. The ship had gotten cleaned up and the equipage stowed. They were ready.

"When sailors get quiet, officers had best get very careful," his father told him once. "It means the men are past the point of words and are contemplating evil doings." Wake had never forgotten that wisdom, and knew it applied in the naval service as well as the merchant service—especially when facing unknown danger and death.

Wake stood by the towing bits at the stern and looked at the swirling path behind them. Pounding incessantly, the steam engine never stopped or slowed. The stack spewed a gritty cloud of soot, some of which fell around Wake. The rhythm of the pounding engine reminded him of the description he had heard once of an African tribe's war drums—never changing, always throbbing along, the self-discipline and inevitability terrifying. Wake wondered if he would ever get used to the sound that vibrated through every part of his ship. The steam engine is in real control of this ship, the men are simply pointing her, he thought as he turned forward again.

He knew where he was going next. The noise grew rapidly as you got closer, until, when one was at the hatchway to the engine room, a man had to shout to be heard just a foot or two away. Inside the hatch, it was like a scene from a newspaper cartoon of a New York madhouse. Communication was done by sign language. Danger was everywhere, with metal arms pulling and pushing, steam wooshing and hissing from valves, and fire raging from the red hot boxes below the boilers.

Wake made his way slowly into this alien world. Even

though the sea was being kind to them with only a three-foot swell, a man had to be doubly careful down in the den of the black gang. A man could fall or trip into the maw of the unyielding monster that demonstrated its strength each second it breathed, slinging those iron piston arms around as the shaft turned.

Schnieders met him by the condensers and put his mouth right up to Wake's ear, unthinkable for deck petty officers to do with their captain.

"Problem, sir?"

Wake smiled as he realized the petty officer had never seen him down in here under way, and was probably afraid something was wrong. Ginaldi would get a full report immediately after Wake left, he imagined.

"No problem, just looking into how you're doing!"

The relief was visible. Schnieders smiled back.

"Oh! No problems, sir. She's chompin' away!"

Behind Schnieders, several coal heavers had stopped shoveling the black mineral food to the steam monster in order to watch their captain. No sign of disrespect, or respect for that matter, showed. Curiosity was what Wake saw on their faces. He made a mental note to come down in here at least once a day. In a pinch, these men, hidden from the sight and sound of a battle above and around them, could be the precise factors in the life and death of every man aboard the *Hunt*. Wake wondered if the disgruntled man Chard was among the ones looking at him. He would ask later, up at dinner. It was impossible to have a conversation in this maelstrom.

Nodding to the coal heavers and receiving a nod or two in return, Wake ascended the ladder to the world of the sailors, breathing in the heavy sweet air deeply when he got to the main deck. Rork, striding past with a coil of line, winked and called out to him, exhaustion no longer discernible in his voice.

"Aye, Captain, been down to hell with the black gang, I see! Those lads earn their keep, that they do, sir. An' they drink up all their keep when they hit shore!"

Wake laughed and could not resist a reply.

"And I thought the bosuns were the tough ones!"

Rork laughed and waved his hand in appreciation of the joke as he lashed down one of the boats. Wake felt a hand tugging at his sleeve. It was Dirkus, who had somehow approached Wake once again with disquieting stealth.

"Mr. Emerson's respects, sir. Sail sighted to the nor'west, two points off the port bow."

Squinting that direction, Wake could see a smudge of pale gray on the horizon.

"Very well. Thank you. Give Mr. Emerson my compliments and tell him I am on my way to the wheelhouse."

Acknowledging the order with an unintelligible word or two, Dirkus spun around on his heel, surprisingly able even on the rolling deck, and walked in his peculiar gait forward and up the ladder, with Wake following.

Wake found them all, Emerson, Rhodes, and Ginaldi, peering off to the northwest with the three telescopes available. They did not notice his arrival until the helmsman said, "Afternoon, sir."

Emerson pointed out the distant vessel and gave Wake his glass. "She's a schooner, sir. Tacking down the coast to the south. No colors showing. We can be over to her in an hour at the most at this speed."

Rhodes was having trouble containing his excitement. "I would say she'd fetch a good amount at the prize hearing, sir, even if she is empty by the looks of her."

Wake knew what was going to come next. He would end that idea. "If anyone thinks we will stop to board her they are wrong. We will not take time away from the men of the *Ramer* for anything other than an emergency. Time is life for our men on the *Ramer*, gentlemen. Continue on course. Thank you for notifying me."

Before they could reply, Wake walked out of the wheelhouse

and down the main deck, turning into the doorway leading to the companionway to his cabin. Once there he closed the door behind him and sat at his desk, reviewing the charts he had of the coast by the Mosquito Inlet. As he sat there, he thought of the yellow jack and its grisly symptoms. He wondered what exactly he would find aboard the U.S.S. *Ramer* in the morning.

It had been a dark night, with a heavy haze obscuring the stars and a humid light breeze coming in from the south. The swells were not large, but big enough to make *Hunt* roll as she labored onward around Cape Canaveral and its shoals. Wake arrived at the wheelhouse for his watch in time to see the sunrise. It was blood red. As it boiled up ominously from the sea, a sudden penetrating sensation spread throughout his body. He tried to shake it off as he surveyed the others around him and saw their reaction was the same.

They stood transfixed at the malevolent sight. Seamen are just far too superstitious, and I'm getting as bad as they are, Wake thought as he calmed himself and attempted to divert the attention of the men on watch to the coastline on the other side of the ship. "Well, men, we should see the *Ramer* soon, we're getting close. I'd estimate we're about ten miles from the inlet now. Should be along up in that area."

The watch-standers dutifully turned and looked in the direction their captain was pointing, but no one said anything. He looked at them again. They appeared terrified, eyes wide and mouths grim, struggling not to give vent to their fears of the sickness they were about to confront—again.

"I want the lookouts doubled, including two aloft. I want to know immediately when she is sighted, understood Bosun?"

The bosun's mate of the watch, Curtis, acknowledged the order and quickly started rousing some sailors idling on the main deck to get it accomplished. Curtis then went to the ship's launch, stowed on davits on the port waist, and began to prepare her for whatever duty would be necessary.

An hour later they saw the surf line at the inlet, but no vessel. The remnants of the old lighthouse that had collapsed thirty years before could be seen as a dot of black on the beach, as well as several crude structures set far back in the woods of the mainland behind the sandy barrier island. Closing with the coast, the men of the *Hunt* saw the outline of the beaches become clearer, but no ship. Trees and bushes were identifiable, and colors were illuminated in the few shafts of sunlight that stabbed through the haze. The *Ramer* was not in sight.

Soon the decks of the *Hunt* were crowded with men straining their eyes and pointing their arms to the coast, so many that she listed to port with their weight. The officers and petty officers, even the engineers, were higher up in or around the wheelhouse, conjecturing about where the *Ramer* could be and what had happened to displace her from her station. Amongst all the busy conversation, Wake heard a familiar voice and looked aloft to the narrow crosstrees of the foremast. There was Rork, standing on one foot while the other dangled in air, one arm crooked around the mast with the other holding a telescope, his entire body swaying with ease as the mast carved a dizzy circle in the air. The young seaman next to him was clinging with both arms intently to the mast and only occasionally glancing around the horizon. Wake was glad Rork was up there. The bosun's eyes were sharp.

Rork saw the color yellow first. One of those rare beams of diffused light from the now white-yellow sun caught the color and made it stand out for a brief moment. Rork brought his arm up on the bearing of the color.

"Deck there! Two-masted ship, with the yellow jack hoisted, dead ahead just off the beach up there. Looks about seven miles away. It's the *Ramer,* sir. I recognize her."

The flag Rork described was caught in the rigging of the distant ship, about halfway up the foremast. Wake could see it now from the wheelhouse deck. Now and then the roll of the ship, or a bit of wind, would unfold the flag so that its yellow color could be seen, as warning to all who saw it to stay away. The fever was aboard.

A cloud of sound rose from the decks around Wake, overwhelming the rumbling noise of the engine, the swish of the bow waves, the hiss of the stack. Officers and men were all talking at once. Some were asking for more information about what exactly had been seen, a few were swearing, others were praying. Wake looked down to the foredeck gun and saw one young boy, a steward's assistant, he believed, with tears in his eyes staring forward over the ocean. One of the originals who had survived the yellow fever decimation on this ship, Wake guessed.

There was no need for any new orders. The *Hunt* was already heading directly for the stricken ship at her best speed, but still the men felt they had to do something. The *Hunt* would take another hour to arrive, but all the preparations had been made already. There was nothing to do but wait, and watch that yellow flag get closer and larger.

Ginaldi, standing on the port side main deck with his petty officers, looked up at Wake, then put his hand on McKinney's shoulder and nodded over to Schnieders.

"Well fellas, time is a-wasting. Let's see if we can help old *Hunt* to get there a bit quicker. Come on below to our little den with me and let's get that main bleed valve tightened a bit to build some more pressure."

Wake knew he had to do or say something also. The age-old order would probably still be the best. In a way—they *were* going into battle.

"Mr. Emerson, since you're here, would you please see to it that the entire crew gets a good breakfast? I know some of them have already eaten, but I want all hands, including those on watch, to have a *good* meal. Now is the time. We'll be very busy later I suspect, and the men will need all their strength and wits."

"Aye, aye, sir."

"And Mr. Emerson."

"Sir?"

"I think that before and after the men have had that good breakfast, *Hunt* would do well to have a good scrubbing down by them. More than the usual morning deck wash. I want well-fed men and a clean ship. You have an hour to accomplish all of that, Mr. Emerson."

"Aye, aye, sir!"

The commotion caused by the sighting, and the subsequent orders, diminished as the men were focused on their task. The conversations about the *Ramer* continued, but the sailors worked hard. Wake heard no more prayers, saw no more tears, saw only grim faces taut with the strain of physical exertion. Leaning out on the starboard wheelhouse railing, he saw Rork on the afterdeck, supervising a detail of men faking down a hawser line. Rork happened to look up and saw his captain and old friend watching. A hand slowly went up to his brow and he nodded, then looked over at the *Ramer* on the horizon. Wake nodded back and grimly smiled.

It didn't take an hour to get there. Ginaldi's assistants had increased the speed enough that they made it fifty-three minutes, a fact noted nervously by Emerson to Wake as they both scanned the decks of *Ramer* for a sign of life. They saw nothing by eye or glass, except the sails and rigging in disarray. It appeared that the mainsail had been lowered but not furled, and the flying jib and lower jib both hung down into the water from the bowsprit. The twelve-pounder gun was secured, but the davit falls on the port side swayed just above the waterline, the block tackles thudding into the hull with the motion of the vessel. The anchor cable held her bow into the wind and flood tide current, but no sign of human habitation could be found. A ship's boat lay fifty feet astern on a painter. *Ramer* was rolling in the swells with the water climbing the sides and then cascading off with each wallow.

The *Hunt* came close alongside to windward of the schooner and stopped, the crew silently watching, straining to hear or see anyone aboard the *Ramer.* The only sounds were the creaking of wood and rigging, the splash of the water cascading off the rolling hull, and those fall tackles incessantly thudding. It was the sight and sound of a ghost ship, and Wake could feel his heart start to beat stronger as his ears became obsessed with the rhythm of the fall tackles thudding against the schooner.

"Please hail her, Mr. Emerson."

"Aye, aye, sir."

The speaking trumpet in his hand, Emerson called out the hundred feet to leeward.

"*Ramer* ahoy! Ahoy there! Anyone aboard?"

Repeating the same litany, louder and louder, he finally stopped and shook his head.

"Anchor her to windward, if you would, Mr. Emerson. Once that is accomplished, Rork and I will go over in the launch to ascertain the situation."

"Sir, I'll go. It's my place to go."

"I'll be the judge of who goes, Mr. Emerson. Now kindly arrange for that boat to be ready. Also, I want every man rowing that boat to be a volunteer. Understood?"

It took another fifteen agonizing minutes to get *Hunt* securely anchored and the boat lowered. Once again, the side was crowded by sailors staring, some with terror in their eyes, wondering if the sickness in the ship to leeward would make the short distance to their own ship, wondering how long it would take. They were feeling the fear again, invading them until walking became a conscious effort.

The boat coxswain stood waiting in the stern sheets of his tiny command, anxiously folding and unfolding his arms, as his crew leaned on their oars and looked glum. Rork climbed down and stood in the bow as Wake, giving final orders to Emerson, descended with as much calm as he could muster to sit on the after-thwart.

The coxswain, a muscular man named Lawson, had the unique distinction of being the only African petty officer Wake had ever seen. When younger, he had served aboard a whaler and learned the art of the harpooner, serving as an alternate boat-steerer when usually only the white mates of those vessels had that authority. He had changed over to the naval service five years earlier, and his seamanship had come to the attention of the prior commander of the *Hunt*. That now-deceased man had promoted Lawson to coxswain of the ship's launch, a prestigious position and one that was noticed by other ships in the squadron. Lawson had never given the captain, or the ship, any cause to regret it.

"Give way together, men," Lawson's deep voice quietly intoned as a swell took the launch away from the ship's hull. The launch only used three strokes of the oars to cover the water to the mystery vessel. "Hold water. Now boat your oars." Lawson looked at Rork, who grasped the foremast chains of the *Ramer* and held the launch as steady as he could in the rising and falling sea. Rork looked at Wake and wrinkled his nose up. Wake smelled it too, the smell of death. Lawson and the boat crew were stolidly doing their duty, saying nothing about the stench that was now engulfing them.

A boat crewman stood to hold the launch as Rork started to climb the chains. Wake put one hand on the substantial shoulder of Lawson and leaped for the strake on the side of the hull. One foot slipped dangerously but the other found its mark, and he was able to ascend using the mainmast chains, avoiding the indignity of falling backward into the launch on top of his own men.

Rork made it first, with enough time to make a spontaneous utterance before Wake reached the level of the deck.

"Oh Jesus, Mary, and Joseph . . ."

Then Wake saw the scene.

The origin of the stench was immediately apparent. A body lay on the deck among some loosened halliards by the pin rail of the foremast, so bloated and blackened that no features could be recognized in the face. The body was clad in an officer's uniform and bore the insignia for an ensign. It had been rotting there for several days.

The forward and after hatchways were open. Barely audible, an elongated moan emanated from the forward hatchway. Wake and Rork instinctively moved slowly in that direction.

"Ahoy *Ramer!* This is Captain Wake of the *Hunt*. Is anyone aboard?"

The moan came again, but louder. Rork reached the hatchway first and descended into the shadows, closing one eye to keep his vision while the rest of his face hardened with determination. Wake followed him down, taking shallow breaths to reduce the amount of fetid air he would inhale.

The space they entered was the berthing deck for the crew, dimly lit by sunlight entering from the hatchway and some dead-lights. Bodies in lines of hammocks suspended from the deck beams swung in unison with the roll of the ship. Dark stains permeated the normally clean hammocks. The deck below the hammocks was filthy and greasy with body fluids, making Wake grip a stanchion to prevent himself from slipping. He could tell that the moaning was coming from several of the hammocks. Rork moved to the closest one. Wake took as deep a breath as he could stand and tried once more, his plaintive voice matching the gloom. "Anyone alive here? I am Captain Wake of the *Hunt*, come to help you."

The hammock Rork was about to examine abruptly opened, revealing two eyes staring from above a beard congealed with blood and vomit. Tears ran from the man's eyes as his mouth opened, tentatively at first, then with sound.

"True? No dream?"

Rork gently took the man's shoulder, helping elevate his torso in the hammock. As he did so, some other men started moving in their hammocks, moans becoming words, words becoming questions. Rork looked around at the voices, then at Wake, and back to the man he held. "'Tis true, sailor. Navy's here now. We'll help ye now. What's your name, son?"

"Nelson, able seaman, foremast . . ."

"All right, Nelson. We're here now. We'll get ye up an' better afore the sun hits the mast truck. Ye've gotten past the worst o' it, son. You'll be pullin' through now."

Wake stood next to Rork at Nelson's hammock. He appeared to be in the best condition of the *Ramer's* men around them, and Wake needed answers. He spoke slowly, leaning close to Nelson's ear.

"Where is the Captain, Nelson? Where are the officers?"

"Captain's dead, I think. Heard somebody say that. Ensign's waiting. He' sick, but he's waiting for you."

Rork glanced at Wake and shook his head. Nelson didn't know the ensign was dead on the foredeck. The sailor couldn't be much help.

"Rork, stay in here and try to determine how many are alive. We need to get them out of here and up on deck right away. I'll go aft and see what I can find."

"Aye, aye, sir."

"And Rork, have Lawson send two men down here, then stand off."

"Aye, Captain. I'd make a bargain with the devil his ownself for a navy surgeon right about now, sir."

"Yes, Rork, I know. We'll do what we can with what we have. I'm going aft now."

In the captain's cabin Wake found the body of a man he thought might be the steward, judging by his clothes, lying as if asleep in the captain's berth. He too, had vomit and blood staining his clothing and the blankets—signs of yellow fever. No one else was in the cabin. The logbook was on the chart table, but Wake decided he should check the whole ship for survivors before reading the last words of dying men. He moved to the starboard side of the ship and checked the petty officers' berths.

Wake heard a voice coming out from the black void ahead of him as he stumbled through a companionway that normally would have a lantern.

"Who's that?"

"Captain Wake of the *Hunt*. We're here to help. Where are you?"

"God! Oh God! Thank you, sir. Gunner's mate Thomas, sir. I'm here in the gunroom, sir."

Wake made his way forward, ducking under the beams and gradually regaining some eyesight after the relative brightness of the captain's cabin. Thomas stood leaning against the doorway to the petty officer's gunroom, saying something to others in the room behind him. Wake went past him into the cabin.

Two other men were in there, both in their berths. Thomas was ambulatory, but even in the dimness Wake could tell he was very sick. The cabin had the same fetid smell as everywhere else on the ship. Thomas was obviously trying to be the petty officer.

"Sir, we are very thankful you came. Peterson here was down for his numbers, but never died, so I think he'll live. And Giles, the lazy bastard of a bosun, he's right and well. Just needs encouragement."

Weak but sarcastic replies came from the subjects of Thomas' comments, which Wake took as a good sign.

"Thomas, where is your captain?"

"He died early on, sir. Weeks ago."

"And the other officers?"

"Only had one sir. Ensign Barnes, sir. Standing watch on deck, waiting for the relief ship, sir. He must've met you, sir."

"The men, Thomas, where are all the men?"

Thomas stared at Wake, saying nothing.

"Thomas, where are they?"

"The ones that lived are here, sir. The ones that died were put over. We was shorthanded to begin with. Only twenty-five to man this schooner. Too shorthanded, sir . . ."

Thomas started to slump down. Wake caught him, lowering the gunner's mate into a berth. The man's breathing was labored and he was clammy to the touch.

"Need to sit, sir. Sorry."

"It's all right, man. Now, when did this start and where are your men?"

Thomas' voice faded, replaced by a gurgling cough as he

struggled to communicate. Wake waited. He had to know.

"Three or four weeks ago, I think. Almost everybody got sick. Harpford went for help in the cutter but . . . no help till you. Dead men overboard."

"Harpford went for help where?"

It was no use. Thomas was now gagging on fluids and doubled over. Wake knelt down on one knee and helped him sit up to alleviate the fluids building, and looked over to the other two in the cabin. They lay there, staring in the gloom at the scene of the officer and their shipmate.

Wake got up from the berth and walked out. He stopped in the captain's cabin, picked up the logbook, and ascended the after ladder to the main deck. The air up on deck no longer seemed as rancid as it had when they first arrived. Compared to below, it was fresh, and he eagerly gulped it into his lungs like a drowning man. He looked over the side and saw Lawson and the launch floating fifty feet to windward. Behind him he heard Rork telling the two seamen to be careful as they lifted another of the survivors up out of the forehatch and laid him out on the deck, his arms instinctively covering his face to shield his eyes from the glare of the sun.

Wake bobbed his head to Rork, then turned to call to Lawson. "Lawson, come alongside for a message for Mr. Emerson."

"Aye, aye, sir."

As the launch glided over, Wake scrawled a short note to Emerson.

Emerson,
Yellow fever struck here. No officers alive. Not sure what happened. Many dead. Maybe ten survivors. Send six more volunteer men by Lawson. Have Lawson lie off afterward. Also send a boat along the shore to look for one of Ramer's boats. A petty officer named Harpford took it to get help. I will remain here for a while.
Wake

He folded it and handed it down to the coxswain, then held up his hand.

"Lawson. Deliver that right now to Mr. Emerson, then return with the detail he sends. After they are aboard, lie off again."

Lawson, sensing the tension in his captain's tone, quickly acknowledged the order and swung his tiller, turning the launch and telling his men to put their weight into the oars. Wake called forward to Rork that he had more help being sent over, then walked aft and sat on the cabin top, opening the logbook in his hands.

He turned to the last entry. It was dated three days before, on Tuesday the eighteenth of October, 1864. It was difficult to make out, the writing was so illegible. The day and date blocks were filled in, as was the sky and wind, but no time of entry. Evidently there were no clouds that day, and the wind was from the southeast at five knots. Wake stared at the remarks section to decipher the writing there. He couldn't get it all, but some of the words came through. His hands started to shake as he understood their meaning, seeing the scene in his mind.

More chain let out . . . stopped the dragging. Can't work ship. Waiting . . . must know by now. Very sick . . . gone . . . more down. Thomas now senior . . . write the log . . . and maintain . . .
   Barnes

Wake looked away from the logbook, trying to think. Thomas had never made a subsequent entry in the log. Neither had Ensign Barnes. After laying it down on the captain's chart table, he had come back up on deck to stand and wait for the rescue they were sure would come. Wake looked forward. Barnes was still waiting there, dead and rotting by the foremast, unrecognizable even by his own mother. The entries for the days leading up to the eighteenth became steadily more garbled as they proceeded to tell the saga of the fever taking more of them.

Captain Stanley was one of the first, dying on the fifth day, going insane from the extreme pains inside his head beforehand. It was on that day they hoisted the yellow signal of fever aboard— Stanley would not permit them to while he was alive, a stubborn refusal to face the sad facts.

By the seventh day a third of the crew of twenty-five men were down with the fever, and more started to die. On the tenth of October, the eleventh day of the sickness, everyone but three men were sick, most in their berths. *Ramer* was anchored off the Mosquito Inlet, a well-known blockade running area, with no one manning the watch. The least sick cared for those who were the worst afflicted. No one had the time or strength to work the ship anymore. They dragged the dead up the ladders and shoved them over the side, recording their names in the log, and the fact that a Christian prayer was said for each.

Harpford left on October fifteenth, and there was no further reference in the log to him or his boat crew of four. It didn't say where he was headed to get help, but probably north along the coast, Wake surmised, toward the small army forces that periodically occupied Jacksonville, a hundred miles up the coast. Wake doubted that Harpford had made it. There were many things, storms and Rebels, and the fever itself, that could have stopped him.

The log told the tale. Painstakingly, Ensign Barnes described who among the men was sick and who was dead, writing an epitaph for the crew even as he must have known he was dying himself. On the seventeenth of October, *Ramer* started to drag her anchor as a southeasterly wind built up, Barnes noting that they could only let chain out, as no one was strong enough to set sail or weigh anchor. They dragged through the day and night with Barnes and Thomas and a seaman named Farah on deck, watching and waiting for *Ramer* to either hold to her anchor or wash ashore and founder. On the eighteenth Barnes made his last entry—the anchor finally had held and they stopped after dragging nine miles up the coast from their original station.

Wake felt exhausted when he finished. The sun was high and hot, sucking strength from the men working on the deck. It had taken awhile, but the survivors had been brought up from below and laid out in the shade, where they were ministered to by some of Wake's men. One of them knelt over a stricken man, giving him a drink from a cup and talking softly to him. Wake saw that it was Dirkus and wondered why he had volunteered for the duty. Other sailors, neckerchiefs wrapped around their faces, were bringing up the dead and laying them out at the very stern, downwind of Wake and the survivors. One of the sailors tending the sick was the boy who Wake had seen earlier on the deck of the *Hunt,* crying at the sight of the *Ramer* as they approached. He was one of the original crew from the *Hunt* who had survived the horror of the fever, but Wake didn't know his name. There hadn't been enough time to get to know all their names. Seeing the boy, eyes showing teary fright above his neckerchief, Wake wondered if he and Dirkus and the others had truly been volunteers for this grisly duty. With the rate of decomposition in the tropics, Wake knew they would have to get them overboard as soon as possible or more disease would generate. He called out to Rork at the hatchway, who came over to his captain.

"Rork, are all these men—Lawson's boat crew and the others—volunteers?"

"Every one, Captain. I was there when Lawson and his crew volunteered. They all stepped forward together, sir."

"And Dirkus and the boy?"

"Aye, sir. The lads told me Mr. Emerson queried for volunteers, and the whole deck division queued up. They said that was when Dirkus stepped forward. Mr. Emerson had three times the sailor volunteers he needed, but he took Dirkus and the lad anyway."

"Very well. I was surprised to see those two, particularly. That boy was pretty distressed earlier, and this Dirkus fellow is a mystery to me."

"Captain, they volunteered because it was you. They trust

you. I wouldn't wish this duty on the English Lord o' Derry, but these lads have got it done. Terrified to come over here they was, sir, but they did it in spite o' that. And they did it for you. Now, by your leave, we've got to finish what we've started here, sir. 'Tis cheerless duty and the sooner done, the better 'twill be for all hands."

"Yes, Rork, you're right. As soon as you have each dead man identified, we'll do a mass burial ceremony and send them over the side. We've got to end this."

"Thomas, in their crew, has got their names down, sir. He's sick too, but he just took care o' that for us. This is sad, Captain. Ne'er seen anything like it."

"How many survived?"

"Got three petty officers an' six seamen laid out alive. Three o' the seamen are pretty bad, though. Coxswain an' four went in a boat for help, so that makes fourteen survivors out o' twenty-five souls aboard. I seen it bad, but ne'er this bad. What'll we do for the lads, Captain?"

"Make them comfortable and clean, Rork. We're not in charge here, God is. All we can do is make them as comfortable as possible."

"What about the ship, sir?"

Wake had thought about that while en route. His first duty was to save the lives of the stricken men. His next duty was to the navy, which meant he had to do everything he could to save the *Ramer* and bring her back to Key West, ready for action. Wake knew exactly what he had to do, and what he had to say. He took a breath and looked at his old friend.

"Rork, you know what we have to do. As soon as we have loaded some fresh provisions from the *Hunt,* we will take both ships back to Key West. *Hunt* will tow *Ramer* until you get her in sailing condition. At that point we will cast you loose and escort you the rest of the way."

"Aye, aye, sir."

Wake knew the question in Rork's mind. "And you will keep

on board the men you have now, along with Lawson and his boat crew. Lawson will be your second in command."

"Aye, aye, sir. Understood."

Wake contemplated Rork. He wondered. Did Rork really understand the consequences of this assignment? "Perhaps you do, Rork. But allow me to clarify anyway."

Rork's left eyebrow rose, betraying his confusion as he stood there, arms akimbo, waiting for the rare event of an explanation of an order. "Aye, sir. Thank ye."

"Rork, you are ready to stand for your examination for acting ensign. Been ready for sometime, actually. This assignment will bring you to the attention of the admiral and squadron staff and probably remind them that you are eligible for the examination board. We need some officers with your experience. Both at sea and in life."

Rork managed a brief smile. "Well Captain, those words are kind, indeed, sir. Much appreciated. Me mum would love to hear 'em, though me ol' rector in County Wexford might not recognize the lad!"

"Yes, well, Rork, we've got unpleasant work to get done here. Tell me when you're ready, and I'll do the ceremony."

"Aye, aye, sir."

Wake rose and walked forward to where the sailors from his ship were caring for the survivors of the *Ramer*. Dirkus, the boy, and another sailor, were tenderly removing the clothing of the still-living victims, throwing it overboard, and covering them with clean sheets found in the captain's cabin. Most of the men were emaciated, doubled up from the pain, covered in their own fluids, and too weak to move on their own. One was hallucinating something about the wintertime and bearskins to keep warm. Another was calling softly for "Lucy."

Wake knelt beside the man as Dirkus washed the strings of vomit from his face. The steward looked over at his captain and shook his head.

"Like us a month ago, only, if anything, even worse."

Dirkus returned to his work, throwing the now slimy rag overboard also. He got another from a tub of water and washed the man's lower torso, throwing that rag over when it became matted with filth. Next to him, the boy was helping another victim in a gagging fit sit up and retch a stream of bloodied black bile into a small bucket. The patient was an older man who appeared to be in marginally better condition. When he was done he croaked out thanks to the boy, then eased backward to the deck, clearly exhausted by the effort. Wake walked over, reached down and put his hand on the boy's shoulder. It was trembling. The boy looked up, grim-faced. He was a boy only by chronological age—not by lack of life experience.

"Thank you for your good work, son."

The youngster's eyes were hard and unblinking.

"This ain't no war, Captain. This here is just dying for no reason. An' we're gonna be next."

Wake's mind went blank with grief for the boy. He knew he should say something to raise the spirits of his men—this brave boy who was facing the ultimate horror of painful death by a mystery fever—but he had no answer to that comment.

It was Dirkus who answered, an edge to his tone. "Stow that bunk, boy. I don't need it, and the captain don't neither. Get on with your job there and help these men."

Dirkus' words stirred Wake, clearing his head and allowing some words to come forth. "Son, I think the fever has piped down here. Chances are we won't get it, and the season is changing now. This fever can't live in cool weather. And Dirkus is right. Now we need to help these men recover. You're doing good work here. Keep it up."

The boy looked back at the row of men moaning as they lay in pools of their own waste. When he spoke, he sounded ten years older. "Aye, aye, sir. Lead or fever, you're dead just the same. Doesn't matter the cause, I guess, an' it sure don't do to think on it none."

Wake nodded and walked aft.

It took thirteen long minutes for Wake to say the prayer and the detail of *Hunt*'s men to lower the remains overboard. Lawson and his boat crew stood in line on the deck as the honor guard and the others under Rork handled the bodies. Dirkus and the boy, who Wake found out was named Sunderland, handled one of the bodies together with another, larger sailor. All three were barely able to get it over the side, as the emotion welled up inside of them. They tried to be as dignified as they could, but it still took its toll on even the hardened veterans as they looked into the victims' faces when releasing hold of them. When it was over, Wake told the sailors to rest for a moment before returning to their duty.

"Rork, make sure you use the supplies I sent over. Get all the decks smoked out with hot tar and sulfur. Throw away all of the clothing, all the water and food. Wash down and scrub every surface with vinegar. The ship must be cleansed of her disease. Give the men fifteen minutes to rest, then get them to work and keep them working. Maybe working will conquer their fears. I don't like the looks in their eyes, Rork. They're terrified that they're next."

"Aye, sir. That's what they're all a-thinkin'. Had the thought me ownself, but it don't help a wit, so there's no sense a-dwellin' on it. We'll do, Captain. We'll do."

"Very well, Rork." He looked at his pocket watch. "I think an hour would be about right. Start to weigh your anchor then, and we'll pass the hawse to you when your rode's short. Good luck, Rork."

As he was rowed over to the *Hunt* he felt as if he were returning to the world of the living. Climbing up to the main deck of his ship, he stopped and looked down at Lawson.

"Good luck, Lawson. Take care of those sick men over there as best you can, help Rork, and thank you all for volunteering. I'll see all of you in Key West!"

"Aye, aye, sir. We'll get 'em home, Captain."

Lawson saluted and turned his attention to his crew and the

other ship. Wake turned to Emerson and Rhodes, who were standing at the ladder to the wheelhouse. The expression on the executive officer's face spoke more than words. It was a combination of concern and dread. Wake jerked his head toward his cabin, leaning forward and speaking with a low tone in Emerson's ear.

"We'll get underway in one hour. Meanwhile, I want you, Rhodes, and Ginaldi to come to my cabin. I'll brief you there on what we found on the *Ramer* and what our plan is. Any word from the launch we sent to search for the *Ramer*'s boat?"

"Curtis just returned, sir. Went fifteen miles further up the coast. No sign of any boat, camp, or survivors."

"Damn. Well, maybe they were picked up by a ship, or made it to Jacksonville. Either way, we have to get *Ramer* and her crew to Key West immediately. All right then, I'll see you and the other officers in my cabin in a moment."

After Emerson acknowledged the summons, Wake spoke loudly to Rhodes. Several of the watch-standers were listening, and Wake knew it would be repeated all over the ship in minutes.

"It's what we thought. It's the yellow jack over there, Mr. Rhodes. We buried several, but I think most of the ones we found alive will make it." Wake's eyes took in the men around him. "We saved the lives of those survivors today. *You,* all of you, saved the lives of those men. Well done. This day won't be forgotten by any of us who were here."

Emerson's facial expression grew tense. "Good God, I'd rather face a battle, than face the damned yellow jack, Captain."

Wake eyed him for a moment. Emerson had said what everyone felt, but Wake thought there was something more to say.

"It was a *battle* for our lads who went over there today, Mr. Emerson. Make no mistake about that at all. It was the toughest battle Dirkus, and Sunderland, and Rork, and Lawson, and all the other men from the *Hunt* who were on that ship, ever fought, and it was against the most sinister enemy we'll ever face."

Rhodes' forehead creased, the question that was forming in

his mind coming out of his grimly set mouth in a low tone, almost in a whisper. "Sir? What enemy is that?"

"The enemy within, Mr. Rhodes. That enemy we each have deep within us. The one that that tries to stop us from doing what we know we should. The one that's called *fear.*"

As he said it, the image of the stained hammocks, with the living and dead in them swinging in unison in the morbid stench of the crews' berthing deck, and Dirkus and Sunderland cleaning and caring for the sick, filled Wake's mind. He turned away from the men surrounding him in the wheelhouse, lest his eyes betray his thoughts. It took all of his self-control to maintain his composure in front of his officers and men, but there really was no choice for Wake. He was the captain. Death was just another factor to be faced, a potential consequence of decisions he made every day. And fear was a luxury no captain could afford to display.

Wake smelled an acrid hint of burning sulfur and spotted an eddy of smoke drifting away from the forehatch of the *Ramer*.

"One hour, Mr. Emerson, then we'll weigh anchor. Officers' call in my cabin in five minutes. We'll go over the plans for the immediate future. Carry on."

3

Force Majeure

Two weeks had drifted by since the *Hunt* escorted the *Ramer* into the quarantine anchorage off Key West. The three-day passage south from Mosquito Inlet against the wind and current had been difficult. As the only man aboard who had been on the fever ship, Wake sequestered himself in his cabin and allowed Emerson to take *Hunt* to Key West—more to allay any fears in the crew than any real concern on his part.

The *Hunt* was dangerously shorthanded with so many men gone and the watch-standers were exhausted at the end of each day. There weren't enough men to fight the ship, should an enemy appear, and tense lookouts scanned the horizon constantly to identify the ships seen en route. Fortunately, duty did not invoke a boarding or a chase—-all the ships seen were benign.

Off Cape Canaveral Rork buried at sea another of the *Ramer's* men, using a Bible found in the dead captain's cabin to find some words to say over the body. The medical condition of most of the sick was at least not getting any worse, and several were improving.

Rork didn't sleep in the captain's cabin. He just couldn't

bring himself to do that, though no one would have objected. Instead he slept on the main deck aft, close if needed, and there was a lot of need for his skills as a bosun and as a leader. It had taken a day for all hands to get *Ramer*'s sails and rigging squared away and the ship fumigated with smoke in an effort to drive the disease out. After that was accomplished, they cast off the tow and sailed her, making long tacks southwest to the beach and southeast to the edge of the Stream. The steamer continued on the rhumb line slowly, watching the schooner as she sailed to the left and right of the track.

None of the *Hunt*'s men aboard *Ramer* grew sick, though they watched each other constantly for signs. As the days went by and no more deaths occurred, Dirkus, Sunderland, and the rest started to feel less fatalistic. Rork, assisted by Lawson, had enough work for them all to do, and even after they had anchored off the naval station, in addition to nursing the sick, the days were filled with repair and maintenance work to get the *Ramer* in fighting trim once more.

Once the two weeks had passed with no new cases of yellow fever, the slowly recovering *Ramer* men were taken ashore to the hospital, and the jubilant men from the *Hunt* were replaced aboard by new drafts from the naval station. An ensign officially relieved Rork with undisguised reluctance—everyone ashore had heard what happened aboard the schooner and no one wanted to serve aboard the *Ramer* now, for she would carry the reputation of a death ship forever.

But Rork didn't care about the ensign's opinions, as Lawson and his launch brought the men home to the *Hunt* to a tumultuous welcome heard by the whole harbor. Sailors and engineers alike lined the decks and cheered the men, and all hands were greeted with a special noonday meal of fresh beef and fruit prepared in their honor. When Rork came up the side Wake greeted his friend with a firm handshake, held for only a moment, knowing anything more would be unseemly. Their eyes met. Wake grimly smiled and Rork nodded. No words were needed. The horror was done and they were home.

Hunt, even with the return of the men, was still not up to strength, but they were now at least able to get her under way and do their assignments, one of which was waiting. There was no time for liberty ashore for Rork and his returning detail of men, for the *Hunt* weighed anchor immediately after the feast, bound south into the Straits of Florida to search for and reprovision the steam gunboat *Whatley.*

Whatley had been on station in the Straits for three weeks, inspecting vessels and looking for those ships about to run the blockade and bring munitions into the Confederacy from Cuba and the Bahamas. In that time, she had found two British schooners and a small Spanish steamer that actually had contraband cargo and false papers. Sending to Key West reports and requests along with the seized ships, the captain of the *Whatley* had asked for supplies and provisions. His hunting area was fruitful, his men were making prize money and were therefore unusually happy. An extension of time at sea could provide more, and the officers and men had no desire to return to Key West at the moment. The admiral was more than willing to oblige, for the *Whatley* was doing well. In addition, as a little added reward, the admiral of each squadron received a share of the prize money gained by any vessel under his command, and he reasoned that there was certainly no reason to diminish that premium prematurely.

The day was fair, a small breeze from the south bringing some movement to the heavy humid air, some low white clouds over the islands dotting the pale blue of the sky. *Hunt* met the low swells out in the main channel and increased speed to her usual seven knots, making the bow wave swish and hiss as it washed aft along the hull. The manmade smells of the island and harbor were replaced by the fresh sharp smells of the sea. The air had a tingling body to it, invigorating all aboard the ship and bringing forth smiles from the hardened men. The freedom of the sea could be tasted in that air, and the sailors of the *Hunt* left the harbor with a much better attitude than the previous departure, for they were on a far different mission than the last. This would be a routine mission of resupply, and that felt good.

Fort Taylor, that grim reminder of the mechanics of war, slid by to port, and later Sand Key lighthouse, symbol of rescue and life, was passed to starboard. The water color changed to darker green and then darker blue as they progressed southerly beyond the coral reefs, until the sea looked majestically royal blue, clear enough that the men could peer into the depths and see the dolphins and fish playing under the bow waves.

It was a beautiful day, especially after the reunion of the men and the feast of fresh provisions. It was the kind of departure that sailors remember in front of a fireplace on cold winter days far from the sea—when their leathered hands hold a mug of rum and their white hair shakes as they laugh, describing the scene for those landsmen who can only imagine it.

Wake stood on the narrow deck outside the wheelhouse and took in his surroundings and a deep breath of sea air. He loved heading out to sea on a day like this.

"Course is set s'west for Bahia Honda on the Cuban coast, sir. Revolutions made for apparent speed of seven knots, and the ship is secured for sea."

The ship's bell rang out twice as Rhodes made his report. Emerson looked over at him.

"And the bosun reports two bells in the afternoon watch struck, sir."

Emerson nodded to the ensign and turned to Wake. "A beautiful day for it, sir. I estimate that we'll be off the Cuban coast in the area of the *Whatley*'s station in twenty hours or so, maybe nine o'clock tomorrow morning."

Wake considered his estimate. It seemed about right. He was still getting used to not tacking upwind. It made navigation so much easier. "Does that include the effects of the Stream, Mr. Emerson?"

"Aye, sir. The Stream and the wind on our port bow."

"Very well. What do you make of the weather, Mr. Emerson?"

The executive officer surveyed the sky, knowing that he was missing something. He had been in this squadron for two months now, one month of that under Wake, and was learning every day from his captain. "It appears to be good weather, no cloud masses on the horizon, sir. Nothing in the offing."

"What about the sea? What is it telling you?"

Emerson looked down at the water around the ship. The swells! The present wind didn't build them, something else did, something to the south. His eyes returned to Wake. "The swells, Captain. They don't match the wind. Something to the south is sending them."

"Exactly. It *is* a beautiful day. But watch those swells as we progress. Could be nothing, could be a storm. We've only had one hint of northerly air come down so far. Storm season isn't over yet. Even though we're in November, it's not autumn. Not down here."

"Aye, sir. We'll keep an eye on the swells, and the wind."

"Very good, Mr. Emerson. You have the deck and the watch. Continue course and speed. I'll be in my cabin if you need me. Notify me of any ship sightings, weather changes, ship problems, or unusual occurrences."

In his cabin Wake worked out his own estimate, which was twenty-one and a half hours, assuming they found *Whatley* exactly where they thought she would be—an assumption that had been wrong every other time Wake had tried to rendezvous with the speck of a ship at sea during the last year and a half. He presumed it would be wrong again and allowed himself four to six hours of searching to find *Whatley.*

In a sailing ship the strike of the bell was audible everywhere.

In a steamer it was only audible close to the wheelhouse, where it was kept. Since Wake's cabin was close behind the wheelhouse on the same deck, he could make out the *ding ding* even above the incessant rumble of the engine. Two bells in the first dogwatch. Dinner would be served soon. His daily paperwork completed, reminding him he was short a yeoman clerk, Wake decided it was time to take a look around the ship. Her motion had changed for the last two hours, with the pitch of her bow becoming more pronounced. Nothing dangerous yet, but noticeable. Wake began his tour at the wheelhouse, where Rhodes was officer of the deck. Curtis spotted him first and alerted the rest by his greeting.

"Afternoon, sir."

"Good afternoon, Curtis. How is everything, Mr. Rhodes?"

"No ships sighted, sir. Sea is starting to build. Nothing too bad though. Cloud haze coming in from the southeast, wind steady at force three from the southeast too. McKinney reports the engine is steady, with no problems. Dinner is being made now, sir."

Rhodes' recital finished, Wake scanned the horizon and the decks, then went out and down to the main deck. Walking aft he examined the starboard launch—Lawson's. As he expected, it was in perfect order. Coxswains were miniature captains in their own way, and their boats were their commands. Wake smiled as he went further aft, where some coal heavers were leaning on the bulwark, breathing in fresh air and getting a respite from the stifling atmosphere below. They straightened up upon sighting the captain approach.

"How is the machinery, men?"

The oldest, maybe twenty-five and his name unknown to Wake as yet, spoke in reply. He had never spoken to a captain before and was nervous.

"Working well, sir. We're just having a five-minute stop, sir. Then we'll go back down. McKinney said we could, sir." He glanced at the other two men. "Time to go back, lads."

"That's fine, but wait a moment. What's your name?"

"Galloway, sir."

"How long in the navy, Galloway?"

"Two years, sir."

"Very good. I'll go down with you men, if you're ready now."

All the engineers knew that at least once a day Captain Wake would appear in the boiler room, asking questions about the procedures and equipment. Usually he would talk to Ginaldi or the petty officer on watch. They were not used to having a conversation with him, and were unsettled by it, even though the captain was smiling. Galloway smiled back.

"Aye, sir. We're heading back down right now, sir."

Wake was always amazed at the men who could work in that environment. The heat was the first thing to assault the senses, then the overwhelming thundering of the machinery itself—different parts thunking and clacking and pinging. Moving deeper into the ship and closer to the metal beast, eyes were diverted by the array of moving arms, pistons, and gears, all of which would dismember a man if they were able to grab him.

Only one man had been hurt in there in the time Wake had been captain. Coming back when escorting the *Ramer*, one of the oilers had been reaching out past the crankshaft to oil the beam elbow, when his own elbow got in the way. The remorseless iron beam smashed down on it, rendering it and the man useless immediately. His scream was heard above the engine all over the ship. Brought up to the main deck for Wake to see, the man writhed in pain, his arm swollen in five minutes to twice its previous size. Wake gave him laudanum from the medical chest in his cabin, wrapped the arm in a splint, and gave the man straight brandy every hour to keep him senseless. He was put ashore at the hospital upon reaching Key West, and never seen aboard again. Wake received word from the surgeons that they were deciding whether to amputate or not.

The memory served as a reminder to walk steady and stay away from the moving parts. On deck, one had a sense of a wave coming. Down in the bowels of the ship all ones' senses were distorted, and lurches of the hull came without warning. Wake wondered why more men weren't hurt in this foreign place.

McKinney suddenly appeared from around the bulk of the boiler, startling Wake. Like everyone else who worked in the engine spaces, he had a cloth wrapped around his head to protect his hearing. The engineer had to shout from six inches away from Wake's ear to be heard.

"HELLO, CAPTAIN!"

Wake nodded in return, for normal conversation was impossible and he was in no temper to shout back and forth, and continued making his way aft to the shaft. McKinney followed, his short thin frame deftly maneuvering through the hot iron obstacles. Wake held his hands up and apart in a gesture of inquiry if all was well.

"NO PROBLEM, SIR!"

Nodding again, Wake peered down into the gloom of the narrow alley abutting the after end of the engine room at the shaft revolving around and around, shoving the *Hunt* into those seas outside this cauldron of sound and heat. It was a bit mesmerizing watching that shaft, for it was the very reason for all of this mechanical and manual effort. That iron rod was the strength of the ship, if it stopped turning she was dead in the water and at the mercy of whatever was out there—an enemy ship, or a tidal current, or a storm. It was an eerie and disquieting thing to ponder. Wake shook his head free of such thoughts and noticed McKinney was staring at him, watching for a question or complaint. He made his way past the petty officer and climbed the ladder out of the heat and noise.

Wake had been below only a few minutes, but the air out on deck seemed almost cold. He felt like roaring with the pleasure of escaping that mechanical hell and getting back where sailors belonged, where they could see and hear and smell the sea. His stomach told him it was time for food, and Wake was making his way to the ladder to go up to his cabin when he heard the report of the lookout aloft.

"Deck there! Smoke on the horizon one point off the starboard bow. I think I see two masts. Vessels look to be heading westerly."

Wake was in the wheelhouse even before Rhodes acknowledged the report. They were now approaching the middle area of the Straits of Florida, a shipping lane for the trade of the Caribbean, the Atlantic, and the Gulf of Mexico. They would see many ships, some of which were running munitions and supplies to the enemy. Occasionally a few of those vessels turned out to be warships in the enemy's navy, well-armed ocean raiders that could, and without hesitation would, immediately sink a small steamer like the *Hunt*. The famous Captain Raphael Semmes had already done that in the Gulf of Mexico, humiliating the U.S. Navy, and every naval officer knew it could happen again.

"Steer for her, Mr. Rhodes. Take bearings and determine the rate of intercept or escape, and advise me."

Rhodes' reply was even-toned. "Aye, aye, sir. It appears the range is approximately ten miles. My bearings on the smoke show an intercept, but it will take quite a while for us to gain on them, sir."

Wake gazed around the horizon and thought about the various factors of the scenario. The wind was now from the southeast at force four, with the swells beginning to break and the height equivalent to a force six. They looked to be increasing still further. The suspect vessel was south of them, near the middle of the Straits, coming from the east and moving west. That put the origin of the vessel somewhere in the Atlantic, for if they had come out of Havana they would have been coming from the south, and if from Matanzas, the southeast. The destination was somewhere to the northwest or west. The vessel was too far north of Cuba, more than fifty miles, to be heading along the coast or down to the Caribbean through the Yucatan Straits. That vessel was fighting the Gulf Stream to go west. Why wouldn't she travel west to the north of the Stream, along the Florida Keys, where there was no current to fight?

"My compliments to Mr. Ginaldi, and have him visit me here, please."

Curtis sent a messenger as Emerson arrived on the bridge. Rhodes presented the facts to the executive officer, who stood next to Wake, staring to the southwest at the smudge on the horizon. Wake wasn't sure yet what he would decide, and said nothing. He needed more information. Emerson assumed a stance of patient interest and waited for his captain to speak. Ginaldi arrived at the wheelhouse, puffing with the rapid effort to respond to the summons.

"Mr. Ginaldi, take a glass and examine that vessel out there."

Ginaldi was not used to being brought from his beloved engine rooms to the bridge of a ship for anything other than chastisement over some failing of the mechanical elements of a vessel. He was very uncomfortable in the role of consultant, especially with everyone watching and listening. He looked at the distant smudge, adjusting the telescope until the image was the best he could make it. There wasn't much to see beyond the smoke. But that smoke told a message itself. Ginaldi put it down and waited for his captain to give an idea of why he was there.

"Mr. Ginaldi, can you give us enough speed to catch her? We'll need everything you have. No, we'll need more than what you have. Can you give me nine and a half?"

Ginaldi glanced back at the other vessel's smoke. It was a fair distance away.

"A moment, please, sir." Ginaldi turned to Emerson. "Sir, has that smoke cloud increased since we've spotted her?"

"Yes, it has gotten thicker a bit. What does that mean?"

"They're burning bituminous coal, sir. That means three things. They didn't come from a northern port, because ships take on anthracite coal there. It means also that she'll be visible in daylight and moonlight because that kind of coal makes a lot of smoke—much more than we do. We use navy anthracite. The third thing is that bituminous is less effective coal. It doesn't burn as hot, and the engine doesn't get the same steam power. That means that we can come up to greater power and speed more rapidly than they can, sir. The increase in smoke means they're already doing their best. We haven't even tried yet."

Wake was impressed with Ginaldi's knowledge. But the question hadn't been answered. "Very interesting, Mr. Ginaldi. But can you give me nine and a half knots?"

"Aye, sir. I can give you that for at the most, the very most, two hours. Then we'll have to back down to what we're doing now."

"Excellent. Do it."

"It'll be dangerous, Captain. Things happen when you do that. Things inside the boilers and the pistons. Things we can't see until they break. The boilers will be extremely hot and the lubrication will have to be watched very carefully. If we burn out a bearing during this, it could be a disaster."

Everyone present had shifted their attention from Ginaldi to Wake. Emerson looked the most concerned, as he should have been. It was his function to ensure the safe and efficient operation of the ship. Wake understood, but he knew that something was wrong with that ship out there. It had to be stopped and examined. Risks had to be taken.

"I understand and duly note your point, Mr. Ginaldi. Thank you for being candid, but my decision stands. Give me two hours of total effort on the part of your men and their machines."

"Aye, aye, sir. That you'll get, and more, Captain."

As Ginaldi departed Wake faced Emerson. "Mr. Emerson, there is something about that vessel's behavior that is suspicious. We will go alongside and examine her, and I want the following accomplished—I want all the hands to have their dinner. It will be a long night. Double the lookouts watching that vessel. I want to know if they see anything new about her. Keep me informed of the rate of intercept, and also the weather conditions. And get Durlon to ready the guns when we get within two miles of her. I want him to handle the forward gun personally."

Wake was glad to see that Emerson was not fazed by the orders.

"Aye, aye, sir."

"I'll be in my cabin. Keep me informed."

Emerson wondered, for the tenth time in a month, how Wake could be so calm after making decisions with such far-reaching consequences. As Wake left the wheelhouse Emerson set about to make sure the orders were followed, then climbed to the top of the wheelhouse for a better look at the far-off ship. Rork was already there, spying through a glass the duty bosun's mate had passed up to him. He moved over when Emerson arrived. With the dull roar of the stack behind them and the whine of the wind in the rigging around them, Rork had to speak up as he greeted the officer.

"Evenin' sir. Another grand chase it seems we've got!"

"Yes, Bosun. What do you make of her?"

"Oh, I believe she would be a runner, sir."

Emerson noted the lack of hesitation in Rork's opinion. "You seem pretty sure. Why?"

"Hard to tell much for certain, what with the light fadin' an' the haze an' all, sir, but I'd say she's not big enough for trans-Atlantic work. Not enough coal bunkers. An' she's not got enough sail area on those wee bitty masts to be much of a sailor. No sir, I'd say she's probably from Nassau, Mr. Emerson. She's got blockade runner in her blood, that one does. She's just made for it. She'll try to lose us in the dark."

Emerson thought about Rork's observations. They were probably correct. "Well, you might be right, Bosun. You just might be right."

Just at that point a woosh came from behind them as a shower of sparks volcanoed out of the stack and floated out over the sea astern of them. The vibration of the engine got faster and the roar of the gasses increased as they were spewed up and out of the stack into the darkening sky. Ginaldi was true to his word. *Hunt* was starting to pitch more and spray was flying from her bow as she plunged into the seas. Rork was grinning wildly at it all.

"Aye, Mr. Emerson. Either way—it will be a grand chase!"

An hour later at his chart table, Wake heard the knock and said to come in. It was Emerson.

"Wind is piping up and the seas are building, both from the south, sir. Wind's up to force six. Haze is turning into heavier clouds. There's a storm out there somewhere. We're gaining on the ship, but she's still about five or six miles off. Getting hard to see her in the dark."

"Very well, Mr. Emerson. Assume for a moment she's a runner. What would you do if you were her?"

"She's figured us out by now, sir. I'd reverse course when it gets completely dark. Probably go southeast, toward Matanzas, maybe south to Havana. Be in Spanish Navy waters well before dawn."

"So then what should we do?"

"Watch her like a hawk, sir. She turns, we turn."

"I see. But there is no light tonight. No stars, no moon. She's burning bad coal, but even so, at that range we'll probably lose sight of her completely in half an hour or so. Best we can hope for is that she flames up her stack for a moment and we spot that, right?"

Emerson wondered where Wake was heading with this line of thought. "Yes, sir."

Wake put a finger down on the chart in front of him. The lantern mounted on the bulkhead above the table cast a yellowish light on his finger pointing to Matanzas, Cuba.

"Look here. They won't go anywhere near Havana because they probably have intelligence that the *Whatley* is patrolling from that area to the westward. Matanzas is the next safest port for them. It's southeast of us. If they wait until complete darkness, which should be in a half an hour or so, then they should be about five miles away from us when they turn from west bound to the southeast, correct?"

Emerson saw it now. Wake saw the understanding in his eyes and smiled.

"We turn before they do!"

"Precisely. We are behind them and in the darkness of the eastern sky. We can turn earlier. Then we head to the course that they'll be on. We'll be there to greet them."

A sudden lurch of the ship made Emerson grip the table. *Hunt* slewed around, descending on the slope of a wave, then thudded hard into the next. Any intercept in the dark was difficult, but especially in the worsening weather. Accurate gunnery with a twelve-pounder at any range beyond two hundred yards, even for a veteran like Durlon, would be almost impossible.

"Good Lord, sir. I think it can work. What about boarding though?"

"We order them to heave to, and keep them close through the night, under our guns. We wait until morning to board. If they even look like they're going to make a dash for it, or dump cargo, we cut them bloody with grapeshot."

"Very good, sir."

"I'll be up shortly, Mr. Emerson. Please explain the plan to the others on watch and ready the crew for action. I want triple the lookouts at all positions. Though we know where she'll probably be coming through, we have to see her coming. Call all hands once we turn. It won't take long once they turn. They'll only be five miles away, moving at seven or eight knots. That means we should intercept at," Wake paused while he scrutinized his pocket watch, "just about the first bell in the last dogwatch, somewhere about three to four miles to the southeast of our present position."

"Aye, aye, sir," said Emerson. The awe and excitement in him was palpable, as he went out the door.

Wake took a deep breath and let it out slowly. If he guessed wrong, that ship would be gone quickly, her cargo well on its way to prolong the Rebels' resistance and thus the war. If he surmised correctly, they would have a very dangerous intercept to accomplish, at night, in bad weather, and she still might escape.

The dim light of the binnacle was just enough to show a man's form, but not his identity until one got close. The gale blowing outside, for it was a gale by then, was shrieking in the doorways and moaning in the rigging. Wake made his way slowly as he entered the small compartment. The wheelhouse was very crowded, with several men on the verge of losing their footing, and the first thing Wake did was to order everyone out who was not essential. That left Emerson, Rhodes, Rork, the helmsman, and Sunderland the messenger. Each was using at least one hand to hold on as the *Hunt* rolled and plunged and shuddered in the fifteen- to twenty-foot seas that were cresting over her. Wake pictured what it must be like in the boiler and engine rooms below.

Water poured over the bow, and the ship rolled severely when a wave rose from alongside. No one spoke. Another thud, and she stopped her bow in the wall of a wave on her port bow, lifting the hull and rotating it to the starboard until that rail was awash. Wake realized that the wind was getting worse, catching up with the height of the waves. They were entering a real tropical storm.

Sunderland rang four bells, the signal Wake had waited for.

"Bring your helm to port. Bear her off till she steers so'easterly. In the trough, helmsman, in the trough. Steady now. Bear a hand there on the wheel, Rork. Mr. Emerson, I believe that two men on the wheel would be appropriate at this time."

Hunt started her turn to port, from the southwest to the southeast, through the eye of the wind and seas. They slid over the first wave without much effort, but the second caught them, and stopped them. The liquid-solid wall and the wooden bow collided with a long splintering crash. Everyone in the wheelhouse fell forward, with curses rising from men thrown into the unnatural positions. Sunderland was quietly whimpering, but the first back on his feet. He went to help on the helm.

A mass of water four feet high flooded the foredeck, carrying away lines and chain, sweeping men before it. It looked as if the *Hunt* was sinking, with only her wheelhouse above water. The forward twelve-pounder crashed backward along the main deck into the deckhouse structure just below the wheelhouse, the sound of the wooden frame creaking loudly with the impact. Tearing loose all eight of its lashings as if they were string, the twelve-pounder slid this way and that, gouging the deck and anything it hit. The gun ended up on its side on the starboard main deck, cracking the bulwarks and blocking the way forward. The wave swept aft along the decks, taking everything that was not part of the structure with it. Rork groaned aloud as he saw the ship's launch, Lawson's pride and joy, torn from the davits and smashed into the deckhouse, pieces of planking, thwarts, and oars flying everywhere.

Hunt was still turning, and the third wave hit them on the starboard bow, washing the forward gun back to the center, forward of the wheelhouse. Wake could see a form, probably Durlon, down on the foredeck lashing down the gun again. Another wave came, but this time rolled underneath them, allowing the water that had filled the main deck to pour out of the scuppers. The course steadied as much as possible on southeast, the *Hunt* smashing into every third wave or so, but none as brutal as that second one.

Wake was concerned with damage and flooding. He needed answers fast. "Mr. Emerson, check for flooding and see how Ginaldi and his engine are doing. Then inspect the magazine. Mr. Rhodes, check the deck and get anything that could foul the propeller cleared away. And make sure that forward gun gets lashed down. Rork, get another man in here to help on the helm, then go out and help Mr. Rhodes. I want reports as fast as you can on flooding, damage, and casualties."

Minutes later a coal heaver came staggering up to the wheelhouse and reported to Wake, holding on with both hands to a handrail as the ship took another roll. It was the first time he had ever been above the main deck, and the first time he had ever talked to the captain.

"Sir, Mr. Emerson, he presents his, his respects, that's it. And he says to tell you that we are taking on water and the pumps are handling it for now. He said to say that Mr. Ginaldi has no problem with the machinery, and has two men hurt. I saw 'em get hurt, sir. Pretz and Guht. They fell onto the outside of the fire-box when the ship moved, while shovelin' coal. Burned up a bit, but they'll be fine. That's it, sir. That's what he said to say. All of it."

Rhodes was next. He had a bloodstain on his left leg and limped in to give his report.

"Both boats are smashed beyond repair, Captain. One anchor was carried away. The rode just beyond the chain tore away. We have the towing hawser stowed again. It was over the side. And there are many cracks in the deckhouse forward, sir. Gun is lashed down now. Old Durlon hurt his arm doing it, but won't show anyone. Foremast looks sprung, and the shrouds and forestay are slack. The stack looks secure, sir, from what I can see."

"And the men, Mr. Rhodes?"

"Oh, I'm sorry, sir. We have three men hurt in the deck division. One looks to have a broken arm, the other two are bruised badly in the ribs. I sent all three to their sacks, sir. Then there's Durlon, sir."

Wake took down a recently lit lantern and held it close to Rhodes' leg.

"I see. What about you? Your leg is bleeding."

"Oh that. Just a cut, sir. Got it when that wave hit. It's stopped bleeding now. I'm all right."

Wake studied the ensign for a moment. Even in the dim light of the lantern, he could see the blood was fresh. The ship slewed down a watery hill and rolled, making everyone hold on tighter.

"Very well, Mr. Rhodes. I have the deck and the watch. Go see if Mr. Emerson needs your assistance, present my compliments, and ask him to return with you to the wheelhouse."

The wind rushed in the open door when Rhodes departed, and Wake saw that it was now starting to rain as well. The seas had not abated, but *Hunt* was riding through and over them relatively well. An occasional collision with a larger than usual wave stopped her, but nothing like the monster that had smashed down on her during that turn. Wake was glad that most of the seas appeared to have a regular pattern now and were easier for the helmsman to anticipate, even though the wind had increased to perhaps force eight, gusting to force nine.

One of those larger than normal waves chose to arrive at that moment, hitting on the starboard bow and pushing *Hunt* bodily across to port. Wake heard a thump, followed by some cursing, and then two shapes fell into the wheelhouse together, struggling to stand.

Emerson helped Rhodes up, who then leaned against the after bulkhead.

"Just came up from below, Captain. We are taking on water, but Ginaldi says the pumps are handling it. He says his engine is doing well, but it's time to bring it back down."

Emerson stopped for a second and caught his breath, then resumed.

"The deck is torn up, fore and aft. Foreward gun is out of alignment with the slide carriage. Durlon's working on that as best he can with those seas coming aboard. His left arm is sprained. Don't think it's broke. The after gun stayed lashed, but the debris around it needs to be cleared away. I put Rork on that. I've got Rhodes here with me. I told him to stand easy with that leg gashed."

Wake noticed that Emerson, obviously tired and physically exhausted, omitted the "Mister" when referring to Rhodes.

Curtis, the bosun's mate who had been standing on the small deck outside the wheelhouse, came bursting inside, bringing in rainwater and interrupting Wake's thought process.

"I smell smoke from windward!"

The wind had shifted to the south, Wake realized. Windward was on the starboard bow—where the mystery steamer might be. On the other side of the wheelhouse, Sunderland, sliding on the deck, struck the bell once, then fell. It was a half-hour into the last dogwatch. The lookout from atop the wheelhouse yelled down to them, his words sounding detached in the screaming wind.

"Deck there! Smoke . . . from ahead. I see something . . . in the darkness a hundred yards . . . dead ahead!"

Wake pushed past Emerson to the helmsmen. "Steady as you go. We want to get close, but get ready to turn to starboard in a hurry."

"Aye, aye, sir," came back in a grim duet as four arms spun the wheel in unison back and forth to keep her on course.

"Mr. Emerson, go atop the wheelhouse and give me your opinion of what's out there, and where it is."

"Aye, aye, sir."

Wake suddenly remembered he had never ordered the engine to back down. He told Sunderland to send down the engine bell signal, then turned to Rhodes.

"Well, Mr. Rhodes. You'll earn the public's money tonight. Go rouse the men and send them to their action stations. Advise Mr. Ginaldi and his men too."

"Aye, aye, sir."

After the ensign left, Wake realized he was in the wheelhouse with just the helmsmen and Sunderland. He was at the mercy of the lookouts to tell him where the other ship was. He wondered what he could do with these seas. The plan he conceived earlier was completely useless in this weather.

"There she is! Over there to port."

The starboard door slammed open and Curtis fell into the wheelhouse again. He grabbed Wake and pointed out the leftmost window in front of the helmsmen.

"Out there, sir. She out there a hundred yards off and dead in the water. She's rolling her guts out, broached."

Wake couldn't see a thing. He pushed open the port side door and stood out on the deck, shielding his eyes against the sheets of rain. The he saw her and dashed inside again.

"Stop the engine and port your helm!"

Emerson slid in from the starboard side, colliding with his captain. "You see her? She's off the port bow. Wallowing. I think she's sinking."

They both went outside again and peered through the dark. Some lightning flashed and lit up the other craft. She was dead in the seas and riding low, wallowing as if swamped and full of water. Each wave washed completely over her, driving her lower. Her stack was canted to one side, with no smoke coming out anymore. The masts were swaying independently, their rigging trailing off in the wind. A group of men were on the stern, waving their arms, yelling soundlessly into the gale.

"Mr. Emerson, bring *Hunt* closer to her stern."

Emerson disappeared inside and the steamer slowly turned toward the stricken vessel. The *Hunt's* bow rose higher and higher, then dropped in a dizzying descent, while Emerson and the helmsmen got her to within thirty yards of the derelict.

Wake made his way forward to the bow, passing Durlon sitting down on the deck holding onto his gun barrel for support, and coming up on Rork, who had gone forward along the starboard deck.

At the bow they could hear the cries more clearly from the men on the stern of the mystery ship.

"We surrender! Save us!"

But there was something else—another voice, commanding, baritone, without fear. It was coming from somewhere forward in that ship, stronger than the pleas from the frightened men aft.

"We . . . do not . . . surrender! Invoke . . . force majeure! Force majeure!"

Wake and Rork looked at each other, wondering, as the bow fell into a wave and solid water washed over them. Sputtering and gasping for air they clung to each other as the bow rose again. The baritone came through the wind another time with the strange words.

"We invoke . . . force . . . majeure!

Now they could see him, standing on top of a deckhouse aft.

A man in some sort of uniform, lit up for a few seconds at a time by the flash of lightning.

"Captain, he's talking like one o' them Frog navy sods!"

"Rork, it's French for 'the law of the sea.' He's refusing to surrender but he's invoking the—."

Another drop of the bow into solid water stopped Wake's explanation temporarily. The cold sea took his breath away. He waited to get some air, then continued by shouting in Rork's ear.

"The law of the sea. Force majeure means the overwhelming force of nature. When a captain invokes assistance because of it, it overrides any other law, even war. He won't be our prisoner. He'll be our protected guest. We can't refuse to help him."

The effort of shouting the words in explaining the phrase was tiring. Wake paused for another breath and to brace himself for another deluge he could see cresting as it rushed forward.

When Wake could see and hear again he looked at the other ship. The men on the stern were no longer visible. Wails for help could be heard from that direction, but nothing distinct. The sounds were pleading in their tone, except that lone baritone calling out, "Force . . . majeure."

Wake grabbed Rork by the shoulders and shouted into his face.

"Come back to the wheelhouse."

Together they crawled aft through the debris strewn everywhere, holding on to whatever seemed solid. The wind rose and fell as it shrieked and screamed in the rigging. The seas were a constant rumbling roar, more massive a sound than even the engine. Wake found it hard to think. He knew he had to make a decision, make several, and make them soon. But he wanted the noise, that penetrating noise, to stop. He wanted the deck to stop moving, the sea to calm down, so he could think.

They made it up the ladder, falling backward at one point, to the port side door to the wheelhouse. Just before they made it inside they heard him again, faintly this time.

"Force . . . ma . . . jeure . . ."

Inside the wheelhouse, they could hear the ship moaning and cracking and grinding, as she flexed with the strains put upon her. Wake found Emerson standing by the wheel. Rhodes sat on the deck in the corner. Even inside the wheelhouse, Wake had to shout to be heard.

"Mr. Emerson. They've invoked assistance due to force majeure. We'd rescue them anyway, of course, but now they won't be our prisoners of war."

"Hell, Captain, they won't be much of anything in a few minutes. They're going down."

"Yes they are. So here's what we'll do. Steam up to windward of them and stream a line with floats tied on it down to them. As we go by, they can jump in and grab it, then we'll pull them aboard. Any questions?"

Outside, Curtis pounded the window and shouted through the glass, "Hold on!" Another wave rolled over the foredeck and washed up against the wheelhouse, making everyone inside get down on the deck. Wake was the first back up.

"Now, as I was saying, any questions? No? Right then. Rork, you and Curtis heave and stream the line off the port side. Let's get this done."

Standing out on the side deck Wake looked but could no longer see the man with the uniform. The French words were no longer heard. No sign of any life came from the derelict ship, whose main deck was now constantly awash. She wasn't even rolling anymore. She was going down, and Wake thought that they were probably too late to save anyone. It had taken too long to get it all ready.

The *Hunt* gradually gained room to windward as the other vessel drifted to leeward. Coming along her weather side, Wake yelled for Rork to put over the float line, which the big bosun did with a heave up and over, letting the wind take the float at the end of the line across. The float actually landed on the vessel's afterdeck house top, and for a moment Wake feared it would foul and drag *Hunt* down, until he saw Rork standing by with his knife, ready to slice it free.

The deckhouse top, stack, and the stubs of the masts were now all that could be seen. No men were aboard her. Another wave washed over the wreck, and then nothing could be seen after it passed on. The mystery ship was gone. It was over. They had failed. Wake turned away as another wave lifted the hull and buckled his knees. As he held on while the deck dropped away he knew it was time to forget them.

"Haul away, Rork. Bring it back aboard."

Wake opened the door and staggered inside to the wheelhouse, shaking his head in answer to Emerson's questioning glance.

"We'll keep steaming forward just enough to keep her head into the seas. I want to clear the debris in the water. We don't dare turn her now and broach. Mr. Rhodes, go below and report back on the flooding and any damage."

The wind continued to veer around to the southwest. Wake knew that meant the storm was to the west and maybe north of them, heading north into the Gulf of Mexico. They were on the eastern side. The change in wind direction caused the seas to be even more confused and irregular, the motion of the ship more unpredictable. It made it even more exhausting to merely try to stand on the deck.

Wake was so tired, so fatigued, that his muscles felt as if they were about to stop functioning completely. He knew that if he sat down on the deck he wouldn't be able to get up, so he leaned against the side of the wheelhouse and tried to think of where their position might be. His mental calculations of course, speed, current, and drift proved useless, and he went into the small chartroom and bent over the chart table, attempting to work it out on paper. He stood there for some time, forcing himself to do the mathematics and then check its accuracy, and then recalculate. It frustrated him, even though it was such a simple procedure.

Another wave rolled under the ship, making Wake hold on to the table. The bell struck two and Wake suddenly realized it must be nine o'clock in the evening. Time had gone by rapidly. The outside wheelhouse door opened, and swirling mists of water rushed in as a blast of storm noise and raised voices filled the room. In the vague light of a lantern Wake saw a shadow fill the doorway to the wheelhouse and looked up. He strained to focus his eyes. It was a stranger he didn't know, a middle-aged man in a dark gray uniform, sodden with seawater. Rork's voice entered the room from behind the stranger.

"Meet Captain William Parkham, sir. We just pulled him and two others from that sinking ship. He's the one that yelled those Froggee words to us."

The stranger held onto the bulkhead, barely able to stand. Wiping his dripping face and beard, he straightened up and cleared his throat, his voice no more than a hoarse whisper.

"Captain William Stephen Parkham, master of the steamer *Vindicator,* at your service, sir. And may I say, most assuredly in your debt, as well."

Wake was stunned. He shook his head, trying to clear the confusion. Rork and Emerson stepped in beside Parkham, both grinning at the moment. Wake started to grin with them at the incongruity of the moment, and he reached out a hand to Parkham.

"Force majeure?"

Parkham returned the smile and shook his hand firmly.

"Yes, Captain Wake. Force majeure. Didn't want you to fire on us or abandon us. Had to invoke the law of the sea. I'm sure you understand, sir."

Wake laughed and felt energy coming back into his body.

"Force majuere! I'm the only one aboard who knew what it meant, Captain Parkham. The teachers at a school in New England had me in their clutches for three years when I was young. I learned that phrase from them in some boring lecture on international custom and law."

"Then someday, sir, I shall raise a toast to the good educators of New England."

Parkham had a southern accent—Virginia, Wake guessed. He was a blockade runner for sure.

"So, Captain Parkham, tell me. Where are you from, and what was your cargo?"

Parkham's smile faded as he looked at Wake. The look in Parkham's eyes did not match his words.

"Why, peaceful cargo, Captain Wake. China and manufactured goods and brandy from England, sir. A shame it all went down."

"And your origin?"

"Maryland, sir. East shore. The part down near Salisbury."

Wake pondered that. His knowledge of Maryland geography was sketchy, but he thought that Salisbury was on or near the Cape Charles Peninsula, an area of considerable Confederate sympathy.

"Where bound?"

"Belize, Captain Wake."

"Where from?"

Wake could feel the deck lifting and a wave coming, and held onto the edge of the table. Parkham started to sway, then he fell to one side, grabbing the table next to Wake's hand, his eyes never leaving Wake's, like a pugilist about to strike an upper cut from below.

"Plymouth in County Devon, in England."

Wake was intrigued by this man who moments ago faced a lonely death in the raging seas, and yet was now playing verbal chess with his rescuer.

"Why the gray uniform, Captain Parkham?"

"A personal affectation, Captain. Blue has been so overused. Besides, it really is but a poor version of gray, sir. Faded and salt-stained beyond its glory, I'm afraid."

"You are well above the course for Belize, Captain Parkham."

Parkham showed no fear. He only shrugged.

"The Stream does odd things, Captain Wake. Was I off course?"

"You were off course when we found you. Then you ran away and we intercepted you."

Parkham's mouth creased, but it wasn't a smile, as he eased forward over the chart table toward Wake.

"Captain Wake, I am sure that you are not accusing me of being a blockade runner. An erratic course during a storm would not support that accusation if you were so rash as to make it, sir. You have no evidence at all, Captain."

Wake could see that Emerson and Rork were watching with interest, but the tension in the muscles of Rork's face was something Wake had seen before. The bosun was right, the repartee had gone on long enough.

"Captain Parkham, you *are* a blockade runner and an enemy of the United States, and I am tired. This conversation is over, sir. You will be shown a cabin by Bosun Rork. You are not under arrest as a prisoner of war because I did not have the pleasure of obtaining the evidence of your transgression prior to your invocation of force majeure—which is a legally debatable point anyway. Therefore, since I do not have any evidence, you are simply a guest. Do not abuse that role."

Parkham's eyes brightened and he raised his hand, about to speak. Wake cut him off. "But, Captain Parkham, let there be no doubt in your mind as to my opinion of you and your intentions prior to the sinking of your ship. You are an *enemy* guest, sir, and I don't like your condescending demeanor. You sound like a sea lawyer to me."

Parkham held his hands out and apart as he leaned back, a triumphant smirk below his cold eyes. "Captain Wake, evidence is the point here, is it not? Without it, I will thank you not to disparage my ship or me, sir. Your tone and words are insulting to a man who has just asked for assistance according to the customs of civilized men upon the sea."

Rork moved in next to Parkham and put a hand lightly upon his shoulder. "Sir, shall I show his Highness his cabin now?"

"Yes, Bosun. Have him berth in with the petty officers."

Parkham bowed up, his chest expanding and his expression glaring, even in the dim light. "Petty officers! I am a captain, sir! I do not berth with petty officers!"

Wake was about to reply when another blast of spray and noise rushed into the chartroom. He heard Curtis' voice calling out for Rork, who told him to enter the tiny space. Curtis wedged his way into the glow of the lantern. He was holding the jagged remnant of several boards nailed together. It was some sort of box or container lid.

Rork saw the pieces of wood and angrily turned to his bosun's mate. "Why are you in here, Curtis? Now's not the time for idle chat, man."

Curtis was excited and breathing hard. He glanced at Wake for a moment, then turned to his bosun. "Beg your pardon, Captain, sir. No idle chat *here,* Bosun. Right here's some cargo lids floatin' from the wreck what just went down. We eyed 'em alongside an' brought up a few. They's all over out there. Thought the captain and Mr. Emerson would want to see these little devils, Bosun."

Parkham stiffened as the others gathered closer to the flotsam in Curtis' hands. The printing was plain to see. Parkham looked away. Rork tightened his grip on Parkham's shoulder and read the stenciled print aloud.

"Well, what do we have here? Let's see what this box of manufactured goods says, sir. Hmmm. . . . '*Enfield Arms . . . fifty-eight cal . . . Rifled . . . Stand of Twelve . . . Birmingham . . . England.*' No doubt they're manufactured goods, Captain," Rork brought his face close to Parkham's. "Manufactured to shoot down our lads ashore."

The sounds of the storm subsided in their ears as all eyes swung to Parkham. He said nothing, and looked at Wake, who, nodded to Curtis.

"Well done, Curtis. Gather up all you safely can. After that, have a talk with the other two brought aboard from the *Vindicator* and tell them they might as well be honest, we have evidence."

"Beggin' your pardon, again, sir, I was about to get to all

that. Already gathered up all we could of those lids, sir. And we already had that talk with the other two we fished out. Thought you'd want me to, sir, so I just went and did it. Didn't mean no disrespect."

"Well done, again, Curtis. That's no disrespect, that's called initiative. Pray tell us what they said!"

"Well, Captain, they was two Limeys, they were, sir. One was a common seaman and quiet as a beaten dog. Sullen-like, sir, wouldn't say a word except he wasn't no part of it. Signed on in Plymouth not knowing what was what. The other one was the bosun. He said he'd done time as a English redcoat soldier, sir, and we could scare him none. At least that was what he was saying until I told we had a bosun too. Told him ours was an Irish bosun what hated Limey redcoats, and would just love to have some time to talk real serious with him."

Curtis grinned at Rork, who nodded for him to continue, then returned his gaze to Parkham. "Well, sir, this bosun fella, suddenly he got real friendly. Sang like a bird, he did, sir. Limey redcoat bird! Said he always liked them Irish people when he was on his duty there. Said he never did nothing against them at all. Then he started saying that Captain Parkham here had loaded up their ship with rifles for the Rebs. Didn't ask none of the crew if they'd sign on for a run on the blockade or nothing like that. Just loaded them rifles and figured the crew would do it. No choice once they's out at sea."

Curtis paused for breath. The storm was still exercising its fury with wind and waves and noise, but everyone in the tiny compartment was leaning forward, straining to hear the bosun mate's report. Wake was impatient.

"Curtis, tell us what else he said."

"Aye, aye, sir. He said they was doing well on their crossing. Got into Nassau ahead of time and picked up some coal and provisions there. They were going to go into Havana too for any blockade cargo there, but word was out about the *Whatley* on that coast, sir.

"Said that the mates and their captain," he crooked his head at Parkham, who threw an angry glance back at the petty officer, "had a big discussion about how to get through the Straits of Florida. The mates wanted to coast along Cuba and pick up the countercurrent down there, take a chance on the *Whatley,* but the captain here said they'd go right down the middle of the Straits, against the Stream and all. Then they saw us today and thought they'd lose us by doubling back and going southeast. Pardon me, sir. I'm trying to remember all the words the man said. Singing fast, he was, sir."

"That's all right, Curtis. Just give us the gist of what he said. They tried to lose us?"

"Aye, sir. He said when they turned they broached and took a big sea aboard. Stove in some of the planks on the forward hatch and flooded the forward hold. Water made its way aft somehow into the boiler room, I'm guessing the hold's bulkhead parted, sir. Anyway, he said somehow the boiler fires got doused and they had no way on. Laid broadside to the seas and he knew they was in trouble then. They got broached again and she didn't come up, kept filling through that hold."

"Then we arrived."

"Yes, sir. The crew was glad to see us, sir. This Limey bosun fella said they didn't care none about no war at that point, they just wanted to get over to us afore they sank with the ship. Said they was a-hollering for us. Some was saying they surrender and such. Said their captain kept telling them to shut up and not to surrender, that he'd take care of it legal-like. But by then they knew the ship was going down and he was a fool—his words, sir, not mine—and they ignored him."

"And the float line?"

"Yes, sir. They are powerful glad that Bosun Rork heaved that line, sir. They was in the water already and grabbed that line fast and held on. Was more of 'em in the water, sir, but they didn't get to the line . . ."

Wake nodded. The other men in the water were gone now.

There was no way to find them in that storm. It would be a lonely death, floating until you lost strength, gasping for air as the seas tumbled you over and down in with the raging wind and mountainous seas. Another sea lifted the *Hunt* and the tight mass of men swayed together in the lantern light as the deck heaved up, then fell away. Wake shuddered at the thought of it all while Curtis finished his recital of the English bosun's story.

"Well, that's that, sir. I didn't write none of it down, Captain. Figured you'd want to know soon as you could, so's I came up to the wheelhouse to tell ya."

"Very good, Curtis. My compliments on getting his story. You may go now. I want that bosun and the sailor taken good care of, with clean clothes and a meal. Treat them right, Curtis."

"Aye, aye, sir."

"Oh, and Curtis."

"Yes, sir?"

"That was a shrewd move to mention our Irish bosun to that man. Well done. Certainly facilitated the conversation, didn't it?"

"Aye, sir. That it did. Bosun Rork has that effect on men, sir."

Curtis beamed at Rork, and made his way out. Wake looked around at the gathering, ignoring Parkham, who had shrunk inside his sodden uniform, his arrogance long past.

"And now Rork, I think that Captain Parkham is quite correct. He should not be in the petty officers quarters. We don't put prisoners of war, especially ones who are dishonorable, in with decent petty officers. Put him in the chain locker and put a guard on the passageway."

"Aye, aye, sir. I'll personally escort him down to that lovely chain locker, an' have all the pleasure of a bishop with a heretic, sir!"

Parkham was spun around and propelled forward into the gloom of darkness beyond the shine of the light. He said not a word as he was pushed away.

Emerson was left alone with Wake.

"Wind's veered to the west now, sir. Not as strong. Seems the storm is laying down a bit."

"Yes, I agree. Probably northwest of us, heading up into the Gulf. We're lucky."

"Aye, sir. What now?"

Wake dropped his eyes to the chart and put a finger on the Cuban coast.

"Now? Now we figure out where we are, then do what we set out to do and complete our mission to find and resupply the *Whatley*. After that we return to Key West and I'll try to explain all this to the admiral."

"Force majeure . . ." Emerson shook his head and sighed. "Think Parkham'll try to use it in the admiralty court to conjure his way free?"

Wake was as tired as he ever remembered being in his life. He looked over at his executive officer. "It doesn't really matter, does it? What matters are hundreds of rifles on the bottom of the ocean, and not in the hands of enemy soldiers. That's real, Mr. Emerson. Force majeure? That's just a couple of words that most sailors don't even understand . . ."

4

Useppa's Call

I t took another day for the winds to lay down enough to make any type of progress. Even then, *Hunt* moved slowly through the upheaval of confused seas. They found their position much further to the east than Wake had estimated. The storm's south-westerly and final westerly winds had combined with the Gulf Stream to put them almost thirty miles away from the dead reckoning position he had deduced, the worst reckoning error he had ever made. As the storm moved north, away from the Straits of Florida, the *Hunt* steamed south, closing the Cuban coast at Matanzas. Wake took her into the port and found no word of *Whatley*, then proceeded west along the coastline.

Off Havana, they spoke the Spanish Navy gunboat *Orgullo de Cuba* and found that *Whatley* had not put in there. The captain told Wake in halting English and sign language that the storm had ravaged the island, and Havana harbor was in total confusion, with debris floating everywhere and two vessels smashed against the sea wall. Wake remembered that harbor very well, and could imagine the destruction. There was no reason to put into that port, so wishing the Spaniards good luck, he and the

Hunt continued west toward Bahia Honda, the original rendezvous point.

The weather started to clear on the third day after the sinking of the *Vindicator,* and the men of the *Hunt* busied themselves with repairing the damage done by the wind and seas. The damage was everywhere aboard the ship, even far below the weather decks. Everything from the guns to the decks required cleaning and renovation.

The steam engine, the most critical element for the *Hunt,* was being operated at low pressure and thus the frustratingly slow speed of three knots. The strain of pushing against the storm could be seen on the metal monster, according to Ginaldi, and the engineers used the respite to renew their efforts to oil the moving parts and clean the fireboxes. Some of the boiler tubes needed cleaning also, but would have to wait until they got to port. Many of the black gang in the engine and boiler rooms were put to work shifting the coal bunkers, making sure the remaining fuel was stowed securely. Just after they had left the Spanish gunboat, Ginaldi came to the wheelhouse and spoke to Wake and Emerson. He had a troubled look that immediately alerted Wake.

"Problem, sir. We used far more fuel than we thought we'd need when we coaled for this mission. We're getting very low."

"How low? How many days steaming?"

"A week at the most at this rate of consumption, sir. At the most, sir."

Wake had heard steamer captains bemoan their tether to coal supplies in the past. He, of course, had used the wind and was free of such constraints. But since taking this command, he grew to understand those laments. But his officers and men would not see that type of behavior from him. Wake beckoned the officers to go with him to the chartroom and do the mathematics while looking at the geography. Once they were grouped around the small table, Emerson entered the conversation, dispassionately calculating a factor that had enormous consequences.

"Let's see. If we find the *Whatley* in the next two days, that would be very good. Then one day to transfer the supplies, or what's left of them after that storm. Then another two days to get back to Key West. That leaves two days' steaming time of coal left for us, sir."

Ginaldi shook his head.

"Perhaps, sir, we should put back into Key West and fill our bunkers, then go in search of the *Whatley*?"

Wake was doing some calculating of his own.

"Thank you for the suggestion, Mr. Ginaldi, but we should project what our course and time would be by staying in this region first. That means, gentlemen, that if we continue at this rate of progress we shall make seventy-two miles a day, and two days sailing westward would put us around the western end of Cuba. That's enough area to find *Whatley*, so there's no cause for concern there. Agreed?"

Both officers replied positively.

"Then we have to figure the return transit of *Hunt* to Key West from the farthest point of that westward track. That would be a leg of approximately," he took the dividers and walked the rhumb line on the chart, "two hundred miles, or about two and a half days, counting the help of the Stream. Agreed?"

Another acknowledgment came from each officer as they watched the man who commanded them think out his decision.

"Therefore, gentlemen, if we take a day to transfer supplies, we are looking at two days westward, one day for transfer, and three days return. That leaves one day leeway."

Ginaldi shook his head again. "Sir, with respect, that's not enough. We're moving at three knots, with the coastal counter-current. What if we have to speed up for any reason, or go out into the Stream and fight it to go west?"

"Excellent point, Mr. Ginaldi. Mr. Emerson, your assessment?"

"Well, sir, weather's settled, but we can't count on that. Mr. Ginaldi has a concern that is valid. I think we could do one day steaming west—seventy-five miles would put us to La

Esperanza—then return to Key West if we don't sight *Whatley.* That would give us another day of fuel for an emergency."

Wake studied his executive officer and engineer. They were right to be concerned. But they had neglected one important factor that called for an extra effort on their part.

"Gentlemen, the *Whatley* has been out here for some time now. She is low on everything, and may possibly be in distress, due to that storm. It is our duty to complete our mission to her if we can. Therefore, we will, and we will follow Mr. Emerson's suggestion."

Ginaldi still looked grim. "Sir, if we have to speed up for whatever reason, we'll eat those two days up in coal fast."

"Precisely, Mr. Ginaldi. That is why we won't head for Key West," Wake paused, bemused as the two subordinates exchanged looks of confusion. "We'll head for the army's coal at Fort Jefferson. That will take almost a day off the return transit time."

Emerson glanced again at the engineer, grinned, then suppressed a laugh. "Sir, I don't know quite how to express this, but are you sure you're welcome at Fort Jefferson?"

Wake's conflict with the former commander of the garrison at Fort Jefferson earlier in the year was common knowledge in both the army and the navy in Florida. Wake laughed at the look of worry on his officers' faces.

"Gentlemen, I see you've heard the story about my special relationship with the colonel who once commanded the fort there. Well, I will only say this. It's all in the past, and he is gone elsewhere and I am here. I don't think even the army will fault me for a perceived conflict with *that* man. They know him better than I did. We'll get coal from them, don't worry."

And so the decision was made and the *Hunt* chugged westward along the coast of Cuba, the dark green mountains rising in the mist four miles away on the port beam. As the sun descended, the mountains changed colors, from green to blue, then to shades of gray and black, with pastels appearing through the low coastal clouds as the sun set flamboyantly into the sea ahead of them. The next morning they saw the *Whatley* inshore, west of La Mulata, and met with her three hours later.

Transferring what supplies were left after the storm, for many had been washed away or spoiled by the seawater, was laborious work for both crews, who sweated over the provisions for seven long hours in the rolling sea. The *Hunt* had no boats left, the *Whatley* had only one, the others having suffered the same fate of *Hunt's* in the storm, which made it even more exhausting. *Whatley's* captain was appreciative of Wake's persistence in searching for them, since *Whatley* was also battered by the storm and was already short of everything in the way of provisions and supplies. Her coal bunkers were much larger than those in Wake's ship, but she would have to return to Key West herself in another ten days at the most, depending on how long they would loiter in the area for prey.

The captain, a lieutenant commander named Raftery who was considerably senior to Wake, expressed approval of the action taken against Parkham of the *Vindicator* and pointed out the irony in that name.

"Odd they chose that name. We have one by that name in our navy, out west on the Mississippi. Did good execution against the Rebs by Vicksburg, and all along that section of the river. That's what I heard from a transiting officer at the Russell Hotel Bar in Key West. He was heading back up north from the river squadron."

"I'd wager they didn't know that, sir. They were in England before they arrived here. Well, we've got to get under way, sir, so I'll say my goodbye."

"Good luck Mr. Wake. And thank you again for your good work."

From the afterdeck of his ship, Wake waived to Captain Raftery as the sun set that evening. *Hunt* was bound to the northeast, and behind them the steam gunboat was silhouetted against a blue sky tinged with gold as she lay swaying in the low swells, waiting and watching for another runner to come along the coast.

Three days later Key West was a welcome sight when *Hunt* finally raised it on the eastern horizon in the slanting light of the late afternoon. They had loaded some coal at Fort Jefferson's dock earlier in the day, with the compliments of the army garrison, who did indeed remember hearing of Wake and his exploits. The *Hunt's* officers and men were in a state of nervous excitement at the thought of setting foot on land again. Banter could be heard the length of the ship, covering the gamut from the possible worth of the lost *Vindicator* in the prize court to paying off outstanding shore debts to the rum purveyors, who handled far more than rum in supplying the needs of sailors ashore.

Arriving at the main naval wharf, the ship was moored and the prisoners removed to the army's custody at Fort Taylor. Parkham was quiet as he left the ship, looking down the whole time, pushed along by the soldiers detailed to transport him to his cell. The two British crewmen were in better spirits, having been assured that because of their cooperation, they would be repatriated to the British Consulate after a review by the U.S. Attorney in Key West. Leaving Emerson in charge of reprovisioning and supply from the warehouse adjacent to the wharf, Wake went ashore to report in to the admiral. Liberty call could not be granted until that had been accomplished, and he hurried to the squadron offices only to find an anteroom full of officers waiting to see the squadron chief of staff or the admiral. Handing his reports to the yeoman, Wake found a chair on the far side of the room and waited.

As he had walked through the naval station grounds he saw a few trees bent over and torn roof shingles strewn about, signs of storm damage, but was glad to see that the island had been spared the worst. In fact, the sky was clear and an almost cool breeze was blowing from the northeast, making the air pleasant for the first time in six months. It was difficult to remember that only a little more than a week earlier a vicious tropical storm churned the ocean into a malevolent mass of wind and water, reaching out to take the weakest ships that dared to venture upon it. But

November was well under way, and Wake knew that better weather was coming. He hoped the worst was behind them.

He had to wait for an hour before the admiral could see him, an indication that his resupply mission had not been that important. Wake learned from the clerical staff that the storm had ravaged the squadron's ships along the west coast, particularly north of Tampa Bay. The admiral was looking for vessels to send up there to assist those in need. After hearing that intelligence, he knew that *Hunt* would not be in port long, contrary to the wishes of her sailors. It was now over a month since they had had liberty ashore, and it appeared that no one was going on liberty this time in port either.

Admiral Stockard had been in the squadron for two months. His predecessor had been in command for only six months when he was summoned to Washington to be given one of the foreign squadrons, usually a signal honor, but now a backwater post of mainly diplomatic and social import. Wake had never met Stockard, but he knew Captain Zachary Morris, the squadron's chief of staff. When the admiral's yeoman told Wake to enter it was Morris who greeted him. As he entered the austere office, which had the same appearance no matter the occupant, Wake gauged the newest man in charge of the East Gulf Blockading Squadron.

Admiral Jonathan Stockard was in his late forties, young for his rank. A man of short but solid build, without any facial hair, he did not have the ferocious aspect that many senior officers cultivated with their beards and mustaches. He was known as a man of action in the western rivers campaign, pushing into areas previously thought unreachable. Extending the power of the Federal government deep into Rebel jurisdictions, Stockard caught the attention of the Republican leadership in Congress, and subsequently the senior officers in the navy. The fact that he rose from the rank of lieutenant commander at the beginning of the war to rear admiral in three and a half years was an accomplishment, and a signal. Stockard was a force to be reckoned with, especially for a career naval officer, as Wake now considered himself. The admiral sat at his desk ruffling through a pile of papers as Wake entered. Captain Morris spoke first.

"Another adventure, eh Wake?"

"Well, sir, no, not really. It was just a storm. And a lucky guess."

"You have a lot of those, Wake. We make our own luck in this profession. Admiral, Lieutenant Wake of the armed steam tug *Hunt* is here, sir."

Stockard looked up but gave no outward sign of pleasure or greeting. Wake saw that his eyes were a disconcertingly light color. Pale gray, they were devoid of expression—like an animal's. The eyes were unnerving as they fixed upon Wake.

"I've read the report of the incident with the *Vindicator,* Wake. Well done."

"Thank you, sir."

"I can't lose any more ships, Wake. I appreciate that you didn't lose the *Hunt* in that storm." The gray eyes left Wake and turned to Morris. "Now, Captain Morris, do you have those orders for Wake here?"

Morris nodded, handing Wake the standard blue envelope with the embossed wax seal that every ship captain knew contained his future.

"Here Wake. Another supply mission. You're heading north along the west coast to Tampa. Stop at Charlotte Harbor on your way up. You have supplies for the *Case* and the refugees at Useppa Island. Check on the status of all blockade ships, reprovision and supply them, and return. You're authorized supplies and provisions for three weeks and to completely fill your bunkers. The supplies for the other ships are being assembled now at the wharf. Stow them everywhere you can aboard your ship. We're giving you quite a lot."

Wake didn't have to open the orders to know they were for an immediate departure. He glanced at Stockard, who was busy reading papers on his desk, apparently ignoring them. Morris sounded impatient.

"Well, any questions?"

"No, sir."

"Good. Depart as soon as possible. We haven't had any communication with many of those ships since the storm. There are rumors about that some of them were damaged badly. Go find out. If they are in need of extensive repair and can't get under way themselves, tow them back here. Be quick about it. You have extra provisions to share with the other ships, Wake, not to dawdle on the coast looking for prize money."

"Aye, aye, sir."

Morris stood close, saying the next words deliberately. "Dawdle on the coast includes time spent at islands, Mr. Wake. Do your assignment, help those ships, and return here as soon as possible. Understand my meaning?"

It was a thinly veiled reference to his wife Linda at Useppa Island, in Charlotte Harbor. Wake struggled to stay calm and slowed his words to a deliberate pace. "Yes . . . *sir*."

Wake saw that Stockard, report still in his hand, watched the exchange without obvious reaction. His gray eyes were neutral, examining the men as if they were interesting bugs pinned on a table.

Morris's face reddened and his jaw tightened.

"Don't take that tone with me, Wake. We've had this sort of conversation before. The fact that you and the girl are now married in some sort of fashion, and that she lives up on that coast with some refugees, does not change the equation one wit. Just get your job done and return as soon as possible. You are dismissed."

There was so much Wake wanted to say in reply to that statement. So much he needed to say. The moment of silence as he thought over his answer gave him time to realize there was only one thing that could be said.

"Aye, aye, sir."

Stockard said nothing, but returned to reading the papers in his hand, while Morris made a *harrumph* sound, spun around and walked to the chart spread out on the far wall, examining the pins with tiny blue flags depicting naval vessels at their stations along the coast and at sea.

Ears pounding with the beat of his heart, Wake left the room and silently marched straight through the anteroom and outer offices of the building. Outside in the waning afternoon light, he stopped and breathed deeply, assessing Morris' words. She's my wife now, he thought, she's a lady not a girl, and not some enemy. The things her father did to assist the Rebels are not her fault. Is it because so many of the officers haven't seen their wives in years? Are they jealous of her proximity? When will their attitudes ever end? What more must I do to prove myself?

Usually when he assessed a situation, Wake could process out the emotional and concentrate on the factual, forming a plan of action that would improve his outlook. But this time was different, and he didn't know why. After all he had accomplished for the squadron and the United States Navy, he thought the petty suspicions had ended, that he had proven himself worthy of trust. Morris' mention of his wife was a reminder that Wake still had a long way to go to be accepted and trusted as a regular officer by the academy-graduated officers who ran the service. He wondered when it would change and grimly realized that it probably never would. Wake strode out along the wharf toward his ship as if he were marching into battle.

His dour face warned the crew of the bad news when he arrived back at the *Hunt*. Rork and Durlon were on the foredeck talking when they saw him come up the gangway. Durlon shook his head and grimaced.

"Oh Sean, I know *that* look. Bad news comin' our way, my Irish friend."

Rork watched as all of the officers were rounded up and then disappeared into Wake's cabin. He shook his head and let out a breath.

"Gunner, I fear that you may be right. The lads won't like this one, whatever it is. Won't like it a wee bit."

The meeting with Emerson, Ginaldi, and Rhodes was short. Wake advised them of the orders, telling them there was to be no liberty and all hands would load the ship. They would depart as soon as possible afterward. The stunned officers had no questions, for their captain's demeanor told them more than his words. They nodded their understanding, and Wake dismissed them without further discussion.

The *Hunt*'s officers had never seen him this way, and they were worried. Like most of the squadron by now, they knew of his marriage to the Key West girl and the rumors that his young wife was a Reb, or at least from a Rebel family. In the short time he had been with the squadron, Emerson had seen the jealousy among some of the squadron's regular officers toward Wake's successes—pure dumb luck on the part of some volunteer, they had opined—and had heard some ugly talk about Wake's wife in the officers' mess ashore.

He suspected Wake's current foul mood was connected to all of that, and he ended Ginaldi's speculations on the cause of the captain's strange behavior after they left Wake's cabin. It was time for them to show some respect and follow their captain's orders, Emerson told the other two men, not gossip like old ladies about him. Nodding in agreement, they parted to start their assigned tasks, each of them feeling fortunate to serve with Wake as their commander, however odd he was acting at the moment.

Rork and Durlon deciphered the reason immediately, having served under Wake the year before on a small, armed sloop, where the problems of one man became known to all, no matter the rank. There was only one thing they had seen make their captain so melancholy. It must have something to do with his wife, Linda. When word came that they were bound up the coast to search for and assist ships affected by the storm, both thought they might see Useppa Island again. They were pleased but confused, for they liked the islanders of that coast and had many shared memories with them, both good and bad. But their commander's face told a different story. He should have been smiling in anticipation of seeing his wife, but instead they saw an angry man going through the procedural duties without his usual infectious zeal.

After a day and a half of smooth sailing, they found the large naval schooner *Case* at Boca Grande, safely anchored on the east side of Gasparilla Island, in calm water. After mooring alongside, Wake went aboard to report to her commander, Lieutenant Lotrell, who was senior in grade to Wake by six months. The main difference between them, however, was that Lotrell had gone to the Academy, class of '60. Wake knew him from their brief conversations during resupply rendezvous. Upon meeting him at the quarterdeck, Wake dispensed with pleasantries and gave the squadron's latest news, then asked what might be needed in the way of supplies, provisions, and assistance. Lotrell held up his hand and invited him below to his cabin, where they could relax away from the ears of both crews.

Over weak tea, the two officers briefly exchanged information on the supply situation of *Case,* then Wake anxiously asked how the storm had affected the area.

Lotrell, knowing that Wake's wife lived on Useppa, explained first that the storm damage to the islands on this section of the coast was not catastrophic and no lives were reported lost. Useppa, higher in elevation than most of the islands, suffered little more than palm thatch blown off their homes, Lotrell advised, and Mrs. Wake was just fine. He had seen her just three days ago when she and some other Useppa ladies had sailed over in an island boat to offer some fruit to the *Case,* a gift that was accepted and very much appreciated.

Wake felt his shoulders relax, as the anxiety over how Useppa had fared in the storm gave way to relief. He knew it was the highest and safest island in the area, definitely far safer than on any ship, but he had still been worried. Wake asked Lotrell how the *Case* had handled the storm—there was no obvious damage visible as they had come alongside.

Lotrell said they had been lucky, the storm had evidently

gone ashore far to the north of them, so they were spared the worst. He told how, misunderstanding the severity of the storm, he had decided to let the *Case* ride it out at anchor under the lee of the islands. In the middle of it they started dragging their anchors. Lotrell admitted he'd been fearful about being driven ashore on the mainland near the old burned down trading post, eight miles downwind to the east. Their visibility had been nil, and they knew they were dragging, but not how far. Finally the anchors had held, almost pulling the guts out of her fo'c's'le with the jerk of the cable, just as they were readying the boats for abandoning her, if necessary. The next morning, as the sky cleared, the astonished men of the *Case* found themselves a quarter mile away from the rocky shoals off the ruins of the trading post. No major injuries or ship damage had been sustained, but it had been close, and Wake could see the tension in Lotrell's face as he told the tale.

Upon Wake telling his own account of surviving the storm, both ship captains agreed they had been extremely lucky and toasted their outcomes with a laugh and clink of tea cups, this time filled with some of Lotrell's rum. The conversation and rum had their effect upon Wake, and the anxiety and frustration inside him over Linda's fate during the storm and his superiors' comments melted away. Linda was fine, and he was now far away from Key West and the pettiness that seemed to flourish there. Wake felt good being back with the men who were the real backbone of the navy.

He was only five miles away from Linda at that moment, and with the pleasant news that the *Case* was in relatively good shape came the realization that he could visit Useppa that very day. He knew it would have to be brief, just enough time to unload the designated supplies, but it was enough to buoy his spirits.

Wake stood to say his goodbye.

"Captain Lotrell, thank you for your kind hospitality. I'll be going now. The transfer shouldn't take too much longer and then we'll get under way for Useppa."

Lotrell extended his hand.

"Please give Mrs. Wake my respects. I'll see you again on your next visit, which will I hope be much longer."

Rork, out on the afterdeck and supervising the swaying over of supplies, heard conch shells being sounded on Lacosta Island across the passage, sending their calls to the southeast, where more conchs called out on Punta Blanca Island. Rork knew that conch shells were being blown from island to island all the way to Useppa, which could be made out in the distance. Soon all the islanders would know that another naval vessel had arrived. They would quickly find it was the one commanded by Peter Wake, who was well known to the people of this coast. Anticipating that he would come to his wife, the pro-Union refugee islanders of Useppa would then be waiting for Wake and his crew after they had completed their duties with the *Case*. Rork smiled at the thought.

Durlon heard the long drawn out wail of the conch shells too, and knowing what it meant, he walked aft to his friend the bosun standing by the boom of the main mast.

"Word's goin' out that he's here. We'll be havin' some celebratin' tonight at Useppa, when we finish here. Maybe that'll cheer the ol' boy up a might."

"Aye, Durlon. Nothing like a wee lovely to cheer a lad an' bring him up from the melancholy. Best medicine there is. Could do with a little cheer me ownself, come to think on it. An' with that black gang's metal monster in our bowels, this ship could make it there in an hour. In time for a dinner o' *fresh* fish, by the Lord."

"Damn, stop that kind of talk now. You're makin' me hungry for anything other than salt pork an' weevil biscuits, ya Gaelic brute. I think I'd kill for some fresh fish, and maybe some fruit."

Wake's change in manner on his return to the *Hunt* was noticed by everyone who saw his face, and the work of transferring supplies was energized by it. In three hours they had gotten under way and were heading east around the shoals at Patricio

Island, bound for Useppa.

It was high noon as they slid slowly through the deceptively clear water across the shoals and came to anchor off the beach on the eastern shore of Useppa Island. Islanders in small boats escorted them the last half mile, shouting words of welcome and tossing oranges to the astonished crew. Conch shells moaned out from the hills of the island and smoke rose from the top of the highest hill, a place where Wake knew special celebrations and dinners were held. The *Hunt* responded with her steam whistle blowing loudly in a staccato series of piercing screams that echoed around the surrounding islands. Of the men aboard the *Hunt,* only Wake, Rork, and Durlon, had been to Useppa and knew of the appreciation the islanders held for the naval vessels that kept the Confederates on the mainland from attacking their place of refuge. They were considered saviors and benefactors, and it was pleasant to see the reaction of the *Hunt*'s sailors to their reception.

Gazing through his telescope, Wake scanned the boats and the island for his wife, finally spotting her standing under the big banyan tree by the dwelling she shared with Sofira Thomaston. She was waving toward the *Hunt.* He hadn't been with his wife for several months, and the effect of seeing her again jolted him to the core. His throat felt swollen and he couldn't speak for fear his voice would break. He could feel his heart beating as he raised the glass again for another look and saw Sofira come out of the dwelling and stand next to Linda.

Thomaston, a young half-Seminole woman whose white husband was a sergeant in the pro-Union militia that had been formed on Useppa, was Linda's best friend on the island. Sofira and her husband had married just two years before the war started, and fled with many others to the island to escape the Confederate authorities. She, more than anyone, understood the difficulties of an unpopular marriage. Sofira, her little girl Rain, and Linda lived in a palm thatch hut on a knoll just up from the beach.

The rest of the settlement, now consisting of old men,

women, and children since the younger men were away at war, spread along the shoreline and up into the low hills of the island. Most of the structures were entirely palm thatch, but a few had the luxury of a boarded roof made from flotsam found on the beaches. The island also had two rainwater cisterns, clinker-built like a boat—but to keep the water in instead of out. The islanders lived on the fruit and vegetables they raised, and by fishing the amazingly bountiful waters around the islands. Three other islands close by were also home to a few refugees, but Useppa was the acknowledged center of refugee activity in the area.

Sergeant Henry Thomaston's regiment, the 2nd United States Florida Cavalry, was currently up the Caloosahatchee River occupying the old Indian war fort. There had been rumors for months now that they would be used for some future attacks at the Cedar Keys or Bayport, maybe even the Rebel stronghold of Tampa. Wake knew Thomaston and the militia regiment well, having fought alongside of them at Myakka River the previous December. He silently wished them well as he watched three-year-old Rain tug on her mother's dress and point to the steamer.

Looking away from the island to compose himself, Wake smiled when he saw Emerson and Rhodes standing wide-eyed in the wheelhouse watching the scene. He felt so much better now that he ventured some humor.

"It would appear that the natives are friendly, Mr. Rhodes."

"Friendly is putting it mildly, sir. I think they're ecstatic."

"Well, regrettably, we can only stay long enough to offload their supplies. About an hour or two, I should think."

"But Captain, your wife? Surely we can stay overnight?"

Wake shook his head. "Thank you for your concern, Mr. Rhodes, but you know we have to check on those ships at Tampa as soon as possible. I don't want to leave, but we have to."

Emerson added his observations of the pandemonium around them as islanders, mostly women, started to climb aboard from their boats. "I don't know, Captain. I don't really think they'll let us go after only an hour or two. We may have to fight our way out of all this hospitality, and I fear the crew will be on the islanders' side."

Wake laughed, but knew Emerson was right that the crew would be upset at leaving such an obviously inviting place. It was time to remind everyone of duty. "Gentlemen, I understand your sense of appreciation for this reception. These islanders really do want us to stay, but we can't. I have more reason than anyone aboard to stay, but even I can't. I want all the officers and petty officers to explain that to their men immediately. This is not a liberty port. We *have* to get to Tampa to ascertain the well being of those ships as soon as possible. We leave when we are unloaded, understood?"

"Aye, aye, sir."

Seeing the smiling dual reply, Wake thought he'd better add another caveat. "And gentlemen, no slacking in the unloading. We unload, and we weigh anchor. We'll return another day. Mr. Emerson, I'll be lunching ashore with the island's leaders and my wife."

"Aye, aye, sir."

"Oh, and two more things. Mr. Emerson, keep a weather eye out for palm wine or rum being brought aboard from those boats. And mind the men that most of these women's husbands are fighting in the Union militia regiment. I want no gross suggestive behavior toward them. They are enthusiastic to see us. Don't let the men translate that into something else. Understood on those two subjects?"

Both officers acknowledged Wake and went to spread the unpopular word. Wake turned to Curtis, the watch bosun's mate, and told him to call away the launch.

Rork watched his captain head ashore as the executive officer told the men to get away from the railing and gather around him. The word was short and strong. They would be there two hours. Only one boat crew would leave the ship. Nothing but food could be brought aboard, and none of the women in the boats were trollops—most had soldiers as husbands—so woe to anyone who treated them that way. Rork, not knowing the content of the ship's orders in detail, was surprised at the brief stay, but surmised that there was something more pressing to make them leave so soon. It would have to be pressing indeed to make Captain Wake leave his pretty bride. Rork swung to with a will and boomed out his best deck voice to the gathered men, as Master Emerson walked forward to check on the working party there.

"All right lads. There's a bit o' a war on, an' it seems we can't have the garden party jus' yet. So let's do this and do it right smartly!"

Amid some low grumbling, the sailors sullenly turned to loading the boxes of supplies into a cargo net while Rork glanced again at the ship's launch closing in to the dock that made its way out from the beach. Wake stood in the sternsheets, waving at Linda who was running down the hill. Little Rain was running too, followed by Sofira at a walk.

She melted his heart. She was so beautiful with her soft skin, her auburn hair done up, and those green eyes that captivated him. Memories of all the stolen encounters in Key West during their forbidden affair came to his mind as he waited while Lawson brought the launch alongside the dock. Linda was standing there, looking more lovely than he remembered. And the irony of it was that now that they were legitimately married, he could stay but an hour.

Surreptitiously, the boat crew was watching the exchange of looks between their captain and his wife. Consumed with empathy for their commander and his girl, the stroke oar failed to backwater in time, making the boat bump into the jetty, and incurring the subdued wrath of Coxswain Lawson, who was constrained from giving full vent to his comments by the proximity of the captain's lady. But none of it mattered to Wake, who bounded up out of the boat and onto the dock in a leap. Then she was in his arms. She felt so small, but strong.

"Peter. I missed you so very much. I love you."

"Linda. I love you too, darling."

She leaned back and looked up at him, beaming with happiness.

"Everyone's excited. They're making a hog roast for your men. Oh, Peter, it's been so long."

He had to say it, had to break the magical spell. It almost broke his heart. "Linda, I only have an hour. We have to get under way as soon as the supplies are unloaded. We're bound up the coast to help some other ships. I can't stay, darling. I want to, but I can't."

She pulled him close again, burying her head into his shoulder, her voice trembling. "You have to stay. You're here now. You have to stay. Just stay the night with me."

She didn't let go of him. The soft warmth of her body was melting his resolve. He was trying to control himself, afraid that if he gave in to his emotions tears would flow, and he would succumb to her pleadings. He managed only two words.

"I *can't*."

They stood there, neither releasing the embrace, not caring that dozens of people from the island and the vessels were watching their heartbreak. Her face tilted up, her lips finding his, and they held the kiss for a long time.

Linda broke away first. She wiped her face with the sleeve of her gingham dress, then straightened out the wrinkles and looked away to the top of the high hill, where thin smoke was still rising. Her voice seemed as far away as her gaze.

"I must tell the people here to stop their preparations. They've been working on them since we got word you were sighted at Boca Grande. It was going to be a grand evening, Peter. You were going to be the guest of honor."

"I'm sorry, dear. You know that I am so sorry."

"I know that. It's just that my hopes were raised when I heard it was your ship, and I had visions of a wonderful evening—the wedding feast we never had in Key West."

The mention of their wedding increased the pain. They were

married in secret by a black Bahamian preacher at the African Cemetery on the south beach in Key West. The exchange of vows was followed by a brief gathering of a few friends around a fire on the beach. There was no formal wedding, no officially sanctioned demonstration of their love that most couples take for granted.

"Linda, I wish more than you know that it was different and I could stay."

She nodded and walked over to Sofira standing on the sand, exchanging words and gestures. Linda returned to Wake and took his hand in hers.

"We'll go to our home. I promise to have you back at the boat in one hour, Peter. But this hour is mine. I'll share your time with no one."

They walked hand in hand up the pathway from the beach as Sofira went among the other islanders to stop the celebration preparations. There would be no party on Useppa Island that evening. The war, which had dictated everything in their lives for the last three years, would not allow it.

One of the things Wake appreciated aboard a steamer was the powered capstan. As a schooner sailor, he had hauled anchor cables and chains many a time. It was back-breaking, time-consuming work. But today he wished the crew had to break the hook out of the mud the old-fashioned way. It would've taken twenty minutes. The steam engine did it in four.

He didn't want to stand around a lot of people listening to banal chatter, so he went to the afterdeck, where three men were restowing some of the cargo on the deck. Emerson had the conn and Rork knew the channel. They could take *Hunt* out. Wake didn't want to talk with anyone right at that moment lest his feelings show, so he ignored the men and stood by the massive towing sampson posts, watching Useppa Island recede in the pale afternoon light. Heartache and anger swirled inside him, making him want to cry and hit something at the same time—heartache at leaving Linda, and anger at the cruelties of war that make such departures so common. He was also more than just a little afraid at his almost succumbing to her pleas on the dock. That had almost happened in Key West, the day he took his first command, a year and a half ago. Linda had a power over him that he had never felt with any other woman. Thankfully, she had stopped her anguished requests at the dock for him to stay, for he wasn't sure he could've denied her any further.

Once they arrived at the thatched hut, she begged him no more. They didn't even speak of his leaving as they lay together in the crude bed. Instead, they talked of everything else in their lives. Linda was very busy on the island, and happy there. She had no desire to return to Key West. On the island she had found friends that understood tragedy, for each of them had a sad story. Sofira's was the saddest, and had just gotten sadder.

Linda told him of Sergeant Thomaston's death a month and a half earlier, killed in an ambush up the Caloosahatchee River where the Rebels had used a slave as bait to lure the Union soldiers. Thomaston and two other soldiers were killed while trying to rescue the black man. Sofira had taken the news stoically, resigned to trying to make a future life for her child alone in the white man's world, since her own Seminole people, and the Thomaston family in upper Florida, equally distrusted her. The islanders had consoled her and offered to let her stay, but Sofira had decided to leave for some other place come the winter dry season. Linda was attempting to get her to stay too, but told Wake she thought it was hopeless and her friend would leave.

Wake told of what he knew about the happenings in Key West, and briefly of his experiences at sea in the last few months. But mainly he just listened to Linda. He loved her dry and gentle humor. He loved to hear the very sound of her voice, a southern accent with just a tinge of her Irish roots showing when she pronounced her "r." It was a soft voice, so different from the loud and brash voices he was used to in his world of men.

In what seemed to be merely minutes, but was actually an hour, Sofira came up and knocked on the simple board door, then walked away. Five minutes later a grim-faced Wake was in Lawson's boat, seated at the sternsheets and staring at his ship, heading away from the island and his love.

The island was now just a green tinge with a few brown smudges. The failing light of the November evening couldn't illuminate the lush colors of the flowers Wake knew were growing all around the settlement. From this distance you couldn't see the proud American flag undulating bright colors from the bamboo pole atop the high hill, you couldn't even tell there was a settlement. There was no indication of the people, or their lives, or loves. It looked to be just another island among hundreds of others on the coast.

The ship's steam engine droned its pounding beat as she rounded the shoals and turned westerly, heading for the Boca Grande Passage and the open sea. Wake moved over to the starboard rail amidships and gazed forward. He never tired of watching the sunsets in Florida. The falling sun was molten copper now, turning the sky into a giant concave prism. Shades of pink and gold and green were emerging from their pale blue background for a moment of luminescent brilliance, then fading back into a gray void. A few high clouds streaked the sky, holding the pastels a little longer, but then they too faded away as the stars came out one by one over the black eastern horizon.

Wake sighed and made his way forward to the wheelhouse. Rhodes had the watch. He watched the captain enter and struggled to find something to say.

"Evening, sir. We should be passing the *Case* in twenty minutes or so, Captain. We've got an ebb helping us."

"Very good, Mr. Rhodes. You may carry on."

Just then Curtis opened the door, not noticing Wake's presence.

"They're at that seashell caterwaulin' again from the islands.

Eerie, I tell ya. Damned eerie." Curtis caught Rhodes' sideways glance, suddenly saw his captain, and became quiet.

The sun was down in the sea now, for all the world appearing to be boiling the Gulf of Mexico. Wake stepped out the port side door and listened. He heard the two-toned, long-winded moans of the conch shells from Palmetto and Lacosta Islands and looked over at the bosun's mate.

"They're saying goodbye, Curtis. Goodbye to the sun, so it will feel needed and return tomorrow. They do it everyday. An old custom, from the original Indians they say."

"Yes, sir."

"And Curtis."

"Sir?"

"It's never failed once in all those years . . ."

The next day they raised Egmont Key at the entrance to Tampa Bay, finding the steam gunboat *Gates,* Lieutenant Commander Williamson commanding, at anchor off the island. Her consorts, the armed schooners *Joslin* and *Taber,* were anchored close by. Wake could discern no damage as *Hunt* approached the anchorage until a half mile away. Then, through the glass, Wake could see the repair parties at work on the spars and rigging of each ship.

Swinging the scope left he saw that the island showed the effects of the storm even more than the ships. The few trees were down, and the scouring effects of a storm surge were apparent in many places. The depot built by the navy had not escaped either. The slat-sided storage buildings had no walls left, and the roofs of most of the four structures were either partly or completely gone. The hastily constructed temporary hospital, built to house the yellow fever patients of the last few months, was almost totally destroyed. The coal bunkers by the wharf were only partly filled, their contents spread out over the island and the bottom of the anchorage. And the wharf itself was a tangled mass of lumber jutting out at all angles. Wake noted that the lighthouse, rebuilt six years earlier to withstand any storm after the original structure had been severely damaged by a hurricane, was still standing tall over the island.

They found no emergency at Egmont Key. Two men ashore had been drowned and several injured, but fortunately most had emerged unscathed. Each ship had casualties, but miraculously no life-threatening wounds. The *Gates* did have two topmen with broken arms suffered from securing a gaff that had gone adrift in the high winds. Wake offered to take them to the hospital in Key West and was thanked. The damage was such that the vessels were well on their way to self-repaired service.

It was anti-climactic for Wake. Even the enemy was quiet. Other than the battery at Pinellas Point which occasionally threw a half-hearted round toward the ships, the Confederates ashore were too busy tending to their own damages from the storm to attack the naval contingent during its weakened period of refit. The provisions and supplies were very much welcomed, however, and two days were spent in transferring barrels and boxes and bags of cargo among the three floating recipients.

In the evenings the captains would visit each others' ship for dinner, and Wake listened intently as they described riding out the storm, the two schooners at anchor off the Little Manatee River, and the *Gates* having gone to sea. Wake found their experiences similar to his, except for the salient point that they had a shore to leeward, a frightening prospect for any captain in a storm. He also realized that they experienced higher winds for a longer period, and that the center of the storm must have gone ashore somewhere to the north of the bay, since the winds never were easterly for very long. The common agreement was that the ships at Bayport and Cedar Keys may have had a more difficult time, being closer to the eye of the storm. Wake was not to go north of Tampa Bay, however, for according to his orders the *Tahoma* was heading there to check on those ships.

The morning of the third day at Egmont Key they weighed anchor and steamed west around Anna Maria Island. Moving down the coast they felt the wind go to the northeast, dry and cool for the first time since the previous spring. It was a clear day, and mile after mile of wide white sand beach stretched out alongside of them as they chugged south, rolling slightly in the low northerly swells. There was a subtle change in the air aboard the steamer. They were finally heading for Key West. The men were sure that they would have liberty this time and spent their day making plans on how to spend it.

The following morning the sun rose over Sanibel Island, five miles to the east of them. Wake looked to the northeast toward Boca Grande, but saw nothing, and was about to leave the wheelhouse when he heard the lookout call down from his perch aloft.

"Deck there! Sail, hull down, three points off the starboard bow on the horizon. Looks to be a schooner. Not cut like one of ours. Headin' south with all sail spread out."

Wake thought about that. The only authorized schooners on this coast were the three navy and one army, and he had just rendezvoused with the navy's schooners, so that one out in front of them most likely was a runner.

"Deck there! She's wearing ship and comin' round to port, headin' easterly now. She's full an' by now an' movin' fast towards the islands."

Emerson had come into the wheelhouse upon hearing the call. He looked at the chart. Wake didn't need to examine the chart, he'd patrolled this area extensively the year before. They were heading east, and that meant only one destination.

"Set your course for the sou'east, Mr. Emerson. We'll get her off Point Ybel before she goes into San Carlos Bay. Tell Ginaldi I want steam for nine knots."

"Aye, aye, sir," replied Emerson as he gave the orders to Rhodes. Then he went off to find the engineer. Rhodes went to the chart and studied it.

"Are you sure, sir?"

"That's where they run to. They're hoping to get close to shore near Punta Rassa or Estero Island and run her aground, get away from her and find some Rebels that will help them. They don't want to end up in Portsmouth Prison."

"Yes, sir."

Wake went outside to watch the other ship. He could see her now from the deck with a 'scope, and what he saw told him some interesting things. She was around seventy feet and had sails that were faded and splotched with patches, so she was a veteran. She was carrying all plain sail and a big fisherman staysail, heeling over and moving fast. No small crew could set or handle that much canvas, so she had a number of men aboard. She was relatively low in the water and stiff, so she was probably loaded down with cargo of some sort. And, as the lookout had said, she was moving fast. Her bottom was clean and her captain was a good seaman. This would be interesting.

Wake thought about her departure point. It didn't add up. If she was heading south, then where did she come from? The runners that left upper Florida, north of Tampa Bay, all headed far out to sea before turning south so they could avoid the coastal patrols. This schooner was much too close to land. That meant that she must have come out from somewhere close. Possibly Tampa Bay? No, she would've been farther out at sea for the same reason. Sarasota Bay? No, the inlet there had been shoaled. That only left . . . No, it couldn't be, Wake thought. They couldn't have come out from Boca Grande Passage, right past the *Case*—unless something had happened to the *Case* to prevent her from stopping the schooner.

Wake could feel the *Hunt* smashing through the waves faster now, the sound of the engines perceptively louder. Ginaldi was working his magic below.

"Deck there! The schooner's hoisted a flag. Looks to be British."

That was nothing unusual—one out of every four blockade runners used a British flag as a ruse. The schooner was still heading east toward the south coast of Sanibel Island, now apparent to all that she was trying for San Carlos Bay. But she wasn't outdistancing the *Hunt.* The steamer was plunging wildly through the waves like a hunting dog on a rabbit chase, making all hands hold on during the sometimes severe rolls when a wave caught them under their quarter. They were closing the gap fast.

"Mr. Rhodes, kindly calculate the time of closure with that ship."

"Ah, yes, sir."

He came up to Wake a few minutes later and reported in a voice that was without conviction. "Sir, I think it will be in forty-five minutes. We'll be within half gunshot of her then."

"You think, Mr. Rhodes, or you know?"

"I know, sir. Forty-five minutes."

Wake had figured fifty minutes to an hour, but allowed the ensign his opinion, especially since he had done the geometry on the chart table and Wake had done his in his head.

"And so, Mr. Rhodes, what do we do until then? And what do we do at that point?"

Rhodes was more certain of this response. "For right now, sir, call all hands to action station, sir. Clear away the guns. Get Lawson and his crew ready with the launch to go over and take possession. When we get there, fire a warning shot, then a rigging shot, then send the prize party to take control."

Emerson was smiling and glanced at Wake. "Captain, I believe Ensign Rhodes here would be an excellent choice for the prize master. He and an experienced bosun's mate with some good men could take her down to Key West."

"I believe you're right, Mr. Emerson. Let's hope we don't have to cut her up too badly and she still has sails for young Mr. Rhodes to get her to Key West."

That got the desired laugh and everyone settled down for the wait.

They waited for forty-eight minutes, with Rhodes pacing like an expectant father, one eye on his pocket watch and the other on the schooner. The schooner captain was game to the end, never even slowing until Durlon shot not only a warning round, but took off the upper foremast with langrell shot as well.

That persuaded the schooner captain to come into the wind and lower his sails. Wake saw no name on her stern, but upon closer examination with a telescope he saw that the transom has been crudely painted over.

A commotion came from *Hunt*'s main deck as the launch was swayed out and heavily armed sailors jumped down into it. Wake glanced back at the schooner and saw a figure at her stern throwing something overboard, then shaking his head at Wake.

"Mr. Rhodes! Mind that man on her stern. I believe he's her captain and he threw something overboard."

Within minutes Rhodes, Rork, and the rest of the boarding crew were on the schooner's deck. Wake kept the glass on the other vessel as Rhodes and Rork quickly detained the captain, his gestures indicating that he was protesting innocence. Then the man's shoulders slumped and Wake smiled, for he knew that the schooner captain had given up his façade when the bluejackets opened the hatch to the hold. Wake had learned long ago in this war to assume nothing, prepare for the worst, and search the suspect vessel thoroughly right away. Soon Lawson was back alongside the steamer. He held the stern of the launch off the steamer's hull with one hand, while saluting with the other.

"Captain, Mr. Rhodes presents his respects and says to tell you that she's the *Emma* out of Nassau, and loaded with lots of cotton, maybe fifty bales of it. And she's got barrels of turpentine. Captain's British and the crew is Reb and West Indian. She came out of the Peace River. Got past the *Case* 'cause the *Case* got grounded chasing her in the dark. Ran the *Case* up on the shoal by Patricio Island at high water. Says he thinks they're probably still there as they was heeled over when they hit."

Unbelievable. What were the odds of that happening? The blockade runner had had incredible luck in running the *Case* aground and then getting out through the Boca Grande Passage. But by the same token, Wake realized, she'd had very bad luck when the *Hunt* came along the next morning.

"Very well, Lawson. Tell Mr. Rhodes to send the captain

here, and secure the other prisoners separately. Then square away for Key West as per his orders. We'll meet him there directly after we check on the *Case*'s situation. Now get that done and be back aboard as quick as you can, I don't want to waste time here."

A few minutes later a very disgruntled British captain was standing by the after gun waiting to be shown below to the officers' quarters and Lawson was supervising the lashing down of the launch. The stack belched a puff of smoke and the deck rumbled as *Hunt* gathered speed, leaving the schooner astern.

It was odd seeing no naval vessel at Boca Grande Passage. Wake had never seen it unguarded like this. But they soon found her. She was an awful sight, lying over on her port side on the shoals by Patricio Island, near where the *Hunt* had crossed just days earlier. It appeared that in the dark, however, the *Case* had misjudged the shoals and run hard aground under full sail while chasing the runner.

There were men in the water walking around her. It only came up to their knees in many places. Other men on the canted deck were manning the capstan, trying to pull her to a kedge anchor set in deep water fifty feet away. They were making no progress.

Wake anchored his steam tug in the deep water and went over in the launch to see the *Case*'s captain, Lotrell. He found him on the slope of the afterdeck gazing astern, holding onto the running backstay. Lotrell was surveying the path the vessel had taken to get where she now lay like a wounded whale in shallow water. The *Case*'s captain was glad to see him and laughed, holding his arms up in the air in a gesture of surrender.

"Well, Peter Wake, of all the ships that could've come in the pass, you're the one I wanted the most. I do believe we could use a tug right about now."

Lawson brought the launch in close aboard as Wake jumped aboard the *Case* and climbed up the deck to where Lotrell was standing. Wake pointed to the kedge anchor.

"Any progress?"

"No, she hasn't budged. It's quite a story. But then I guess we have time, don't we?"

"Actually, we heard the story, sir. From the horse's mouth, as it were. I have the blockade runner captain aboard the *Hunt* right now. We had the very good fortune to spot them just this morning off Sanibel Island. Thought it was a very queer thing to see them this close in. Then we found out about your mishap. Sorry to hear of it."

Lotrell's mouth fell open. When finally able to speak, he said, "You got him? Well, I'll be damned. What a stroke of luck! Excellent news. The best that could be heard."

Wake couldn't suppress a smile. It had been pure dumb luck.

"We need to get you off, but even the *Hunt* can't do it until extreme high tide. We'll have to wait until tomorrow morning."

"Yes, you're right. Somewhere around five o'clock in the morning. We'll get *Case* prepared, then at half past four we'll take your hawser and take up the strain."

Wake studied the angle between the heading of the *Case,* southwesterly, and the route to deep water. He pointed out the route he would pull her through.

"We'll need you to keep her well heeled, sir, with halyards to anchors set ahead if necessary. Then we'll pull your bow around to the northwest and break the suction of the mud. Then we'll try to drag you through the mud about fifty feet, maybe sixty, to that deep water right over there."

"Very good, Wake. That sounds like a good plan. All we have to do is wait the sixteen hours until then."

Through the noise of men shouting orders, Wake absent-mindedly heard something in the distance as he answered Lotrell. "Right, sir. We'll wait around here."

Wake heard someone on the steamer calling his name and looked over to see Curtis pointing to the south. He was calling to Wake, who could now make out the words.

"The seashells, Captain. They're calling for you! They want you to return."

It suddenly struck him. Conch shells were sounding on the

islands nearby. In the haste and gravity of the moment he hadn't thought of Useppa since they had glanced over at it when coming through the passage. Now it flooded his mind, and his heart accelerated. He stared south toward Useppa four miles away. Linda was there. Four miles—he could be with her in forty minutes. . . . Wake suddenly shook himself to awareness, for he realized that Lotrell had been speaking to him.

"I said, Wake, that you're not needed here until we start the work at four in the morn. I suggest you go over to Useppa and see that wife of yours until then."

"Well, ah, Captain Lotrell . . ."

Lotrell smiled and held up a hand, shaking his head. "*Hunt* will be fine, Wake. Your man over there is right. Useppa calls. Go. I am the senior here, and I give you permission to leave your ship in the charge of your executive officer until four A.M."

Lotrell was making a very kind gesture as the senior officer, for a captain could only leave his ship overnight with permission. Wake concentrated on Lotrell's eyes, finding no deception. Wake thought about Morris' words about dawdling at Useppa. He smiled as he decided that Morris' words were not applicable in the present circumstances.

"Thank you, Captain Lotrell. I shall take your kind offer."

Lotrell laughed again and slapped Wake's shoulder. "Good Lord, Peter Wake, take advantage of the moment, man. If I had a wife on that island, I wouldn't have waited for permission. I would've just gone."

Wake decided that Lotrell was sincere. At any rate, he had been given permission and time was wasting.

"Well, sir. I didn't want to violate regulations. But you are certainly right, and again, I thank you. I'll depart directly in our launch and be back at four. Then we'll get you off and floating."

"Very good, Wake. Never disappoint when a lady calls. Please give her my regards and respects."

Wake was already sliding down the deck and halfway in the launch when he replied. "Aye, aye, sir!"

Lawson had no knowledge of the conversation between the two officers but saw the complete change in his captain's manner as he helped Wake to the sternsheets.

"Lawson, take me to the *Hunt* for a moment, then get me over to Useppa Island as fast as you can."

Lawson caught Wake's euphoria and was glad the man was going to get over to his wife. Sentimental as most sailors, Lawson allowed a grin to spread across his face as he urged his men to make the dream come true as fast as they could.

"Aye, aye, sir. Lay your backs into it, men. Two strokes to the *Hunt,* then a race to Useppa!"

Lawson's boat crew was as good as his word. In two powerful pulls of the oars they were at the steamer and Wake was bounding up to the main deck. Emerson greeted him there with a report on their preparations.

"Sir, we're pulling out the number one hawser and faking down a cable length on the stern. I think six hundred feet should do it. Looks like it'll be at least four tomorrow morning before the tide's high enough that we can start to pull her off. I recommend we stay anchored until then. Ginaldi wants to do some maintenance work on the boilers anyway, and the bosun can get some of his mending work done too."

"Very well, Mr. Emerson. I concur with your preparations and recommendations. Carry on with them. Now, Captain Lotrell has given me leave of the ship for the night, so you are in command. I shall return aboard by four A.M. and then we'll get the *Case* off her ground. Have the launch at Useppa Island beach at three A.M. Understood?"

Emerson's eyes crinkled as he nodded. "Aye, sir. The boat'll be there and we'll be here. Don't worry about a thing."

Wake didn't wait for Dirkus to pack some belongings. There was no time for that. He grabbed a few necessities, and five minutes later he was carrying a small bag into the launch, which now had the double-masted lug sail rig stepped, sails luffing in the breeze. Lawson shoved them away and the boat crew simultaneously hauled in the sheets and pulled on their oars.

The sailors on both ships' decks stopped and watched the display of seamanship as Lawson and his crew sailed and pulled the launch ever faster through the water. The sailors were still rowing strongly as she sailed, a feat few seamen could achieve, and making the heeling launch speed as fast as the steamer could go. Lawson, standing like a statue in the stern, swayed with the roll of the boat. With one arm on the tiller and the other pointing forward, he directed the trim of the sheets and steered the boat over the shoals toward the island as the spray from the bow started to send a sweet-smelling mist of saltwater over them.

It was exhilarating sailing in the strong sunshine. Wake couldn't remember a finer moment as he watched the men at their work. Their eyes did not meet his, regulations forbade that, but Wake could still sense that they were willing him to the island with their minds as much as with their muscles. One of the *Hunt*'s men would get to visit his wife, and all of them wished him well. It was their gift to him.

The different tones of the conch shells became clearer as they grew closer. Sounding in conjunction with each other, Wake thought they had a primitive musical quality. By the time Lawson told Wake to hold on, for they were going to sail the boat right up to the beach, thirty people had gathered on the sand in front of them. Linda and Sofira were standing by the big banyan tree, its huge twisted trunk looking like a monster next to their delicate proportions. Wake waved to her and received a wild wave of both arms in return. He could see her wonderful smile more prominently than anything else. Wake loved her smile. He struggled to hold his emotions, not sure that he would be successful as they closed the distance to a few feet.

A spontaneous roar from the crowd went up as the launch stopped with its bow crunching on the dry sand, the sailors forgetting their discipline and doubling over, laughing and slapping each other in congratulations. Lawson looked down at his captain, took the bag from his hand, and swept one massive arm toward the island.

"Captain, we have arrived at Useppa Island. Sir, I do believe you are welcome here."

"So it would appear, Lawson. So it would appear."

The two men made their way forward through the thwarts and over the bow, dropping down onto the beach, where they were met by an older woman who immediately introduced herself.

"Welcome back to Useppa Island, Captain Wake. I am Esmelda Carmichael, the elected leader of this island. My husband's with the regiment on the mainland fighting the Rebs. Your wife is waiting in her home for you." Her hand pointed at the low hill and the hut behind the banyan tree, as she continued. "And we would be greatly pleased if you would honor us with your presence later for an early dinner tonight."

"Ah, well . . . ma'am—"

"We know that you'll be busy with Mrs. Wake, Captain. We do not mean to intrude. We mean later, when everyone has rested."

The crowd consisted mainly of women, with a few elderly men standing on the fringes. The women laughed at the mention of the word "busy" and Wake felt himself turning red, which brought forth more guffaws. He didn't know what to say, or how to say it.

"Madam, I fear you have me at a disadvantage here. I can't make a social commitment before consulting with my wife."

The moment he said it he knew it sounded ridiculous, as if they were in Boston or New York, or Key West for that matter. Carmichael, old enough to be Wake's mother, slowly shook her head as a rueful expression filled her face.

"Captain, don't worry. Your wife helped to plan the dinner. She'll let you come, not to fear, sir."

This last maternal affirmation got more laughs and Wake realized it was time to surrender and do what the woman wanted. No wonder she was elected the leader.

"Thank you, ma'am. It would appear that all is taken care of then. I would be delighted to have dinner with all of you."

His submission earned him another roar from the crowd, and a grin from Lawson, who saluted and returned to the boat, shoving it off into deep water for the return to the steamer. Several of the women waved to the boat crew, who enthusiastically returned the gesture. For a moment Wake worried about them coming ashore, but then saw the look on Lawson's face as he reminded his men of their duties. Wake turned and walked up the path.

She met him inside the doorway, wearing the faded green dress that in its prime had matched her eyes. Closing and latching the door after her husband entered the darkened interior of the thatched hut, she motioned to the crude straw mattress. Neither said a word—they didn't need words to communicate their thoughts.

Hours later, the sun pierced the veil of unconsciousness Wake had fallen into. It intruded through gaps in the closed windows and doorway, making strange patterns of light on the thatch-matted floor and walls. The breeze made its way through the thatch, cooling the room and bringing the deliciously incongruous smells of flowers and marinated roasting meat. Feminine laughter floated in from the island around them. It was all so different from the world he lived in. The sounds and smells calmed him.

They lay there holding each other gently, neither knowing when they would be able to do so again. A short time later they left the hut and joined the others at the top of the hill. The feast had already begun and the ladies and old men were sitting at the collection of tables stretched out for thirty feet. Food covered the table from one end to the other.

The smell of freshly grilled grouper, snapper, and red fish, accented with orange, lime, and lemon, filled the air as they arrived. A round of applause started and Wake thought for a moment it was for Linda and him, but it was for the hog roast that was being brought forth. A large pig had been spit roasted for twelve hours in a special marinade, since the *Hunt* was first spotted early in the morning coming through the pass, and was now laid, with great ceremony, on the table already piled with food. Wake suddenly realized he was famished.

He and Linda were placed in the seats of honor at the center of the table next to Esmelda Carmichael, who officially opened the repast with a prayer of thanksgiving for the feast before them and supplication for the safety of their men, wherever they might be. Then they all started to eat. Every type of fruit and seafood was piled on the table. Wake had never seen so much food. He had been out of the company of women for so long that he felt oddly ill at ease at first, as if he might embarrass himself or them with some faux pas. He soon forgot all his qualms, however, as he became the center of attention, the women listening intently to his narration of the latest war news and his opinions regarding the future of the conflict.

It was grand, and in between bites, Wake conversed and laughed with a dozen of the ladies. Linda smiled as she watched him deal with it all, so very proud of her husband and of what she had come to think of as her island. Several of the ladies complimented her on her man and expressed their aching to have their men back, if just for an evening as Linda did.

Darkness started to gather in from the east as the sun descended, and a dessert of fruit pies came, enhanced by palm wine and strong Cuban rum. Dusk softened the scene, the women remembering their men, and feeling the loneliness of the coming night. He and Linda excused themselves, thanking the many ladies individually, and then walked slowly with his arm around her waist back to her hut on the lower hill. Each was silent, wishing with all their hearts that the joy of this dream evening would not end, but knowing that a mere eight hours later they would return to their forced separation. They had eight hours to create memories to hold them through whatever the future held.

Before he fell asleep in the pitch-black hut, Wake heard the sound that he would forever associate with Useppa Island. It was a conch shell that briefly cried out from Mondongo Island, high-pitched and plaintive, almost questioning. The answering call came from a deeper-throated shell on Useppa, low and strong and reassuring. The long moaning wail transcended all other sounds and filled the recesses of his mind, swirling and echoing as Peter Wake drifted off into the softness of his dreams, far away from the war that ruled them all.

5

The Enemy's Kindest Regards

December 1864 was the most pleasant month the officers and men of the *Hunt* had experienced since Wake took over command. After getting the *Case* off the shoal by Useppa Island, a task requiring an hour of exertion on the part of the steamer's engine, they departed for Key West. Arriving the next day, the *Hunt* was assigned to the Tortugas run, which meant that twice a week they took supplies out to Fort Jefferson and would enjoy liberty ashore in Key West once a week. The effect on the crew's morale was immediate and impressive. It didn't take long for the sailors to spend every cent they had, enabling the lending shysters in the naval station detail ashore to attach themselves to the crew's future pay, with interest. Wake worried about them, but was glad that that was the worst of his concerns.

Other news arrived that also cheered them. The vessel they took off Sanibel Island was taken into the Admiralty Court and scheduled for adjudication. It appeared there would be a successful prosecution and almost everyone in the crew, including the captain, was pondering what their share of the prize money would be. A survey of the ship and cargo was under way and everyone looked forward to the result.

Momentous news affecting the nation arrived from outside Key West via the Northern newspapers. Lincoln had won re-election. It had been a close run during the campaigning and "Little Mac" McClellan looked like he might bring the Democrats back to power, throwing the future of the war into doubt. But in the end Lincoln and the Republicans had taken the day, and according to the pundits' opinions in New York and Philadelphia, the balance was tipped by the vote of the soldiers and sailors who supported their commander-in-chief overwhelmingly. Wake was pleased, since he and most of the navy men he knew had cast their absentee ballot for Lincoln—they didn't want the sacrifice of the last three years to be used as negotiating fodder for anything less than a total surrender of the enemy.

The Confederate sympathizers among the people of Key West took the news resignedly. Long ago they realized that Federal strength was too overpowering for Florida or the other Southern states to gain independence. The election sealed the fate of any hope for negotiating a partial autonomy. The Key Westers congratulated the naval and military men on the island on the victory of their man and went back to the business of a port town. The pro-Union islanders, however, were ecstatic, and several threw parties for Federal officers on the Saturday after the news arrived.

One other mysterious bit of intelligence came to Wake the day they arrived from Boca Grande. It was a peculiar communication from an adversary in his past, but Wake wasn't sure of its author's authenticity, nor what to make of it.

It came to him after reporting in to the squadron offices upon his arrival in port, when Wake was approached at the officers' landing by a lanky petty officer who said he was Bosun's Mate Harpford from the fever ship the *Hunt* rescued at the Mosquito Inlet, the schooner *Ramer.*

Wake remembered the name. He was the petty officer who had taken a ship's boat off to look for help just before the *Hunt* arrived at the *Ramer*—the boat they had never found. He nodded for the man to continue.

"Well, sir. I had three men with me in the boat, and we went south toward the Mosquito Inlet to see if we could find anyone to help. We went ashore and made a camp on the beach and kept a watch up, day and night, sir. We watched real hard for any help, sir, but we was getting sickly our ownselves by that point."

Harpford looked uneasy as he told the story in one breath, finally stopping to inhale again. Wake couldn't understand Harpford's expression. The man appeared frightened.

"All right, Harpford, I can understand that. Go ahead and tell the rest. How did you get rescued? We searched, but couldn't find you."

"Aye, sir. You's couldn't find us 'cause by then we was captured by them Reb runners, sir. They came up quiet-like in the dark and caught us at gunpoint. Twarn't a thing I could do, sir. The boys and I was sickly and them Rebs had us quick."

"I understand that, Harpford. What happened that you came to return to Key West?"

"Well, sir, that's the strange part. Them Rebs was from a blockade runner that was anchored just up the river from the inlet. Snuck her in at night when *Ramer* was just a-laying there at anchor up the coast, sir. We never saw her go in, sir. By that time we was just trying to stay alive, Captain."

"Yes, Harpford, you're not at fault. Continue."

"Well, sir. Some of the Rebs, they wanted to send us to the Reb militia on the mainland there, and they'd a sent us off to one of them war prisoner camps up in Georgia they got. But this here leader of the Rebs, he says no. Don't turn them over, he says. They'll go to that hellhole at Andersonville. We'll keep them, he says. Well, Captain, some of those boys didn't want to do that, wanted to get rid of us, but this man said no. They ended up doing what he said, and took us over to their ship. Should'a seen that darlin' sir. She was something!"

"Describe her to me."

"Don't know her name, sir. Twarn't none on her, and they never called her nothing but 'the ship.' But she's a new steamer, maybe five hundred tons, two hundred feet. Sleek like a racing dog, she is, sir. Got two low schooner-rigged masts, raked well aft, and new canvas what looks like it's not ever been used. Holds fore and aft of the bridge and funnel. Painted all black. Everything. Hull, cabin tops, masts and spars. No guns that I saw. The way they was talking about her, she sounded like she's almost new built. They run her out of Nassau. Fly the Brit flag when hailed. Heard them say about how it's a day and a half run. That's about it for her, sir. They kept us down in the cable tier under guard, until we got to sea."

"They took you to sea?"

"Yes, sir. That man said he would hold us until they got free and clear of the coast."

"Describe that man, Harpford."

Harpford set his jaw and raised his hands in submission, as though he was afraid Wake would physically attack him.

"Captain, please don't get upset. I mean no disrespect, sir. But I think the man is a friend of yours. That's what he said to me, sir. Said he was a friend and to give you a message when I saw you, sir. I didn't know what to think, Captain, but I got that message and I done like he said to do. I ain't told nobody about him or the message to you, sir. It's just a secret atween us three."

Wake was stunned and confused. Harpford did not appear to be a lunatic, but what he was saying sounded crazy. Wake was getting angry at this circumventive narration. It was time to get to the meat of the matter.

"Harpford, what on earth are you talking about, man? I don't know any blockade runners, much less am friends with one. Who in the hell was this man?"

Harpford shrank back and pulled an envelope from his pocket, thrusting it toward Wake as if it had the plague. "Captain, please, I meant no disrespect. That's just what the man said. Here's the message, sir. Nobody's seen it 'cept you. He gave it to me when they cast us off in our boat to go back ashore, and he said to give it directly to you when I next saw you, sir. And that's right now. I heard you was in port today."

Wake took the envelope from Harpford. It was sealed with red wax embossed with two reversed "J"s with no other markings. Wake looked up at Harpford's face for a clue that he knew the contents. The man was intently watching as if he didn't know what would happen next.

"Thank you, Harpford. Whoever this man is, his sense of humor has us both in its grip right now, doesn't it?"

Harpford relaxed and managed a smile. "Well that it do, sir. That it do. The whole affair was curious, Captain, but all the same, I'm grateful not to be in some hellhole prison in Georgia. Whoever that man is, he saved me and the boys' lives by not letting them send us off to that there prison. And then he let us go."

Wake wasn't listening to Harpford ramble on. He was carefully slitting the envelope open with his pocket knife. Then he slid out the two sheets of paper and read them. Wake couldn't believe it. He read them again, examining each quilled word, trying to decipher any hidden meaning of the message.

My dear Captain Wake,

Should you be reading this missive, it will mean that I have been successful in my endeavor to lessen, if only in this miniscule manner, the horrors of this unfortunate conflict by allowing some of your compatriots to go free and live yet another day. I must say, it was a pleasure to do something constructive and peaceful in the midst of this devastating and bellicose time we seem to have found ourselves in.

It was made doubly pleasurable by the certain knowledge that my most worthy adversary over the last year or so had inadvertently assisted my efforts by arranging to take the federal ship Ramer, *and his own ship* Hunt, *away from my location so I could make good my departure. This departure was a particularly profitable one, so in the spirit of the moment I thought I would allow the federal sailors we captured to go free. Of course, admittedly, I wouldn't send a dog to one of those prisoner camps.*

I understand from my acquaintances here and there that you have been promoted and now command that steamer. Quite an accolade for a "mere volunteer officer." Wake, you are making those veteran regulars who lounge about Key West in the Russell Hotel bar look woefully inadequate. Congratulations, you certainly deserve the recognition for your successful work to date. I also understand that felicitations are in order for your new matrimony. What wonderful news! I offer my warmest wishes for a long and contented life for both you and your dear lady.

It would appear from the intelligence coming out of Richmond and Atlanta, and from Washington for that matter, that the time for our little competition of cat and mouse may be nearing an end. That is truly a shame. It has been intriguing for me, especially that time in Havana when you convinced them to arrest me. How very Machiavellian. You forgot one thing, however, Captain Wake. Not everyone shares your allegiance to principles. Regrettably for you, and very fortunately for me, it is a sad fact that most of the human race will succumb eventually to material temptations.

I would wish you good luck and good hunting, but by the looks of things you don't need any further assistance from me. I will wish, though, that we could meet someday in less acrimonious times, as friends and not enemies. I would take it as an honor to buy the first drink.

Please know that I am your most respectful and admiring adversary,

Jonathan Saunders

Wake realized that Harpford was still staring at him and saying something. "I said sir, is that who you thought it was? He was a right gentlemen, that he was, sir."

"Harpford, I hadn't a clue who it was until I read this letter. But now I know. It's a Rebel blockade runner I thought was dead or gone. Obviously he isn't either."

Harpford grinned and ventured an unsolicited opinion. "Well thankee to the Lord he ain't, Captain, or I wouldn't be here to talking with you."

"Yes, well, Harpford, I agree that was a good outcome."

"Aye, sir. Will there be anything else, sir? I'm on watch at the magazine dock soon. That's where they's keeping me working till *Ramer* gets back to port."

"No Harpford, that will be all. I'm glad you and your mates made it alive. And thank you for delivering the letter."

Harpford saluted and loped off as Wake read the letter a second time. He knew what he would have to do, and dreaded doing it—dreaded the looks, the innuendoes. But it was the right thing to do, and there was still time before the office closed. He turned toward the late afternoon sun and headed over to the squadron offices.

Captain Morris was in his office, reading a mound of reports on his desk. He didn't look up as the yeoman reported Captain Wake of the *Hunt* entering the room. "Damned busy right now, Wake. Make it quick."

Wake walked over and put the envelope on the top of the pile. Morris glanced at it, and then up at Wake. "Mail call?"

"A very unusual mail call, sir. To me, from Jonathan Saunders, the blockade runner."

Morris put down the report in his hand and picked up the envelope, turning it over in his hand, examining it carefully before extracting the letter inside. A slight sneer formed at the corners of his mouth as he looked up again at Wake. "Well, well, Wake. You don't say? Your old nemesis writing little notes to you?"

"Yes, sir. It would appear he is. It also appears he is still very active in our area, and has informants in Key West. It's all in the letter, Captain."

Morris's eyebrows furrowed as he read the letter twice through, his mouth changing from a sneer to a scowl at the finish of the second reading.

"How did you get this?"

"Harpford, the petty officer of the detail of men they captured, brought it to me minutes ago, sir. Saunders gave it to him, to give to me personally as soon as he saw me."

"I see. It would seem he is well informed of events in your life, Mr. Wake. What do you make of that?"

Wake knew what Morris was thinking—Linda's family was informing the enemy.

"Captain Morris, I think that there are hundreds of people in Key West who know that information, and that anyone sitting in a tavern could pick it up through idle gossip."

Morris leaned back in his chair, one arm draped over the desk, the other holding the letter. His features relaxed and the tone of his voice lost its edge.

"I thought you'd say something like that, Mr. Wake. You may very well be right. You may also be wrong. It appears that this man has paid particular attention to your career and life. Why would that be?"

Wake had been intensely pondering that himself. "Captain, the only thing I can come up with is that I'm the one that got him, or almost got him, several times."

"Yes, there was that time off Sanibel."

"Yes, sir. That was the first time, about May of last year. I had no proof and let him go."

"Right. Then there was Havana, of course."

Wake would never forget *that* assignment. He thought Saunders would be dead within a day after he was captured by the Spanish authorities. "Yes, sir. Last I saw him, the Spanish Navy was leading him away to an interrogation and prison. Turns out he bought his way out."

"Yes. Regrettable . . ."

The moment he said it, Morris remembered that was the word Saunders had used in the letter. Morris shook his head slowly. "He is a devil of a character, isn't he, Wake? Later on, you damn near had him off Yucatan in Mexico, didn't you?"

Wake remembered that one well also. That time Saunders had paid off the French Navy. "Within moments of capturing him after a three day chase, Captain Morris, but he made over to a French naval vessel and we were in their waters. That ended that. I also missed him in the Bahamas, but he had been long gone by the time I was there."

Morris nodded, showing surprising empathy. "Well, you certainly have tried. This looks like some sort of personal contest between you too. He plays the part of a gentleman, but I'd be careful Wake. You had him chucked into a Spanish gaol, if only for a short time. I can only imagine what that cesspool was like. And it must have cost a fortune to get out of that mess with the Spanish authorities. He may want a little personal revenge. He may be playing with your mind, Wake."

Wake had considered that and rejected it. Saunders clearly could have done something to Wake in Key West by now if he had wanted to. The letter showed that he had at least informants there, and maybe henchmen. No, there was more to it all. Wake wasn't sure, but he had an idea.

"Captain, I think he grudgingly respects our side in this. He's making lots of money out of misery. I think he was educated as a gentleman and is ashamed of his role in all this. The letter, and the release of the seamen, is a small atonement for that. I don't know for sure, of course, but that's my opinion based on what I know of him."

Morris's laugh was cynical. "How chivalrous, Wake. But the *gentlemen* in this war were all killed off years ago."

Wake shrugged. It did sound ridiculous. "Yes, sir."

"Thank you for bringing this to me. We'll have Harpford and those seamen in here straight away and find out what they know. If I remember correctly, they were picked up off the beach by one of our vessels after drifting for days. I don't remember them reporting any of this when rescued."

"I think it was in gratitude for being freed, sir. They were sick and scared. I can understand that."

134

Morris eyed Wake. "Yes, you probably would, Mr. Wake. Nevertheless, we will have them in and find out what they know, now that we know they know something."

Wake knew Harpford and the others were in for a rough time, but Morris had a point.

"Is that all, sir?"

Morris' mind was already on other things and he dismissed Wake with a wave as he started pulling open desk drawers searching for something. Wake seized the moment and left quickly.

In the three weeks since that day, Wake had heard nothing more about the letter, but had thought about it, and the author, often. He had discussed it with Rork, who agreed on the probable motive. "Almost like a limey gent, but don't let your guard down," Rork had opined.

Christmas was coming in a week, and the *Hunt* had been given the unusual and appreciated task of being the harbor guard vessel since the boiler on the regularly assigned steamer, the *Honeysuckle,* was being repaired. That meant every night at the wharf, with a third of the men on liberty until sunrise. Living alongside the wharf was a luxury in many ways, but a burden in others. With their money gone and the next pay not due until the end of the month, most of the men spent their time in less troublesome pursuits, but a few would end up being delivered back aboard by the provost patrol of soldiers. Somehow they would get rum, and then they would find trouble, and Wake would have to pronounce disciplinary action the next morning.

Two days before Christmas Wake received a letter from Linda. She told of how all the island ladies were taken with him and envied her having her husband so close. Many of theirs were now fighting with the militia regiment in upper Florida. Most had not seen their husbands in three or four months. She went on to describe how the ladies had decided to invite the officers of the *Case* to a Christmas social day at the island. Linda described the preparations in detail, reminding Wake of the wonderful feast he had had with them, and he knew the Christmas social would be one the officers would never forget. He ached to be there with Linda. They had never shared a holiday together. They had never done so many of the usual things that husbands and wives share, and it hurt deep in his heart. But the important thing, he told himself, was that she was well and safe and happy on Useppa.

The same mail pouch brought another letter, this one from his mother. That was unusual—his father was the usual writer, with his mother sometimes adding a short postscript. He tore open the envelope and read her halting hand. It confirmed his fears.

His father was dead. His will power, and his health, had been worsening in the months since his son James was killed aboard a monitor gunboat in South Carolina, and previous letters had hinted that his physical condition was serious. James' death had broken his heart, which had finally given out. His mother wrote that he had died in his sleep on November 21, at age 61, and that he had finally looked at peace. The letter was longer than any Wake had ever gotten from her. It filled both sides of two pages.

The oldest son, Luke, five years older than Peter and a schooner captain who had been considering joining the navy as his younger brothers had done, presided over the funeral arrangements. The funeral was on a rainy day at the cemetery by the church. His mother said she visited the grave often and talked to it, for she had no one else to talk to about certain matters. She hoped that wasn't a sign of senility. Luke, she was glad to say, had abandoned his notion of joining the navy and was now running the family business, or what was left of it.

They were down to one schooner, which was employed often on the New England–Canadian runs, but their income was sharply down, what with the insurance rates so high and the cargo rates so low. She wasn't sure how much longer Luke could hold out.

She closed by hoping that he and Linda were happy and well and that someday what was left of her family would gather once more and bring some warmth to the old house overlooking that cold sea, perhaps with little grandchildren to add some gaiety and love. And she reminded her son to attend church on Christmas if he could, as the family always had when he was growing up.

Wake was surprised that he couldn't cry for his father, and felt a little ashamed of that, as if he were somehow failing in his duty. But he loved and respected his father and accepted that the old man had probably decided it was time to go. The man had a rock strong will, and his death must have been part of that. Instead, he said a silent prayer and acknowledged his father's departure from this life, and sat at his desk to make plans to send a portion of his monthly pay to his family's bank account in Massachusetts.

An hour later, to break the melancholy, Wake rose and took a turn about the ship. In the wardroom he found the officers gathered, reading their letters aloud to one another. Ginaldi's letter from a young lady in New York, who apparently thought they were engaged and whose letter was more than just a bit dictatorial, was being narrated. Ginaldi, with his gift of humorous repartee, was providing potential replies to each of her instructions. Laughter that could be heard over half the ship was the result. It was hilarious and just what Wake needed. As he stood in the passageway waiting for them to invite him in, he thought of how lucky he was to have these particular men as his officers. Their invitation came not as a duty, for no wardroom would refuse to ask their captain in, but as a sincere request for his companionship at the most happy of their times—receiving mail from up north.

The Christmas Eve service at the Episcopal church on Duval Street was attended by many of the naval officers in Key West. Wake squeezed into a pew at the back, just as the rector was beginning the prayers. It had been a long time since he had been to a church service—years earlier in Massachusetts with the family. Wake looked out over the chapel and wished Linda could be there with him, the two sitting proudly together as husband and wife. The serenity of the scene almost overwhelmed him. The flickering glow of a hundred candles, the sweet scent of the wax and the incense mingling with the flowers placed everywhere, the delicately tranquil sound of a chorus of young girls singing "Amazing Grace," all reminded Wake of better times long ago. He started to feel his throat constrict with emotion.

At the end of the service he said three silent prayers—one for his father to finally know peace, one for his mother to have strength, and one for his wife to be content in their marriage, as strained by absence as it was. Afterward, he walked down Duval Street with a hundred other men, all silent. The taverns and bars did no business that night. No one was of that mind.

Aboard the steamer later, Wake found his officers sitting on folding chairs at the stern, smoking cigars and talking. He joined their group and they talked for hours about many things. They agreed that the war couldn't last much longer and that they would all be home by Easter. That brought forth talk of what they would do upon arriving home, and in what order. It was a pleasant conversation and even the quiet and shy Rhodes was exuberant. Up forward a sailor sang a German Christmas hymn, and for a few minutes they sat silently, listening to the words they could not understand, but comprehending fully the respectful tone of the man singing them.

They finally said their good nights when the bell struck the second watch, each man going to his berth immersed in his own thoughts of home. Wake went into his own cabin feeling a mixture of emotions—appreciation for having officers of their caliber with him, and sadness at being apart from his wife on this most emotional of evenings. Crawling into his berth with the cool air of the Florida winter funneling into his cabin, he desperately missed Linda, missed touching her soft hair and feeling the warmth of her body. Later that night in his dreams, they were together again in a world at peace.

6

Heros and Scoundrels

It must be some error in communication and the squadron's chief of staff is mistaken, Wake thought as he stood in Morris' spartan office. The *Annison* was missing? It didn't make sense. He had seen her only a week or so ago. They had sailed together on many operations and he knew several of the men in her crew, including Ensign Henry Waller, her commander. But apparently something had happened to her, according to Captain Morris.

She'd left Key West bound for Boca Grande four days after Christmas. It was now the fifth of January and she had not arrived at her assigned station. The schooner was well found and well armed with a veteran crew of men, and should have had no problem on that voyage, although she did have a new commander. The run was one that Wake knew well, and the weather was nothing that could have produced a calamity. He couldn't fathom it. Perhaps she'd put in somewhere else or went off chasing a blockade runner. Morris then told him further news that completely shocked him.

"In addition to our schooner *Annison* missing enroute to her assigned station at Charlotte Harbor, we've lost the steamer *San*

Jacinto in the Abacos. She shipwrecked there on New Year's Eve and we just got word this morning. All hands were saved, but the ship is totally destroyed. There are also some unpleasant rumors that we will be addressing. Right now, however, I need to know about the *Annison,* and quickly. Two ships lost at the same time is highly unusual."

Wake looked over at his friend James Williams, who had once commanded the *Annison,* though now he was in command of a large schooner, the *McVeigh.* Williams was standing next to the chart displayed across the wall. His face grimaced as he thought of his former ship and crew. He and Wake had suddenly been summoned to the chief of staff's office an hour earlier. Now they knew the reason. They were to assist the ships on the west coast of Florida searching for the missing schooner.

Wake thought of what Morris had just said, and looked at his superior. "Rumors, sir? Anything we should know that would help in the search, if the two events are related?"

Morris shook his head, slowly letting his breath out while looking intently at Wake and Williams, obviously gauging whether to tell them. "It has been said by the Bahamians who delivered Captain Meade's message reporting the wreck that many of his men either mutinied or deserted after the shipwreck. They went over to and joined a Confederate blockade runner anchored nearby on the other side of the island."

Wake looked at the man incredulously. "I'm stunned, sir. There must be some error or miscommunication. The Bahamian must be confused."

"He said he wasn't. We are sending two ships right now to Meade. At least we know *where* he is. Meanwhile, I need to know about the *Annison* and what happened to her. I don't know that anything bad has happened, but you needed to know that rumor, in confidence, of course. In the unlikely case it is true with the *San Jacinto,* it might be true with the *Annison.* If there *is* some mutinous skullduggery afoot, I want it quashed, decisively and quickly. The admiral and I will not stand for that. Now, as I said before, Wake, you'll search from Cape Romano south to Cape Sable. Williams, you'll take the northern edge of the Keys east to Cape Sable. Other vessels are searching from Romano northward. Any questions?"

Williams and Wake said no. Morris nodded, then held up a finger. "And remember, gentlemen, what I have told you is confidential."

Both lieutenants chorused their acknowledgement and departed, walking quickly out of the building and to the wharf. Neither said much, their minds reeling with the necessities of getting under way and accomplishing their mission. They were still in a state of disbelief.

"We'll find her, James, don't worry. She probably went off station on a chase like you used to do."

"I don't know, Peter. This sounds bad. She's a good strong ship, and a week is a long time to be missing."

Reaching the wharf, each wished good luck to the other and shook hands, then parted ways to their own vessels.

When Wake went aboard he relayed to Emerson the information of the missing ship and their orders to search for her. Two hours later, liberty men rounded up and extra provisions brought aboard, they backed away from the pier and moved through the harbor. Wake stood on the deck outside the wheelhouse watching the anchorage full of ships slide by and tried to imagine the various scenarios that might have played out on the schooner *Annison*.

The thought of mutiny was so alien as to be ridiculous, and he dismissed it in both ships' cases. The *San Jacinto*'s wreck would be clarified soon, so he did not dwell on that issue. But the *Annison*. Where was she? There had been no storm in the area to founder her. There were no known Confederate armed naval vessels in that area to capture or sink her. She could have been overwhelmed by a blockade runner's crew when coming alongside or afterward when they were prisoners aboard her. She might be hard aground in the maze of islands south of Cape Romano on

Marco Island. It was shallow on that coast, with some strong tidal currents. Only a few traders and fishermen were scattered along the coast there, with the occasional Seminole coming out from the Everglades to fish or barter, so there would be no settlement to summon help from or to which they could get a message. The Confederates were not known to venture that far south in the peninsula, so no shore boat could have come out and captured her. Piracy was a romantic notion, but not a practical reality. There hadn't been any true pirates there for forty years.

As they steamed northwest up the channel, increasing speed now that they were away from the anchorage, Wake decided *Annison* would probably be found aground among those islands, her new commanding officer embarrassed but appreciative of the *Hunt's* help in getting her free. Two months from now it would all be a joke in the Key West petty officer taverns.

At the Northwest Channel Light, Wake issued orders for the steamer to head northeast and told Rhodes to come up with proper turn of shaft revolutions in order to make a landfall at Cape Romano the next dawn. That was enough to keep Rhodes and Rork busy for some time, with Emerson checking their calculations.

Wake retired to his cabin and started in on the stack of administrative and pay statements that needed approval, disciplinary cases that needed resolution, and periodic operational and log reports that needed to be written. He despised the mindless paperwork of the navy—the merchant marine had nothing remotely close to it. Wondering who, if anyone, would ever actually read the documents, he was tempted by the sarcastic side of his personality to imbed some inane comments in the reports. The idea quickly passed as he plunged into the work at his desk, but not before a smile crossed Wake's face. For a brief moment, he imagined some bureaucratic gnome at a desk in the bowels of the Navy Department building in Washington inadvertently really reading the report and falling out of his chair in an apoplectic state when he found that the United States Steamer *Hunt* had expended all of her ammunition at elephants on the beach, who had then promptly surrendered.

The frivolity evaporated when Dirkus announced that Mr. Rhodes presented his respects and was ready with the calculations of speed and arrival. Welcoming the chance to escape the paper drudgery, if only for a little while, and do some navigation, Wake patted a surprised Dirkus on the back and strode out of his cabin back to the wheelhouse.

They were watching the remnants of a beautiful sunset as he entered. Rhodes spun around and saluted.

"Turns for five knots, sir. That will put us there at sunrise."

"Very well, Mr. Rhodes, make it so. And double the lookouts. I want all hands to understand we are searching for one of our own who might need help. Call me immediately upon anything being sighted."

"Aye, aye, sir."

"Mr. Emerson, would you care to take a turn around the ship with me?"

"My honor, sir."

They started forward along the starboard side, past the repaired gouges in the deck from the storm and on up to the anchor cat. It was a cool evening and the wind over the deck was starting to feel cold. It was delicious after the humid summer and fall.

"Rhodes seems to be coming along well. What do you think?"

"Aye, sir. He had the knowledge before, but it was book knowledge mainly. I think he passed his examinations for the volunteer commission by studying, rather than by doing. But he's come a long way since this summer. Much more confident."

"Good. I thought so too. I think he'll leave when the war is over, though. Go back to his home and go into business."

"Yes, sir. He's talked about that. Wants to marry that girl he keeps talking about. Wants to have children and live the dull but happy and safe life."

Emerson smiled at the thought of Rhodes as the head of a family with wife and children. Wake nodded and sat on the bulwark.

"What about you Stephen? What are your future plans or wishes?"

Emerson started to reply, then paused. With any other captain than Wake he would have been cautious instead of candid. He looked Wake in the eye as he spoke. "I'm not sure yet, Captain. But I think I'll get out too when the war ends and go back to riverboatin'. I'm not thinking the navy will have room for me, and I want to go back to Illinois and the Mississippi. Anyway, I'm not much of one for those foreigners and far off places, ya know."

Wake could understand that completely. The challenge and intrigue of naval life for an officer was not for everyone. Squadron assignments usually meant foreign stations and a cruise of two years or more. The amount of sea time far from home had deterred many.

"Well, Stephen, you've done very well as executive officer aboard the *Hunt,* and I appreciate your considerable efforts. I'll support you whatever your decision."

Emerson breathed a visible sigh of relief at Wake's reply. "Thank you sir. I was hoping you'd understand. I haven't said my thoughts to many. It would look bad."

"Not with me."

"Thank you, sir."

"Come along, let's go see what Ginaldi's black gang are up to this evening. I haven't been down there since yesterday sometime."

Rhodes' face was beaming with accomplishment as he stood outside the starboard door of the wheelhouse, gazing at a black line stretched across the eastern horizon while the sun rose above the gray of the sea. As they steamed closer they could make out the white beaches of Marco Island. On the starboard bow was Cape Romano. Wake turned to Emerson, who was showing a flicker of a smile himself.

"It appears that our ensign has not led us astray, Mr. Emerson."

"Aye, that it does, sir. We may make something of him yet."

Rhodes addressed the two superiors standing next to him with a strained attempt at an unruffled air.

"Sir, I just applied the logical navigational factors to the problem and it came out as expected."

Wake and Emerson looked at each other and laughed, with Emerson slapping a perplexed Rhodes on the upper arm. Wake regained his composure and replied to the ensign's comment. "Mr. Rhodes, Mr. Emerson and I laugh because the logical factors are frequently not the most decisive ones. It's those illogical, immeasurable factors that are the very devil to take into account. They're the ones that'll throw off the best navigation calculations. And only sea time can give you the understanding of those. But still, you did very well in estimating the time, course, and speed. Well done, Mr. Rhodes."

Emerson leaned in close, the windy January air was cutting through them. "A second of that from me, Mr. Rhodes. Good landfall. Now, you've got an hour of watch left, so set a course for the northern point of the island. Then we'll close to within a mile and turn south." Emerson glanced questioningly at Wake.

"Quite right, Mr. Emerson. Carry on, Mr. Rhodes. I'll take the deck in an hour, after my breakfast. Make sure those lookouts are changed frequently, and that they examine everywhere. Let's find our missing ship and men."

"Aye, aye, sir," acknowledged Rhodes as he went inside to give the course to the helmsman. Wake scanned the horizon with his glass, finding nothing except a seething mass of waves and miles of white sandy beach with green jungle tangled behind. He handed the glass to Emerson, who focused upon the island.

"If they did wreck, let us hope they've made it ashore and will set a signal fire when they see us coming. How about firing a signal gun every half hour, sir?"

"Excellent idea, make it so."

"Deck there! Small boat putting off from the beach to the south, broad on the starboard bow."

Every man turned in that direction and Rhodes came rushing out of the wheelhouse.

Wake saw the tossing object through the telescope. It was a small boat, a dinghy, with no more than one or two men, and it was headed out toward the steamer. He could see nothing on the beach. The naval schooners in the squadron carried a small boat such as that.

"Mr. Rhodes, alter course to the boat and increase to full speed."

They met the dinghy a quarter mile off the beach, bobbing in the two- to three-foot seas. One disheveled older-looking man, soaked with salt spray, was in her. He was pulled up to the main deck by Lawson and deposited in front of Wake. As the man shook himself out he produced some yellow-stained papers from his coat pocket and held them out.

"Johnny Robertson, Captain. Too old to fight, but still a true Union man, sir. Got my papers right here that say I took the allegiance oath an' everythin'. I got another paper that says I can stay on this here island an' fish an' raise a little castor bean crop. Signed by the head army man at Key West. I'm waitin' for a boat to come by an' take me an' the crop down to Key West for to sell it."

Wake surveyed the man before him. His clothes and manner matched the story. The papers appeared valid. There were several fishermen and farmers granted permission to try to make a go of it on the desolate islands of this coast. Robertson glanced around him and saw the intent stares of the sailors on the deck, others peering out in all directions from the masts aloft.

"Somethin' happenin,' Captain? Are there Rebs about?"

"Why don't you tell us, Robertson? Are there any Rebs about here?"

Water flung off as the old man vigorously shook his head.

"Nary a one, Captain. They got nothing down this far south on the coast. They's all up by Fort Myers and Charlotte Harbor way. You's the first I seen in weeks that come by this close. I thought maybes you's were a army supply steamer that could take me an' my crop down Key West way." Robertson paused from the effort of the explanation, then started in again. "Well, sir, could ya?"

"No, Robertson. We're not the army steamer and we can't take you and your beans to Key West. You say you haven't seen a ship in how long?"

Robertson's face fell at the denial of his request. He pulled his chin trying to think of the amount of time that had gone by since the last ship had been close enough for him to recognize. "Saw a steamer headin' south the day after Christmas, Captain. Yep, it was the day after Christmas. I remember that 'cause I celebrated Christmas, an' it was the next day."

Wake could guess how the lonely old man celebrated Christmas on the deserted island, surrounded by his beans. Palm wine was a staple on this coast.

"No other ships since then, until us?"

"Nope, nary a one, Captain. Them Rebs getting desperate now, ain't they? Are they hidin' in these here islands, Captain? Ya lookin' for a Reb runner?"

"No Robertson, just checking on this section of the coast. How long have you been on the island?"

"Nigh on to six months, Captain. I was really hopin' you could take me and the beans off'n here an' back down south. I got 'em bagged an' ready to load, Captain. No bother about it. Just take me an' a couple of your hands an' that big boat you got on the deck one trip to bring all my things. Maybe's a hour, sir. That's all."

The man looked and sounded desperate himself. Wake thought about what it must be like to spend six months alone, fishing and trying to raise a crop of castor beans, waiting for the ships that might, or might not, come someday.

"No, Robertson. We're not your ship. But if I see that army supply steamer, I'll tell them to come here and pick you up on their way south."

Robertson lurched forward and grabbed Wake's hand, pumping it up and down with a filthy fist. "Oh God, Captain, thankee, sir. Thankee. You don't know, Captain. You jus' don't know."

Wake disengaged his hand and backed up a step. "Quite all right, Robertson. You keep a sharp eye for any vessels that come close ashore here. Let the next naval vessel or the army steamer know if there are any wrecked or suspicious vessels in the area. Same goes for any men you may see ashore. Understood?"

"Yes, sir. I understand that. Understand that good, Captain."

Wake wondered if Robertson would even remember the conversation the next day. "Very good. Mr. Emerson, see that Robertson here gets a couple days of food provisions from the galley. And have that dinghy bailed out. Good bye and good luck, Robertson."

They continued making their way south along the beach, keeping off a half mile or more, sweeping the seas and the sand with eight pairs of eyes at all times. The cool morning became a warm afternoon, but the wind and seas were still from the north, making the steamer roll gently. Mile after mile of white sand beach went by, with no sign of the schooner or her sailors. They passed the abandoned Cuban fishing camp just inside the beach at Caxambas. Going close inshore to within two hundred yards of the beach, they examined it through the glass but saw nothing. Wake wanted more than a perusal through a telescope though, so he sent Rork and Lawson ashore to examine the old camp. They came back a short time later, reporting that it looked like the Cubans hadn't been there since the war started, and it was obvious that no one else had either.

The *Hunt* continued to steam south when they reached Cape Romano at the southern extremity of the small island just south of Marco Island, instead of following the shoreline around as it backed away to the east. The shoals here were famous for having strong and unpredictable currents, so Wake kept the steamer headed away from the island to get out around the shoals. When the leadsman called out two fathoms at about five miles offshore, they put the wheel up and turned easterly, proceeding up into Gullivan Bay at a slow pace.

Islands were spreading out on both sides of them now, Cape Romano and Marco Islands to the port, and the Ten Thousand Islands all along the coast to starboard. The water depth was diminishing rapidly, until they had only two feet under their keel and were advancing at three knots. Ginaldi came up to the wheelhouse and reminded Emerson that the intakes for the pumps might get silted if they got into any shallower water, and Wake agreed to keep her offshore a bit further.

Seeing nothing of note near Gullivan Key, they turned southerly again and made for the island protruding the farthest out from the rest, Indian Key, an old trading point with the Seminoles. Wake had never seen a full-blood Indian, didn't really know much of anything of the Seminoles, and didn't know how they would even communicate with them, but thought it was worth a try to look into that area and ascertain if any of them had seen anything unusual.

He was relying on a sketch of the area given him at the squadron office. The author and date were unknown, but since the government charts showed no detail at all of the coast below Cape Romano, it was all he had to go by. The islands were a jumble of mangroves, many with groups of taller trees and several with long beaches. Comparing what he saw to the sketch was useless and he quickly saw that it was a vague depiction at best. He decided to have Rhodes and Rork do a new sketch chart of the islands as the *Hunt* moved slowly south.

The two became engrossed in their assignment, a large sheet of paper spread out and tied down to a makeshift table set up by the forward gun. Rork was drawing and writing the data, while Rhodes was taking the bearings of islands.

"Deck there! Smoke on the island on the horizon, narrow on the port bow."

Emerson was already on it with his glass and gave a report. "Thin wisp of smoke, Captain. Not much at all. Oh, there it goes again."

Wake looked himself and saw the column of smoke. It was on Indian Key. "Very well, maintain this course and speed."

The water was deeper as they approached the island, almost two fathoms close into the beach. The current was ebbing strongly and Wake didn't want to get caught aground, so they went in very slowly, with all eyes watching the shoreline of the long thin island. No smoke had been seen since the second waft was spotted blowing away from the island. Now that they were close, it was as if they had made some mistake in identifying which island had emitted the smoke. There was nothing here.

Emerson glanced at Wake and shrugged.

"I presume we'd better look, sir?"

"Yes. Anchor in this deep water and send Rork and Lawson and a boat crew over to look through the island."

Wake waited for a moment, sensing that something was wrong. He held up a hand to stop Emerson. "And send the men to quarters, Mr. Emerson."

Emerson couldn't hide the surprise in his voice. "Quarters, sir? Aye, aye, sir."

The bell rang out the constant clang for quarters—*Hunt* didn't rate a drummer—sending dozens of men to their stations for battle. Durlon and his gun crews ran to their two twelve-pounders fore and aft and got their powder charges and shots ready. Seven minutes later, shouted reports of readiness were heard from along the decks and a messenger came up from Ginaldi's den below. *Hunt* was no longer a benign vessel transiting the coast. She was now a very dangerous machine ready to dispense death. Wake felt a chill flow over the skin of his arms and chest.

There was no apparent enemy in sight, but no one asked the captain why he had issued the order. After the noise of the men and equipment preparing for battle, the intense silence was unnerving. Except for the lookouts, all hands on the weather decks looked to the wheelhouse and the one man who would decide their fate. Emerson reported to Wake that the ship was at quarters and ready for battle.

"Very well, send the landing party ashore. Cover the island with the guns, loaded with grape."

Emerson acknowledged the order even as he strained to see anything on the island with the telescope at his eye. Wake could hear the boat crew shoving off and starting to row against the current to the island a hundred yards away. Suddenly he thought of something else.

"Mr. Emerson. Pass the word *not* to open fire until ordered. They may see someone ashore, but do *not* open fire unless ordered."

The executive officer passed the word and returned to his position next to Wake. The boat was now almost ashore, crabbing into the ebb tide. Two men in the bow sat with muskets leveled forward. Rork stood in the stern, colt revolver in his hand. The launch crunched on the thin strip of crushed oyster shell beach and then stopped. Rork urged his men forward and over the side.

While four men crouched on the beach watching the tree line, the other six sailors pulled the launch further up on the beach, but not so far that they couldn't shove it out in a hurry. Rork placed Lawson and six sailors in a perimeter on the beach around the boat, while he and the other four headed east along the shore to the end of the island just three hundred feet away. Wake could not shake the feeling that something was odd as he watched the sailors walk down the beach.

The movement was so smooth and subtle, it seemed like

magic. One moment there was the green twisted mass of mangrove trees, stark against the white of the shell beach, the next moment the forms of five dark men appeared. One was armed with an ancient large-caliber musket, which he held pointed to the ground but ready to raise, and two of the others had long cutlasses of some type. All the men were short and muscular, covered somewhat with ragged cloth trousers and faded sleeveless unbuttoned shirts.

Wake realized that the Indians had come out of their hiding place after Rork and his detail had walked past, within a few feet of them. Rork and his men heard a shout from a sailor aboard the *Hunt,* and turned to face the Indians. Wake could hear Rork saying something to his men and was relieved to see the sailors' muskets pointed downward as well. Now all parties ashore stood and stared at each other, with the sailors aboard the steamer leaning into their guns. Wake trusted Rork to handle things ashore, but he was worried about the steamer's guns and called out fore and aft in a calm voice.

"Steady now, men. They appear friendly. No cause for anything rash right now."

Wake wondered if there were more hidden in the mangroves. If there were, he wanted them to see the guns manned and understand the consequence of assaulting his sailors. He saw Rork move over to the Indian with the musket, the tallest and darkest of the group. Soon they were having an animated discussion. It didn't appear to be a hostile exchange. The Indians and sailors relaxed their postures a minute later, and Rork yelled across the water.

"Ahoy, the *Hunt!* These men are Seminoles. They're fishing the area and hid when we came up, worried that we're the army. Seems they're afraid of those army pogues, sir. Something about them takin' these here boyos off somewhere far away. Not too sure on that. They're not too fancied that we're navy, though I tried to tell 'em we're different from the army, an' friendly. Said they're headin' back up the river near here to their village. Not a problem over here, sir."

Wake cupped his hands and shouted back. "Very well, Rork. Ask the questions and we'll be on our way. Ask if they would like some of our provisions as a token of good will."

More animated discussion occurred, Rork using wild gestures and Wake comprehending with a smile that both men were trying to use sign language to communicate, albeit with some difficulty.

"Ahoy, Captain! They say no to the provisions, sir. They don't eat our kind of food. Say they appreciate the offer, but it would offend many of them to take it. Something of that sort."

Wake was getting impatient. This was not why they were here. "What about the schooner, Rork? Have they seen her?"

"No, sir. Not seen any ship or sailors other than us. Been here a few days, I think."

"Very well. Get their names and come aboard."

Wake was anxious to continue onward to the south. He felt sure that the *Annison* must be somewhere along the coastal islands. The schooner had been missing now for two weeks. If the crew was shipwrecked ashore they would be in dire straits and need help as soon as possible. There was no time to lose.

Rork made his report as they weighed anchor and proceeded south again. The bosun was excited, like a schoolboy telling his classmates of a visit to a strange place. No one on the steamer had ever seen an Indian, and Rork was the only one who had ever communicated with one. Officers and petty officers pressed close around as he told the story to Wake.

"Well, sir, the head man with that ol' blunderbuss of a musket, his name was something like Gabootee. He spoke for the rest. Had a little English, like 'day' and 'soldier.' They live in a village up some river called Faka-something-or-other and they said there's a white trader what lives near there. Some others live on a big island or cape far to the south, but nowhere else. Gabootee says no water soldiers, that's us, sir, have been in the area."

"Do you believe him?"

"Yes, sir, I do. They were curious and a bit nervous around

us, wonderin' if we're like the soldiers they've run into, but not scared like they had killed or robbed any shipwrecked sailors. If they had done something evil against a sailor I would've felt it from 'em, Captain. Not that they couldn't, sir. They're tough lookin' little buggers. I wouldn't want to have the little devils perturbed at me! And they can have this place if they want it."

Wake dismissed Rork, leaving him to regale his messmates with detailed descriptions of each Seminole and a verbatim narration of the conversation on the beach. Wake knew that tale would make the rounds of the taverns in Key West on their next liberty, but probably considerably enlarged as to the number of Indians and their armament. He could imagine Rork at the Anchor Inn, telling how he had met the famous Seminoles and made friends with them.

They secured from quarters and steamed south, still moving slowly and now almost a mile off the beaches of the islands, due to the shallowness of the water. They passed a dozen small islands, the gaps in between showing more islands further inland, each with an identical maze of mangrove jungle. They tried counting them as they moved down the coast, but gave up after counting over a hundred in forty minutes. Rhodes and Rork continued making their own sketch chart, with bearings on the islands and points of land and place names they made up on the spur of the moment, to the amusement of those watching.

They reached Ponce de León Bay and the Shark River several days later. Wake had been on this section of the coast before. The year before, he had found a shipwrecked vessel on the beach a couple miles south of the river mouth. It was in the summer and he remembered the incredible swarm of insects that crawled over them, entering their noses and ears and driving them mad as they worked to float the beached vessel. His skin crawled as he recalled the feeling of the tiny invisible biting sand fleas. It had been terrible, and he had only been on the beach during one morning—the shipwrecked sailors had been there for three days and were covered with oozing infected sores from the bites. He remembered the horrific look in their eyes as they told of the incessant onslaught of the insects infesting their bodies for three days, and he prayed that the men of the *Annison* had not shared that fate here.

The *Hunt* continued south, searching for days, peering end-lessly at the islands and rivers, and sending landing parties trudg-ing up and down suspicious beaches. They searched conscien-tiously, slowly. But it was all without result. At the end of their track south, Wake turned the *Hunt* around and they reversed their path, steaming north at four knots while the lookouts scanned the beaches and mangroves they had already examined. A week and a half after they left Marco Island on their trek south they returned to it again, edging up into Gullivan Bay's shallow waters to scrutinize the islands in that area again. They were about to head west from Gullivan Key, out around the Cape Romano shoals, when the foremast lookout saw a canoe darting between two islands to the south, by Panther Key. It took half an hour to come up to the island and anchor while Rork and Lawson went about their routine of going ashore on the beach on the opposite side of the island. Wake decided this time not to call the crew to quarters, but did have Durlon stand a gun crew by their piece. Wake could hear Rork ashore, calling out Gabootee's name on the chance it was him in the canoe, but he couldn't see the bosun through the thick trees.

Soon the ship's launch came surging back around the island, heading directly at the steamer at a fast pace. Rork leaped up to the deck before the boat was even secured alongside. He was grin-ning at Wake as Lawson climbed up and stood beside him.

"By the God above, Captain, you were right as a' Irish rain to come back this way! That was Gabootee the Indian over on the island. Bugger tried to hide from us, but then he saw it was me an' Lawson an' he come out from the bushes." Rork gestured at the coxswain. "Said he would trust us, sir, 'cause the black sailor man trusted us! Said all the black men he knew were slaves run-nin' away from the white man, an' if we were the kind of folks Lawson could trust, then he would too. Spoke a bit more English words than he did before. I fancy that he talks even more than he showed today, too. That Indian ain't what he appears to be at first, sir. 'Tis no ignorant savage, no sir, not by a long shot. These Indian folks are amazin' as a first day in Derry, Captain."

Lawson was smiling at Rork's narration. Wake understood the Irishman's fascination with the Indian but needed the information they evidently had gained.

"Continue, Rork. You look as if you have something important to say, so say it, man."

"Aye, aye, sir. Sorry, sir. It was just that it was more than a bit o' irony about ol' Lawson here's presence getting the little devil to talk. Anyway, Captain, the ol' boyo Indian said they saw some sailors in a small boat sailing by out there, offshore, three days ago. Said they was wearing blue jackets like us, sir. Headin' up toward the Cape an' Marco Island."

Wake considered this new information. The wind was from the southeast. That made it a fair reach up the coast to the naval vessels blockading by Sanibel. The *Case* was up that way. One day, maybe two at the outside.

"Excellent. Let's get under way and around to the western coast of Marco Island. Maybe that Roberston man saw them also. Perhaps they're with him."

The sun was dropping as they headed west. Wake made his course purposely farther to the southwest to round the shoals farther offshore in the dark. He estimated dawn would come as they approached the beaches where Robertson had his crude camp.

That night many of those men off-watch stood on deck and looked out over the sea. There was a slight breeze during the evening, bringing the heavy smells of vegetation out from shore. The stars' reflections flickered in the small waves, occasionally appearing like the cast of a lantern light. Several times men cried out that they had spotted the boat, but further investigation would show it to be well-intentioned but false.

Two hours after the dawn the lookout broke the silence. "Deck there! Smoke on the beach ahead."

The smoke was rising off the western beach of Marco Island in the area of Robertson's camp. Wake and his men had scanned the sea and land for any sight of the reported small boat with bluejacketed men, but found nothing. Wake was thinking about what to do if Robertson reported no sign of anyone, when the lookout hailed again.

"Deck there! Steamer off the starboard bow, hull down. Gray smoke."

Wake swung his telescope in that direction. Gray smoke meant navy coal. He spotted the smudge on the horizon, but couldn't tell much. Emerson asked the question Wake was thinking.

"Lookout! Direction of travel and speed?"

"Deck there! Heading southeast toward us, sir. Looks to be moving fast."

Wake knew that the schooner *Case* had examined the coast from Boca Grande down to Marco Island. Who was this ship?

"Deck there! She's a big steamer. Gun boat. I think she's the *Hudnall,* sir."

Emerson was shaking his head. "Captain, as of when we were in port the *Hudnall* was assigned from Tampa to Cedar Keys. If she was bound south to Key West from Tampa she'd be fifty miles to the west of us here."

"Deck there! She's got a bone in her teeth and moving fast."

Why would the *Hudnall* be this close to shore this far south? Wake could see her now, two miles off the beach on a southerly course at a fast speed. They would pass close aboard in a few minutes. It took eighteen minutes for them to meet and Wake to shout into the trumpet at Lieutenant Robert Cummings, the *Hudnall's* commander.

"Ahoy *Hudnall!* Captain Cummings, any news of the *Annison?*"

Cummings leaned over the rail and cupped his hands to his mouth. "No, Captain Wake. I take it you have none either."

"We've searched sixty miles of coast twice. Saw nothing, but got a report yesterday from an Indian who saw a small boat sailing by several days ago with bluejackets in it heading north. They were about fifteen miles south of here."

Cummings listened, then turned to converse with two officers next to him for a moment.

"Captain Wake, since you're here inshore, we're going to search around off the Cape, then head so'west to Key West. We were bound there from Tampa Bay and decided to come closer in and look about for the *Annison* while passing the coast. Good luck in your search, sir."

"And also to you, Captain Cummings."

The two ships parted and were soon far apart. Wake brought *Hunt* close in to the beach where the smoke was sighted earlier. He saw Robertson standing there staring at them, but making no gestures. Lawson was sent in on the launch and was seen conversing with the old man, then returned after only a few minutes. He was shaking his head as he approached Wake on the deck.

"Hasn't seen anyone or anything, sir. Cantankerous old fool. Doesn't want no part of us since he heard we won't give him passage south."

"Very well, Lawson."

Something was not right, Wake thought. It wasn't adding up. The small boat of bluejackets might be up the coast, but they would've come across the *Case*. And then the *Hudnall* would have let Wake know that. If they were on the western beach of Marco Island, Robertson would've known of them. Where did they go? Why were they not on this beach, waiting for rescue or signaling?

Wake took the steamer up the coast for ten miles, then returned south to Cape Romano, finding nothing. The sailors were frustrated and tired, but Wake had a feeling that the answers to the disappearance of the *Annison* would be found in that area, and he was determined to find them. He was explaining that very point to Ginaldi when a muffled thump was heard from out to sea. They looked at each other, then went out to the starboard deck.

"Deck there! Gun fired from the *Hudnall,* far off to the southwest. I can see her at the horizon, sir."

Wake lost no time. A single gun was probably a signal. A signal to come fast. "Mr. Ginaldi, get to your bailiwick and give me speed."

"Aye, aye, sir. Speed you'll have, Captain."

"Mr. Rhodes, set a course for the *Hudnall.*"

At full speed it took two hours to reach her, fourteen miles southwest of the point at Cape Romano, and when they got close what they could make out from the telescopes stunned them.

The *Hudnall* was using her derrick boom to lift something alongside, out of the water. It was a small schooner.

Or what was left of one.

The *Hunt* came to within fifty feet and stopped, drifting in the gentle swells. Her decks, as were the *Hudnall*'s, were solid with men in dark blue staring at the grotesque thing in the grasp of the *Hudnall*'s tackle.

Cummings shouted over the water. "It's her. Obliterated."

Wake yelled back. "Any sign of survivors?"

The answer was short and devastating. "No."

Wake anchored the *Hunt* and was soon on the *Hudnall*'s maindeck, peering over at the mangled vessel awash in the water below them, as sailors searched through the mass of splintered wood and tangled rigging. Wake had never seen anything like it. He spoke to Cummings.

"Captain, what have you found? Anything?"

Cummings lowered his voice and nodded over his shoulder toward his cabin door on the afterdeck. "Back there, Peter. Let's talk in my cabin."

Cummings didn't wait for an answer and headed aft, ducking in a doorway under the after gun on the poop.

They made their way through the dark passageway to the captain's cabin, where Cummings closed the door. When he spoke, his voice was still lowered. The theatrics puzzled Wake, but he sat down at the chart table and waited for the man to start.

"Peter, it's not so much what we found. It's what we didn't find."

"All right, go on."

"No sign of the crew or the boat they usually trailed astern. No sign of the twelve-pounder. The hull is blasted apart. Magazine obviously went—obliterated the ship. Only the forward section by the foremast is still held somewhat together. Everything else is gone."

Magazines were dangerous, Wake knew, but they could operate, and were operated, normally without a catastrophic explosion. Cummings moved closer, holding a small pile of blue uniform cloth that he picked up from the deck next to his desk. It was soaking wet and had formed a puddle.

"The one thing we did find was this. Only the bosun who found it, and the executive officer, know about it."

Cummings handed the cloth to Wake. It was an officer's shell or waist jacket, the buttons relatively new and shiny, with the lace of an ensign sewn on the sleeves. Henry Waller had a small physique. The shell jacket was a small size. Wake looked at Cummings, who pointed to the jacket.

"Examine it closely, Peter. There's more."

Wake held it up between his outstretched arms and looked it over again. He shot a glance back at Cummings, who nodded and sighed.

It was a slit. A vertical slit, an inch and a half long, with a jagged bottom. It was the same width as a standard-issue navy cutlass and was in the area of the left abdomen of the wearer of the jacket, an inch from one of the brass buttons. The cloth had a dark brownish-black stain, which had congealed, making the fabric around the slit stiffer than the rest of the jacket. Wake felt around the cloth again, not knowing what he was trying to find, but feeling that maybe somehow he would be able to get some understanding of it all.

"Unbelievable . . ."

Cummings sat down at the table and slumped forward, across from Wake. "Yes. It is."

"Robert, where did your man find this?"

"Lodged up against the scuttlebutt, forward of the deck-house."

"Odd place for the commander's jacket."

"That's exactly what I thought, Peter."

"No sign of bodies or limbs or anything?"

"None. No sign of bandages either. No sign of personal belongings. This is the only piece of personal effects we found."

Wake stood for a moment. He paced the seven feet to the bulkhead and stopped, one hand in the air. "But from what I just saw of the wreck, some of the crew's berthing deck forward must have been still visible under water, down in the hull."

Cummings's brow furrowed and his eyes met Wake's. "Yes, you're right, it was. We found part of that still held together, barely, but there was nothing in there. It was empty of everything to do with the men of the ship. No hammocks or personal articles were found."

"Was it blasted and scorched?"

"No. The fire was just aft of that. Blew the deck up and burned it aft and amidships, but not forward. The forward berthing deck was torn apart but not burned."

"Well, Robert, what do you make of it?"

"Probably the same thing you do, Peter. The last thing any captain wants to think about. Mutiny and murder."

"We'll have to tell our officers."

"Yes, and we'll have to report this to the admiral, right away."

Wake's mind jolted him at that moment with an idea. Cummings saw the change of expression.

"What are you thinking, Peter? You look like you have some notion about this."

Wake sat down at the table again and leaned forward, chin in his hand, elbow on the table.

"Well, Captain Cummings. I don't know if it's a valid notion, but I do have an idea of something we could do."

Cummings leaned back in his chair, cocking his head warily.

Wake was his friend, but had a reputation for dangerous ideas.

"I'm listening, Captain Wake."

"Well, reviewing the facts as we know them, I've come up with this. You spoke with the *Case* at Sanibel Island on the way down the coast yesterday, and they hadn't seen or heard anything from the *Annison* or a small boat of sailors, right?"

"Right."

"The weather's been fair, so if a small boat of sailors had passed by here four days ago they would've made it to the *Case,* or old man Robertson's on the beach at Marco Island, or would've seen us and signaled. Right?"

"That sounds logical. Yes."

"The only sailing vessels on this coast would be naval vessels, the occasional blockade runner, or a very occasional Cuban fisherman. Of those, only navy sailors would be wearing blue jackets. Right? Only sailors from the *Annison.*"

"Right again, Peter."

"Robertson, the old man on the beach at Marco Island, said he hadn't seen anyone come by in the last few days. Now, Robert, that old man's been looking out for months for a vessel to take him back to Key West with his crop for some time, so he'd be keeping a good lookout. He'd spot them if it was daylight, and maybe at night, if they were sailing past his camp."

"Sounds correct. What are you getting at?"

"Robert, I think they're ashore at his camp. I think they have him hostage somehow, or he would have told us."

"Well, Peter Wake. I imagine you have some scheme cooking inside that head of yours. What do you propose?"

"You are the senior of us. It's your decision and I'll obviously abide by it, but I feel strongly that we need to investigate Robertson's camp. It'll be dark in a couple of hours or so. We can use the cover of darkness to investigate it tonight."

"All right, I'm listening. Continue."

Wake paused, mentally adding details to his plan before verbalizing them. "We head the steamers off to the southwest, toward Key West, with plenty of smoke showing our departure. After sunset, we reverse course and approach the island with lights doused and the fireboxes tended well so no sparks illuminate us. About five miles offshore we each send a launch with extra crew, well armed, to pull inshore to the island. They should land on the beach somewhere around ten or eleven o'clock. The wind's from the south so we should land the boats to the north of the camp. That way the sound won't travel."

Cummings was nodding his head with each point. "I see. Then we search the camp and catch whoever is there while they're asleep."

"Precisely. They'll be lulled by seeing us in the last light heading off away from them."

"Very well, let's do it. Now, who do we send in charge of this expedition?"

Wake sat up, his hands spreading apart as his eyebrows furrowed together. "Me, of course."

Cummings pursed his mouth. "Now Peter, wait. This is an assignment for a junior officer, either your executive or mine."

"No, it's not. It might get complicated, and while both of those men are fine officers, this is a possible mutiny and deserving of a ship's captain—a man who can give the order to use deadly force against another navy man. It has to be a captain, Robert, and you're the senior and therefore can't leave the ships."

Cummings knew Wake's suggestion was the correct one, but he wasn't happy with it. "Damn it all, Peter Wake, if you don't sound like some poxied sea lawyer!"

Wake grimaced at Cummings' statement. That type of remark was usually enough to start fisticuffs. He knew he needed to explain further.

"Listen, I will follow your orders, either way. But we both know that it might come to the ultimate decision of shooting fellow sailors on that beach. It's got to be me."

Cummings sighed and stood up. "All right, I agree. You'll take command of the boats. We get under way in thirty minutes, heading southwest. At nine o'clock we will reverse to the north-east and douse lights. We in the *Hudnall* will take the lead and anchor in eight fathoms off the island, which should be far enough offshore. Once we're both anchored, you take the two ship's launches. My executive will go as your number two. I'll stay with the ships offshore tonight. But at daylight I'm bringing both ships in close to the beach and coming ashore myself. Understood on all of that?"

"Aye, aye, sir."

"I suppose it's too much to hope to find Henry Waller alive. Did you know him well?"

"Not that well, really. He's only been in the squadron for a few months from Philadelphia. James Williams thought he was a decent sort though. Definitely not the type to drive his men to . . ."

Wake paused, trying to think of another word than the one in his mind. Cummings finished the sentence.

"Mutiny."

The word still stunned Wake. Even in the small vessels he had served in, the age-old discipline of the navy had been observed. Certain lines of conduct had not been crossed, as if both officers and enlisted men knew that once lost, the self-control needed for their dangerous work could not be regained. Submission of one's very life to another man's opinion and decision was necessary. It sometimes had amazed Wake—the fact that one man, completely outnumbered, could order others into deadly situations and they would immediately go, with not a whisper of hesitation. Was it fear of discipline? Was it resignation to one's fate? Or was it commitment to ideals?

"Yes, mutiny. What an unbelievable scenario. I keep asking why, though. Why do the one deed where there is no turning back, no possibility of a second chance?"

Cummings rubbed his eyes, shaking his head.

"We don't even know that it was mutiny for sure, yet. We don't need any rumors either. Tell the men there may be deserters on that beach. They've dealt with those before and won't hesitate.

Do not use the word *mutiny* with anyone enlisted, below chief petty officer, Peter."

"Aye, aye, sir. It sticks in my craw too much to say, anyway."

"Yes, mine too. Let's hope we're somehow wrong on this, and Waller was hurt some other way."

The two boats headed for the strip of beach far ahead. Wake and Rork were in the *Hunt's* launch, with *Hudnall's* executive officer, Master Jordan, and one of his bosuns in the other launch. In the starlight they finally made out a pale line between the sea and the sky, after rowing for an hour and a half. Wake had them pulling at a slow but steady stroke, but the men were tired and he was glad to see their destination come into view at last. The big passage into the Marco River lay on their port bow, and the broadening expanse of beach spread out to the starboard. Another hour of rowing brought them into the surf line, where they quietly slid over the gunwales into the knee-deep water and pushed the boats forward until they took the ground and stopped.

Wake had briefed the men in the launches as they floated together by the steamers offshore, when first put into the water. He told them that there were possibly men on the beach who had deserted the shipwrecked *Annison,* were slacking in their naval duties, and might have robbed Robertson. He reminded them of the need for silence as they ascended the beach, and was thankful to see their nodded acknowledgments. None of the sailors looked perturbed or uneasy. They had been assigned to track down deserters before and had no sympathy for men who shirked the duty others were resigned to do.

Wake realized that none of them asked about the sole officer of the *Annison,* or what had happened to the schooner. They had all seen the destroyed hulk, but none had asked the question that was burning in Wake's mind. If they were wondering, they didn't show it or ask questions of their officer—it would've been a breach of courtesy. Another example of naval discipline, Wake thought. A merchant crew would've asked. As the group walked through the shallow water, Wake slowed his pace briefly, holding Rork behind and whispering to him his more detailed suspicions, with a final admonition to watch everyone, in all directions.

On the dry sand of the beach, the two officers gathered the twenty sailors around them and ordered a detail of four to guard the boats, while the others started to make their way up into the treeline.

Once there, they formed a column and trudged through the sand southward the mile to Robertson's camp. Wake sent Rork and two sailors out ahead to scout for any sign of trouble. Twice he had Jordan silence men and take their names for future punishment. They moved slowly in the darkness, the trees and bushes making strange shapes outlined against the sand. Overhead, the stars glittered brightly in between the branches of the buttonwood and seagrape trees. The inevitable noise produced by so many men and their equipment was partially obscured by the sound of the surf periodically crashing along the beach, and the swish of the trees' leaves and branches. Wake was glad it was at least a crisp January night and there were no insects. In August it would have been unbearable.

A tall dark form detached itself from the trees ahead, followed by two others, and walked up to Wake, who recognized his bosun's rolling gait. Rork whispered. "Robertson's camp is up ahead about a hundred yards, sir. There's a small fire that's almost out. I don't see pickets about, but I do see a boat pulled up into the bushes behind Robertson's thatch hut. It's not his. His is down on the beach. From where I stood, this one looks larger—size of a small launch or cutter. Maybe *Annison*'s."

"Anything else?"

"That's all I can tell in the dark, Captain. Might be some men in there, but I can't tell unless I get closer."

Wake felt Jordan come up beside him. Wake motioned them all to kneel down and he used his finger to draw a diagram in the sand.

"Very well. Here we are, and there the camp is. We will creep forward until we are as close as we dare. What do you think, Rork?"

"Fifty feet, sir. No closer or they'll hear us."

"All right, until we're fifty feet away. Then we'll form a line perpendicular to the shoreline. Mr. Jordan, you will take your bosun and five men and form here," Wake's finger poked the sand, "at the beach end of the line. As Rork and I advance with the other nine men through the trees, you will start to advance along the beach and cut off any escape to the boat or the water. Mr. Jordan, your captain has told you of our suspicions regarding the *Annison*'s men and their captain, correct?"

"Yes, sir."

"Yes, well, there may be some resistance. We will be in an L shape, with your people along the shoreline and ours perpendicular to it. Be sure you know where we are. If there is any gunfire, control your men and make sure of your targets before returning it."

"Aye, aye, sir. I understand."

"Very well then, any questions or suggestions?"

There were none.

"Then let's get this done. I want those men captured and lashed securely, with gags. I don't want them talking to our men."

They gathered the sailors close into a circle, where Wake explained the upcoming maneuver and then split them into two sections, nine with Wake and five with Jordan. Both sections then crouched and walked forward toward the camp, each step measured and as quiet was they could make it.

Rork held up his hand and whispered to Wake.

"We should form here, sir. Make the dash into the camp from this point."

Wake nodded to Jordan, who led his men out from the shadows into the pale gray of the beach. Wake took a deep breath and stepped forward, drawing his Colt revolver. He looked left and right and saw the sailors spread out into a line, with Jordan's men moving quickly along the beach. Wake glanced at Rork standing beside him. The bosun was leaning forward, waiting for the command.

"Forward men. Watch that flank on the port side there, Rork."

The sounds of the wind in the trees and the surf crashing on the beach was broken by the rattle and thumps of men crashing rapidly through bushes with no further attempt at silence. In a few seconds they were bursting into the clearing of Robertson's camp.

Just as Wake was about to shout out the presence of the U.S. Navy, another man did it for him—but with fear, not authority.

"Oh gawd, it's the navy! Run, you bastards! They're here!"

A dark shape darted out of the bushes onto the beach, where he was clubbed by the butt of a musket and crumpled to a heap. Two more lewd shouts came from the woods inland, with Rork leaping over and through bushes with two of his sailors toward the sound of the curses. Another man was jerked up out of a palmetto bush as he tried to crawl under it, by a sailor who laughed as he punched him in the face. Wake made his announcement, but got no reply.

Wake counted four men found so far and wondered where the others were. Besides the commander and the bosun, there had been twelve men aboard the *Annison*. And where was Robertson? Wake called out to Jordan, as the other sailors in Wake's section prodded the bushes and trees with cutlasses.

"Mr. Jordan, any more over there?"

"None yet, sir."

"Come in from the beach and search the boats, then."

Wake walked into Robertson's hut, where he couldn't see anything in the pitch black.

"Robertson, are you here? It's Captain Wake of the *Hunt.* Can you hear me?"

A sinister laugh came from the far corner of the gloom, making Wake recoil. When it spoke again, the voice was low and graveled and menacing, the very opposite of Robertson's.

"I don't think the old son of a bitch will be hearing much of anything, *Captain* Wake."

The words turned into a maniacal laughing scream, and the unseen man rushed solidly into Wake, crashing him backward through the thatch wall and out of the hut. The animal-like howl continued, inches from Wake's face, as large, iron-strong hands reached up, grasping for his throat and locking down onto his trachea. Wake was on his back now, twisting one way, then the other, but nothing could break the grip of the monster, whose putrid breath was spitting with each shriek.

Wake tried to call for help but couldn't get any air, and he felt his resistance start to weaken, his arms and hands refusing to do what he needed them to do. His head was being shaken deliberately and savagely, smashing back into the sharp shells of the beach time after time. As his head was lifted and smashed down again, he saw a long shadow swing across the stars.

A mushy thud hit Wake in the face. The screams of his attacker grew muffled and then stopped, his face and hair lying on Wake's left shoulder. The fingers crushing his throat flexed and let go. A warm liquid from beneath the assailant's hair was flowing down onto Wake's cheek and left eye as the maniac went limp and became dead weight atop Wake. He tried to move, to get away before the next attack, but he still couldn't move his hands, arms, or legs. They wouldn't respond and he was on the verge of panic.

The weight was pushed to one side and rolled off him, and another face came down close to Wake. He couldn't focus on it, but the sound of the voice was familiar.

"Captain? Can you move, sir?"

The voice moved away, speaking to someone else. "He's breathing, I saw his chest move. But he looks damn near dead."

Another voice spoke with a different sound to the words.

Wake realized it was Rork calling out, coming through bushes.

"All right Chard, that'll be enough o' that kind o' talk. He's a tough lad an' been through far worse than this. Make a hole there and let me to him."

Chard looked back down at the splayed figure of his captain. "Jus' worried I was too late, Bosun."

Wake saw Rork standing over him now, hand on Chard's shoulder. "Better late than never, boyo. Ya did good an' saved the captain's life, son. Now see there, he's moving a bit. He'll be fine as frog's hair in no time a'tall. Ya did good, Chard."

Rork knelt down and moved close, whispering as he held the back of Wake's head while another man put a shirt beneath it for a pillow.

"Captain, can you hear me?"

Wake moved his arm, willing his hand to touch Rork's. An attempt to talk came out as a gasp. His throat couldn't form a word. He could think now, and the fluid was dripping away from his eye so he could see better.

"Lay easy there, Captain. Mr. Jordan got the rest of the bastards rounded up. He'll be along shortly. Lay easy an' let your strength come back."

He lay on his back looking up at the stars, trying to bring more air into his lungs with slow deep breaths. He could feel his body start to regenerate its strength, and his fingers and arms began to move. The feeling of panic left him, and he gripped Rork's hand tighter to show him he was recovering. Jordan arrived at the circle of men standing over Wake, puffing from exertion. A moment later he knelt down next to Rork, who gave him a questioning glance. Jordan paused, then looked at Wake as he spoke.

"We got them, Captain. There were eight of them—two are dead, three are in bad shape. Three just stood there and cried like babies for mercy. They told us what happened. We have three wounded, Puglisi with a small gash on the arm, Younger has a cut leg, and you. You're the worst off, I think, but you'll be all right in a while. Are you strong enough to hear what happened, Captain? It's one horrible story."

Wake was able to move his head slightly up and down. He croaked out a sound. He had to know.

"They'd all been paid off after the capture of the big cotton schooner they captured last year by the Suwanee River. Got almost five hundred dollars each. I remember the word spreading through the squadron about the sailors of that small schooner getting all that prize money. Everyone said they were heroes and such. Got mentioned in the Gazette up north.

"Well, evidently, right after they left Key West on this cruise, they got to talking up on the foredeck and just decided that since they had all that money, they didn't need the navy anymore. Decided to take the *Annison* down to Central America, to one of them new countries that are always coming up down there. They'd live like kings with their money. They would try to get Ensign Waller and bosun to go along with them, and if they didn't want to, they'd get sent ashore in those deserted mangrove islands south of here."

Jordan stopped. After a breath he resumed his narration as Rork stood up and got the sailors to working on relashing the prisoners and searching the camp for further evidence.

"In the middle of the night, they jumped the bosun and the ensign as they slept. They didn't count on much of a fight, but the bosun fought hard. They ganged him and slit his throat. Ensign Waller never had a chance I guess to use his Colt, and he tried to reason with them, but they refused to listen. They took him up to the main deck where he told them they would all be hunted down like dogs if they killed him. They would never have a peaceful day. Then Alfonso Churchwell, Acting Gunner's Mate, that's the one that attacked you, went raving mad and ran Ensign Waller through with a cutlass.

"The one singing like a canary here, Ronald Tape, Ordinary Seaman, said that him and some of the younger ones took the ensign's jacket off and tried to bandage the wound, but he pumped out of blood fast and died right then. They got scared and dumped the body overboard and then the whole lot of the scum had a discussion as to what to do next.

"Churchwell evidently was the leader of the group. He went crazy mad again at them and told them to take all their belongings into the schooner's boat. There was an argument between Churchwell and his men, and the others who wanted to take the schooner. All of them were in on it, and all of them got their hammocks up on deck, but several of them still wanted to sail her to the Spanish countries. Tape said that Churchwell all of a sudden got agreeable and shrugged, said to take the damned thing and go. He'd go ashore here and make his way back north with a new name and new life. Churchwell wanted to live where they spoke his lingo, Tape said. That sounded better to this Tape fool so he got into the boat with Churchwell and his brethren and rowed off. The ones on the *Annison* were laughing at them as they pulled away. Then they blew up. The whole schooner just blew up and disappeared. As a gunner's mate, of course, Churchwell had access to the slow match coils. He must have lit one before he got into the boat. Had it all planned, I guess. Tape said Churchwell laughed when the *Annison* exploded. Tape is hoping to spare his life with this, Captain, and he's telling the whole story. It doesn't get any better as it goes along, though. How are you feeling now, sir?"

Wake propped himself up on his elbows and was able to get some words out. "Go ahead."

"Right sir, well, Tape says that they went in the boat to some island south of here, but didn't like it, so they figured they'd come up here and go by Robertson's camp and steal some of his food. They'd come across him a couple of months ago while patrolling the coast here. Robertson saw them in the schooner's boat and thought they were here to help him go down to Key West or something, asked where their steamer was. Churchwell said it was coming soon and asked where his food and drink was, but by then Robertson had seen through the lies. They got into an argument just as the *Hunt* hove into view. Robertson said he'd tell the navy what was happening. That set Churchwell off again and he threatened to kill Robertson if he told anyone they were there.

"When your man, Lawson, came ashore and spoke to Robertson, they were all in the bushes watching. They told Robertson to deny they had been there or that he'd seen anyone. Said they'd kill him and the *Hunt's* boat crew where they stood if he told. Well, we know that he didn't, and Lawson and his boat left.

"As soon as the *Hunt* was out of sight, Tape says that Churchwell called Robertson over, put his arm around him like an old friend, smiling and everything, and rammed the cutlass up into his gut. Was laughing like a hyena, says Tape. By that time they were all scared of Churchwell, thought they might be next if they crossed him."

The palmetto bushes rustled and a shadow appeared close by, squatting by Jordan. Suddenly Rork's deep somber voice intruded into Jordan's pause. "I've heard before—down in Key West at The Anchor—that he was a mean-spirited bastard. But this all shows him to be the devil himself. You were lucky Chard came along when he did, Captain. Churchwell was reaching for his cutlass when he had you down in the sand. An' Robertson's body was in that hut with Churchwell."

Wake felt a chill run through him as he nodded to Rork. Jordan continued on in his dry manner. "Quite true, Rork, I was coming to that part. Should I continue, sir?"

"Yes."

"Very good, sir. Well, Tape says that they were drinking up Robertson's palm wine last night. Churchwell was making them all sing songs and eat the old man's food. Said they should be gay for a night because they deserved it for all they'd done to get free. Tape said that a few of them got really drunk, Churchwell most of all. Didn't think we'd be back, even when they'd seen us stop at where the wreck of the *Annison* was, out offshore there. Saw us head off to the southwest and began to celebrate. Tape says he and a couple of them drank a few cups and pretended to be drunk, but Churchwell and his main cronies crawled into that hut with Robertson's body and howled the night away. Evidently they found some rum hidden away in there. He says he heard them talking to the dead body and laughing at some unknown jokes, that it scared him more than any Rebel minie balls and he regretted getting into that boat with Churchwell. If you can believe him, he says he'd rather he'd blown up with those that stayed aboard.

"When we came into the camp he tried to surrender straight away, but one of Churchwell's men named Mills was watching him, so he just hid in the boat up in the bushes. That's where we found him. That's all we got out of Tape. Two of the others are talking and saying the same thing about Churchwell. That's pretty much sums up the information we've got, sir."

Jordan stopped as some sailors clutched Churchwell's feet and started to drag off the bound and gagged body next to Wake. Feeling more able to breathe and speak, Wake croaked out a question. He pointed an unsteady finger toward Churchwell's head as it leaked a dark bloody trail in the pale starlit sand.

"Is he . . . alive?"

Rork put his hand on Jordan and answered. "Yes, sir. We left that un' alive. Barely, but he's a breathin' an' he's got one eye what opens. He's gonna live long enough ta' dance at the yardarm, Captain. Methinks it'll be a nice long slow dance, too."

"Good. I want . . . him . . . kept alive. For trial."

Jordan stood up. He seemed so far away to Wake. "Not to worry, sir. All prisoners are being kept separate, and they're under heavy guard with a petty officer watching at all times. They'll all swing—everyone of the worthless bastards."

"Very well . . ."

"Captain Wake, I must beg your leave, sir. Dawn is coming and I want to get things ready for re-embarking to the ships when they arrive. Rork here will take care of you."

The sun came up through the trees behind them, bringing

into sharper focus the scene of the brief nightmarish fight. Jordan had gotten the prisoners down to the water, with the boats bobbing obediently in the shallow surf water. Rork helped Wake stand and walk down to the water's edge as the *Hunt* and *Hudnall* rounded to and splashed their anchors down. For the first time since Churchwell was pulled off him, Wake saw Chard. The stocky coal heaver was sitting on the sand staring out to sea, his bare arms showing the muscles that tore away the death grip of Wake's assailant.

Wake walked over and lowered himself onto the sand next to Chard. His voice was returning, but still raspy. He held out an opened hand to the coal heaver.

"Thank you, Chard. You saved my life."

Chard smiled, taking his captain's hand.

"Nah, sir, twarn't no such glorious thing. I just did what I'd do for any shipmate. An' you'd a probably got him anyway, sooner or later."

"I don't think so. He had me. And you . . . got him."

"Well, thank you for the thank you, Captain. Ya know, I was just sittin' here thinkin', Captain. It's all strange how things turn out sometimes."

"How's that, Chard?"

"Well, sir. Before I came aboard the *Hunt* I was a thinkin' of jus' takin' French leave of the navy. Had it with the navy an' all its trappin's, sir. My enlistment was up an' nobody cared, nobody would send me home. Got a bit worked up about it, Captain. Did some bad things and got blamed for even more. Guess I was on the same course as Churchwell there."

Chard leaned his head toward the lump stretched out on the sand fifty feet away. "Didn't want to come aboard the *Hunt,* but wasn't no other choice. If I'd a stayed in Key West another day, I'd a' been in irons, sure as hell. Decided ta jus' try to stay alive on your ship till I could get home, proper-like, and get away from saltwater and blue jackets and brass buttons. . . ."

Wake let him take his time. Chard was obviously struggling with the words.

"I'm taking the oath agin, Captain. I'm re-enlistin', God help me. I been a scoundrel, jus' shy of Churchwell's type, all my enlistment. Been not much use to Uncle Sam's navy, but since I been on *Hunt* I been thinkin' things over different.

"I ain't no hero, Captain, like some's saying this morn. Don't feel like no scoundrel, like I used to, afore I came on *Hunt*, but I ain't no hero neither. Jus' did what I'd do for any shipmate. Point is, Captain, before in the navy I never felt like I had any shipmates. Nowadays I do. Got a home. No reason ta' leave no more."

Chard brought his eyes up and gazed out to sea, beyond the anchored ships. He was probably twenty-one or twenty-two years old, Wake surmised, but at that moment the coal heaver looked like an old man, with the weight of the world in his mind.

Wake put a hand on Chard's massive shoulder and pushed himself up off the sand with a groan. The sailor looked up at him, and Wake sighed a final comment before he walked away to greet Emerson who was arriving ashore.

"Chard, I understand what you're feeling better than you know. Thank you for staying with us, sailor."

Wake took a few steps and stopped, slowly rotating his body back around since his neck couldn't turn.

"And Chard . . ."

The sailor stood up and faced his commander.

"Sir?"

"Any time you save any shipmate's life, no matter who it is, you're a hero to the rest. There's nothing you can do about *that,* Chard. Those other scoundrel days of yours are long gone. Put them in the past."

7

The Taste of Evil

An oyster sky arched over them, the mackerel scales of the high clouds streaming westward with the wind as the *Hunt* made her way into the short steep seas off Deadman's Bay. It had been some time since Wake had been on this section of the Gulf coast of Florida, where it bends from vertical to horizontal on the chart. It was a shallow and featureless coast, to which he did not relish returning, but the recent events in Key West were such that a sea voyage, with clean salt air and limitless horizons, was absolutely needed for the captain and crew of the steamer *Hunt.*

Two months earlier the trial of Churchwell, Tape, and the others had gone quickly and predictably. Senior officers, some brought in from other squadrons, formed the court and were presided over by Commodore Silas Jericho Gunn, a bewhiskered ancient brought to Key West from Washington specifically for this purpose, who was as grim as his name would suggest. Called from retirement, Gunn's function in the war was to travel and preside over the most serious and politically threatening trials of naval discipline.

His stooped frame disguised a keen mind and sharp tongue,

which had inflicted itself upon several of the squadron's staff officers who foolishly underestimated the old man. Gunn outranked everyone except the admirals, and few of them would challenge the decisions of a man with his backing. Within an hour of his arrival in Key West, he had determined that the charge would not be mutiny, which was too attention-getting and flammable. Instead, the prisoners were all charged with murder, a crime that was more common and had less effect upon the ears of the public and the fleet. It was a gross bow to political perceptions and offended many of the officers and petty officers, but the orders had come down from on high and they had no say. The punishment and the outcome, of course, would be the same as if it were mutiny. Death was the common denominator of any serious naval crime.

Testimony was heard and pieces of evidence examined, while the accused sat glum and disinterested. They already knew what the result would be and simply wondered why the charade was pursued. But the rituals were observed, with stentorian rhetoric by some of the officers, and all involved in the proceeding performed their roles in the manner prescribed by naval regulations. The officers detailed to present the defense had the most difficult parts to play. Madness caused by war was their excuse, and mercy their request.

Wake, his voice restored by rest but his neck still aching, testified his about involvement. A charge of attempted murder had been added to Churchwell's list of crimes to cover the attack on the beach. The court leaned forward and listened intently as he described nearly dying at the hands of Alfonso Churchwell. While he was showing his seniors with his own hands how Churchwell had been crushing his throat, Wake caught a glimpse of Churchwell looking at him, a slight smile lifting the corner of his mouth, as if fondly reminiscing the moment. It was the only emotion Wake saw him show.

In two days the trial was completed and the expected decision rendered. It was approved by the admiral commanding the squadron thirty minutes later. The findings and sentences of the court were immediately sent to and approved by Secretary of the Navy Gideon Welles, a former newspaper man, who only wanted it done and forgotten before any sensationalism appeared in print.

Tape had testified against the others, showing the only remorse of the proceedings. He portrayed himself as a victim of Churchwell and therefore was the only man spared the "traitor's dance" at the yardarm. Instead, he got life at hard labor at Portsmouth Naval Prison, which to Wake's thinking was worse than the five minutes of torture on the end of a rope with the fleet watching. The executions were not carried out in the usual manner for a murderer, who would have been hanged or shot in a prison yard. The death sentences for these men were carried out as if they *had* been convicted of mutiny. Gunn had seen to that, for he was from the old navy.

Churchwell had gone to it dull witted and uncaring—the head wound he received from Chard's crashing a musket butt into his skull ensuring that he didn't understand or even wonder about the confusing official ceremonies that began the end of his life. When he was stood up in the boat bobbing alongside the U.S.S. *Dale,* ordnance ship for the squadron and appropriately square rigged, the monster of Marco Island more closely resembled a confused child who had to be led through the ceremony of having the noose tightened around his black-hooded head.

Above them, on main deck of the *Dale,* the bosun's whistle called to the twenty men lined up, each holding a section of the hangman's rope in their hands, and they trotted forward over the fifty feet of open space, swiftly running the line through the blocks on the yardarm and lifting Churchwell effortlessly up and out of the boat below. He soared skyward until two blocked hard beneath the main yard's outer starboard end. Wake had never seen a naval hanging, and he thought the ascent appeared almost like some sort of legerdemain. But then magic ended and the faceless torso, arms bound behind, started its wiggling, kicking jig. Eventually the grotesque gestures diminished to a gentle slow sway, synchronized in motion with the ship. The thing hung there all day, and by the next morning was gone. But each day after breakfast another of them ascended the sky, with all hands in every vessel present ordered to watch. And not all of the prisoners were as silent and cooperative as Churchwell.

Wake felt no pity for them, nor remorse for his part in their death. He just thought it was quicker to use a bullet and didn't think it useful to waste time each day seeing any more men swing. The United States Navy had its traditions, however. He knew they existed for a reason, but he wondered if it really would have a deterrent effect upon the truly demented determined to follow in their footsteps. When the orders came for him to head up the coast and see about some pro-Union refugees that were in an area of which he had some prior knowledge, he hadn't hesitated. He needed to see and do something else, something useful.

The war was grinding on but no one thought it would last much longer. Wake had read in the newspapers that Lee was in retreat in Virginia, Sherman was roaming at will through the Carolinas, and Confederate Florida was plunged into chaos. "The End is Near!" had proclaimed the *Philadelphia Herald-Star* to Wake as he ate breakfast at the Russell Hotel with some other officers just before departing Key West. Sitting there reading the banner headline and the accompanying article, he wondered if the correspondent was really on the front lines. It was late March and the campaign season was about to start with the change in climate, as it always had. After years of seeing banner headlines touting imminent victory, and then reading of Confederate victories or stalemates, Wake disbelieved any bombastic headline. The Rebels were tough, and had so many times in so many places made a resurgence, that he didn't believe the papers anymore. Lee would no doubt somehow fight on, dodging a Federal deathblow and frustrating the army generals for another summer.

Florida was a case in point. On the face of it, she was finished. U.S. Naval vessels controlled most of the coastline, and

Union Army troops had made incursions and occupied bases of operations at several places. Blockade running had ceased entirely and the economy of the Rebels was predicated upon a primitive barter system. Money meant nothing. Bands of renegade deserters were ranging up and down the interior of the peninsula, ignoring the dire threats of the governor and the state and county officials, and robbing at will. Florida was a mere shadow of what it had been four years earlier.

And yet, with all of that, they hadn't surrendered. In fact, they had fought tenaciously each time the Federal army had tried to invade en masse. Just a month earlier, at Fort Myers on the Caloosahatchee River, a battalion of Rebel cavalry had even attacked a fortified force of black and New York regiments three times their number. Wake knew in his bowels the war was very far from over and wondered what it would take to get the other side to lay down its arms. Tallahassee was still Confederate, and the enemy forces in the state were grimly hanging on, powered by sheer stubborn determination alone. As much as he despaired of further mindless fighting, Wake grudgingly respected them for their tenacity.

While in Key West he had also received a letter with the large rounded feminine script he knew so well and always read time and time again for weeks while out at sea.

March 2ⁿᵈ, 1865

My darling Peter,

All is well here, what with the weather being so beautiful and the fishing going so well lately. But the real morale stimulator is the war news that it may all soon be over. The women here talk dreamily about their husbands returning to them and going back to their homes on the mainland.

They go on in romantic ways about resuming their lives in their former homes, but I don't know if that will be the outcome, Peter. I don't think anyplace will be the same, and when they go back to their towns I don't think the people will welcome them back. They'll prob-

ably hate them for leaving, and for being on the winning side. I saw so much hate in Key West—too much to end just because the fighting's over.

It seems as if almost all of them are planning on leaving this island and returning to wherever they came from. They're tired and miss the civilized parts of life, and I can't blame them. They just want to go home.

Darling, what will we do when the war ends? Key West has too many bad memories and hostile people for me. Maybe there is somewhere else we can call home.

Sofira and little Rain say hello.

Must end now! More later in another letter for I must send this off with the steamer now.

Your loving wife,
Linda

They were passing off the mouth of the Timucuahatchee River, above Deadman's Bay and away from most of the settled parts of Florida. Wake had fought there the year before, and wondered just what he would find now after another year of war. He was sent because his was the only vessel available, but with the added factor of his knowing the waters and people better than some other officers in the squadron. His mission was to make contact with the pro-Union people and ascertain where the U.S. Army could land and march upon the state's capital at Tallahassee. The Union leadership in Key West and Washington feared an indecisive end to hostilities that would transform into a guerilla war. It was decided after the army's defeat at Natural Bridge that perhaps another route to the capital could be found. Wake was to use his knowledge of the place and the people to find it.

They anchored in two fathoms beyond the rocky reef, three miles offshore and five miles north of the Timucuahatchee. The normal March winds were absent, and the *Hunt* lay on her hook in calm water. Wake felt that he needed to go ashore himself, due to his knowledge of the area and the people, but Emerson had been persistent in his requests to lead the party. He was correct, for normally the executive officer would have been the one to go. Finally, however, Wake decided to go himself and explained the reasons to Emerson, who acknowledged them in the neutral mien of a man who disagrees but will obey. Wake wondered if he thought his captain was vain, but the necessity of getting the mission under way soon replaced any lingering doubts.

Wake took Rork for the same reasons. Only ten sailors came with them, since this was to be quick and not very far inland. The pull to shore was a long one against the tide, and Lawson had the boat's crew take up a slow steady rhythm. By the time they pulled the launch and the gig up on the beach under a six-foot-high shell bluff three and a half hours later, they were exhausted. Lawson and Rork stood guard while the sailors fell to the sand and rested for an hour. Wake walked the beach but saw no sign of anyone. This was the location he was directed to by his orders. Refugees had reported that loyal Unionist Floridians came to this bluff frequently to watch for naval vessels and seek transport to one of the settlements established for them, like Useppa Island three days steaming to the south. As he paced, Wake pondered whether the swirl of events in the state had influenced the situation in the area, and decided not to wait for the people to come to him. He would seek them out and find out the status of the people of the coast and determine if there was a viable way of getting a major expedition ashore and into the heart of the peninsula to Tallahassee.

Greeleyville was a small hamlet four miles inland from the bluff. There was no road to Greeleyville from the beach, only a meandering footpath. After a night spent upon the beach, Wake left Lawson and four men at the boats and led Rork and six sailors up the path and into the dense hardwood forest. With the elevation, there was no marsh or swamp. Wake was grateful, for he remembered well the swamps south of there where he and his men had fought off the Confederate regulars the year before. This path was well used, apparently recently, which made him uneasy, and he repeatedly reminded the sailors to be silent and vigilant.

Two hours later they arrived at the sand road which Wake's handmade diagram, furnished by a refugee in Key West, depicted as running northwest and parallel to the coast. It was named Carmen Plantation Road on the diagram and ran through Greeleyville a mile north of where they now stood. Carmen Plantation, marked at the edge of the paper, was ten miles further distant to the north. Road was a rather grandiose description, it was really more of a cart trail, Wake thought as he remembered the proper roads of New England.

They walked close to the edge of the underbrush, ready to hide if an enemy patrol was sighted. Pine and palmetto spread out on either side of them in a tranquil setting that belied the fact they were on an enemy coast, far from the protection of their ship. A bend in the road ahead revealed some clapboard and thatch dwellings and a field, cleared but not planted, with a few emaciated cattle slouching here and there. Greeleyville was barely a hamlet, typical of the settlements in the area. No one could be seen outside the dwellings but voices could be heard within— women's voices, then a man's, deeper and slower. Wake motioned everyone behind some palmettos, where he had a conference with Rork and directed him to take one man and scout the hamlet.

Rork came trotting back alone ten minutes later, a puzzled look on his face as he knelt next to Wake and made his report.

"Man an' two women in the far house over there, Captain. Having a hell of a row."

"Over what?"

"That's the queer part, sir. Sounds like they're arguing over slaves. Something about killing them or selling them. Something about Havana. Couldn't catch it all."

"Who is saying what?"

"Older woman is askin' something about why. Younger one is cryin' an' sayin' a name, maybe o' a slave. Man is telling her it's necessary or whatever. That's all I know for certain, sir."

The sailor left to observe the house now came running back and slid to a stop by the bosun, who gave him a severe look of disapproval for his lack of decorum.

"Sir!" he whispered in a hoarse tone, "They's gone now. Lady folks left in a buggy rig, yellin' about Moses and the Israelites, or some Bible thing like that. And then the man got under way on a black horse. Looked like he could kill with his eyes when he left. Ladies was bound up the road and moving fast. Man was bound down southerly on the road, moving faster."

Wake couldn't understand it, but knew it might be significant. "Rork, take two men and search that house, and those other buildings. Let me know what you find."

Rork acknowledged the order and set off with two sailors, one guarding and the other searching. It was awhile before he returned.

"Nothing much, but I did find this letter, sir. Appearin' like it may be meanin' somethin' with the words I heard. Looks like the lady might've dropped it in that cabin house."

Wake read the note. It was short, a paragraph of scratched ink, slanted so far over as to look almost like a foreign alphabet. It took him a moment to make it out.

To my wife Cynda Williams,
Carmen Plantation
Harney County, Florida
You know the war is over and everything is done for. Even Nassau is drying up. The only thing left is the blacks at the house. Havana will take them. Not for much, but it'll be at least something. S. Basic will do it, then come here. Use the money in the lock box— it should last a while. You're welcome to come to Exuma if you wish, but you will have to adjust to my way of life here. Let Basic know your decision. You'll ride with him.
Your husband,
Cadworth W. Williams
Georgetown, Great Exuma Island
Bahamas, West Indies

Wake considered the letter, and the conversation. He had heard of Carmen Plantation, but not been there. It was a large plantation that primarily grew cotton and sugar cane. He didn't know the man Williams or anything else about the plantation.

He was intrigued by the letter. It bothered him—more by what it did not say than by what it said. He suddenly realized it was a business letter. Apparently written to a wife separated from him by the war and hundreds of miles, it contained none of the expected endearments and only spoke of financial arrangements. Very odd indeed, Wake thought.

"I'm going to see that hamlet myself. We'll move into Greeleyville and spend the night there. I want four men on guard at all times. You and I will stand watch also."

Wake was in the dwelling only thirty minutes when the lookout called out that horses were approaching fast from up the road. The sound became clearer the closer it got, and soon they could make out a single horse landau bouncing along under the control of a woman wearing a black skirt, jacket, and brimmed hat. Wake moved the sailors out of the hamlet and behind the bushes on the side of the clearing. The roan was lathered as he abruptly stopped in front of the dwelling Wake had just evacuated. Throwing the reins around the brake, the woman leaped down and was inside the cabin in three strides.

"Stay here men. Rork, come with me and stand at the front door."

Wake walked in quietly behind her as she started to move the crude chairs and look under the plank table in the middle of the room. She was a diminutive woman, but her clothing displayed the femininity of her figure with stunning effect. Her blonde hair was done up, with several strands escaping from the confines of the hat. She didn't hear him enter.

"Looking for this?"

She turned around and faced him, not with surprised fright, but with ferocity on her face. His quick examination registered that she looked to be in her middle or late twenties—his age. Her glaring eyes took in the letter he held in his hand.

"A thief? I should have known someone like you would take a lady's letter. You Yankees are well known for that type of behavior."

She walked toward him, and he thought she might slap him from the look in her pale blue eyes. They showed no warmth, no feminine charm. Emanating from those eyes was only cold calculating hostility. He raised his hand holding the letter in a plaintive gesture. She stopped five feet from him as he spoke.

"I am afraid ma'am, that you have me at a disadvantage, for I do not know who you are. Allow me to introduce myself. I am Lieutenant Peter Wake, captain of the U.S.S. *Hunt,* United States Navy."

He waited, but she made no reply. "And *your* name would be what, ma'am?"

Several seconds passed before she finally spoke, during which time her face softened. Her voice came out in a tone more cordial than before. "I am Cynda Denaud Williams, of Carmen Plantation. You have my letter, Lieutenant, or should I say Captain?"

Her eyes had tangibly darkened their hue, and the change in tone and facial expression completely altered her appearance. Cynda Denaud Williams was a beautiful woman, and for a moment Wake couldn't think of what he should say.

"You may call me either, Miss Williams."

She held up a glittering left ring finger, and as she did so moved closer to Wake, looking him in the eye—almost drawing him into her.

"It's Mrs. Williams. Now, Lieutenant, kindly hand the letter back to me."

"Of course Mrs. Williams." He brought back his hand with the letter as she reached for it. "Just one courtesy from you, if you would be so kind?"

She was in front of him now, her perfume faintly evident, her eyes locked into his. Her voice maintained its silky smooth flow, the Southern-accented words weighted with meaning.

"Now it is you who have me at a disadvantage, Lieutenant Wake. Do you often place a woman at a disadvantage? What must I do to gain the return of my letter?"

He couldn't take his eyes off her. Heat was surging through his limbs and he had to concentrate to keep his hand from shaking as it held the letter in front of her. He didn't want to use her married name, it felt somehow wrong.

"No, I do not take advantage of women, and I find it hard to imagine that you have ever been anything other than in the position of advantage with everyone, Cynda Denaud Williams. I just want you to explain what he meant in the letter."

She was touching the letter, and his fingers.

"You're the naval officer that got the loyal Union people out of here last year, aren't you?"

"Yes."

"And the one that fought the regular soldier regiment the state had resting down here earlier this year?"

Wake became aware she was holding the letter and both his hands. He tried to pull them back, but they wouldn't respond.

"Yes. What did he mean in the letter?"

"Just what he said. That's what he always means. He has no sense of humor, or anything else for that matter . . ."

Wake heard Rork cough behind him. "Rork, make the rounds of the men, make sure they're vigilant."

The reply contained a speculative tone. "Aye, aye, sir. *Vigilant* . . . Back in a moment, Captain."

"I believe your man didn't want to leave you here with me. Is he worried about my safety?"

Wake almost grunted with the effort to make his hands return to his side. The letter was in hers. "Probably mine."

"You have quite the reputation, Lieutenant Wake. A lot of men in Florida would like to see you dead."

"And they may well get to have that pleasure, but for now I want to know about that letter and what exactly it means, and about the argument you had with that man here earlier."

Williams gasped and the color left her eyes. Wake thought it amazing and more than a little chilling. This woman was dangerous.

"So, in addition to being a thief you are an eavesdropper, a common voyeur!"

Her ploy did not ring true to Wake. He was losing his patience with her game. "No, not a common voyeur, just a wartime one doing a thing known as surveillance. I think it's time to leave the niceties aside now, Cynda Denaud Williams. Time for you to either be a cooperative citizen, or an enemy. I would much rather think of you as a willing citizen helping your navy."

She waited, then turned away, looking out the single opening to the dwelling, the doorway. "Cadworth left when the war started. Went to Nassau. He said he would make some money and be back, but never came. He set up a little house with a black girl in the islands, some trollop who likes his money, playing tropical king and making money off the misery here with blockade runners. The overseer became the top dog around here and ran the plantation for him. More like a cur, to be precise. He's a Yankee too, from New Jersey. He terrorized the hands and alienated the neighbors, but he kept the production up so Cadworth liked him, even though I loathe the heartless tyrant. We did reasonably well until sixty-three when the state took forty of our blacks for labor up St. Marks way. We haven't seen them since. Right about then the bottom fell out of the market. We have twenty-eight workers left, but there's nothing to work except a few vegetables. The main fields are all fallow and there's nobody with any money to buy anything we grow anyway.

"Cadworth's ordered Stephen Basic, that's the overseer, to gather up our people, the blacks living at Carmen Plantation, and take them to Havana to be sold. That was Basic I argued with today. He gave me the letter from Cadworth and told me to make up my mind right then and there, said they were already aboard a Spanish slave schooner and leaving right away from the Suwannee tonight."

Williams paused and looked at the rough wood floor. When she resumed, her tone became pleading, and to Wake's ears sounded sincere, though he couldn't be sure.

"Those people have been living here for two generations. There are children and grandparents among them. They've trusted me and need me, and we never had any trouble with any of them until Basic showed up and began to run things for Cadworth."

"When was that?"

"Basic came down to Carmen Plantation in sixty-one. Three years after I married Cadworth. It seems Cadworth met him on one of his business trips to Charleston and took to him straight away. I always wondered why. I asked one time and got a nasty answer—the man gets things done. Just like that, nothing more.

"When Cadworth left, Basic took over everything. He ignored me and what I wanted. He said I didn't count anymore and should be happy just to be able to live there. He especially hates the blacks. He cares absolutely nothing about providing the most necessary things for them. He just uses them until they drop, like he uses everybody. He's a bully who uses his strength and will to cower everyone, white or black.

"It all makes me so sick—the whole war and slavery, and Stephen Basic and Cadworth Williams, just all makes me sick to my stomach. There, now you know my miserable story, Lieutenant Peter Wake of Abe Lincoln's high and mighty navy."

She slumped into a chair, drained of energy and emotion. Wake saw that she was crying.

"Why do you have them as slaves if you care about them so much?"

"Because I can't free them. They're owned by Cadworth, not me. Basic doesn't listen to me. He didn't tonight. He only listens to Cadworth, but with everything ending here I wonder how long that will last."

"Why did you come back here tonight?"

"My little sister and I drove off from Basic very angry, then

I thought of the letter and returned from Carmen to get it. I thought it might be better to have with me. It might prove helpful one day. My sister Mary Alice is at Carmen Plantation now."

"Why meet him here at this place? Why not at the plantation?"

"I was curious why he wanted to meet here. Now I know it was because he was closer to the schooner here. He knew what he was doing when he left a note for me to meet him here. Some of our former white workers live here. We can't pay them anymore, so those that aren't off fighting moved away to get other jobs if they can. Basic wanted to be close by that filthy slaver so he could leave. When I returned to Carmen, the blacks were already gone, all of them. The silver plate and guns and tools are gone too. It was all planned out."

Wake was thinking of the various possibilities of actions to take when he heard Rork's boots clomp on the planking as he entered.

"Men are in position and vigilant, sir."

Wake looked over at the bosun and glanced sharply to the doorway. Rork gazed at him without indicating acknowledgment and walked outside. Wake sat down at the table opposite Williams.

"So now he is at the Suwannee River and leaving for Cuba to sell the slaves and the valuables, and then pocket the money? Theoretically he'll sail to Exuma and give the proceeds to Cadworth Williams there?"

Her reply emerged as a quivering murmur.

"Evidently that's the plan, but Cadworth'd be a fool to trust that shady scum with his money. I can't bear to even think of our people being sold in some filthy barbaric market in Havana. Captain Wake, I presume I really should call you Captain since you have your own ship, I just don't know what to do to save them."

Wake ignored her obvious flattery. What he needed was more information for the plan that was beginning to form in his mind. He must know the civil and military situation in this area, and he needed to know it immediately. There was no time to lose.

"What kind of relationship did Basic have with the authorities here?"

"They loathed him too. But they put up with him because of Carmen Plantation and Cadworth's influence."

"And your relationship with the authorities?"

"They know I hate the war. They know that I think slavery is morally wrong and productively stupid. But they've put up with me too, because of Carmen Plantation and Cadworth. Now I suppose even that will be gone."

"Do you know any Union people here that would come to the aid of Federal forces if they landed?"

Williams regarded him carefully, her tone petulant when she replied.

"You want to use me for your military purposes? This conversation is all about that?"

"Your problems are secondary to the war effort, Mrs. Williams. Until I'm shown otherwise, I will regard you as an enemy civilian. Now, do you know of any loyal Union people here who would help us?"

She paused for a moment, annoyed at being dictated to, but then she grudgingly answered the question.

"Yes, there are several. They'd help, especially nowadays. The end is near for the Confederacy, even if some of those fools don't know it."

"I'll need their names and addresses. Now."

"And what do I and my sister Mary Alice get out of this? She's only seventeen, and I'm all the family she has now. Our parents died of the typhoid at Gainesville two years ago. Your Yankee blockade stopped the medicine and nobody could help them." Williams looked down at her hands, then away. Wake sensed that it was no act, that she was reliving some scene of despair in her mind.

"Mary Alice has lived with me since then and she's all I have.

Cadworth's demonstrated his disloyalty, of course, so Mary Alice and I are alone now. If I help you, can you help us get away from here? This place is dead to me now."

"I'll get you and the other Union people passage to a pro-Union settlement, but I need to move fast on other matters first. I need further intelligence of the enemy."

She stood and leaned over the table, looking at him with those eyes. "And those poor people on that slaver. What will you do to rescue them?"

"We'll go after them directly. I need that other information now."

Her voice took on a sharpness, an edge that contrasted with the vulnerability in her eyes. "Captain Wake, you'll go after the slaver right now, or she won't get caught. Free those people and I will do everything in my power to rally the people of this coast to your flag. My family, the Denauds, were prominently known and respected here and in Gainesville. Daddy was a banker and commissioner. If I speak on your behalf, they'll believe in your cause. But I'll do that only if you go after that slaver right now, Captain Wake. Right here and now to save those black people. There's no time to dawdle, Captain."

"Tell me the disposition of the regular and militia forces in this area, the names and political leanings of the local government leaders, and names and addresses of any loyal Union people. The faster we get that done, the sooner I can leave to intercept the schooner. The future of those slaves is not my primary problem right now, Mrs. Williams."

Her stare never left him as she touched his hand. The tone of her words was low, almost husky. "Take Mary Alice and me with you tonight and I'll write out all the information you need and swear to it. While I am writing it out, send your man out there to Carmen Plantation in my buggy and bring her back here. By the time she's here, my essay on the situation in this area will be completed. Captain Wake . . . I'll trust you if you trust me."

Wake knew she had bested him. And he knew that she knew

it. It had to be done.

"Mrs. Williams, it seems for a second time tonight you have me at a disadvantage."

Her other hand came to join the first in touching his. He couldn't get his own to obey the command to back away. He also couldn't look away from her eyes as she smiled at him.

"How very kind of you to acknowledge that, Captain. And please be even more kind and don't use my last name again, it makes me think of horrid things. Call me Cynda, please."

"Mrs. Williams, now I must—"

"Cynda, Captain Wake. My name is Cynda."

"Yes, well, uh, hmm . . . I suppose that I could call you Cynda. I'll send for your sister now."

"Thank you, Captain. May I call you by your first name?"

Rork scuffled into the room, making Wake wonder if it was by some sort of telepathy.

"Sir, did you want me for anything else? I'm about to check on the lads."

Wake withdrew his hands from her clasp abruptly, standing up and nearly knocking over the chair in the process.

"Yes, Rork, I do want you for something. Take a good man and use the buggy outside to go to Carmen Plantation. Get Mrs. Williams' sister Mary Alice, who is there now. Tell her to pack some things for herself and her sister Cynda and bring her back here as soon as possible."

"And my explanation to the young lady, sir?"

"We are taking them both to freedom tonight, and time is of the essence. I want this done quickly, Rork."

"Aye, aye, sir." Wake could feel the thinly veiled suspicion in the reply.

As Rork had left the room, Wake heard a scratching sound and turned to find Cynda Williams sitting at the table, dipping a quill pen and writing on the blank frontispiece of a moldy book she had taken from the shelf on the wall. Looking closer he saw it was a Bible. She saw him staring and laughed. It was a dainty, fragile laugh that didn't match her tone of a moment earlier.

"Appropriate, isn't it, Peter? Using a Bible to help you to save those wretched people on the way to their doom."

He ignored her use of his first name, but then he realized that he liked the way she said it.

"Let's hope that I can do more than just save *those* people. I have other matters to deal with too."

Cynda Denaud Williams looked up again at the naval officer standing tensely before her, arms folded in front. It made him very uncomfortable when he saw that she was smiling.

"Of course, whatever you say. You're the captain."

The sun was lightening the eastern sky when the lookout called down from the foremast head.

"Deck there! Shape on the horizon two points off the starboard bow. Distant maybe five miles or less."

Wake glanced at Ginaldi, who was making one of his rare visits to the wheelhouse.

"Well, Mr. Ginaldi, in this wind she'll be making a good speed. How is the boiler? Can it make a sprint?"

"A short sprint, Captain. Remember, it's been needing a decent cleaning and overhaul now for three months, sir. Full speed for ten, maybe fifteen minutes, is what I'd recommend, sir."

Emerson shook his head. "Ten or fifteen minutes! Hell, you were bragging about the damned thing in the wardroom just yesterday."

Ginaldi shrugged. "Just because it needs a little care doesn't mean it's not doing its job, sir. And it's been doing that pretty well in storm and calm for us for a lot of months."

Wake was mildly amused at the banter, but then returned his attention to the geometric problem of an intercept and the time needed for full speed.

"Deck there! She's a schooner. Full an' by on a broad reach. Bound southerly, setting more sail now. Heelin' over an' makin' speed."

Emerson was focusing the telescope as Ginaldi opined. "I bet she *is* setting more sail now. She'll get every rag and trouser up on that mast if she's a slaver. Doin' six, maybe seven, I'd wager."

Emerson yelled aloft the question in Wake's head before he could ask it himself—the sign of a good executive officer.

"Lookout! Do you recognize her?"

"Deck there! No, sir. Don't know her. By the cut an' color of the sails, I'd say she's a Dago, sir. Cuban most likely."

Wake thought about it. It was probably the slaver. The vessel traffic out of the Suwannee River had been drastically cut since the blockade increased its grip on the coast. At this position, and on that course, she was obviously outward bound from the river. Since she wasn't navy, she must be enemy. There were no authorized merchant vessels in this area.

When he had brought the women aboard earlier in the evening, Wake had briefed his officers and petty officers about the slaver. Their reaction was the expected one. Naval sailors hated slavers and slave ships. The U.S. Navy had been intercepting and capturing them around the world, most particularly off Africa, for over twenty years now, since the '40s, and Wake knew that the men would double their efforts for a chance to free the trapped victims aboard a slave ship. They absolutely hated the men who sailed the ships that carried the "black gold" cargo. The hostility was almost visceral when they spoke of it.

Most of the men on the *Hunt* had joined since the war started and thus had never seen slaves or a slave ship. Wake had never seen any himself until his mission to Havana two years earlier, when he saw the liveried black servants of the Spanish crown's governor serve dishes and drinks at a formal ball. Those slaves, elegantly costumed in heavily gilded, ancient-looking European uniforms, had acted like mute toy soldiers, silently gliding in among the elite to attend to a request. Wake wondered at the time what those people were really like, what they really felt. The rumors in Key West were that the slaves in Cuba were treated much worse than those in the American south.

He was about to issue the order to beat to quarters when a voice interrupted his intention.

"That's her? That's the boat with our people on it? Catch them, Captain, please hurry!"

Cynda and Mary Alice stood in the starboard wheelhouse doorway, the color of their matching red cotton day dresses a contrast to the brown and blue of the men's clothing. They both looked first at Wake, then strained to see the distant vessel. Wake was not amused by their presence.

"Mr. Ginaldi, on your way to the engine room to bring her up to full speed for twelve minutes, kindly escort Mrs. Williams and Miss Denaud below to the engineering petty officers' quarters. That's sufficiently protected by the coal bunkers in the event of enemy fire, I believe?"

"Aye, yes sir, it is," Ginaldi replied, then wheeled around with a gallant turn and half-bow toward the women. "Come along now, ladies, the captain has a ship to command, and he absolutely needs to have his full concentration. Can't afford to be distracted by beauty at a time like this."

The two females obliged Ginaldi with a small giggle for his compliment and departed aft with him, leaving Wake wondering how much of the engineering officer's remark was innocent jest and how much was satirical jab.

"Beat to quarters, if you would please, Mr. Emerson."

In a few moments, Wake could feel the invigorating difference as the *Hunt* surged forward with the engine changing from a constant strumming to a loud rhythmic pounding, the sound overpowering all others. Along her decks, men ran to the two twelve-pounder guns and readied other positions and equipment.

Danger and power were strong narcotics to some, Wake decided, and he was not immune to the feeling himself. He leaned out the starboard door and watched Lawson and his boat crew preparing the ship's launch, while above him Rork ascended the ladder to the wheelhouse top. Wake felt a welling of pride for his crew. In his years in the merchant marine he had never felt anything like it. In the confusion of the ship going to quarters, Wake heard Durlon's raspy voice call up to Rork, then saw Rork climb down and stride over to the gunner at the forward gun. The bosun then quickly met with the executive officer, and Emerson came up to Wake.

"Gunner's Mate Durlon requests permission to speak to you about the slaver, sir. He was on the Anti-Slavery Patrol off Africa evidently and wants to tell you something about them."

"Very well, have him come here."

When he arrived, Durlon smiled uneasily, then set his jaw. "Sir, I know about them slave ship bastards. They's an evil lot, Captain. They know what we think o' them, and they'll do anything not to be caught. *Anything,* Captain. I know that most aboard the *Hunt* here never's met up with one o' them types before, and I just wanted to pass along that we shouldn't treat it like a normal blockade runner, sir. These black birders will shoot us, kill the slaves, do any damned thing they can to keep from going to the jail. They're not human, sir. They don't think like us. When ya get aboard of that hell ship you'll understand, Captain, and you'll never forget in all your days what ya see and smell."

It grew quiet in the wheelhouse, only the helmsman moving as he turned the wheel to match the waves. Wake noticed the look in Durlon's eyes. They showed a mixture of anger and tragedy. The veteran gunner was obviously quite deeply affected by his memories.

"Thank you, Durlon, for your good advice, which we'll act on. You may return to your station now.

"Mr. Emerson, call away a well-armed boarding party. If she doesn't stop peacefully for our boat to go over to her, then we'll come alongside with the steamer and board her by force."

Emerson nodded, his voice a little louder than usual. "Aye, aye, sir, and *I'll* command the boarding party."

Wake smiled and nodded back. He would've said the same thing in Emerson's place. "Of course, Mr. Emerson. It is your privilege as the executive officer to command a boarding party. You may take whom you wish as your assistant."

"Rhodes, sir. And Lawson with his crew, supported by a half dozen other sailors."

Ensign Rhodes beamed at the prospect of participating in some action and as soon as Wake gave his approval, dashed out to the starboard deck to supervise the preparations. The steamer was moving at nine knots now and closing steadily on the schooner, spray bursting from the *Hunt's* bows as she plowed through the waves. The sun had risen enough to make the horizon clear all around and the details of the schooner easily visible.

Wake watched her as they approached. There were men standing at the stern, looking at their pursuer, pointing at her and conversing. She was a large schooner for the Suwannee River, perhaps eighty feet, drawing five or six feet at the most in order to get in the river. Even then, the captain must have timed the tides carefully, Wake surmised, as he studied her rig and sails. They were old and faded and in disrepair, but she was sailing to the best of her ability, which was fast in these conditions. Her captain was by all appearances no fool, and Wake remembered the look in Durlon's eyes.

"'Twill be an interestin' thing to bring her alongside that 'un in these seas, Captain."

Wake turned to see Rork taking advantage of his right as bosun to go anywhere while at general quarters by coming in the wheelhouse and standing with his captain. They hadn't talked about the prior evening when Rork had seen Cynda Williams with Wake in what some might consider an inappropriate gesture. Wake was perturbed about it but had had no time to talk with Rork. There was no time now either. They would talk later.

"Yes Rork, you're right. With the wind and seas from the east and her heading south, we'll have to come on her weather side. We'll have to come alongside and grapnel her fast—get our men across before the slavers can resist. Durlon may be right on this, Rork. We'll have to be fast and overwhelming."

"I'll take care o' the grapnel irons my ownself, sir. I'll have Curtis and Jones do the stern, I'll do the bow. We'll hold her for the lads, sir. By the by, Captain, I hear I'm not goin'."

"No. Lawson'll be the petty officer."

Rork grinned. "Splendid decision sir. Serves the bastards right to get caught by a black sailor man!"

Wake realized that he had not even thought of the fact that Lawson was black. He had only thought of Lawson's strength and judgment.

"Well, Rork, that wasn't part of the criteria, but it will certainly be part of the satisfaction, won't it?"

Rork laughed at that and Wake felt the tension building within him ease. He loved to hear that full Irish laugh.

"Captain, the look on their slaver faces when they're seeing our lad Lawson with a cutlass an' pistol chargin' toward 'em, 'twill be givin' me more than jus' mere satisfaction. It'll be better than a pint o' the old stuff by the fire at the pub on a misty day in County Wexford. Why, back in Eire I'd almost pay good money to see that show, an' here I'll get it all for free!"

Rork went forward and got the multi-pronged grapnel iron ready, looping several large easy coils in his left hand and standing there waiting, swaying with the motion of the heaving foredeck. Wake had Durlon fire a warning gun when they got to within a hundred yards. The men on the stern of the schooner ignored it. They weren't looking aft anymore, just staring forward as if refusing to acknowledge that a warship was bearing down them. A white and gold flag emerged from behind the mainsail, blowing off to leeward from the topmast. It was the flag of Spain, but that would provide no protection. Any ship carrying slaves was fair game for the United States Navy, especially on this coast.

Wake leaned out the wheelhouse window.

"Mr. Emerson, ready your party on the starboard deck. I want this done quickly."

Emerson got his fifteen men ranged along the side deck, each armed with a cutlass and a pistol. Rhodes and Lawson had the forward half of the group, while Emerson had the after half. They would leap over and secure both ends of the slaver simultaneously. Durlon already had both ship's guns trained to starboard in readiness to fire.

The *Hunt* was closing rapidly. Very rapidly. Wake was gauging the closure rate, knowing that there would be no second chance to overwhelm the slaver crew and free the blacks before they were killed to prevent their testimony. He had to do it right the first time.

A wave lifted them as they approached the schooner's port quarter. Wake saw that the slaver had no name on her stern and her crew wore no uniform—in fact they wore little clothing at all. There were more of them than the normal complement for a schooner of that size, a dozen in plain sight, another sign she was carrying the most horrific cargo known to man, for all slavers lived in fear of their cargo rising up in revolt and killing them.

Wake could see two large hatches, fore and aft on the main deck. They were closed and battened down with lumber. The crew was milling around on the deck, some forward, coiling lines by a pile of crated oranges, and some amidships fiddling with some cotton bales on deck—all of them steadily ignoring the steamer that was now a mere thirty feet from their hull.

"Reduce revolutions to ahead full," Wake said to the seaman to his left, who then rang the engine bell on the annunciator twice. Wake moved forward to the man at the wheel.

"Steady your helm on her port bow, standby by for the crunch when we hit."

"Steady the helm on her port bow and standby for the crunch when we hit, aye, sir," the helmsman echoed. "The helm is steady on her port bow, sir."

Wake then called out to the men on the starboard deck. "Grapnels over and haul!"

Three iron grapnels arced through the air, their rope tails

undulating as the coils unfolded. As they hooked on the schooner, details of sailors put their weight on the lines and man-handled the ships closer as the bow of the *Hunt* crashed alongside the port side of the schooner at her foremast shrouds. The jolt of the crash caused men on both ships to stagger and fall. Then Wake swung his attention to the men on the schooner's deck. Many of the seamen were raising their hands in the air in gestures of submission and staring at the steamer and her crew. Wake saw several men at the stern calmly watching the navy bluejackets as they raised their arms. They looked oddly different from the usual crew about to be boarded. In his experience in boarding blockade runners, Wake usually saw crews looking fearful or dis-gusted or angry. This one didn't. Durlon's words came to mind.

He leaned out and called to Emerson. "Away the boarding party!"

Before the order was finished Emerson was standing on the gunwale and leaping over the heaving four-foot space between the two moving ships. A wave surged up and reached for him, making the vessels crash together, then push apart, but he was already on the schooner's deck and heading for the men on her stern. Rhodes was jumping over to the men on the slaver's fore-deck, with Lawson beside him.

As Wake watched it all unfold he sensed instinctively that something was not right. The slaver crew was backing up along the deck, hands high in the air and apparently submitting, but it didn't make sense. He couldn't define it, but Wake knew some-thing was ominously wrong.

Wake saw Rork climbing up on the starboard fore gunwale, preparing to leap over to the other ship and pointing to one of the men on the schooner's foredeck. The man appeared different from the others, wearing a gentleman's brown shirt and black trousers, taller and stouter and calmer than the men around him. Wake wondered if that was Basic, then saw the man look from the steamer looming next to him, to a figure at the stern of the schooner. The man forward nodded, then looked directly up at

Wake and leered. A chill instantly rushed through Wake and he knew the man was Basic, the slave overseer from Carmen Plantation.

Suddenly it all registered in his mind and he understood what was about to happen. The slavers were calmly backing away to the bow and the stern, away from the bluejackets, who were now between the two groups. The sailors were in some sort of trap.

Wake looked aft along the schooner's deck and pointed at the man he thought might be the schooner's master, as he yelled out to his executive officer. "Mr. Emerson! Seize that man now, before they can—"

His words were cut off by two sharp bangs coming from four-pounder swivel guns on the schooner, one concealed by the orange crates forward and the other by the cotton bales aft. Their buckshot charges, intended to devastate any slave revolt coming up out of the hatches, swept across the schooner's main deck like a farmer's scythe through wheat. Blue-jacketed sailors crumpled and fell into lumps on the deck.

The flash and smoke of the swivel guns stunned everyone on both ships for a fraction of a second, and in a tableau Wake would never forget, he caught sight of Rhodes' head exploding into a heavy red mist, his torso still falling forward in a crouch toward the muzzle of the slavers' gun and collapsing in spasms at their feet. Basic was still holding the gun's firing lanyard, laughing hideously as he fired a pistol and shouted to the other slavers to fire their pistols. Two *Hunt* sailors standing next to Rhodes at the moment of the blast were also down, splayed unnaturally on the deck and not moving. Others, led by a bleeding and screaming Lawson, were holding their wounds but attacking the slavers on the bow while some of them were frantically trying to reload the gun.

At the same instant he saw Rhodes being destroyed, Wake realized the after-boarding party was also hit badly by the swivel gun at the cotton bales. Several navy men were down, but the scene was further confused by an immediate huge flaming blast from the afterdeck of the *Hunt* as the twelve-pounder there roared out, and the canister load plowed into the schooner, annihilating every one of the slaver's crew standing there. The main mast and sail were also shredded by the shrapnel, making the schooner's rig lean crazily off to the leeward.

The remaining sailors on *Hunt*'s main and gun decks, led by Rork and Curtis, swarmed over onto the schooner, hacking and shooting at any slaver still moving. The slave ship's crew forward fired a few pistol shots before being subdued, but it was over quickly. Wake's last image of the fight for the schooner's foredeck was of Lawson, standing with his massive legs wide apart, blood splashing out from his mouth as he screamed an oath, both ebony arms outstretched and swinging his cutlass in a fast wide arc. It sliced into the neck of a wide-eyed Stephen Basic, who stood holding a pistol a foot away from Lawson's stomach as his head was severed and launched overboard in a spray of blood. Lawson staggered from the effort of the blow, then fell down on the deck next to the twitching body of the slave overseer that was still pumping blood out of the cleaved mess that had been his neck.

And then, abruptly, there was silence, except for the pounding engine and the rush of water. The *Hunt* dragged the schooner forward, the grapnel lines straining to hold them together.

Wake was still stunned but knew he had to get her stopped. He shouted into the wheelhouse. "Stop engine! Maintain your course, helmsman."

He made his way down to the main deck and across to the schooner, where Rork was kneeling by Emerson, who was clutching his abdomen and gasping, his hands opening and closing spasmodically as he rolled on the deck in pain. Wake grabbed Rork by the arm.

"Are you wounded?"

Rork looked away from the executive officer. "No sir, but Mr. Emerson took some in the gut. Mr. Rhodes is dead, sir."

"I know. Rork, get the slavers that're still alive secured and under guard. I want them kept alive. Do it now. Understand?

And send Mr. Ginaldi and Durlon over here. Tell them to bring my medical chest."

Wake knelt down and held Emerson by the shoulders.

"It's all right, Stephen. You've got the hero's wound, friend. You'll be out of the navy and telling sea stories soon. . . ."

Emerson looked at him but couldn't talk with the pain. He managed a grimace and a nod, as he gritted his teeth and made a sound between a growl and a groan.

Wake leaned close to Emerson's ear. "We're going to get you some laudanum, son, and then you won't feel that pain. Then we'll get that wound bound up and you to the surgeon at Egmont. You need to stay strong, Stephen."

The pool of blood was appallingly large on the deck around Emerson. Wake knew it meant the wound was fatal. Ginaldi arrived carrying the medical chest.

"Mr. Ginaldi. Give him two doses of laudanum, then get that wound bound up fast. Stay here with him. I'll see to the others."

Durlon was tending to two wounded sailors aft. Wake could feel his eyes on him as he passed by walking up to where several bleeding bluejackets sat on the foredeck.

"Durlon, get laudanum from my medical chest for their pain, then bind their wounds. Any venal bleeding?"

"No sir, it's oozin' and not pumpin.'"

Lawson was bleeding from his face and arms as he helped Rork lash the three slavers, wounded but still alive. All the others were dead. Wake touched the coxswain on his shoulder, moving his hands over gashes on the man's muscular arms and shoulders, examining the wounds, then checking a cut across his face.

"Lawson, are you wounded anywhere else?"

"No sir. I'm not hurt bad, Captain. They're hurt worse." He tilted his head toward two men sitting up against the foremast.

"All right, Lawson. See Durlon and get dressings on those wounds. Then take two men and see about the slaves below. Bring them up and have Mr. Ginaldi treat any that're hurt. I want your wounds dressed right now, Lawson."

"Aye, aye, sir."

Rork and Curtis came up and reported the prisoners lashed and secured.

"Very well, Rork. Curtis here will be the prize master. He'll take the schooner with the prisoners, the ladies, the wounded, and the slaves, to Egmont Key and meet with the senior officer there. Lawson will assist him. Give him a dozen men."

"I can take her in, Captain."

"No Rork, you're now the acting executive officer of the *Hunt*. I need you with me. We're going back to the mainland and completing the mission."

"Aye, aye, sir."

Rork turned to his bosun's mate. "You heard the captain, Curtis. Gather your gear and get your men told off to their duties. Pick good ones you can trust. Make your course south-easterly, then follow the coast southerly till ya reach the naval vessels at Egmont Key off Tampa Bay. They'll give you help and direction there."

Curtis acknowledged the order and made his way over to the steamer, now rolling in the seas next to the schooner, whose sails were making a thunderous protest as they luffed into the wind. Wake noticed Rork looking at him oddly, then realized there was a strange sound rising above the noise of the sails and sea and engine. It was coming from below them.

Lawson was smashing the lumber battens from the forehatch top with a belaying pin, finally prying one up with a brute strength Wake found amazing in a wounded man. The sound was getting louder. It was a groan, or a wail, a sound unlike anything Wake had ever heard. Rork sniffed the air.

"Jesus, Mary, an' Joseph. I can smell 'em now too, sir. I heard tell o' that smell. The stories were right."

The smell was from the ship itself. The wood of the deck smelled. It was everywhere, like sewage and rotting death. Durlon appeared beside Wake and Rork.

"Mr. Ginaldi's got Mr. Emerson and the others knocked out on the laudanum, sir, and the wounds bound as good as we could. Three dead—Mr. Rhodes, Johnston, and Moorer. An' Mr. Emerson is mortal wounded, sir. I'm sorry, but I can't do anything for him more than give him laudanum. No one can."

"I know that, Durlon. Just keep him knocked out so he doesn't suffer any more. Who all are wounded?"

"We've got five with bad wounds, Surrey, Giles, Updike, Shoap, an' Wanicka, but they'll live if kept clean. Another three have some cuts, sir. Sewell, McInerny, an' Ring."

A splintering crunch raised the hatchtop next to them and an ominous sound and smell welled up out of the hold. Lawson stood at the hatch, looking down at the mass of bodies.

"Oh Lord in Heaven . . . Captain, I'll need help with these people."

"Durlon, get some men and help Lawson get those people up out of there."

The odor made the air heavy, and like a fog you could almost touch it. Durlon was shaking his head and swearing every oath he knew as he pushed sailors down into the hold to help the slaves emerge. It smelled as if the hold had never been cleaned out, as if a lifetime of misery and torture was emerging from the hole in the deck. Sailors were coughing and gasping as they reached down to pull the blacks up onto the deck and into the sunshine.

The slaves staggered around on the swaying deck, freed from the chains and exercising their legs for the first time in twenty-four hours. In that time they had not had food or drink, or the ability to handle their personal hygiene needs. According to what Cynda Williams had told Wake the previous evening as they arrived at the steamer, the blacks of Carmen Plantation had never been on a ship, or even far away from their homes on land. The women among them were crying and the men visibly angry. The restraint of that anger showed in the flexing of powerful arms as they closed and opened their fists while looking down at the deck, not daring to look into the eyes of the white men around them.

Lawson explained to them that they were now free like him. Looking at the blood and gore scattered everywhere, their faces showed that they slowly realized that they were the object of the fighting a few minutes earlier, which they had heard on the deck above them but hadn't understood. When Lawson further explained that sailors had died, *white* sailors, to free them, many started to pray and wail. They listened to Lawson intently, as he told them what he needed them to do to help the bluejackets.

Slowly, as they began to understand that they were no longer slaves, stunned smiles appeared. Several came up to Wake, knowing immediately who was in charge, and thanked him for making them free. After he shook their hands they retreated to the security of their group, speaking rapidly in the patois of their language to the others, conveying more about freedom than Lawson ever could in his Massachusetts-accented English, for though he was obviously of African descent like them, he was as foreign as the whites in his demeanor and speech.

Wake felt drained and overwhelmed. He had to get things back under control. This was all taking too much time, and had taken far too much blood. There was blood everywhere. Ginaldi came up to him.

"Sir, I've had the remains of our men brought back aboard the *Hunt*. They're sewing them up in their hammocks now. I thought we'd do the service as soon as we could, Captain."

"Yes, you're right, Mr. Ginaldi. Rork will be the acting executive officer. You know that engineers are not authorized for that."

"Yes, sir. No problem with me on that. He can have it."

"And we'll need to transfer some of the men in your division to the deck, to fill in some of the vacancies. I want Chard to be one of those."

"Aye, aye, sir. I'll pick them right now."

When Ginaldi left, Wake found himself alone. Everyone was accomplishing some task, getting the people treated and the vessels repaired. He thought of the service he would have to conduct, and suddenly he felt exhausted, drained of emotion and strength.

A wail from behind made him jump and he turned around to find out what his next problem would be. It was Mary Alice Denaud, standing on the deck of the *Hunt* and looking at the human carnage spread out over the schooner. Cynda Williams grabbed her younger sister's hand and dragged her along the deck. Before Wake understood what they were doing, the two women had leaped over onto the schooner and were coming toward him.

"Captain, I'll start helping with those wounded, and Mary Alice will help with our people."

"Now Mrs. Williams . . ." The look on her face stopped the rest of his thought and he relented. "Yes, well . . . thank you, ma'am."

"We women have a sense of duty just as well as you men, Peter. And stop calling me by that damned last name. I hate it. Call me Cynda."

He let out a breath, taking a moment to think about her. He wouldn't call her Cynda. That would start something he dared not even contemplate. She faced aft and was looking around, searching for something or someone.

"Is that horrible bastard Basic dead? If he's alive I want to see him. I want to spit in his face."

Wake considered telling her that Basic's face didn't exist anymore, but he didn't have the strength to explain it. "No, he's dead . . ."

"Thank God above for that."

Wake nodded in agreement, then started to the railing. His body felt as if it had a hundred pounds of weight attached as he wearily made his way back to the steamer.

The wind and seas had lain down a bit and the *Hunt* was no longer smashing into the schooner as they lay lashed together. Wake stood looking at the sky and realized he would have to tow the schooner to windward, closer to the coast, so she could make good time on a broad reach to the mouth of Tampa Bay, the closest location of a naval vessel with a surgeon aboard.

An hour later the confusion abated enough for all hands to assemble for the funeral services. The three hammocks, sewn up around their owners with twelve-pounder shot at their feet, were placed on boards on the port afterdeck. Every man of the *Hunt,* except those guarding the prisoners and tending the engine room, stood on the main and after gun decks, hat in hand, as Wake read the service for the dead. Ginaldi and Rork stood next to him, and he was glad for the strength of their proximity.

The slaves, now properly considered freedmen, gathered on the side deck, behind the sailors. They knew the funeral was for men who had died to free them, and their emotion was visible as they tried to maintain their silence through the age-old ceremony. Some of them were looking at Lawson, bandaged and leaning to one side, but standing proudly in the ranks, a symbol of true equality. Wake could see the wonderment in their eyes and hoped they could summon the courage to handle their newfound freedom. Standing with them were Mary Alice and Cynda, both with tears streaming down, holding each other up to stand.

It should be deeper, Wake thought as he gave the command to let them go. Twenty feet of depth wasn't dignified for a sailor's body to be let down into, but that was where they were, and it would have to do. It was just another part of the unfairness. The war was winding down, and as the three bodies splashed into the Gulf of Mexico, he wondered if any more of his men would die before the idiocy ended.

"Ensign Terrell Rhodes, Seaman Michael Johnston, and Seaman Bernard Moorer died today fighting an evil which has plagued the world for centuries. They were victorious in that fight, and twenty-eight people were freed because of it. Those people will marry and raise families, and their children will marry and raise families, and those children will have children, until hundreds of people will live free because of our shipmates' sacrifice.

"In all of this sad war, there is no nobler cause, no more important fight, no more long-lasting victory. And while we here on the *Hunt* must continue to do our duty and hope we fulfill it well, they are already victorious, and have assumed their places in Heaven.

"Terrell, and Michael, and Bernard are no longer troubled . . ."

Later, in his quarters, Wake put down his pen. He had to take a break from the letters. The one to Rhodes' parents was the worst. How does one say what happened, he pondered. As he wrote, it felt false trying to comfort good decent people who had no idea of the horrors their son had seen and endured. He kept seeing Rhodes' head being atomized into gore and tried to think of positive things to say in the letter. And he knew that by tomorrow at the latest there would be another funeral, this time for Stephen Emerson. And another letter to write.

The letters to the families of Johnston and Moorer were completed, the one to Rhodes' on its fourth draft. It had been three hours since the schooner had departed and the *Hunt,* now quiet except for the hum of the engine, as if the ship herself was in mourning for her boys, had reversed course for the coast not far from Carmen Plantation. Wake still had work to do ashore there, contacting the loyal Union people and ascertaining if an expedition to Tallahassee would be feasible from that location.

He had started writing the families but was now hopelessly depressed. He needed to get some sleep also, for with the losses of manpower he was going on watch in an hour. Desperately tired, he rose from the chart table with the notion of seeking out some food when Dirkus entered his cabin with a tray, putting it down on the chart table.

"I thought you might need some fuel for your body, sir. You've had a long day and go on watch soon."

"Thank you, Dirkus. One more time you've read my mind. I certainly am tired, and do need some food."

Wake sat back down and looked at the meal as Dirkus silently padded out of the cabin. It was salt pork and peas. He stared at the food, but the scene of the swivel guns' destruction of his crew filled his mind. Wake raised a fork full of the solidified pork to his mouth, willing himself to block out the mental sights and concentrate on getting some nourishment, but then the stench of the schooner's hold inexplicably filled his nostrils.

Durlon was right. It was something he would never forget—the bilious taste of absolutely chilling, inhuman, evil. . . .

8

Last Man to Die

April was a swirl of experiences for the East Gulf Blockading Squadron generally, and for Peter Wake personally. The squadron's sailors at Key West reacted to the news of Robert E. Lee's surrender in Virginia with unrestrained pandemonium. Naval gun salutes, homemade fireworks, ceremonial dinners, musical concerts, and carousing in the streets were but some of the manifestations of the joy felt by the bluejackets that the war was finally over, and they could all go home. Everywhere in Key West soldiers and sailors in blue drank and sang and yelled on the Saturday night officially proclaimed to be the day of celebration. Many of the islanders joined them, some true Unionists, others pragmatic businesspeople who knew the smell of easy money in the air.

One part of the population did not rejoice, however. Those were the people, numbering a quarter of the islanders, who had sons, brothers, or fathers, in the Confederate service. No mail had been received in Key West from the early enlistees in the Florida regiments since the summer of 1861. For four agonizing years the families on the island did not know if their loved ones, far away in Virginia and Tennessee and Georgia, were alive or dead.

During that time, each triumphant headline in the pro-Union island newspaper proclaiming Northern victory and thousands of Confederate dead in particular battles had meant a resurgence of anguish for those Key Westers with family fighting in the states to the north. The toll was sadly high among those waiting, with illness and death coming for many who couldn't cope with the gnawing fear of the unknown. When the large Confederate armies finally surrendered, a slight hope rose in the hearts of the families that their man might be among those who survived and he would soon be headed back to the island. On either side of the political question, emotions were running high in Key West by the end of April, and smiles were seen more often than any time since April of 1861.

Wake felt these same emotions regarding the war and his part in it. An empty sadness and guilt filled him over the deaths of Emerson and Rhodes and the seamen. Questions swam through his mind about whether he could have done the boarding differently, or should have done it at all—given the nearing end of the war. Was freeing twenty-eight Negro slaves worth the lives of those good men? Would the families of the men killed understand and agree that their deaths were worth it?

Prior to the boarding, Wake had believed that the rumors that Lee would surrender were false, that he had not been beaten down enough. After all the years of false hopes and proclamations, he thought the speculation of February and March was just more of the same that he had heard bandied about for so long with no result. But with the confirmed capitulation of the famed Robert Edward Lee, the man who led an army with nine lives, the hoped-for had finally happened. Still, it was hard to realize that it was over, that the fighting was done, that no else would have to receive a piece of hot metal flying through the air to slash into his flesh and stop him, leaving him maimed or dead.

After stopping at Useppa Island again on the way, Wake had returned with the *Hunt* to the Deadman's Bay coast and met some of the pro-Union people of the area to ascertain their numbers and abilities. He was not impressed by what he saw. A meeting at Carmen Plantation netted a total of thirty-one persons, most of whom were women whose men were off fighting for one side or the other. They told him stories of renegade bands of deserters and of state conscriptors roving across the land, stealing or confiscating—the result was the same—livestock and property from the women who were desperately trying to hold on to their family's land and possessions. The people at the meeting demanded not the ouster of the Rebel authorities, but merely protection from everyone who was stealing what they owned.

The laments of the women showed Wake that their motives were self-serving, not out of loyalty to the Federal government centered a thousand miles away to the north. He came away from the meeting convinced that the area was not conducive or receptive to a Federal expedition, and that the situation was far too fluid in political terms to risk a substantial force that could become mired in a guerilla war in the swamps of upper Florida.

He returned from his reconnaissance mission of the coast to Key West in early April to find several things out of the ordinary. Curtis and Lawson had made port with the slave ship, which was undergoing Admiralty survey for adjudication. Although she was in sound condition and seaworthy, no naval officer wanted her because of the awful stench. The newly freed black people were living in the old slave barracoons on the far side of the town, doing labor for the army and navy, and receiving food and some supplies in return. Lawson had been spending much time with them, explaining how to handle their new lives and the manner in which they should conduct themselves in a legally equal society. Lawson became their de facto leader, a position he did not relish, for absent the common color of their skin, he shared no other bond, being born and having lived free all his life. But he knew that everyone, white and black, expected him to do it, and he patiently tried to explain the intangibles—attitude and responsibilities—of freedom to his charges.

Two other events affected Wake's life, both having to do with beautiful women.

He encountered Cynda Denaud Williams at the Russell Hotel dining room, in an appropriately unusual way, while he was finishing an evening meal there with Lieutenant Wyatt Walker of the steamer *Bonsall.* The two officers had been discussing the drawdown of the fleet, with many of the vessels of the squadron being sent north for long overdue repairs or decommissioning out of the navy. It was the subject of all of the conversations among naval officers in April, volunteers like Walker for the most part wondering when they could be released from their obligations to the navy, and the regulars like Wake wondering if there would be any place for them in the drastically reduced fleet. His regular commission, one of only a handful from among the original volunteer commissions, was junior to almost every other lieutenant, and he was worried about retaining command of his ship. Walker had no such concerns, waiting and eager to go home to New York.

She came up behind him, her sultry voice alerting him at the last moment before her cool soft fingers gently squeezed his shoulder, caressing their way up his neck to the scar by his right ear, making him twitch when she touched it.

"Why, my Lord! The man who saved my life. Captain Peter Wake himself."

She stood there in a simple pink cotton dress, filling it admirably and looking femininely dangerous while presenting her most delicious smile as she rested one hand on his shoulder and leaned over, placing the other in his hand, which rose automatically to take it. The effect, which he was sure she had calculated, was of her almost embracing him and was so obvious that he could see Walker almost wince in reaction.

"I merely provided you transport, Mrs. Williams. That is all. That hardly justifies such a magnificent comment. How is young Miss Mary Alice?"

Williams was not fazed by the gentle rebuff and turned her

attention to Walker, who sat there grinning at the scene.

"Now Captain Wake, or should I say Peter—considering *all* we've been through—your Yankee manners are becoming deficient. Are you going to introduce me to this gallant young naval officer sitting with you?"

It was all Wake could do not to shake his head in disbelief. Cynda Williams was a woman with no outward fear or timidity. She will need that trait in the post-war chaos to come, he thought.

"Certainly, Mrs. Williams. Allow me to introduce Lieutenant Wyatt Walker of the United States Steamship *Bonsall*. Lieutenant Walker is her gunnery officer and a friend of mine. We were just ending a relaxing dinner."

"A friend of Peter's? Well, I presume, Lieutenant Walker, that being a naval officer and friend, you have long been well aware of my hero's stalwartness, but I, of course, was not. Let me say that Peter Wake showed me true bravery," she batted her eyes at Wake as she slowed down the sentence with her Southern drawl, "and I am here today because of it."

It was getting to be too much. Wake couldn't stand it.

"I did no such thing, Mrs. Williams, and you know it. Wyatt, she was aboard when we boarded that slaver and lost Emerson and Rhodes and two seamen."

Walker nodded seriously, understanding the connotation, but when he replied to Williams his face lost its frown.

"Well, ma'am, it *is* true that my friend Peter here has quite the reputation in the fleet. If you think that was a dangerous situation, I could reveal to you further some of his other exploits that would absolutely make you cringe with fright to hear!"

Wake stood up, interrupting any further banter. "Excuse me, you two. I am done with my meal and regretfully have some other duties to attend to right now. Mrs. Williams, Lieutenant Walker and I would be honored if you would take my seat. And again, how is young Miss Mary Alice?"

Williams glided smoothly down into Wake's chair as she

answered. "She is busy all day long with our black people. Clothing and teaching them, helping your colored sailor man getting them ready in every way for their place in society, whatever that might be. She views it as some sort of holy mission."

Wake sensed the lack of enthusiasm in her tone. Her previous solicitations on behalf of her former slaves had been fervent, but this description of her sister's endeavors was almost mocking. He started to wonder how Cynda Williams had the money to be at the Russell Hotel, Key West's most exclusive place. As he replied he also noticed she had subtly moved her hand across the table and closer to Walker's.

"Well, please tell Miss Mary Alice I admire her sense of duty to those people, and I am sure they appreciate her devotion to them. I must take my leave of both of you now, for my own duty calls. Thank you for buying my dinner, Wyatt. Reciprocity in the future, of course, my friend."

Walker's jaw dropped a bit with Wake's surprise thank-you for an unoffered dinner. The Russell Hotel dining room was not the place where naval officers, without other independent income or means, could routinely buy dinners for others—it was far too expensive. Wake smiled at his friend, who he could see was mentally adding up the bill for two persons already, with a third probably coming.

"Yes, well . . . ah . . . you're welcome, Peter. Sorry you have to go just as a lovely lady can join us."

As he walked away, Wake turned around to see Williams holding one of Walker's hands, captivating his attention with those china blue eyes of hers while she ordered something from the waiter. Wyatt's evening will not be dull, or cheap, ruminated Wake with a slow shake of his head, stepping out onto the busy street and heading to the officers' landing to catch the shore boat to the *Hunt*. In reality, he had no urgent duties awaiting him, other than getting away from her. Her beauty was a weapon, and she wielded it far more effectively than most of the soldiers he knew ever managed a sword or cutlass. He breathed a sigh of relief to be free from her presence as he entered the naval station gates. For some reason he couldn't fathom, he felt vulnerable around that woman, and he didn't like to feel vulnerable about anything. He would apologize later to his friend for leaving him with her—and pay him for his dinner—but Wake had had to leave when he did to maintain his composure.

His arrival aboard came an hour after the mail was delivered. Rork knocked and entered his cabin holding an envelope, which he handed to Wake.

"Evenin' sir. A wee bitty envelope from the paradise o' Useppa for you. I hope it's fair tidin's from your lovely lady, Captain.

"All's well aboard the ol' *Hunt* while ye've been ashore. No foul word from the liberty party, an' no news is good news on that horizon, I'd say."

"Thank you, Rork. Sit down and rest a bit whilst I read what Linda writes. She's worried about you, you know. She always asks how you're doing. She also wants to know about that one girl from the Anchor Inn you used to see."

"About me? That dear sainted lady mustn't worry a drop about me. I'm as fine as a bishop in his best on a Sunday in Derry. An' as for a young lady from the blessed Anchor Inn, well I'd have to inquire which one she'd be referrin' to, sir. There were two or three, if ya remember."

Wake laughed as he remembered the night in the Anchor Inn on the far side of Key West by the Bahamian quarter when he and Rork had decided that a wedding should be held—that very night. Rork's lady companion that night had helped with the hurried preparations. He opened the envelope carefully, as he always did to preserve it, and began to study the contents of the short letter within. There was only one paragraph, which was odd since she usually wrote several pages' worth, filling the paper completely with the comings and goings of the island community, but even though brief it was the most momentous letter he had ever received. He was so stunned he almost dropped it, but regained his composure enough to hand it over to his friend Rork, who was watching with concern. Rork read it aloud, reinforcing the import of the message.

May 5th, 1865
Dearest Peter,
The boat is leaving now for the steamer, and I don't have much time, so will make this brief note to tell you of the news. With all the stories and confusion coming from the war lately, I've waited to tell you something. I wanted to be sure before I did, and now I am. Oh darling, we are going to be parents. A precious little baby will be arriving sometime in December, I think. I can feel it already, and am sure that it is a boy. Sofira and Rain and all the islanders are as excited as I am, and they all send their best wishes to you. I love you and miss you and can't wait for you to be here with me and our little child. You will make a wonderful father. More details with the next boat's mail . . .
With all my love,
Linda

Rork held the letter in silence and looked at Wake. A smile spread and he slapped his hand down on the chart table. "Well, by the Lord above and all around, this is the most wonderful news I've heard in years. After all of this war and the grief you and the lady have endured, a little baby will be born to the two most deservin' people on the earth. Why, this is nothin' short of a sign, a holy sign, my friend. It deserves a true recognition in the finest fashion!"

Wake smiled too at the sight of Rork's lopsided grin and spirited proclamation.

"Well now, Rork, perhaps we could do that, but another time. I'm tired and—"

"Nonsense, my dear Captain Wake! Why this calls for a drink at the finest establishment that can be had, here in Key-for-saken-West! The Russell Hotel, by God sir! Right now . . . we'll go there right now an' hoist the finest nectar they have in honor of the littlest Wake bound o'er the horizon."

Rork's enthusiasm had Wake laughing until he said Russell Hotel. The words conjured up Cynda Williams, which brought to mind that night ashore when Rork had walked in on them at that table in the cabin. Rork stopped his comments when he saw the changed look on his friend's face. Wake sighed and tapped the table with his finger. "Rork, ah . . . there's something I need to say. Something I need to explain . . ."

Rork was taken aback by the sudden change in demeanor for no apparent reason. He leaned forward, intently listening. "Very well then, what seems to be the matter?"

"It's about that night ashore, when you came up to the cabin and saw Cynda Williams and I there at that table . . ."

Rork nodded slowly, "Aye, I remember that night, an' comin' into the cabin there where you were."

"Right, well, it probably appeared to be an improper situation, but that was not my intent nor action."

Rork's mouth lifted in a wistful smile. "I never thought it was, Peter Wake. I fathomed right off what she was about, an' I know for a fact what you are about, an' n'er would I think you'd succumb to that. Not the man I know. That she tried, of course, I have no doubt of. But you've got a thing she doesn't have, nor won't in her life. You got a love an' trust that's as solid as I've seen, an' more than a match for what that Williams woman can offer."

"Well, I know it probably looked odd."

"Aye, it looked like what it was. She's tryin' to use what she's got to get her way. Now we've both seen that a hundred times, haven't we?"

"Yes, we've seen that." Wake was feeling better and regained his smile. "I just ran into her again at the Russell this evening and it reminded me of that night when you walked in. Thought I'd better get that cleared away. Glad I did."

"Aye, 'tis not a thing to be worried about. Now I me'self might succumb to her charms, but then she'd not waste time on a lowly petty officer. No indeed, my friend, she's eyein' more valuable targets, that she most certainly is. Why, the admiral him ownself will probably be under her sway by the week's end. He won't have a heretic's chance in heaven, the poor sod, if she gets five minutes with him."

The thought of the wily Williams weaving her magic on the old admiral was a comical image, but Wake thought that Rork was probably right. She *was* hard to resist. "Rork, my friend, thank you. Maybe we can haul down a few next time ashore, once at the Russell Hotel and once at the Anchor Inn. How's that sound?"

Rork knew that most officers would never drink with an enlisted man, even a senior petty officer, but then Peter Wake was not like most officers. Rork nodded his appreciation of the offer.

"An offer made an' accepted, by God! Next time ashore together, a celebration for the sainted Mrs. W, and the newest addition to your clan."

Later that night when Wake climbed into his berth, he thought of Linda and the coming baby. It was dangerous for a woman to have a baby, especially in the tropics of Florida, and he was torn between joy and worry. At least she was with friends, and according to Linda on other occasions, Sofira had some sort of native knowledge of herbs and forest medicines that could help in such situations. Though there was no medical doctor on Useppa Island, Wake thought that perhaps Sofira might be even more beneficial. From what he had seen, and personally endured, he didn't have much faith in the medical doctors in the islands.

And there was another factor that relaxed him. The war was over. It was finally, almost unbelievably, finished. The over-whelming pain and fear that ruled everyone's life would end. His wife and baby would never have to see and feel the evil of civil war again. Mean-spirited people would not be ranting slogans or epithets against each other in the same community. Families would not spill each other's blood. Someday, the people of the country would be united again, or at least tolerant of each other. And the insanity of the last four years would become a memory, buried away deep in his mind, in a place he never wanted to revisit.

Wake went to sleep wondering what it would be like to be a father and have his little children listen to his stories of the majesty and power of the sea, as he once had with his father. His mind conjured a vision of him with a grandchild on his lap, laughing at a story while his own son, a grown man, sat by his side. Wake went into a deep sleep, his face relaxed, dreaming of his family two generations hence.

Lieutenant Alexander Sibbald was a Scotsman, born and bred in the cold hills just north of Glasgow. Though he had been in America for fifteen years now, his accent was as thick as his barrel chest, which sometimes made it difficult for him to be understood, especially when he was excited. Wake and he were at the back of the room, dripping with sweat and chafing their necks in their uniform coats and buttoned-up shirts. A dozen other captains crowded in next to them in the meeting room of the squadron offices. Captain Morris, the fleet captain and chief of the squadron staff, had just started speaking to the assembled officers and what he said had created a buzz of conversation, but Wake hadn't made out the man's words or Sibbald's reaction to them.

"Alex, what did you say?"

Sibbald realized with a frown that his accent had overwhelmed his speech, and spoke more deliberately. "I said . . . Toos' a suicide ordarr . . . Peter. Nothing short o' that."

Wake became aware that Morris was speaking again, and whispered to Sibbald.

"What did he say that was a suicide order? The war's over. There's no more enemy to fight."

Sibbald said nothing, but pointed to the tall man in front, who had raised his voice to gain attention. Wake could hear him clearly now, for the room was absolutely still, the officers actually leaning forward slightly in an attempt to catch all that the man said.

"And so, gentlemen, it would seem that the unthinkable has happened, and the men in this squadron must go to Havana and prepare to try to stop, or more likely at least slow down, the raider until reinforcements arrive from Mobile and Charleston. The admiral has asked for them, and I'm sure they are on the way, but it is up to us to be the first in the breech, as it were."

As Morris paused, Wake suddenly realized what had happened. He had heard the speculation about the new Confederate ocean raider *Phoenix,* last seen on the Spanish coast in March by Commodore Crandon and the Navy's European Squadron. Now it seemed that she had gotten away and just arrived at Havana. The *Phoenix* was said to be the most formidable ship in the world, recently launched from a French yard, with iron armor thicker than any other vessel and new British guns that were heavier and more accurate than the Union's. Nothing in the squadron at Key West would last five minutes against her in battle. There weren't even any ironclads in the squadron. There were barely any gunboats left.

It was incredible, Wake almost said aloud to himself. The war was over. Lee had surrendered a month ago. Sailors and ships were already heading home. The enemy was gone. The fighting was over everywhere and the Rebel national leaders were running for their lives. Even the soldiers at Fort Jefferson and Fort Taylor were reducing the garrisons. There was no effective Confederacy left anywhere—except. . . .

In Havana harbor, aboard a ship that could defeat anything the U.S. Navy could send against it. Indeed, Wake had already read about how Commodore Crandon had refused to do battle in Spain with the solitary *Phoenix,* even though he had two ships with him, and there were rumors that a court martial was being considered. Wake had wondered when he read it at the tremendous courage that decision had taken.

Morris suddenly boomed out in a quarterdeck voice, startling the officers. "Make way there for the Admiral!"

Silence again descended in the sweltering room, as a portly short man with a huge mustache, wearing the gold-braided cuff rings of a rear admiral, made his way through the crowd to stand next to Morris. Admiral Cornelius Stroud raised his hand and pointed at Captain Samuel Gibbs, of the gunboat *Providence,* the largest vessel in the harbor.

"I have just returned from the general's quarters and relayed the information to him. He is standing up the regiment, manning the Martello Towers and Fort Taylor here on this island, and Fort Jefferson out at Tortugas. Now, Captain Gibbs . . ."

The distinguished-looking Gibbs half-bowed toward his commander. "Yes, sir?"

Stroud's eyes fixed upon the man.

"You shall have the honor of taking the three heaviest ships we have here at the present with you and blockade off the harbor at Havana. Besides the *Providence,* you'll take the *Bonsall* and the *Nygaard.* It will not be called a blockade, for the Spanish sensibilities, of course, but that is damn well what I want you to do. Understood?"

Lieutenant Commander West of the *Nygaard* grimly nodded, as did Lieutenant Commander Erne of the *Bonsall.* All eyes turned toward Gibbs as he registered his calm reply, as if he'd been told to lead a parade for the annual Independence Day celebrations.

"Quite well, sir."

Stroud continued to stare at him for a brief moment, then turned to Morris. "I want the others to spread out to the steamers on the coasts and tell them to go to Havana at once. *Immediately* to Havana. Do not stop anywhere on the way, including here. And when they get there, report to Captain Gibbs and prepare for battle."

"Aye, aye, sir."

"Now, while you are taking care of those assignments, I want Captains Gibbs, Erne, and West in my office. Oh, and Captain Wake also."

Wake felt eyes on him as he followed the others into the admiral's Spartan working quarters. As the door closed he could hear Morris quickly naming ships and their coastal assignments to notify steamers. He still was trying to adjust from the relaxed atmosphere of the last month to the near panic in the men around him in the building.

Stroud gestured at the large table covered with charts, bidding them to sit in the chairs grouped around it. He sat down with them, yelling for his yeoman, who came in the room almost at a run.

"Yeoman, bring me the British bottle. And six glasses."

No one spoke as they watched the skinny bespectacled clerk dash out and return with a tray holding a bottle and six glasses, which he set down in front of the admiral. The yeoman lifted the bottle but was stopped by Stroud.

"You may go. I'll do it."

Stroud poured a dark golden liquid out of the black bottle, the label of which was faded and tattered, indecipherable even as close as Wake was to it. When each glass was full, the admiral placed it in front of a man, including Morris who just then entered and sat on the edge of the desk across the room. The last glass the admiral poured for himself. He looked around at the officers.

"This is a fine Barbados rum, gentlemen. A gift to me seven years ago by a Royal Navy acquaintance who appreciated some help I gave his ship. It is appropriate to drink it now. He said I should wait until a moment such as this. Until today's news, I thought I'd not have an occasion to broach the bottle since the war was over, but, of course, the *Phoenix*'s arrival has changed that."

Stroud held his glass up and rotated it, surveying the rum inside and letting out an audible breath. "Sixty years ago, Admiral Lord Nelson shared a drink and a game of whist with his captains the night before they went into a battle called Trafalgar. The next day he was dead, they were national heroes, and the seas were made safe for three generations of Britons.

"We won't play cards, gentlemen, there's not much time for chivalrous niceties, and it may well be one or all of you who are dead soon, but the sentiment is the same from me to my captains, my band of brothers, as it was with Nelson. This will be a time for steadfast duty, gentlemen. A time for you to be smart, and to be strong. We aren't much in this squadron, I know, but we are all that there is between the *Phoenix* and the nation we serve, and that's enough reason."

Stroud, mouth firmly set, lifted his glass higher and looked at each man at the table in turn. Then he spoke, gently and with his eyes visibly moist, as he stood up.

"To our country, our navy, and our sailors . . ."

They rose as he said it, echoing the words while clinking glasses. No one smiled, no one said anything. They were all veterans and knew what the orders meant.

Stroud poured another round and spoke again as they regained their seats. "Captain Gibbs, you will maintain a close watch on the harbor with all three ships, from just over the three-mile limit. When she comes out, you will do everything you can with all of your vessels to sink her, by ramming if it comes to that. You will not let her away from Havana undamaged. Do all three of you gentlemen understand that?"

Gibbs, West, and Erne chorused, "yes, sir," leaving Wake wondering his part. He noticed Morris watching him. Stroud turned to Wake, a brief hint of a smile curling his mouth.

"And you, Captain Wake, I'm sure are wondering your reason for being here."

"Yes, sir, I was wondering that."

"You're here for the intrigue, Wake. You're good at that evidently, and now's the time, if ever there was one, for someone who is good at that."

"Intrigue, sir?"

"You know your way around the Spanish and around Havana, I'm told."

"I was there two years ago, sir, and did briefly meet with the

Spanish Navy admiral there. I can't say I know Havana, or the Spanish, particularly well though, Admiral."

Stroud's voice showed an edge for a moment. "Well, you know the bastards in that sewer of a port better than any of my other officers, don't you?"

"Yes, sir."

"And so you will have a tough mission, Captain Wake, and if by chance you are successful, then these men," the admiral waved around the table, "won't have to die in an impossible fight trying to slow that monster down."

Morris stepped over. "Shall I explain, sir?"

Stroud grunted an affirmative.

"Wake, you do know the place better than anyone else. Your mission is to immediately go into the harbor and make contact with the captain of the rebel raider. We think it's Roger Payne, who was in our navy and left to be with the Rebels in sixty-one. He had a good reputation and is no coward. He'll come out and fight, for honor like Semmes did at Cherbourg, if for no other reason. You have to convince him that there is no reason to do that, that there is no honor in that. You will carry a written appeal from me to him and await a reply. We served together on the old *Vandalia* in fifty-four, and I am hoping he will understand the sentiments in my letter and come to his senses."

"Yes, sir, I understand that mission."

Stroud harrumphed as he poured more rum in the glasses from another bottle that he had ordered from the yeoman. He slapped his hand down on a chart.

"Yes, well, I don't think Captain Morris' letter or his sweet sentiments will put a dent in Payne's armored ship or his ego. So you will also carry a letter from me to the Spanish Captain-General of Cuba. And that letter will not be friendly or sentimental in the least, Wake. In fact, when that regal worthy reads my letter he just might clap you in irons and chuck you down into old Morro's dungeon!"

Wake didn't know what to say. Glancing around, he saw that

the other officers around the table appeared as perplexed as he. Morris laughed, apparently at the reaction of the men to the admiral's comments, which sent a flicker of anger through Wake. Stroud, having stopped for an effect, resumed speaking.

"Yes, that's right. He won't like my letter, but he damn well better take it to heart. For my letter is giving him a specific and personal warning, gentlemen. A warning that since the *Phoenix* no longer has an official government in being, she is no longer considered a legitimate international combatant according to the rules of war, and therefore she is a pirate. And anyone who harbors, assists, or enables a pirate to pursue their destructive ways, is to be considered a pirate also, with all of the severe connotations that particular designation carries. My letter will further point out that though the squadron in Key West is diminutive in stature, it is part of the second largest navy in the world, most of which is rushing to Havana as we speak, just to deal with any pirates that emerge from that place."

Stroud smiled broadly for the first time that day. Wake was stunned. What Stroud was doing was practically issuing an ultimatum to war if the Spanish did anything to assist the Rebels in Havana, or even if they merely let them leave. There could be no official authorization for the admiral to issue such an ultimatum in there wasn't enough time for Washington to approve. Wake smiled back at the admiral, amazed at the man's initiative and mettle.

"I understand *completely* now, sir, and I'll make sure he does too."

Admiral Stroud looked around at the gathered officers, who were grinning at him and at Wake. The admiral raised his glass again and was joined by the others.

"Gentlemen, here's to Peter Wake and his coming confrontation. May his be successful, so you won't have yours. Now drink up and go, time has run out."

All of them were clapping Wake on the shoulder and suggesting various ways to verbally enhance the admiral's message.

By the time the second bottle was emptied and they all made their way out of the squadron commander's office, the sun had turned into an orb of molten copper, pouring out on the western horizon. Wake was dropped at his ship first by the other officers in the harbor boat, the warm feeling of the rum spreading throughout his body and making him light-headed as he climbed up to his main deck. Calls for good luck and offers of drinks from them in return for his success in the mission came from the boat as it left to return the others to their ships.

Rork watched the arrival with wary eyes. He had observed the other ships in the harbor departing and had already heard the news of the raider. Wake's unusual return aboard was the final clue that the *Hunt* and her men would be part of something. And Rork knew that with Peter Wake it would not be something boring. The bosun didn't wait for orders, but called forward to the crew clustered at the foredeck.

"There's some real navy work still needin' to be done, lads, so get her hook hove short an' ready to go. . . ."

Master Charles Hostetler had been aboard for one week as the new executive officer of the *Hunt*. He was obviously nervous as he reported the landfall to Wake in the gloomy cabin.

"Morro is dead ahead about eight miles, sir. We should be entering in about an hour or so. *Providence* is in sight off the port bow and *Nygaard* and *Bonsall* are off the starboard. They're all around three miles off the coast—just outside the line."

Wake regarded the large-framed Hostetler closely as he made his report. A second-generation Dutch-American from Pennsylvania, Hostetler had been a third mate on a river steamer in Philadelphia. *Hunt* was his second naval assignment and most probably his last, since the navy was releasing most of the volunteer officers.

Wake could tell that Hostetler was a gregarious type of man, but had kept his humor in check because he was replacing the much-respected Emerson, whose image was still strong in the crew's memory. There had been no replacement for poor young Rhodes. Wake shook himself from gruesome memories of his own as he realized his executive officer was waiting for his reply.

"Ah yes, we're approaching the harbor. Very well, then. Lay a course to pass close aboard the *Providence* and then for the southern side of the entrance and loiter a mile off if no *guarda costa* boat comes out before then. We'll have to wait for them to lead us in."

"*Guarda costa,* sir?"

"Yes, it's their version of the revenue marine, a sort of coast guard. Should be a two-masted lugger of about ten tons or so. They'll meet with us offshore most likely."

"Aye, aye, sir."

"Mr. Hostetler, have you been to Havana before?"

"Me? No, sir. Never south of Norfolk before this war, sir."

"Yes, well, me too. I first came here with *Rosalie* in sixty-three. I guess we're all getting some geography lessons courtesy of the U.S. Navy, aren't we?"

Hostetler's voice shed some of its tension with the captain's attempt to lighten the mood.

"Yes, sir. That is so. The navy surely does give a man quite an education."

Wake had briefed him on their mission earlier, but without the admiral's nuances about Wake's previous experiences, leaving Hostetler wondering why *Hunt* had been chosen for this almost impossible assignment.

"And send de Alba here. I want to talk with him for a moment."

"Aye, aye, sir."

Like over a third of the crew, Hernando de Alba was a foreigner. His English was learned in his native Palma de Majorca when he joined the U.S. Navy's European Squadron at its winter base there. Five years and three ships later he was on the *Hunt*.

Most of the foreign men aboard were Irish, English, or German. De Alba was the only Spanish speaker, and he would be Wake's interpreter. It was time to go over any last-minute details. There might not be a chance later and Wake wanted no misunderstanding by de Alba as to what would have to be accomplished. Ten minutes of conversation was enough to assure Wake that the thin young Spaniard understood the mission and had no last questions.

To the soldiers at Fortress Morro, the *Providence* and her consorts probably looked impressive cruising up and down off the harbor entrance, Wake thought as they neared Gibb's ship. But a naval officer could see them for what they were—hollow floating crates with small-caliber weapons, ready to crack from one round of the *Phoenix's* massive main battery. *Hunt* passed *Providence* fifty yards off her starboard side and Wake could see Gibbs slowly waving from the bridge walk as he heard the detached voice float out over the rolling seas.

"Good luck to you, Peter Wake, and God be with you . . ."

Wake waved back, knowing that Hostetler and Rork and the others aboard were watching him—everyone knew the mission and the consequences of failure.

"Thank you. We'll see you again in Key West, Captain Gibbs. And this time you're buying!"

Wake was rewarded with some laughter from his own men, and saw several of the *Providence's* crew nodding their heads and looking to their captain. *Providence* was receding rapidly astern of them on the opposite course, but Wake could see Gibbs lean out from the bridge walk, fist pumping up in the air and yelling through a trumpet across the cobalt blue heaving mass between them.

"Will be my pleasure . . ."

Hostetler touched Wake's shoulder. "It would appear they are coming out to us, sir."

Wake turned and saw a brown-sailed lugger bent over in the easterly breeze and charging fast out to meet them. The white and gold standard of the empire of Spain streamed out to leeward from the top of her main mast.

"I am Lieutenant José Roberto Monteria y Córdoba de Sevilla, of Her Most Catholic Majesty's Imperial Navy, under the command of His Excellency Vice Admiral Don Roi de Rodríguez y Costabela, commanding officer of the naval forces of Her Majesty in the Faithful Isles of the Caribbean. I am the captain and commander of the harbor coastal guard vessel and welcome my United States naval colleagues to Her Majesty's empire, and the faithful island of Cuba. I am most humbled to meet you, sir, and am at your service."

Wake didn't need de Alba for this conversation. The elegant speech was entirely in good English and accompanied by a demeanor as colorful as the uniform Lieutenant Monteria was wearing. With his white trousers and jacket, blue cross belt, gold sash and sword, red under vest, and black plumed tricorn hat, Monteria looked every inch a Spanish gentleman of the court. Wake wondered how an intelligent articulate man such as the one standing before him was assigned to the dirty and thankless job of harbor guard in the filthy port of Havana. Monteria had somewhere made a mistake in his life, Wake surmised, a considerable mistake.

"The United States Navy welcomes the distinguished representation of Queen Isabella aboard and thanks him for his most elegant hospitality upon our arrival at the beautiful island of Cuba, pearl of the Spanish Empire in the Caribbean."

Monteria bowed in reply and smiled at Wake's attempt to be as grandiose as a European. "And how may I assist the famous and well-respected navy of the United States, sir?"

Wake was uncomfortably aware of the officers and men around him watching the spectacle, as if a comedy was being played out on a stage before them. This is ridiculous, he thought, but I have to get through it.

"Our needs are very simple, Lieutenant Monteria. We only need to enter the harbor and moor in the general anchorage. I have communications for various personages ashore. I don't imagine we will be in port more than a few days, and won't require any provisions or repairs."

Monteria's gracious mien started to disappear, his eyes hardening and the smile fading. "Then there is no emergency aboard this vessel as a result of a disaster of the sea, and no request for succor according to the precepts of international courtesy and law?"

Wake knew something was wrong. The situation was changing, but why, and how? "No, Lieutenant. There are no emergencies or requests for help. Why do you ask?"

Monteria seemed to be standing taller and straighter. The tone of his voice was lower and his dark eyes bore into Wake. "Because those were the only conditions upon which your vessel could enter the harbor, Captain. The Empire of Her Most Catholic Majesty does not wish to see further bloodshed among the North Americans and will not permit even the possibility of that bloodshed occurring within her waters and in her ports. There is already a Confederate ship of war in the harbor. No vessel of belligerency against her will be allowed in close to her. No officers of mutual belligerency will be allowed in proximity to each other either. Therefore, you cannot come ashore by any vessel, and visitation to the port in person would be imprudent, sir. The tenets of caution demand our unusual policies, sir. I am certain that you understand, of course."

Wake eyed Monteria closely and decided he was parroting the words of his superior. There was no way to get them to change their mind, and a small vessel such as the *Hunt* could not force her way. The only thing to do was to send a reply as tactfully as possible and think of another way to get ashore to accomplish the mission. No one had thought of the Spaniards closing the port. It was an unheard-of action. Wake would have to be innovative.

"Please convey my most heartfelt thank-you to your leaders for the very high compliment of thinking that my small and humble vessel, or my own person, could be of any threat to such a powerful ship as the *Phoenix*. The navy of the United States has always held the officers and navy of Her Most Catholic Majesty in the highest esteem, and would be honored to accede to this rather . . . unusual . . . request to prohibit a small steam tug from intimidating a large ocean raiding cruiser from a defunct political organization. We will now depart this area, but I have one most sincere request of you and beg that you fulfill it."

Monteria bowed again. "If it is within my power, it will be done, Captain."

"Thank you. Please pass along my profound and sincere respects and admiration to Admiral Rodríguez, and tell my old friend that I will be speaking with him, one way or another, very soon. I look forward to his kind company and wise counsel in a very important matter. I shall now have to leave for consultations with my superiors."

Wake was pleased to see the look of surprise that briefly showed on Monteria's face.

"So you are acquainted with our most respected commander-in-chief? I will pass along your message through my harbor commander, sir. Thank you for your understanding of my most delicate position. I shall not impose upon your ship's hospitality any further, Captain, and will depart now. The admiral will have your message upon his return from Cienfuegos tomorrow. He is on an inspection there."

An hour later and two miles northward, the *Hunt* and the *Providence* were stopped a hundred yards apart, rolling in the swells. Gibbs and Hostetler were with Wake in his cabin studying a chart of the northern coast of Cuba. Gibbs was unfamiliar with the coast and searched the chart. He pointed to the area just west of Havana.

"With the winds out of the east and dropping, you could go ashore at Chorrera. There are uncharted coral rocks off the coast, but you could avoid them and land on the beach, then go by road to the city. It's only a few miles."

Wake shook his head. "They are watching us now and can see over to Chorrera from Morro. If I do that, it will appear clandestine and be an affront to them. Remember they are very sensitive about Americans sympathizing with the Cuban rebels, and I think I remember something about rebels in that area."

Hostetler laid his beefy hand on the chart with the index finger resting on Matanzas. "This looks like a decent-sized port. Nothing clandestine about that. Go there and take the road into Havana. Looks about forty, maybe fifty, miles. Chart shows a road of some type between them. We could be in Matanzas by dawn at the latest. On a carriage or wagon at eight knots on a good road you could be in Havana tomorrow evening. Is Matanzas a rebel town?"

Wake studied the chart. Hostetler might have something there.

"Not to my knowledge. Yes, I think that might be the solution. There probably is good transportation and it's the quickest way to get into Havana. We will steam north and appear to be returning to Key West."

The officer aboard the *guarda* cutter at Matanzas was the opposite in dress and demeanor from Monteria. The sun was starting to lighten the sky and it was obvious that the revenue officer had not had much sleep from whatever occupied his attention the evening before. De Alba translated Wake's request to put in for coal and stay three days, then leave for Santo Domingo.

The anchorage at Matanzas was open and uncomfortable. Wake did not envy Hostetler and the others who would have to endure the incessant roll of the ship while loading coal and cleaning up the choking dust that came with it.

"Mr. Hostetler, please make sure the coaling goes slowly, which shouldn't be hard judging on the activity I've seen in this port since we anchored. I need three days at least. I will send Curtis back with a report on how we are doing. If you hear that the *Phoenix* has put to sea, then do not hesitate. Go out and get up to where our ships are and do all that you can do to help them. Any questions?"

"No, sir. Be careful, and good luck."

"Thank you, but now is not the time for any of us to be *careful.* Now is the time to take chances. But I'll definitely need the luck."

Rork met him as he was preparing to go down the side into the boat.

"I can come too an' watch your stern, sir. A fair amount of unsavory buggers ashore in these parts, and they frequently come up from behind."

Wake shook Rork's hand, a gesture that was in the face of the social rules between commissioned officers and enlisted men.

"Thank you my friend, but the ship and Mr. Hostetler will need you aboard. If she has to go against the *Phoenix,* I want you to help lead the men."

Ginaldi and Durlon appeared on deck and said good luck, the thoughts in their minds clear to see. Everyone knew that if the captain failed, the crew might well pay the ultimate price.

"De Alba, tell him I have two gold dollars and he will get one now, and one when we reach Havana. I am not going to waste more time with him. There's a man over there that looks capable of getting us to Havana, and we'll talk to him next."

The wagon driver on the dock was obviously trying to drive up the price, but understood Wake's gestures toward the other driver even before de Alba translated. He immediately started to load the two sea bags of the Americans onto the wagon and spoke to the sailor in Spanish. De Alba laughed as he reported to his captain.

"His Spanish is atrocious, Captain, but he says that he would be most honored to help his new friends avoid the services of that pirate over there. Says that we might get robbed by the other driver."

The road was the best on the coast, according to the driver, Miguelito. But the eight knots of Hostetler's prediction were diminished to maybe five, according to Wake's estimation. He realized they would arrive late at night, if at all, after bumping along the rutted dusty road as it climbed and descended the coastal mountains and wound its way through the villages where people would stand and stare at the unfamiliar uniforms of Wake's party. Word went out in front of them, and soon at each village the inhabitants would line the road and point at the *marineros del norte* as they clomped by.

The heat and the dust, which transformed the dark blue of their uniforms into a shade of reddish gray, made it almost unbearable, but Wake saw that his small band of de Alba and Curtis, the bosun's mate, was holding up. De Alba was busy teaching Curtis words for the less gentlemanly aspects of Cuban society, and the petty officer was demonstrating considerable ability in pronouncing them. Curtis's proficiency progressed to the point that Wake had to remind him there would be no time to test those phrases in actual conversation, and that their mission did not include pleasure. Even with the tension of his assignment, Wake had to smile at his preposterous situation and wondered what the taciturn old admiral would think if he saw him now.

It was well after sunset when they came onto a rise in the outskirts of Havana and saw the lights of ships in the harbor several miles away. Since they were on the eastern side of the harbor, they still had to make their way around to the old part of the city, where Wake speculated the Confederates had moored the *Phoenix.* He thought it logical that they would be near the governmental center of power, the better to show off their powerful warship and gain any advantage they could from her formidable appearance.

Miguelito plodded his way through the winding streets and cart lanes, looking as tired and ready to drop as his old horse.

Wake was grudgingly impressed as they stopped at the main commercial wharf—his doubts about their ability to actually make it to Havana had grown during the journey to the point of resignation to failure. Miguelito stood in the wagon and with a flourish of his hand worthy of Lieutenant Monteria, announced that he, Miguel José Soto, had done the impossible and brought the naval sailors all the way to Havana in one day. De Alba translated and added that apparently Miguelito hadn't really thought they could do it either and was as surprised as his passengers.

Wake's pocket watch showed it to be just before ten o'clock. The streets were still full of the sounds of people: Spanish guitars and African drums from a tavern, a girl's tired laughter from a window, a drunken man's roar of disapproval from the alley behind them. They all brought back to Wake images of his last visit to Havana, especially of a sinister evening spent searching out Confederates operating a blockade-running organization. Then, as now, the smells of the port were a mixture of sewage, fish, and cooking oils.

They walked along the wharf until they found a harbor wherryman who would row Wake out to the *Phoenix*. The warship was anchored by herself by the naval docks close by the commercial wharf. It was late and most definitely not the proper time to call upon a naval vessel's commander, but Wake knew that time was of the essence. What if he delayed until morning and they weighed anchor tonight? No, it had to be done now, he told himself, and readied for the confrontation as he dropped into the boat's stern. De Alba told the boatman to row the officer to the warship and wait with the wherry off the ship until called for the return trip.

As the silent old man heaved on his oars Wake surveyed the infamous ship looming ahead. She was intimidating. Her solid iron hull looked impervious even in the darkness, concealing the Armstrong 300-pounder rifled main gun that could take on any ship in the world. Wake glanced back at the shore, but Curtis and de Alba were lost in the shadows. Curtis knew what to do if Wake didn't return. He was to take the admiral's message to the consulate and try to have them convey it to the Spanish Captain-General who governed Cuba for the crown. Neither Wake nor Stroud thought the diplomats at the consulate would have the courage to do that, but it was worth a try if Wake was taken captive.

A movement on the stern of the *Phoenix* was accompanied by a shout from a man with an English accent. "Boat there! Stand off and identify yourself!"

Wake tried to sound calm and reasonable. "Peter Wake, with communications for Captain Payne from Captain Morris."

The voice was doubtful. "This late at night? The captain's asleep below. Who are you again, and where are you from?"

"I am Peter Wake, and I'm delivering an urgent communication from Captain William Morris to Captain Payne. Obviously it's important or I wouldn't be out here in the middle of the night."

The exasperation in Wake's tone did the trick, and the officer of the watch bade them to come close alongside to the Jacob's ladder that was dropped. Once the old man had propelled them to the side of the iron ship, Wake looked up in preparation for the climb to the deck and found himself staring into a .58 caliber Enfield rifle's muzzle that was three feet from his face. He heard a click and saw another barrel from farther forward swing over the bulwark and down toward him. Wake held up the blue envelope, obviously official, with the red tape and wax gold seal.

"Easy now . . . This is an official communication from Captain Morris to Captain Payne. Let's not accidentally shoot the messenger, boys. Request permission to come aboard and personally deliver this as I am bound to do."

He could hear several men speaking, then the English voice came down to him, wary and hostile.

"Open your coat there, navy man. Then come up here and explain why you didn't say you were in the United States Navy before."

Wake did as he was told, holding his coat out so they could see he had no weapons, having anticipated that problem before- hand and given Curtis his pistol. He knew he never would have been allowed to get that close if they had known he was a Federal naval officer during their approach. Wake continued the vague tone in his voice. "I didn't think I had to. We're in a neutral port. I hold no threat to you. I'm just delivering a personal message, that's all."

He slowly climbed the hull, feeling the oddity of it all. The iron was dented slightly in a few places, and it was still quite warm from the heat of the day. There were no seams, no grain, just solid plates of iron riveted together into a massive, unyield- ing barrier. Unnatural was the word for it, thought Wake. This ship is unnatural and intimidating, a mechanical monster. No wonder the world was frightened of her and Commodore Crandon had refused to give battle to her in Spain.

The scene on the main deck was equally unnerving. Huge canvas-covered shapes, that Wake guessed were the famous Armstrong main guns, occupied the foredeck and afterdeck. Three men with rifles aimed at his chest watched him look around. Two others, appearing to be officers, stood further aft, one of whom was a large man with the gold cuff stripes of a cap- tain. The watch officer with the English accent stepped forward and spoke first.

"All right, now we know you're an enemy naval officer, but why *exactly* are you here, and where is your ship?"

Wake ignored his interrogator and watched the other two officers. They were silent and letting the first man do the talking. Wake looked at the one he presumed, by the clothing and the age, to be Captain Payne.

"I am Captain Peter Wake, of the United States Ship *Hunt,* which is lying at Matanzas. This," he held the envelope up for all to see, "is the official communication I have been ordered to pres- ent to Captain Payne, of the *Phoenix.*"

The watch officer made a move to take the envelope, but

Wake held it back. "I said I will present it to him personally. Those are my orders." Looking at the older man, Wake walked two steps and held out his hand. "Captain Payne?"

The man's weary answer had a sense of nostalgia in it as he shook Wake's proffered hand.

"Yes, I'm Payne. You say that message is from Willy Morris?"

"Yes, sir. Captain William Morris, Fleet Captain and Chief of Staff of the East Gulf Blockading Squadron."

"I'd heard he was at the Key West squadron. How is Willy? Is he here too?"

Wake detected a Virginia tidewater accent. "Captain Morris is fine, sir. No, he's not here in Cuba."

Payne chuckled. His laugh had a softness that was incongruous with his size and commanding bearing. He looked as formidable as his ship. "Oh, I bet Willy is chomping at the bit, wanting to be *here*. Guess old man Stroud wouldn't let him. I'm glad he's not though. Always liked Willy. No joy in getting him mixed up in this situation. No joy at all."

Payne was nothing like Wake expected. He acted like a man going to the gallows. There was no bravado, no strong-willed front. Wake handed over the envelope.

"Here is the communication, sir."

"Thank you, son. Have you had dinner? Would you care for some coffee and a bite to eat? I know it's late, but then again here in the Spanish islands they eat late, you know."

Wake was taken by surprise by the offer, but realized that his mission was to end the bloodshed and enmity—not exacerbate it. Besides, he *was* very hungry.

"Ah . . . no sir, I haven't had dinner. Thank you for your kind offer, and I would be very pleased to have something."

"Good. Come below to my cabin, Captain Wake, and we'll relax while I read Willy's letter. And where exactly is your ship, the *Hunt* was it? We saw no naval vessel come into the harbor here. You said Matanzas?"

As they descended below, Wake started to worry that Payne

was a master at surreptitiously eliciting information from unwary guests. For an ocean raider captain constantly being hunted down across the globe, it would be a valuable skill. But he concluded that his tug's location was not a material secret that would alter the situation.

"Yes, Captain, she's merely a tug, and she's at Matanzas, down the coast. The Spanish wouldn't let me in the harbor here. Inferred my little vessel would heighten the tensions."

Payne laughed again and nodded. "Yes, they are a bit nervous right about now."

Wake expected to see metal bulkheads in Payne's cabin, but instead found it to be richly paneled in mahogany and teak. The table was inlaid cherry. It was a magnificent commander's cabin. Payne looked at him surveying the place and understood his thoughts.

"Yes, Captain, it is a beautiful cabin. Not like the others I've had, which were probably much like yours. But this one is more than my office and sanctuary. This cabin is meant to impress dignitaries I meet in foreign ports."

"I'm sure it fulfills that function admirably, Captain Payne," Wake said, unable to repress a smile.

The steward brought sandwiches and coffee, and Payne poured a gill of rum into both cups. The light in the cabin was very dim with the lamp turned as low as it could be. Probably low on lamp oil and everything else, Wake guessed. Payne sat in a padded easy chair in the corner reading the letter under a bulkhead lamp he turned up, illuminating more of the cabin. The substantial desk next to Payne was inlaid with blonde wood of some type in the design of an anchor. Wake had never seen a desk that large on a ship before. A painting of a frigate flying the Stars and Stripes of the United States was mounted on the transverse bulkhead above the desk, forming an ironic backdrop for this man who had turned his back on the Federal Navy in which he had spent twenty-one years.

Wake sat at the table, watching him read and sipping the

rum. The letter was written on both sides of two pages and Payne read it through twice, showing no reaction until he had finished and looked up. A long sigh came from him as he pursed his lips and slumped back in the chair. Payne adjusted the lamp, dimming the light again.

Wake could see that his eyes were sad. Payne shook his head slightly and looked down. When he spoke, it was with paternal tones.

"How long have you been in the navy, Captain Wake?"

"Two years, sir."

"Two years? You were a seaman before that, I presume . . ."

"Yes, sir. Ten years on New England schooners. Third mate when the ship was sold in sixty-three. Joined the navy then."

"Ah, yes. Sixty-three *was* a bad year for the Yankee merchant marine. Wake? Hmm. I've heard that name somewhere."

"Probably my father or older brother. They were well-known schooner captains on the east coastline."

"No, I've heard in connection with the navy. You've seen some action, I believe."

"A little, sir."

"In these waters, even a little can be deadly."

Wake ate the last of the sandwich and chased it down with the remnants of the coffee. Payne did not offer more, and Wake realized that what he had just eaten and drunk had come out of a rationed supply. This was not going as he had anticipated. It was time to bring up the matter at hand.

"Captain Payne, I am here to deliver that letter, but also to speak to you about ending the bloodshed. It's time to end all of this, sir. You know that, I'm sure."

"Yes, well that's what Willy said in his letter. Seems they all are thinking that, north of here. You know, I've been in the navy for twenty-five years, sail an' steam, Captain Wake. Willy and I served as midshipmen together on our first ship, the *Columbia,* back in forty. She was new then, but it seems a hundred years ago now. Went off to Africa straightaway in her, then saw the world.

The navy taught us both many things in all that time. Willy and I learned that it was amazing just what all you could endure.

"I saw and did things over those years that I never would've dreamed of that first day when Willy and I stood shaking in the gun room as the warrants inspected us like newly arrived vermin. Those old warrant officers taught us to be tougher than we thought we could be, and *never* give up. Only the strong survive in the navy, young Captain Wake, and only the strong and smart get promoted."

Payne stopped suddenly and looked at Wake, curiously, as if seeing him for the first time. "And they taught us something of the old ways of honor, too. Duels and fights were common then, illegal of course, but common. You could get in trouble for doing it, but the man who didn't go through with it and defend his honor suffered far worse than anything the captain could give out."

Wake felt he had to oppose Payne's course of the conversation, bring in the reality and futility of the present situation. "But Captain Payne, honor has responsibilities beyond merely dying for a cause. There are responsibilities to live onward, to live honorably and productively. To not waste your men's lives."

The corner of Payne's mouth lifted, crinkling his face. "Captain Wake, honor is something Southerners cherish. Honor is the core of our souls. Honor is the reason we do what we do. Do you think Semmes didn't know the odds last year at Cherbourg? His ammunition was faulty, his hull was fouled with growth, and he needed to overhaul his boiler. He did what he did for the honor of his country and navy, to let everyone know that no matter what the odds, we would fight, always fight, and that no one anywhere could intimidate us into doing something against our wishes."

"Yes, sir. But he lost to the *Kearsarge,* and men were killed. For what, Captain Payne?"

Payne's voice rose as he explained his point. "For what? To send a *message,* Captain Wake. To deter you from attacking us again, because your cost would be too high for you to stomach, even though you probably would win. That is what this war is about, Captain. Sending a message to stop trying to get us to change our ways and to submit to yours. That we will make it so painful for you that you shouldn't try to invade us or threaten us. What do you think Bobby Lee has been doing for the last four years?"

Wake struggled to keep calm and rational. This wasn't going well. "General Lee has surrendered, sir. The war is over. There is no reason for anyone else to die."

Payne leaned forward in his chair, elbows on his knees, hands outstretched for added emphasis. "Until the message has been received and taken to heart, it's got to be made again and again. There are other Semmes and Lees to send that message. This isn't over yet, not by a long shot."

"Captain Payne, please do the reasonable thing. Don't leave this harbor and get men killed for no cause. Your government is on the run or has surrendered. There is no Confederacy left. It doesn't exist. You can't win. One ship against an entire navy? Please, Captain, think of your men's families, their children."

"You mean like Crandon did with me at Corunna two months ago? Do the logical, safe, reasonable thing? I am a naval officer! I don't get paid to do the *safe* thing. I'm not in that kind of business and neither is anyone among my officers or men. I'd rather die than be humiliated like Crandon was. And he did it to himself. He outnumbered me two to one, and he backed off. He, and your navy, will always be known for that in Europe. Hellation man, they're talking about that here in Havana. His misery is just beginning because of that."

It was obvious to Wake that Payne was not listening, that he didn't even understand Wake's argument, or the hopelessness of his position. "Captain Payne, you'll be destroyed, along with your men, and it will be for nothing."

His eyes devoid of emotion and his voice lowered, Payne leaned forward toward Wake—a dangerous man in command of a dangerous ship. "We shall see, Captain Wake. We shall see who gets destroyed."

It took every shred of self-control for Wake not to show the chill that flooded through him at hearing those words. He forced himself to ask the one thing he needed to know, a question that would probably not get answered.

"A regrettable situation, sir. And now a final question, sir, if I may. When is it that you are going to depart the harbor?"

Payne sat back in the easy chair, aggressive stance gone, looking like a grandfather telling a sea story to his family in the parlor. "Now, now, Captain Wake, that wasn't very subtle at all, was it? I shall get underway at the time of my choosing, of course. Though I am loath to leave my Spanish friends here. Their hospitality has lived up to its fame.

"But it is getting late, Captain, and I am a busy man these days and the morn comes early. Unlike you young bulls, I need my sleep, and ask your forgiveness that I must beg to ask you to depart the ship. One other favor though, if I may?"

"If I can, sir, then certainly."

The hardness left Payne's words and he cast his eyes down. "Please tell Willy that I appreciated his letter. More than I can say. It brought to mind many happy memories and made this old man forget the tribulations of the moment. Tell him I wish I could do what he asks, but that it is simply not within me. Tell him that I always considered him a friend. And that I said a heartfelt goodbye."

It was a final statement from one old warrior to another. Wake felt the chill again, not for Payne, but for the hundreds of others who would die also.

"Aye, aye, sir, I will do that. I'll depart the ship now. I must get back to mine and it's a long way."

Wake stood. It was terrible and fascinating at the same time—to watch and listen to this man and know what was soon to happen, but to be unable to stop it.

"Captain Wake, do not judge me harshly. Just know that I

have no real choice."

Wake shook his head and walked out of the cabin past the sentry, who had to run to catch up with him. Moments later he was in the boat, the old Cuban wherryman staring at the *yanqui* officer quizzically as he strained at the oars to get them to the dock where Curtis and de Alba waited.

When Curtis heard that the effort had failed, he laughed.

"Fools. They'll get some of us, but we'll get all of them. They're positively lunatic, Captain, to think they can get away with it forever."

"Yes, well, fools they may be, but they're fools in a very strong and well-armed ship. Because of that, Curtis, we've got more work to do, and we've got to do it right now. Follow me, men, we're heading for the admiralty."

Curtis looked askance but said nothing.

"I know the time, Curtis, but time is not on our side in this thing. De Alba, as we walk along try to find us a ride of some sort. I want to get there quickly."

Wake led the way, trying to remember the route from two years earlier. Though it was midnight, the sounds of the port hadn't diminished that much, with pedestrian and wagon traffic still moving about. Two streets further de Alba found a cart driver who took them on their way. It wasn't commensurate with his rank and position, but Wake didn't care. He was already thinking about how he would get in to see the admiral, and what he would say when he did.

"I am Captain Peter Wake of the United States Navy, commanding officer of the U.S.S. *Hunt,* presently at Matanzas, with an urgent communication from my admiral to Admiral Rodríguez. I know the hour is late, but lives depend on this, and

Admiral Rodríguez knows me and trusts me. Do not delay. Notify him that I am here immediately."

He hoped it sounded urgent enough to make the sergeant of the guard at the Spanish naval station rouse his officer, but Wake worried that it might have lost something in the translation. The uniqueness of an American naval officer showing up in the middle of the night was enough, however, to make the old sergeant run to get his officer. The lieutenant was impressed enough to rouse the chief of the admiral's staff, and by five in the morning, when even Havana's streets were sleeping, Wake was walking through the halls of officialdom of the imperial navy of Spain.

The chief staff officer was Admiral Santiago, a *contra-almirante* or rear admiral, and assistant commander to Rodríguez. The earliness of the hour only increased his wariness at the very unusual request from a Yankee naval officer, and a mere lieutenant at that. He spoke in good English to Wake.

"You say, Captain, that you have a personal message for Vice-Admiral Rodríguez, and that he knows you? By your insignia I see that you are merely a lieutenant. In our navy, admirals do not associate with lieutenants."

"The admiral knows me from another urgent situation here in Havana two years ago. He will see me if he knows I have requested it."

"I know nothing of the event you speak of, Captain."

"It had to do with Cuban insurgents and their foreign sympathizers. I assisted the admiral with eliminating a festering problem here in the city."

The Spanish officer was visibly impressed by that description of the event, which had involved Wake getting Admiral Rodríguez to round up John Saunders and the Confederate blockade-running organizations as sympathizers with the Cuban rebels that plagued the island. Wake had left Havana secure in the knowledge that one of the most successful of the enemy blockade runners was neutralized, only to find out several months later that the wily Saunders had somehow emerged from the dungeon of

Morro Fortress and departed Cuba, apparently without official approval. It was a lesson learned for Wake in the ways of the Caribbean. A lesson he hoped to capitalize on now.

"Time is of the essence, sir. My admiral is in communication with Washington and expects an answer from me. Great events are in motion, sir."

The officer shouted a fast command to his aide out in the hallway, then turned to Wake. "For your sake, Captain Wake, I hope that Admiral Rodríguez is as fond of this memory of you as you say. He just got into the city from a rail trip late last night and will not be amused by an unneeded intrusion into his rest. My aide is notifying him now."

Curtis and de Alba were staring at Wake, clearly in awe of his intrepidity in gaining access to the highest naval officer of the Spanish Empire in the Western Hemisphere. Wake was nervous and knew that the admiral was not his final destination. He also knew that Payne's demeanor indicated that he might move quickly. His words to the chief of the staff were accurate—time was of the essence.

Suddenly Wake's pensive thoughts were interrupted by a booming voice. No knowledge of Spanish was needed to understand that a junior officer was announcing the entrance of the senior naval officer of the empire in the New World. De Alba translated with all the fervor of the original rendition.

"His Excellency Vice Admiral Don Roi de Rodríguez y Costabela, Admiral of the Oceans of Her Most Catholic Majesty's Empire in the Americas, Commander-in-Chief of all Naval Forces in the Ever Faithful Isles of the Caribbean Sea, Knight of the Order of Cadiz, Defender of Spain, and Faithful Servant of the One True Church of Our Savior!"

Dressed in a red satin robe, the subject of this magnificent introduction did not match the rhetoric. Admiral Rodríguez was an average and pleasant-looking man who had the wrinkles and tan of a seaman, but the expanding torso of an aficionado of fine food and drink. He waved the junior officer away and spoke quickly to his number two in Spanish.

"My English is not sufficient. You will translate. Dismiss all others in the room."

When de Alba conveyed this to his captain, Wake told him to take Curtis out in to the hall. Only Rodríguez, Santiago, and Wake remained. Rodríguez shook Wake's hand and waved for all of them to sit.

"Captain Wake, congratulations on your promotion from master to lieutenant. Also from sail to steam, I understand. Welcome back to Cuba. I remember you well. And of course, your enemy, Saunders. He is still out there somewhere, is he not?"

"Yes, Admiral, I believe that he is. Thank you very much for seeing me like this. I know of the inconvenience, but you know I would not be here unless it was truly important. I have an important communication, sir."

Rodríguez nodded slowly. "Concerning the large iron warship in our harbor, no doubt. The wonder of the naval world has come to us here in Havana."

"Yes, sir. About the *Phoenix.* I have to get to the Captain-General of the Antilles, Viceroy Dulce, immediately with an emergency message from my admiral. Washington is waiting."

Rodríguez would make an excellent card player, Wake thought, for he showed no reaction, just amused tolerance for the interruption of his sleep.

"To pass messages onward you disturb me? Why not go to the palace and rouse them up over there? Why awaken me, young man?"

"Because sailors' lives are at stake, and you are a sailor, sir. You understand better than anyone here what that ship is capable of doing, and why she must not leave this port. I need you to get me into the palace and in front of the Captain-General. I cannot get there any other way in the time that I have."

"And your consulate people, they do not have access to the diplomats of the palace?"

"Yes, but not in a timely way. And they also do not understand the naval aspect of this, of what will happen three miles outside of your harbor if that ship leaves."

Rodríguez showed the first reaction of the meeting. "Yes, she will crush your vessels off the harbor. They are nothing to a ship like her. Your navy will eventually catch her though and then crush her."

"But sir, in the meantime, hundreds of men will die, and for nothing. The war is over. There is nothing for the *Phoenix* to fight for."

"So they sent you here to persuade me? I'm persuaded. It would be folly to have a battle now."

"Yes, they sent me, but to persuade the Captain-General. You command the naval forces, but not the army. Not Morro. Only the Captain-General commands the garrison and artillery of Morro. Only the Captain-General can order the artillerymen at the fortress to sink a ship to prevent it from leaving."

"And why would we shed blood? We have no quarrel with those people on that ship. They hate you, not us. If we let them go, no Spanish or Cuban blood will be lost."

Rodríguez was studying Wake as the comment was translated. Wake knew it was a crucial point. This was not the Spaniard's problem. He also knew that Admiral Stroud's message would in effect make it their problem. It was how to make the delivery of that message that was the question in Wake's mind.

Stroud made a direct threat, almost an ultimatum of war. It was a last resort message, to be given when all else failed. Wake agonized as the Spanish officers looked at him. Was it time yet to use the final resort? But the threat to brand the Captain-General as aiding and abetting piracy was one that had best be made to that man in private at this point—let him have a way out that no one knows. Open knowledge of the message would negate its power.

Wake decided not to tell Rodríguez the contents of the message.

"Admiral Rodríguez, you know me. Obviously, I have the confidence of Admiral Stroud at Key West or I wouldn't be here.

When I say that I have a most secret message from Admiral Stroud to the Captain-General, you know you can take my word of honor. I must see the man right now. Sir, you must get me in to see him. More than even the lives of American sailors is at stake here."

Rodríguez slapped the arm of his chair and laughed. "You have the fortitude of a matador, Captain Wake. Each time I see you I know that something of momentous importance is about to happen. I think you are a magnet for such things. I also think it will get you killed one day, and I will lament that when I hear of it.

"We will notify the palace we are coming. It will be only the three of us. In matters of secrecy more than two is a gamble, more than three is a surrender ahead of time. We will go now, and I will get you in to the Captain-General's presence. There I will watch you work your ways with him.

"But I warn you, my young impetuous friend, Captain-General Domingo Dulce did not get to where he is by being a fool. Your message had better be very important to him. Let us go."

It took half an hour for the entourage to gather up and make its way to the palace, a distance of only a quarter-mile, and then inside to the apartment of the Captain-General of the Antilles. The sun was lightening the sky outside the window as Dulce walked into the room, his manner anything but hospitable. He spoke immediately in a deep voice that intensified his authority. The hostility was clear by the tone even before Santiago translated the words.

"Very well, I am now disturbed and awake and ready to spend five minutes on whatever this trivial matter seems to be about. Explain yourself."

"Your Excellency, I have a message here from my commander, Rear Admiral Cornelius Stroud, commanding officer of the East Gulf Blockading Squadron of the United States Navy. It is meant for me to deliver to you personally. It is only for your eyes."

"I will determine whose eyes will see my letters. Now where is this thing from your commander?"

Wake handed over the blue envelope sealed with gold wax and red tape.

Dulce, reading spectacles perched on his nose, ripped the envelope apart without any niceties. Wake saw that it was in Spanish and wondered who on Stroud's staff had translated it. Dulce read it slowly, frowning more and more as he went along. At first, Rodríguez had a pleasant expression, but it too changed as he watched the Captain-General's face cloud and redden. Dulce looked up at Wake, glaring.

"You know what this says?"

"I have been told the general idea of it, sir."

"Do you agree with what it says?"

Wake realized that this was the moment of truth. His heart was pounding and he felt almost faint as the blood warmed his face. "It matters not what I or some others think, sir. What matters is that Washington agrees. And also whether Madrid thinks you made the right decision to place the Spanish Empire in a place that is difficult to return from. And for what? To show allegiance to a dead cause that wasn't even yours to start with, against the will and power of the world's largest standing army and second largest navy—all within a few days of here. I am but a messenger bearing a grave personal warning to you, sir. No one else has seen it, only you. The consequences are yours, and time is running out this morning. I await your reply."

Rodríguez and Santiago had set their jaws and were looking at Wake as they would an enemy. Rodríguez glanced at the captain-general.

"Your Excellency. May I be permitted to read the message and offer my opinion?"

"No. It is private, for me as Captain-General and Viceroy, and for the Crown in Madrid." Dulce turned and stared at Wake. "And the Crown will have this as soon as possible, so they know without a doubt the true feelings of the government of the United States."

This stunned Rodríguez and he showed it. That a junior American naval officer should rouse them all out of bed and hand the representative of the queen a message that had angered him—then not allow the commander of naval forces to read it—was preposterous. Wondering what could be in the communication from the American admiral, Rodríguez regarded Wake closely as Dulce went on, his narrowed eyes belying the apparent kindness in his words.

"The points made in this communication are well made and have import for the Empire of Spain and Her Most Catholic Majesty. We thank the United States for its demonstration of support and are particularly pleased to be of assistance in ending the needless fraternal bloodshed of our neighbors to the north. It is our hope that we may be successful in our endeavor to stop further violence, and that all parties may work and live together in a future that knows peace.

"Write that down right now in English, Admiral Santiago, for my signature and then give it to the American here."

Santiago translated the communication into English for Wake. Afterward the Spaniard paused. No one made a sound. Wake knew they were all watching for his response.

"On behalf of the United States of America, I thank your Excellency for your kind words, and can assure you of the never-ending amity and respect of the American people and government for the people of your empire."

Dulce's scowl remained in place as he added one more comment. "I will have a messenger send word to you at our admiralty when we have success. Wait there."

"Thank you again, your Excellency."

Wake bowed and walked out of the room before anything else was said. He didn't breathe until he made the hallway and saw Curtis and de Alba.

Wake had been waiting in an anteroom of the admiralty, beside himself with worry and periodically checking to see if de Alba had returned from his lookout position a block away at the naval signal tower where he had a clear view of the harbor. Curtis was stationed outside the front of the admiralty building and was to let out a loud whistle if he saw de Alba running their way. De Alba, perched atop the tower with the duty Spanish Navy signalman, was to notify Wake if he saw the *Phoenix* weigh anchor and start moving. Wake didn't know what he would do if she started out, but he felt he had to know. His mind worked to try to come up with a plan of action to stop her himself, but he couldn't think of one.

At 10 o'clock in the morning, while he was pacing in the side portico, Wake heard the whistle from Curtis.

De Alba was out of breath when he came running up the steps, startling the guards until he shouted out that he was an American sailor with a message for his officer. Curtis and Wake reached him at the same time.

"She is moving, Captain! But not out the harbor. She is moving here!"

"Here? Here where?"

"Here to the naval docks. I saw Spanish soldiers and sailors on her too. She is coming alongside the wharf now, over there. . . ."

Ordering him to stay at the building in case a message came, Wake started walking rapidly in the direction de Alba pointed, with Curtis following. They began to trot as astonished onlookers watched the men in the strange uniforms move quickly through the naval station area. Rounding the corner of a warehouse they saw her there, a black iron monolith towering over the wharf with her auxiliary square rig and unusual retracted bowsprit. Workmen were securing her lines as a dark cloud of soot belched out of her stack with a final gasp of her engine as steam was released.

Green-coated Spanish soldiers were positioned with bayoneted rifles every twenty feet on the wharf in front of her, but Wake could see by their relaxed attitudes they were there more for show than for action. A Spanish naval officer resplendent in white was visible above the bulwark on the main deck, talking to four other men in dark blue. Wake walked up to the line of sentries and stopped, examining the ship and men aboard her. A bosun's whistle called, and all the men on the main deck walked aft and formed in two lines, facing away from the wharf. Wake could distinguish Payne's voice rise and address the men formed on the deck. Individual words could not be discerned, but the tone was somber. When the speech finished, a man shouted "Salute," and the bosun's whistle called again, as a drum rolled, with quick beats that slowly decreased in volume.

Curtis pointed to the afterdeck, where the Confederate naval ensign was descending from the peak of the spanker gaff. When it reached a sailor on the deck the whistle and the drum stopped. Another shouted command and the group disbanded and made their way forward to the waist.

"Your enemies are no longer a threat, Captain."

Wake turned around and saw Admiral Santiago standing behind him, a stern look on his face as he continued.

"It would appear that the secret message from your admiral, and your manner of delivering it, were successful in persuading the Captain-General to induce the Confederates to parole themselves and their ship."

"Ah . . . yes, sir. It appears that they have turned her over to you."

"But Captain Wake, there is more than that. Each member of the crew was paid off his outstanding wages with Spanish gold, the officers receiving double what they normally would receive."

"That must have been very expensive, Admiral. We are grateful."

"Oh, I am sure that you will be grateful, Captain Wake. Make sure you remember how grateful you are, in the future. Admiral Rodríguez presents his compliments and regrets that he will not be able to say goodbye to you. He said that you always have provided unique challenges for him when in Havana. He admires your initiative. And he appreciates that he now has a new ship, for a very cheap price."

"Thank you, sir. I will be leaving as soon as I receive that note from the Captain-General."

"The note has already been given to your man de Alba, who is being taken out to the American warships offshore as we speak. The Captain-General wanted no time wasted in getting that note to your superiors in Washington. He does not share Admiral Rodríguez's admiration of you or your initiative. In fact, you seem to have displeased him greatly. He seems to feel that you took pleasure in your message," Santiago paused, a sneer transforming his face, "and his displeasure with you is highly personal. You are very fortunate you are an American. A carriage is waiting for you at the admiralty building right now and I would suggest that you get in it with haste. You will be immediately driven to your ship at Matanzas, so that there will be no delay in your ability to leave Cuba and return to Key West."

Santiago spun on his heel and walked away. Curtis pointed to the *Phoenix* again. A line of men was filing off her, down a gangway that had been set up amidship. Some were laughing but many were quiet. Wake saw Payne come down the gangway at the end of the line. He didn't look back. Seeing Wake, Payne walked leisurely over to him.

"Well, you seem to have won, Captain Wake."

"I think we all won today, sir. By the way, when were you going to weigh anchor, anyway?"

Payne sighed. "An hour before high noon today. Had the steam up and was ready to engage the capstan when I got a message from the Captain-General."

"A message, sir?"

"Yes, Captain Wake, a message. It said that if we got under-way we would be considered pirates without a country, and never get past the batteries of El Morro Fortress. A pirate, he called me. Can you imagine that? A pirate! Twenty-five years a naval officer and gentleman, and it all ended by being branded a pirate by a third-rate trumped up martinet—"

"With heavy artillery at point blank range, Captain Payne. It would've been a one-sided slaughter."

"Yes, that's what I thought. I turned her over to them. It's over."

"You made the right decision, sir. The children of hundreds of men will thank you someday."

"No, I hope not. If I'm lucky, Captain Wake, no one will remember me or the *Phoenix*."

"What will you do now, sir?"

"I don't know. Maybe someone, somewhere in the world, needs a naval officer."

Payne walked off to rejoin his officers. Curtis stood there, looking all around them and marveling at what he had seen and heard in the last two days.

"Captain, does this mean the war is really over?"

"Yes, Curtis, I guess that's exactly what it means. All this insanity is really finally over. Nobody else dies. Come on, let's get that carriage and get out of here. I want to go home to our ship."

9

Upstream

The cabin was lifting slightly with each entry of the bow into the gently rolling seas as Wake examined the scanty charts of the coasts ahead of them one more time. Swaying shafts of sun came through the overhead skylight and slid across the chart table, alternately focusing a spot of light on the island of Hispaniola, then the island of Puerto Rico. Full-bodied salty air from the strong January trades filled the cabin, so thick with moisture Wake could feel its weight as he waved a hand. Through the open hatch above Wake heard men laughing at some joke-ster's comments as they worked on recaulking Lawson's launch, with the Scottish apprentice cook humming some unfamiliar Celtic tune in the background as he dumped the ashes from the noon cooking overboard. It was a good day to be out at sea, Wake thought, and all the pleasant sensations surrounding him remind-ed him of how quite a few things seemed to be going better than they ever had for him.

The war had officially ended eight months earlier in May, and most of the volunteer officers Wake had known were subse-quently released from the navy when their obligation ended. The few officers who were left in the naval service did everything they could to get a sea billet, but the fleet was already a shadow of what it had been just months before. The Congressional allocation of money for the navy dwindled as soon as the political winds in Washington changed from fighting the war to the reconstruction of the Southern society and economy. Ships were scarce now, and even the funding for coal was so diminished that captains were admonished to use their auxiliary sails as much as possible.

Even so, against all the odds and primarily because of his wartime successes, Wake had managed to retain his commission and command of the *Hunt,* and was very grateful for it. With a soon-to-be-expanded family—Linda being due at any time now—Wake needed the increased pay of a sea command. The prize money he had won during the war was safely in a bank account, providing a little security in case of hard times, but he was still concerned about his future. After this cruise, the powers in Washington might rotate another officer into command of the steamer, leaving Wake on retainer half-pay, waiting for another assignment. A friend of his, Lieutenant Jeff Nibarger from the old *Bonsall,* was still waiting for an assignment in Baltimore on half-pay, doing clerical work at an ironworks to make ends meet. Wake knew of a dozen officers in the same situation. Those men were at least single, though. When he was unmarried, Wake had barely gotten by on his pay. Now he had to make it provide for three people and he was worried, for there was no regular way to increase it. Prize money was a thing of the past, except if they were lucky enough to come across the rare pirate or slave runner. Still, many men with families were in worse shape, and Wake realized he should accept his good fortune and not dwell on things in the future he could not control.

The *Hunt* herself had had good fortune. She was in good condition, the shipyard in Pensacola having completed the work requested with no problems. That was in July, just before the budget cuts, and the comforting rumble of Ginaldi's engine was still steady and strong. Their coal bunkers were topped off and they had enough to get to their destination easily. Though it was powdery inefficient stuff they got at Santo Domingo, it would get them back with plenty left over. The last decent anthracite coal they'd had was at Nassau, two ports ago, and they'd get some of that again on their stop there returning to Key West. *Hunt* had also provisioned in Santo Domingo, bringing aboard fruits, vegetables, and that most precious commodity to sailors, fresh beef.

The weather had been almost perfect, with a trade wind blowing up the Mona Passage from the southeast on her bow, but not so strong as to slow her down appreciably. The trades that time of year blew steady in the sunshine, with the little white puffs of clouds scudding along forming a backdrop for the momentary rainbows caused by the spray bursting against her. The sight and feel of that wind was enough to make the grizzled salts smile. The doldrums summer in the Gulf of Mexico seemed far distant, as distant as the war.

For the first time in years, she had a full complement of men in every rating, although many were foreigners, the Americans having gone home at the end of their enlistment. Even better, the morale problems that were so obvious during the war were now just memories. Every man was there because he wanted to be there, because the navy was his home, and he was just glad to have a berth when so many ashore were without work.

All in all, 1866 was starting out with a pleasantness Wake hadn't felt in years, and he should have been happy, but wasn't. Wake was nervous not so much because of where they were heading, but mainly because of *who* they were heading for. He had a sense of dread, as if the war hadn't really ended, and would never end for him.

The *Hunt* was almost to the area of the Caribbean where their objective lay hidden. He wondered exactly what he would find when they reached their destination, and exactly what he would do about it when he found it. The mission was ill defined and potentially dangerous, as the admiral had pointed out quite clearly to Wake and his fellow captains when he explained

Washington's orders to the squadron.

Wake sensed that Stroud himself was not impressed with the orders that sent five of his dwindling number of ships off on searches throughout the Caribbean Sea, but the man had dutifully given out the assignments. *Hunt* was the smallest ship assigned, but since she had recently completed a boiler and engine refit the admiral thought she could carry it out, with proper coaling support along the way to fill her meager bunkers. He didn't have much choice, since she was the only ship left to him that was in any kind of condition to make a two thousand-mile voyage out and back.

In theory, it would be very simple: find them, ascertain their viability and plans, return to Key West, and send the report quickly to Washington. Wake read the sheaf of papers again, trying for the tenth time to discern what the powers in Washington wanted him to do if he found a hostile situation, either with the subjects of the search or with the Spanish. The bureaucrat who had sent the orders, however, had probably never been in the Caribbean, never dealt with the myriad of variables that confused situations there. He probably never had to consider Latin prestige and honor, which could leave the best-laid plans dead in the water.

Of course, now that there was no war between the American states, and no easy money to be made from it by supplying the Confederates, the Spanish imperial officials in the Caribbean were far more cooperative than during the previous four years. That should have eased Wake's mind, but there were nagging doubts about how the Spanish would take to his search of their island for people who might now be considered Spanish subjects—people who shared the Spanish government's belief in the institution of slavery and its so-called economic benefits, and who had paid the anemic Spanish treasury a fair amount of money to relocate there.

Wake read the actual orders to the ships' captains themselves, as copied by the squadron's clerks.

Specific Orders and Requirements:

Ship commanders will go to the reported locations of former Confederate rebels who have apparently set up settlements and plantations at the following places: Puerto Garcia in Quintana Roo, Mexico; Bahia de Lafitte in Jardinas, Cuba; Anasco in Puerto Rico; near Porto Bello in Darien; and Black River in British Honduras.

The commander will personally ascertain the physical facts of said settlement assigned to him, including the description of their population and whether they have slaves from their former estates or newly acquired slaves; the economic nature and future viability of their colony; the military nature and potential of the settlement; the relationship with local and national authorities there; the official category of citizenship these people claim; their attitude toward the United States; and the future plans of the former rebel people living there.

Cooperation with such national government authorities as may be found in those areas visited will be expected, and confrontations that would harm the image of the United States with said authorities avoided. Diplomacy as is the norm of foreign station naval officers shall be followed.

This shall all be done with the utmost expediency, and the support of all attending United States organizations and offices, both naval and civil, including consular officials by order of the Secretary of State, consistent with standard naval practices.

The assignment shall culminate in the submission of a comprehensive report from the individual ship's commander, documenting the aforementioned indicators of the former rebels' current status. The report shall, upon completion no more than two days after arrival at Key West naval station, be immediately transported to the Department of the Navy and the sole and confidential attention of the undersigned person.

Signed/ R. S. Stanwell
Senior Deputy to and for the
Assistant Secretary of the Navy
Gustavius Fox

Staring at the paper in front of him, Wake remembered the afternoon in Key West he drew the assignment to go to Puerto Rico. He knew nothing of the island of Puerto Rico, except that it was one of the oldest colonies of the Spanish Empire in the Caribbean, and that it was a very long way from Key West—and against the trade winds at that.

Wake spent the next three days asking officers at Key West if they knew anything about Puerto Rico, the route there, or a place called Anasco. No one knew anything helpful. On the third day he was referred to a Cuban merchant in the town, who in turn knew of a schooner captain from Santo Domingo who happened to be in Key West at that moment picking up cargo. The Cuban said the schooner captain sailed to Puerto Rico often and would know the way and the coasts.

Wake was rowed out to the decrepit craft and went aboard with the only Spanish speaking man in his crew, Rogelio Aragón, a quiet Spaniard of middle age who had joined the U.S. Navy at the Canary Islands to gain citizenship at the beginning of the war. Like de Alba, who had been released from the navy in October, Aragón was unused to being around officers, especially the captain. The sailor was obviously uncomfortable when his captain informed him of his new duty as translator, but nodded his head and said he would do his best.

Upon hailing the vessel and receiving no reply, Wake and Aragón boarded her and stood on the deck by the main mast. The smell and sound of goats came from the foredeck where five sullen-looking men sat ignoring them, engrossed in a card game and passing around a jug. Finally, after Aragón yelled down the after hatch for the captain repeatedly, an evil-looking gaunt man with a wrinkled face blackened by beard and grime emerged from the after deck hatch saying that he was the ship's mate. When asked about the location of his captain he pointed down the hatchway, shrugged with a rueful look, and led the way below.

They found the ancient captain drunk and unconscious on the deck of his filthy cabin. The mate offered no explanations and left Wake standing there with Aragón as the leathery old man snored and gasped, fumes of rum mingling in a fetid concoction with the smell of a body unwashed for some time. Wake's anger with the situation was building rapidly and he called out for Lawson, waiting in the launch, to send aboard some hands to take the comatose figure aboard the *Hunt* and get him conscious and talking. To Wake's surprise, no one in the schooner's crew said a word or showed any reaction as the bluejackets dragged their captain along the deck and down into the boat alongside. Wake got the impression they had seen it happen before.

It took four hours for Rork, Lawson, and Aragón to get him semi-lucid. They finally got the old man, who acknowledged to Aragón that everyone called him Tonto, or "fool" in Spanish, to the point where he could answer questions relating to their mission. Tonto admitted that he did know the way, and the coasts of Puerto Rico. As he sobered and understood that he had naval men asking him for advice, his voice rose, expounding with great emotion on the hazards of the voyage. With great flourish Tonto told of the hazards of a voyage to Puerto Rico. He described in ominous detail places to be avoided, like the capes of Haiti and Santo Domingo where the winds would sweep around the points of land at the same time they would descend from the mountains—catching a ship in a mortal attack from two sides.

The most important information gleaned from the old man was that he did know of a place called Anasco. It was on a desolate shore along the western side of Puerto Rico, up the coast from a town called Mayaguez. Tonto had not been to Anasco, but had heard of it, and knew where it should be. There was a river by the same name that went far inland, used to bring out sugar cane and rum in small boats to ships anchored off the coast. Tonto laughed as he remembered this last information because he had drunk some of that very rum while in Mayaguez a year ago and thought it was some of the worst he had ever had. The laugh turned into a gasping, hacking cough and Rork had Aragón take the old man away.

That was all Wake would learn in preparation for his mission, and the next day the *Hunt* steamed away from Key West, bound to the southeast and the Great Antilles Islands of the Spanish Empire.

Sitting in his cabin two weeks later, reading the orders again and remembering the primary source of information on where he was heading, Wake was angered by the fact that it was coming from a man who was unable to even stand without assistance, a man commonly called "fool." It sounded like some theatrical satire of a government idea, but unfortunately it was very real, and he, Lieutenant Peter Wake, U.S.N., was the man responsible for the mission's success or failure. Returning to the chart, a frayed and faded thirty-year-old Spanish publication obtained at their last port of Santo Domingo, he perused the unnamed bay that extended in a broad curve to the north of Mayaguez, noted on the chart as a small village. That bay would be where they would start their search for the river, the village of Anasco, and their former enemies. If the weather held, they would be at the bay in two days.

"Deck there! Land on the eastern horizon. All across the horizon!"

Wake heard the yell and opened his eyes. The sun hadn't risen yet, but there was a dim glow in the sky that filtered down into the cabin, making objects faintly visible. Dirkus knocked on the door and entered, advising that the officer of the watch, Hostetler, had told him to present his respects and tell the captain that Puerto Rico was off the bow, about twelve miles ahead.

"Deck there! Land astern! Large island," came a faint call from aloft.

Wake sat up when he heard that report. There were only two large islands off the coast, Mona and Desecheo. Mona was a hundred miles away. Desecheo was around twenty miles off Punta Higuero. They were far closer inshore than anticipated and might be standing into shoal water, Wake thought. He dressed quickly and went forward to the wheelhouse, ignoring for the moment the breakfast being laid out by his steward. As he entered he found Rork, Hostetler, and Jones staring at the island astern. Rork had a telescope to his eye.

"An eerie sight that, Mr. Hostetler. For all the world it looks to be the moon itself! 'Tis the surface an' roundness o' the moon, exactly like it's settin' into the sea."

Hostetler, looking through his glass, slowly shook his head. "I'll be damned if you ain't right, Rork. It does look like the moon setting. I've never seen an island that looks like that. We must've passed it in the dark. Never saw it." A low whistle exhaled from him. "Lucky we didn't fetch up on it."

Wake saw what they were describing and had to agree—behind them to the west, the island of Desecheo was a huge, perfectly rounded rocky mound, devoid of much foliage, that was reflecting some of the new light coming from the east. It really did look like a moonset.

Wake's appearance finally noticed, three telescopes were thrust his way with apologies. Wake took Jones's and examined the island, finding no sign of habitation among the rocky shore and hills, then swung it around to the east along the coast of Puerto Rico, which loomed massively like a giant wall covering the entire horizon.

The shore was still in the dark shadows and no detail could be seen, except for a beach that ran for miles, faintly visible in the gloom. Wake called for the lead to be sounded. The chart indicated deep water close in, but he wanted to be sure. The bosun's mate reported no bottom with the deep-sea lead, meaning they had at least six hundred feet.

That information generated several opinions as to their location and best course. The excitement of a landfall, especially one that appeared to be precisely where they had predicted, even if a little earlier than planned, had excited the men in the wheelhouse and the conversation became animated with Hostetler's Pennsylvania accent competing with Rork's brogue and Jones's southern drawl. Action was coming soon, and every man knew that before the day was out they would see some sights new to them all. A lull in the noise level took his attention from the approaching shoreline and Wake saw that his officers were looking for orders. He pointed toward the coast.

"Mr. Hostetler. Kindly keep the lead going. Maintain this course and steer for the center of that beach. Try to identify any headlands that become visible and notify me when we sound bottom at six hundred feet. Dirkus is waiting for me and I'll be having breakfast, gentlemen."

Wake got the reaction he wanted when a set of grins spread across the others' faces. Hostetler chuckled with his reply as Wake got to the wheelhouse door.

"Aye, aye, sir. And you're quite right about breakfast, Captain. It wouldn't do to keep ol' Dirkus waiting. You know how he gets!"

As Wake exited the wheelhouse and got to the main deck he heard Jones say to Rork, "He's a calm one, ain't he? A two-hundred-mile dead-on landfall from Santo Domingo on an unknown coast with a mystery mission to do, and he's having breakfast like he's just crossed the harbor to the squadron dock!"

Wake was anything but calm on the inside. The voyage here was the easy part. Now came the difficult phase. The rest of the day should prove interesting, he predicted as he entered his cabin. Wake was greeted with a grandiose salute by Dirkus, who presented him with a full breakfast laid out on his chart table. The steward, pride evident in stature and voice, held the chair out as Wake sat down.

"Congratulations, Captain, on your navigation and landfall. I thought today would be a good day for a decent breakfast for you. I hope you enjoy it, sir."

"Dirkus, you must be clairvoyant. Today is the perfect day

for a decent breakfast, thank you. It looks excellent."

"Very good, sir. I'll be outside if you need anything," said the steward as he departed, leaving Wake alone to contemplate the wonderful assortment of eggs, bacon, fruit, and toasted bread before him. He started in on the eggs and drove all thoughts of former Confederates from his mind. Those problems would be paramount soon enough, but there wasn't anything else to be done at the moment, so he concentrated on eating Dirkus's feast, and savoring the tastes.

They found the bottom two hours later. Soon they had to switch from the deep-sea lead to the regular one, the bottom rose at such a steep angle. The sun was now high enough in the sky to burn away the shadows and show the details of the long undulating sandy shoreline and the layers of hills that rolled behind it. Still further inland, forming an immense dramatic backdrop, was a mountain range. It started at a headland on their left and went far back into the interior of the island, curving around until it met the sea again as a series of hills, many miles to the south.

Hostetler and Rork established, by triangulation of the headland and Isla Desecheo, that the prominent point on their port bow was Punta Higuero, and thus knew where precisely they were on the western coast of Puerto Rico. Mayaguez was somewhere to the south, about twelve miles. The *Hunt* closed to within a mile of the shoreline, in one hundred feet of water, then turned southerly and slowly steamed along the coast, closing in toward the beach as she went past the jungle. Wake had never seen anyplace like it in his life.

From time to time they could see a few thatched huts and small boats on the beach, but generally the coast looked deserted of any notable structures. The water was a clear dark blue changing to a lighter shade as they got into shallower water, much like crossing the over the deep reefs in the Florida Keys. The sand beach was not white like a Florida beach, but a rich brown color. It was about a hundred feet wide for most of its length over several miles, backed by groves of waving coconut palms and huge shade trees.

Behind that initial façade of delicate greenery came a thick lush jungle that covered everything, everywhere one looked. The sheer strength and depth of the colors made the Florida coastline look faded and weak by comparison. Four or five hues of green jumbled together in a mosaic puzzle that was interspersed with the bright reds and pinks and yellows of flowers. It was the flowers that struck Wake the most. Many of the trees had huge royal red flowers covering them, making a stunning carpet of flamboyant color up and down the slopes. Out of the whole palette of light blue sea, light brown sand, rich green jungle, and multi-colored flowers, it was those red-flowered trees that captured the eye.

With the wind still coming generally from the southeast and off the land, the smells of those flowers and trees and dark earth, of the soil itself, floated out to the men of the *Hunt*. They stood on deck and drank in huge draughts of the rich sweet air, full of exotic scents, as they gazed shoreward at the magnificent sights. Occasionally, they would catch the smoky smell of someone ashore roasting a meal on a cooking fire, which made Wake think of Linda as he remembered a similar aroma from Useppa Island.

Once, when passing through cooking smoke, they heard the distant sound of drums and strange stringed instruments. The music had strong percussion, as much African as Latin, and the sound reinforced Wake's other senses in telling him he had entered an exotic place, where he was the intruder and at a disadvantage for it. He caught a glimpse of Lawson standing aft on the main deck, leaning against a twelve-pounder and looking intently at the lush colors passing by ashore. Wake wondered what the black man was thinking when he heard those drums. Lawson was from snowy New England like his captain, but those drums, Wake pondered, did they send a different message to him? What do they mean for him, especially after he had just spent several months at Key West helping the men the *Hunt* had freed. Lawson showed no apparent emotion and just stood peering, as if he could decipher the drums and their meaning but would keep it to himself.

It certainly was a strange and beautiful land they were approaching, Wake thought, as he admitted to himself that he was overwhelmed by the beauty and mystery of it all. He thought Puerto Rico must have been what the Garden of Eden looked like.

The lookout intruded into his reverie and Wake cocked an ear aloft to hear over the bow wave and the stack's exhaust.

"Deck there! Brown water dead ahead. About two miles, I'd reckon. All over in front of us."

Wake gave the order to stop the engine and they slowed down, gliding forward while all hands on the foredeck searched the water ahead for shoals. Hostetler anticipated Wake's next order and offered that the leadsman had just reported showing forty feet. A check of the chart showed that the slight bulge in the shoreline half a mile opposite them was called Punta Cadena, and therefore that Mayaguez, as yet unseen, must lay six or seven miles to the south, around a slight protrusion of the land.

Wake felt they had to be close to the river called Anasco, but no mouth could be seen. They would have to go closer to shore, entering that brown water. He remembered that Tonto had said the tidal rise and fall was a meter, more or less, and remembered further that the Spanish imperial meter was a little more than an English yard. *Hunt* drew six feet, so Wake resolved to stay in at least ten feet of water. But Tonto had said nothing of a shoal this far offshore, or of brown water. The lookout suddenly interrupted his thoughts again, with even more interesting information.

"Deck there! Boat putting out from shore, abaft the beam."

All eyes went toward the beach. Wake focused the glass and saw a small boat with lugger rig being launched by a dozen men on the beach. There were drag marks from back in the shadows, under the trees, and he wondered how many other boats and huts were there of which they were not aware. The men with the boat looked like fishermen, and certainly not like any type of government officials. That gave Wake an idea.

"Deck there! He's coming out under sail and oar. Headin' right for us."

Hostetler abruptly snapped his glass closed and looked over at Wake. "Orders, sir?"

Wake smiled at his executive officer's barely restrained enthusiasm. Hostetler had asked his question as if he expected the answer to include clearing for action and preparing for battle. Wake decided to set the appropriate tone for the forthcoming expedition. They were not at war with anyone anymore and were merely visiting another sovereign nation's colony in order to greet some former countrymen. Appearances were everything in the Caribbean, and he was determined to present the least bellicose one he could. The idea in his mind was starting to fill out and have some interesting possibilities.

"Orders, Mr. Hostetler? Yes, I do have orders for you. When they get here, get Aragón to invite them to my cabin for refreshments. In the meantime, why don't we save them some effort and anchor here. Short scope. Do not, I repeat do not, clear for action. Try to appear as *amiable* as you can. But do keep a sharp lookout. In fact, double the lookouts. Let me know of any developments or sightings. I'll be in my cabin awaiting our visitors."

"Amiable . . . aye, aye, sir"

"And pass the word for my steward to lay out on the wardroom table the best claret, pudding, and tinned delicacies he can muster up. Ah, yes, and some whiskey, if we can locate it somewhere," Wake cocked an eyebrow, for whiskey was illegal in the navy now, "and I want all that done straight away."

Hostetler acknowledged the order, but looked confused.

"Mr. Hostetler, think on it. They already have rum and fruit and fresh meat. They won't be impressed by those. So let's try to give them something they don't have," Wake grinned as his number two started to understand, "so that they can give us something we don't have. Like the location of the Confederates' settlement, for instance."

"Aye, aye, sir. Understood. And quite clever, Captain. I'm glad you're on *our* side!"

"There are no sides anymore, Mr. Hostetler. We're at peace

with everyone and merely checking on the well-being of our former countrymen. . . ." Wake said with a humorous tone as he walked out of the wheelhouse.

Hostetler turned to Rork as Wake departed. "The man is always one step ahead of the rest of us, Rork. He must be a fierce sporting man."

"Well, Mr. Hostetler, sporting games I don't know much of, but Captain Peter Wake is a subject I know well. I don't think he'd like sporting, sir. He's not much of one for a game. His best success is when he's up against another man an' his mind, an' the odds're heavy. Those sporting contests are far too tame for such as he, sir."

Hostetler eyed Rork closely, then nodded. "You've been through a lot together, Sean Rork, haven't you? He's lucky to have you with him."

Rork knuckled his brow in a salute to the executive officer of the ship. "Why 'tis I that're lucky to have he as a captain, sir, no doubts on that. Now, by your leave sir, I'll pass the word for Dirkus to get that Yankee feast underway and the deck watch to be ready to bring our esteemed guests aboard."

"Certainly, Rork. I have a feeling this will be a very interesting day."

Aragón was in a clean uniform and appearing to be far more important than a seaman as he translated Wake's greeting to the three men standing in the wardroom. Roberto Gómez and his two sons were fishermen living with their large extended family on a hill behind the beach. Dressed in patched and faded clothing, it was obvious they were barely making ends meet, but still they had a dignity that Wake admired. He greeted them as fellow men of the sea and bade them to sit and relax and enjoy the hospitality of his humble ship.

Gómez's bony weathered hand clasped the wine chalice—there were only two aboard—as his eyes, wrinkled from years of squinting into the sun, calmly took in his surroundings. Only after the food was brought out and his sons, grown men themselves, had started in on the meal, did Gómez open his veil of wariness. Aragón translated while sitting at the table and eating. He had never been in the wardroom, much less sat at the officers' table and partaken of their considerably better provisions. Gómez bent forward and looked into Wake's eyes between bites of tinned ham.

"Thank you, Captain. We did not expect this. We came out to see if you wanted some fish. Your hospitality is appreciated, sir."

"It is our honor, Captain Gómez. We would very much like some fish and will buy what is in your boat alongside. Have you ever met a Yankee warship, sir?"

"No, I've never been on any warship. The Spanish would never let us come aboard, and they never pay for fish." Gómez's tone darkened. "They take it out of my boat as 'the queen's tax,' as they call it. I don't think the queen gets to eat that fish they take."

Wake found that interesting, but didn't want to dwell on the excesses of the imperial navy. It was time to steer the conversation toward the Confederates.

"Yes, well, ah, we believe in paying for fish. A fair price now, of course."

Gómez raised his brown hands in a gesture of agreement, his face crinkling into a huge smile. "But of course, Captain. A very fair price, especially after hospitality such as this."

"And you have met no other English-speaking sailors recently?" The term American or *yanqui* might not apply to former Confederates, Wake thought suddenly.

The fisherman shook his head no and Wake went on.

"I am surprised, Captain Gómez. I thought you would have met our former countrymen who live here."

Gómez's grin disappeared and he leaned back in his chair. "You said recently, Captain. Yes, there were some *confederados* here, but that was many months ago in the last year. They said not to tell anyone," he locked eyes with Wake, "especially

English-speaking men. They were polite and paid gold for the fish. Spanish gold coins. Are you still their enemy?"

Wake sought to dispel Gómez's concern as he might alert the Confederates, making them disappear into the countryside.

"No. No, all that is over. We merely are seeing to their well being. Our country is reunited and we have been sent to see if they are doing well. Perhaps they might wish to return. It is a mission of good will."

"Good will to an enemy, Captain? I never heard of that. They are doing well, I think, but we do not see them often anymore."

"Do they live close by here?"

"Oh no. They live up the river in the hills. They had a camp here for a couple of weeks. Then they went up the river and started a farm there. A big farm. They sent cane down in boats to the coast a while ago and put it on ships from Mayaguez."

"How many are there?"

"I do not know, Captain. Many dozen. Women and children too. They tried some fishing but had no skill, so they went up to the hills."

"The Anasco River? Is it close by here?"

"Yes, they live up that river, Captain. It has a mouth a kilometer along the beach. Follow the brown water that comes out of it."

Wake tried not to show too much interest, but there was another question in his mind. "Captain Gómez, who did they buy the land from?"

Gómez slowly shook his head and took a drink of whiskey. "From the only person who owns land here. Don Fidel León of San Germán, the Viceroy's *comandante* of the region. He owns all of the land. He does not sell it—he allows people to farm it or fish from it for a price, just as I do. Those *confederados* would not be here if Don León did not approve. You will not be here long, Captain, if Don León does not approve, and I do not think he will approve of *yanquis* coming into his area to check on his *confederados.*"

There it was. What Wake had been concerned about—the official reaction to his visit. This would be delicate.

"We mean no harm to anyone, Captain Gómez, and there is no reason for Don León to disapprove of our visit. This is a good-will visit."

Pudding spat from his mouth as Gómez harrumphed and slapped the table when Aragón translated. "Don León does not know good will, Captain Wake. He will distrust you. Be careful."

"Thank you for your advice, Captain Gómez. A last imposition, if I may. How far up that river is the *confederado* settlement?"

"Two or three very long days rowing against the current. They will already know you are here. You may be very unwelcome there, Captain. They may not have as much good will as you have."

"Yes, well, Captain Gómez, we and the *confederados* are like brothers who have had a disagreement and now should regain our fraternal amity. I can only try."

Gómez rose, signaling his sons that it was time to depart. His hand went forward to Wake's and he stood close. The man was old enough to be his father, and in fact reminded him a bit of the elder Wake, with the same leathery skin, strong grip, and direct manner.

"Captain Wake, I don't think that brothers who have tried to kill each can have that kind of amity again. Blood lost is a barrier no good will can bridge. Good luck to you until we meet again."

The two ships' boats rode the flood tide through the narrow opening of the river that snaked its way through the broad beach to the sea. Wake, Rork, and Aragón were in Lawson's launch in the lead, followed by Curtis in the small cutter. Hostetler had

asked to go but Wake said no, he wanted him aboard the steamer to notify the consulate in San Juan if things should go wrong.
Even Ginaldi volunteered, desperate for some activity other than
his engine room, but had been declined. He was far too valuable
to the ship. Wake's plan was to send word down the river with
Curtis of what they found, then descend themselves after delving
into the settlement in detail. So far, there had been no problems,
but Wake knew they had only begun.

The tide was still strong enough to get them past the second
curve inland of the beach with only the coxswain steering, but
then they had to man the oars. Wake kept the pace slow, they had
a long way to go and there was no hurry. After all, he told Rork,
it wasn't war, just a friendly visit. The bosun grunted with raised
eyebrows.

They were very lightly armed, merely sidearms—pistols for
the petty officers and Wake, cutlasses for a few of the men. They
brought provisions for themselves and some offerings he thought
the ex-Rebels might appreciate: newspapers from Key West and
New York, *Harper's Magazine* and *Frank Leslie's Illustrated,* some
tinned meat, and what was left of the whiskey after Gómez had
sampled it.

The land along the banks of the river was flat at the coast,
with palms trees jutting out of a thick jungle matting of vines and
ferns and broad-leafed plants. A loud drone of insects was the
background for raucous noise from colorful birds of all sizes flying suddenly from their perches in the trees, startled by the sailors
as they pulled their way up the river. The jungle here was thicker
and more exotic than anything Wake had seen in Florida.

No sign of people could be seen, but Wake had the strange
feeling of being watched. They pulled for two hours then nosed
the boats into the bank and rested for a while. It was hot and
humid, for there was no air moving on the narrow green-walled
river, the trees cutting off visibility too. They could only see across
the fifty feet of water to the other shore, and as far forward and
aft as the next bend, usually no more than five hundred feet. But

they could hear things moving around them, usually small and sometimes heavy. Occasionally a brown- or black-colored creature dashed quickly across a rare shaft of sunlight that came through the trees, as if the animal knew how dangerous it was to be seen in that environment and wanted to minimize its exposure. The claustrophobic encroachment of the jungle, combined with the unknown attitude of the locals, made them all very nervous.

It was high noon by Wake's pocketwatch when they stopped again. The men were exhausted and needed far more than a fifteen-minute rest on the thwarts of the boats. Curtis took two men ashore and cut out an area with their cutlasses where the sailors could stretch and lie on the ground. As the others collapsed sweat-soaked in the muddy red dirt, Rork climbed one of the trees with the lush red flowers to have a look around. His face was grim as he descended and took Wake aside.

"Captain, I can still see the *Hunt* anchored off the beach. We've been goin' in circles. We're only two miles inland, at the most."

Wake had been keeping note of their progress with the small boat compass and knew their course had twisted and turned.

"No, not circles, Rork, but enough twists to make me wonder how far we had actually gone. How far off are the hills?"

"Maybe three more miles, but who knows how far on this river, which ain't really much of a river, sir."

They pushed off an hour later, right after one of the sailors let out a curse and flailed away at a four-foot-long mottled yellow snake that had curled up beside him on the ground. No one was in the mood to stay any longer following that, and they continued upriver, the flood current no longer helping them. The rhythmic dip and pull of the oars accompanied Lawson's incessant cadence of "stroke . . . stroke . . . stroke." It was just as he said the word that a crack rang out up the river. It was somewhat like a gunshot, but not deep like one. They looked for smoke or splash but saw neither, and kept rowing.

Then they heard two more pops crack in rapid succession further up the river. Rork stood in the bow, one ear cupped. "Signalin' sir. Some sort o' word that we're comin' up the river."

"Yes, well, that is to be expected, Rork."

They saw a crocodile on the next bend, sunning itself on a log jutting out from tall marsh grass into the water. It was longer and thinner than the alligators they had seen so often in Florida, and somehow seemed more sinister. To Wake, Puerto Rico was appearing far more sinister the further upriver they went. They had penetrated that coastal façade of beauty and entered a dark and increasingly malignant world. Though it had only been that morning, it felt as if it had been days since they had felt the open air of the sea. He wondered what the Confederates thought of their new world.

The sun's descent in the late afternoon lengthened the shadows enough to plunge the jungle into an even darker gloom. Not relishing being enmeshed in that tangle during the coming night, Wake was considering anchoring out in mid-stream when they heard another crack, this time very close to them from ahead. It was echoed by others upriver.

They stopped rowing and drifted into the left bank, sitting in their boats with hands gripping their revolvers and cutlasses, looking around but seeing nothing but the living green tentacles of the wilderness. Rork looked at Wake and slightly tilted his head to the opposite bank, almost whispering.

"Two men watching us, sir. I do believe one of the little buggers has a musket. I would not advise any sudden movement, lads."

Wake was facing Rork but could see the men peripherally. "Yes, Rork, I see them. Aragón, call out to them, very politely, and tell them we are visiting here and would like to impose upon their hospitality for information."

Aragón stood reluctantly and spoke to the men, who did not move or show any gestures of greeting as they replied. After several exchanges of words across the river Aragón reported.

"They are militia, sir. On patrol for bandits and they want to know who we are and why we are here. I haven't told them yet, Captain."

"Tell them we are Americans who come peaceably and are going over to their side of the river to talk to them."

The boats slowly made their way across the sluggish current as Aragón explained Wake's intent to the men in the trees. He got no answer. They remained standing there, the one with the musket keeping it pointed down toward the ground as the launch slid into the shadows of the overhanging limbs. As the bow touched the bank the sailors heard four loud double clicks from other unseen muskets in the gloom. The two barefoot young militia, clad in brown disheveled tunics over ripped and patched trousers, stood silently, waiting with a dispassionate manner that told Wake the actual man in charge was somewhere in the darkness.

"I want to speak with your commander."

Aragón shrugged at his captain when he got no reply from the militiamen.

"Repeat it, Aragón," said Wake as he walked along the thwarts to the bow, then leaped onto the bank in front of the men. They did not move or say a word. Aragón's voice started to break.

"Captain, this is not good, sir. These men are peasants. Something is wrong here, Captain, and I think we should leave." Aragón talked louder as he continued. "Leave now. I don't like this place, Captain."

Rork put a hand on the sailor's shoulder. "Stand easy there, Aragón. The captain decides those things, lad. You just translate—"

"No need for that any further, Captain Wake."

The startled Americans turned to the sound of Spanish-accented English coming from the darkness twenty feet away in the jungle. A short solid man in the green uniform of Spanish imperial infantry stepped into the half-light and tilted his plume-hatted head forward.

"I am Captain Julio Agusto Velásquez, of Her Most Catholic Majesty's Faithful Guard Regiment of Foot of Santa Maria de las Montañas, and am responsible for the peace and tranquility in the Anasco region of the Department of San Germán, in the Viceroyalty of Puerto Rico. I have enough English to be sufficient for you to understand, I presume?"

Wake, taken aback by Velásquez's use of his name, tried to remain calm and extended his hand. It was ignored.

"It is an honor to meet you, Captain. I am Captain Peter Wake, commanding officer of the United States Naval steamer *Hunt,* anchored off your island. Thank you for your welcome, and your English is very good, sir."

"My English must be not that good, Captain Wake, for I did *not* welcome you. I am here to determine why you are here. And, of course, I already know your name and other things about you."

Obviously Gómez had passed information along to the authorities. Wake could hardly blame him. Velásquez was barely concealing his hostility, but Wake sought again to ease the situation.

"We have merely come to visit our former countrymen. Our country is trying to rebuild our unity, and in that spirit we are seeing if they need any help. We will only be here a few days."

"And who authorized this visit?"

"I am told that the consular officials of both nations know of the visit. We are visiting all of our former countrymen throughout the Caribbean."

"I know of no such authorization. It must come from Don Fidel or the Viceroy himself."

Wake gauged the man. He had met many like him in his life, petty bureaucrats who lorded their power over small areas, even more so when they were isolated. He looked at Velásquez and imagined what he would be like as a colonel. Wake decided it was time to reverse roles in this conversation and get things moving in the right direction.

"The authorization came from the president of the United States of America, Andrew Johnson, who communicates not with your Don Fidel, or even the Viceroy in San Juan, but personally with Queen Isabella in Madrid herself. I have noted your name and your attitude, and your shocking lack of the hospitality for which the officers of the imperial forces of Her Most Catholic Majesty are justly famous, and will report it through my commander to the president upon my return.

"Now, Captain Velásquez, will you give me the basic assistance which I seek—or should I add another item to the list of your insults to the flag of the United States?"

Wake saw that Velásquez was cowed a bit, more by his tone than the words. The Spanish officer appeared uncertain, but kept the imperious tone in his reply.

"Very well, I will allow you to continue on your journey while I consult with my superiors. What information do you seek?"

"How far to the settlement of the former Confederates?"

"Another day, at least," Velásquez looked disdainfully at the sailors resting on their oars, "if your men are strong enough. The current gets stronger the farther upriver you go."

"Have you been to their settlement?"

"Of course."

"Are they doing well?"

"Yes."

"Who is their leader?"

"I cannot remember his name."

"Are there any villages to stop at and rest between here and the Confederates?"

"No."

"Are there any shoals or rapids ahead of us?"

Velásquez did not understand those words and Aragón translated, engaging in a long, heated conversation, then explained to Wake.

"Captain, he says there are some shallow places and one rocky spot."

"Aragón, he was doing too much talking for just that. What else did he say?"

Aragón cast his eyes downward as he answered, while Velásquez gazed without reaction at the Americans during the translation. "He asked me why a man with the proud name of a Spanish kingdom would be working like a dog for the *yanquis*, sir. He asked me where my pride as a man was."

That got the attention of all the other sailors, who now were watching Velásquez with unveiled anger. Wake's eyes met those of the Spanish officer.

"And your reply to Captain Velásquez was what?"

"I told him that I am a free American now, proud of my Spanish heritage but prouder of my American freedom. I never had personal freedom in Spain."

"And his reply to that?"

"He didn't say anything, Captain."

Wake knew he had to remain calm, but it was a struggle as he spoke to Velásquez. "Our talk is done now. Your insult to an American sailor is also duly noted. Your conduct will be addressed in the future by officials far above your minor position. Goodbye."

Velásquez said something under his breath in Spanish and turned away as Wake stepped back into the launch, touching Aragón's shoulder.

"Very well done, Aragón. Spoken like a true American." The sailors responded with loud shouts of "huzzah" and slaps on the back of the sailor, who grinned at his fame.

A moment later they were pulling their oars again, as another crack sounded from close by and was repeated several times up the river ahead of them.

"Confound it all, but I cannot fathom what that sound comes from, Captain," Rork muttered, shaking his head.

"I presume we'll figure it out as we go, Rork."

The shadows covered the jungle in an ominous gloom. On the river it was already evening, but the mountains in the distance, just visible now, were still bathed in the glow of the sun. There would be no glorious sunset display here, Wake thought, as he had the exhausted sailors stop pulling and anchor the launch in mid-stream, the other boat lashed alongside.

He ordered that all hands should eat and drink now, then rest, with only two armed men on a watch to maximize the recuperation of those off-watch. No light was to be shown and gauze mosquito netting was to be slung over oars set up as ridgepoles.

As the light faded from the mountains to the east, the faint zephyr of wind that had touched the treetops lay down and everything became still. The drone of insects now became the predominant sound, interspersed with an occasional splash in the water or a rustling bush on the bank. The dark mass of vegetation around them became an ill-defined mosaic of shadowy little movements. It was all so mysterious that the men, even as bone-tired as they were from pulling against the current, couldn't sleep at first. After a few hours of quiet speculation about what the morrow might bring, they dropped off to sleep on their folded arms or a hard wooden thwart, one by one, until only the men on watch remained alert.

"*Halt!* Who goes there?"

The cry from the bow jarred Wake from his unnatural position of slumber on the stern seat. As his eyes adjusted to the darkness he heard Rork murmur, "Where away, lad?" and saw the lookout point ahead.

"Small boat coming down river, sir."

Wake touched Aragón's shoulder and nodded. The seaman shouted in Spanish to the boat approaching quickly with the current. The reply came softly, barely audible above the insects.

Aragón whispered to his captain. "He says he's a friend, and must talk with Captain Wake."

"Tell them to come alongside."

Seconds later several wary sailors, with revolvers leveled, stared uneasily at three young peasants in a small canoe that held on to the side of the launch. The one in the stern was, by his demeanor and his speech, the leader, and did the talking to Aragón. Wake listened to the translation.

"He says he is Octavio Soto, one of the leaders of the Patriots of Puerto Rico and follower of Doctor Ramón Emeterio Betances, the future president of a free Republic of Puerto Rico."

"What in the world does all that mean, Aragón?"

"Captain, I think he is a revolutionary against the Spanish. A rebel, sir."

"Damn, I don't need this. What does he want?"

More Spanish was exchanged at a rapid rate between Soto and Aragón. Finally, it was explained to Wake.

"Captain, this is a very difficult situation for us. It seems we are in the middle of something very complicated here."

Rork, sitting next to Wake, shook his head. Wake took a deep breath and looked at Aragón. "Get on with it, Aragón."

"Captain, Soto here is part of a movement to bring freedom to the slaves here and liberate the island from Spanish control, or 'occupation' as he calls it. He said this man named Betances is the head of the organization and they have many friends in America who are supporters."

"So what does that have to do with us?"

"He believes that we all share a common belief in the abolition of slavery, sir. Soto and his revolutionaries are against the ex-Confederates starting a settlement here, because they don't want to see slavery expanded to new farms. The Spanish government leaders do, and hope to make money from the Confederates by selling them land, supplies, and slaves. Soto says the Spanish government is very close with the Confederates."

Wake caught a glimpse of Lawson eyeing him as he listened to Aragón's words. It was personal with Lawson, it couldn't help but be personal—like when he had assisted the freed blacks from that slave ship. The petty officer wasn't saying anything, but the intense look in his eyes conveyed his emotion.

Wake returned his attention to Soto's description of the situation in western Puerto Rico. It sounded logical, but he understood the Caribbean enough by this point to know there was always more to an issue than was readily apparent.

"What about this Captain Velásquez?"

"He is a lackey of Don Fidel and hates Puerto Rico. He runs the militia and keeps the people in place. He goes to the Confederate village often. Soto has been fighting him for three years, since Velásquez was assigned here as punishment for an infraction in San Juan. Soto says Velásquez does not want you to go to the Confederates' settlement because you might convince them to go home and the local Spanish would lose money."

"And what does Soto want from us?"

An involved discussion ensued between Aragón and Soto, with the American sailors watching the interaction intently. Wake thought about his mission as he calmly waited. He was only to obtain information, not take any action. Certainly not take any action that would cause the Spanish imperial authorities to complain to Washington. He must avoid any appearance of siding with the revolutionaries.

"He wants us to leave and take the Confederates away with us."

"That won't happen. We can't make them leave."

"I told him that, Captain, and he said that if we won't help the true patriots then we should leave now. He said we would only confuse the matter here, and might get caught up in something that is not our fight. He spoke strongly about that, Captain."

Rork exhaled and rubbed his chin. "I'll be damned if I don't feel a bit like an Orangeman in Derry Cathedral—I do believe *nobody* wants us here, Captain. It's a certain wager our former enemies the Confederates don't want to see us. An' I'd bet Lawson's pay for a year," Rork smiled at the serious black man beside him, "that ol' Captain high-and-mighty Velásquez has already made sure the folks at the Confederate settlement know we're coming to visit."

Wake wasn't in the frame of mind to appreciate Rork's humor, but did agree with his assessment. Wake and his sailors were a thousand miles from the United States, up a jungle river in unknown territory of a foreign empire, heading for the new settlement of a former foe to ascertain their intentions and capabilities. So far, the local government and the local anti-government entities had both expressed their desire that Wake and his men should leave, and the subjects of the search would no doubt echo those sentiments.

The drone of the insects seemed louder when no one was talking. Wake broke the silence as he wiped the sweat from his face. "Very well, tell him that we are only here to check on the well-being of our former countrymen, not to become involved in the internal troubles of his island. We will be gone in a few days, and wish to avoid any confrontation with anyone. Tell him that."

Aragón reported back a moment later. "Soto says he will not stop us from going up the river, but that we should not side with the Spanish occupiers or the Confederates in any way. He says that his men could not be controlled if they thought that the Yankee sailors were assisting the Spanish in spreading slavery. He is implying the Puerto Ricans would attack us if they thought that, sir."

Wake looked at Soto. The man was around thirty years old, with intelligent eyes that belied his ragged clothing. His voice was calm and considered. Even through the difficulty of translation, Wake could tell Soto was trying to establish a good relationship with the Yankees. An idea came into his head.

"Tell Soto that I understand his concerns and that we are neutral politically, but that we share his hatred of slavery. That we just fought a long bloody war and slavery was part of it. To show my respect for him, I will request that he send a man to carry a message from me to our ship at the coast. For payment, of course. Will he honor my request?"

Even in the darkness of the starlight, Wake could see Soto sit up taller in the canoe as Aragón reported that the request was granted. Wake asked for a candle and bent down over a sheet of paper laid out on the thwart, pencil in hand.

Mr. Hostetler,

We are several miles up the river, with another day or so of heavy rowing against the current before we come to the subjects of our journey. So far we have met an imperial army officer named Velásquez, who has displayed ill-concealed contempt for us but let us go on our way. No real information yet about the settlement. No contact yet with the inhabitants either.

We have also come across guerrilla revolutionaries under the command of a man named Soto, who has also let us continue our journey. We are staying neutral in our behavior, though we agree with the Puerto Ricans in our abolitionist beliefs. They appear to be honorable people and may be successful in their bid for independence.

We should be back to the coast in a week or so. If not back in two weeks, go to our consulate in San Juan and report the situation. Should the Spanish Navy visit the Hunt, *remain courteous but firm unless outweighed considerably. Remind them of President Johnson's personal interest in our visit.*

Give the bearer of this message a half-dollar and send a reply under seal.

Peter Wake, Lt. U.S.N.

U.S. Steamer Hunt, Cmdg

Rork read the note as it was being written. When Wake finished his signature, Rork said, "I doubt whether Mr. Hostetler will be the first to read that message, Captain. Me thinks that others will peruse it beforehand," and glanced at the men in the canoe.

"I certainly hope so, Rork. I wrote it with that in mind. These revolutionaries may very well be our guarantors for passage back down the river to the *Hunt.* No harm in them reading some compliments. Might make them friendlier if we do need them, if you follow my drift. . . ."

"I do indeed, Captain, an' a smart drift it is, sir."

Wake leaned across the gunwales of the boats and put the envelope containing the letter in Soto's hand. Nodding at Wake, the Puerto Rican carefully wedged it down into a shirt pocket.

The man is a peasant fighting an empire, but he's got a bit of dignity, thought Wake, as Rork extinguished the candle and spoke suddenly.

"Say there, Aragón! Ask Mr. Soto the Revolutionary what those loud cracks were that we heard all day. Signals of some sort, but from what? An' what the devil are the messages in 'em?"

Soto's reply to Aragón was more expansive than his previous. The sailor explained with a worried tone.

"He says those signals are bamboo logs about a fathom long that are being bent to crack apart. They make a loud sound like a gunshot. The government militia made the signals to alert the whole area to our presence. They send the signal as we go up the river. Everyone knows that foreigners are coming. Two cracks means strangers approaching. Three cracks close together is the signal to attack the strangers. He says it's an old system of signals from the days of the raids by the English navy. Sir, he says he has only heard two cracks so far, not three." Aragón sounded tired as he continued. "Soto wants to go now, Captain."

"Very well. Present him with my compliments and tell him I look forward to the day when all of the Spanish Empire is free of slaves and Puerto Rico is led by Puerto Ricans. Until that day, and while we are here, we are neutral in their conflict."

"He says to say thank you for your good wishes and he will have the letter sent down river and out to the ship, sir."

10
Aldea Por Fin

They started before the sky above them got light. Rowing while the boats were still covered in the netting was trying for the men, but necessary because of the clouds of mosquitoes hovering around them as they pulled their way upriver. Lawson called out the cadence and four hours and two miles later they were into the hill country. The current grew sluggish, and around the bend they found the shoals Velásquez spoke about.

By that time the sun was broiling the air and the men were soaked from the sweat of exertion. Wake watched the men closely, looking for signs of sickness or reluctance but finding none. They disembarked and walked the boats through the shoals, Wake observing that the banks of the river showed high water marks three feet above the current water level. Once they returned the boats to deep water and started to row again they heard two cracks echo from the top of a hill beside the river. Rork, seated in the bow, looked at Wake and raised his eyebrows as he grinned.

"They're sayin' we're on schedule, Captain. Just like a proper riverboat!"

That raised a laugh from the men, who pulled for another hour until they rested at the next set of shoals. This one was rocky, as Velásquez had described, and they had to carefully negotiate the narrow channel. Wake had seen no rain in the days since they had arrived on the coast and started to worry about the water level falling enough to prevent their descent to the coast. He wished he had asked Soto about that. Where did the river come from? A lake or rainwater?

The shadows were lengthening earlier than before since the river was cleaving through steep-sided hills that blocked out the sunlight sooner. Wake was considering whether to anchor for the coming night when he heard a single crack close by, low on the river bank.

A seaman nudged Rork and pointed to the starboard bank a hundred yards up the river. The first man they had seen since Soto's canoe was standing on a log protruding out over the water. The dark-skinned man, dressed in peasant rags, beckoned them over to him.

Rork turned aft toward Wake. "Trap, Captain?"

"Who knows, Rork? Aragón, speak to him and ask what he wants."

A moment later Aragón reported. "He's hard to understand, sir. He speaks Spanish with a lot of Creole words, or maybe part Indian, I think. I did understand him say that Octavio Soto has a message for us."

"Very well. Take us closer, Rork, but stay off the bank."

They backwatered the oars ten feet from the man, who bent down on the log and called out softly to Aragón. The dialogue was short and then the man sauntered back along the log, his toes clasping the narrow limb like a topsailman walking a yard, as he disappeared into the gloom of the jungle.

"He said that Soto says to tell you that the Confederates know who we are. That he doesn't know why, but they asked the Spanish to let us through. Soto also said the letter made it to the ship. The peasant here said the settlement is two bends up the river."

292

Wake looked around at the sky and hills. It was getting too dark to try to make it tonight. He wanted to make his appearance at the settlement peaceably, in the daylight. He ordered the boats to anchor in midstream, which meant thirty feet from either shore, and follow the same precautions as the night before.

All night long they heard sounds from the dark void of jungle on the right-hand bank of the river. There were heavy sounds of movement through the bushes with no attempt at concealment, of low voices so indistinguishable the language could not be discerned. The one sound they feared—a volley of gunshots—was not heard. But the tension was such that sleep would not come to the men in the boats and they lay on the seats and bottom boards in uncomfortable positions, waiting through the interminable hours for dawn to arrive and shed light on their quarry.

They passed the two bends quickly in the morning light finding a renewed energy and, like sailors everywhere, wanting to demonstrate their strength and skill in seamanship in front of strangers. The speed with which they propelled the launch and dinghy up the river would have done them proud in a squadron harbor race.

Rork saw it first. "Well, I'll be. Will ye lookee at that!"

Around the bend was a sight Wake was not prepared for. He had expected a collection of crude hovels, a subsistence-level gathering of refugees like those of some of the pro-Union people he had seen on the Florida coast during the war.

A village of twenty or more neatly arranged log and thatch dwellings covered the easy slope coming up from the right side of the river. Organized into three wide streets that rose from the waterfront to the top of the hill, and crossed by side streets terraced along the face of the hill, the village gave off an air of prosperity and permanence. Two sturdy docks stood out into the current, with an assembly of a dozen men on the longest one.

Wake waved and had the boats steer for the men on the dock. The men were dressed in long-sleeved white shirts, brogans, and broad-brimmed straw hats that shaded their faces. One of them, taller than the others, waved back with a long lazy wave that one would reserve for a returning friend.

The sailors were armed and ready for trouble, but Wake couldn't get past the feeling that he and his men were being *welcomed.* Scanning the shoreline, he saw women standing by the dwellings and waving also. Children could be seen playing together at the top of the hill, their laughter floating down over the scene. Other men were gathered at a large open-sided thatched building from which hammering echoed out into the hills. A ramp led from the building to the river and Wake guessed they were building a boat. It was a most unwarlike vision.

Rork brought the launch alongside the dock with Curtis sliding the cutter up outboard of the launch. A chorus of hellos in Southern accents came down into the launch as hands reached down for the lines. A moment later Wake was climbing up and standing on the dock, shaking hands with several men, Rork just behind him. Each man stepped forward and stated his name and former state as he shook hands with a friendly enthusiasm. Most were from Florida, Georgia, and South Carolina.

Wake was dumbfounded by the unexpectedly kind reception and was struggling to say something appropriate when one man, Wake remembered his introduction as Nelson from Manatee River in Florida, gestured toward the foot of the dock to a man approaching. It was the tall man who had first waved at the boats. Clad in the same attire as the others but carrying an air of quiet authority, he made his way through the parted crowd and stopped in front of Wake. Smiling as he put out his hand to Wake, he took off his straw hat, removing the shadow and illuminating his face in the bright sunlight.

It was Jonathan Saunders.

Wake fell back a step in shocked recognition of his most persistent foe of the war. For two years he had chased and maneuvered and tried to capture or kill Saunders. The same Saunders who had written the note to him about the *Ramer's* men. Wake couldn't speak. It was as if confronting a ghost.

Rork was quicker and took a step forward to stand slightly in front of Wake. Saunders shook hands with Rork and then with Wake.

"Welcome to Aldea Por Fin, gentlemen. I am the mayor of the town, Jonathan Saunders, but then again I think you have already figured that out. All of us here at Por Fin are all very glad to welcome you to our new home. Captain Wake, it is my particular honor to welcome you, sir. I respect you greatly and always have. May I be forgiven for saying something obvious at the outset? The war is over, gentlemen, thank God. We need to look to the future and celebrate our many similarities instead of dwelling upon our disagreements in the past. Captain Wake, please know that you and your men are our honored guests."

Wake recovered from his shock enough to almost laugh at the irony of it all. "Mr. Saunders. I don't know what to say. I didn't know you were here."

"Well, imagine my surprise when we found out that *you* were here, Captain. Almost like the old days. Started to feel a bit apprehensive, then remembered all that is over and long gone. You know . . . you've made quite the impression upon Captain Velásquez. I don't think he likes you."

Wake glanced down into the boat. His wary men were waiting for orders. This was not the way they had anticipated the first meeting would go. Wake told Rork to have them come up on the dock and stand easy. It would be their first exit from the boats in two days.

As the sailors stretched their arms and legs, groaning with the effort, Saunders took Wake and Rork up the hill to his home, showing them a dwelling prepared for them to stay in, and another for the sailors. Saunders said a feast had been prepared for the late afternoon, and that they were all encouraged to rest until then.

"This evening I would like to sit and talk with you—to explain what we are trying to do here. I think I know why you are here, Captain, and I'll help you all I can. Perhaps we can reminisce a bit also. Now please, gentlemen, you and your sailors rest for the day. Here in Latin America the siesta is a standing rule. This afternoon we'll have a pleasant reconciliation."

With that said he left them standing in front of their designated thatched house. Wake looked at Rork, who shrugged his shoulders. They walked into the dwelling and found a wooden floor with simple furniture in the main room. There were two sleeping rooms leading off the main room. Clearly, this was a house for a family, and Wake hoped no one had been displaced by his arrival.

He was stunned by what he had found so far at Aldea Por Fin. Old habits were hard to forgo, and he ordered Rork to post an armed man at the boats and another at the sailors' house to watch over both of their designated dwellings. He also told Rork to have Lawson see about getting their water casks filled with good water, in case of the need for a sudden departure.

There was a slight breeze up on the side of the hill and it was actually comfortable standing in the shade of the flamboyant trees by the front of the dwelling. Wake stretched, feeling aches in his muscles, and glanced back inside at the sleeping room.

"You take the first off-watch, Rork. I'll sit here and complete my report to date, then wake you up in two hours and you can walk around and see what seems to be what around here. Go ahead."

Rork regarded his commander, raised an eyebrow and laughed. "'Tis one hell o' a situation we've found ourselves in, Captain. Who'd a thought it? A wagerin' man would ne'er o' put his quid down on this bet! Wish Durlon were here to see this."

"Beyond strange, Rork. Of course, a man like Saunders wouldn't go back home to the South. There's nothing left there for him. A lot of men like him are heading to Latin America. Not that unusual he'd head here. Rork, we'll work all this out later. Get some sleep now."

"Aye, sir. I fancy some shuteye after that damned river. A bit o' rest will do my weary bones some good. Two hours now, sir. Not a tick more. You need your rest too."

The smell of roasted meat woke him just as Rork was entering the room.

"'Tis quite a feast they've built up out there, Captain."

"See anything sinister?"

"Nary a thing. They all seem to be playing the role o' innocent farmers."

"Any slaves?"

"None in sight. I walked around a bit but saw nothing military or threatening."

It was the most curious thing Wake had ever seen. The former rebels had been transformed from fearsome fighters to farmers in six months? With no slaves to do the hard work?

"Let's go, Rork. I want to see more of this place."

They walked past the sailors' house and down to the boats at the dock. All was well at those places so they ascended the slope. They were breathing hard by the time they reached the top, two hundred feet above the river.

The trees had been cleared and they had an unobstructed view to the west and south. They could barely see the sunlit Caribbean Sea and occasionally a ribbon of the river that had brought them to the settlement. To the east, the green mountains rose ever higher in waves. In the flat land below them to the west stretched a mosaic of field after field of tall greenish-brown stalks. Must be sugar cane, thought Wake, who was uncertain since he had never seen it before.

"We bought a lease for it all from the Spanish," Saunders said as he came up from behind and stood beside them. "The political leader in this region is Don Fidel León. It means 'faithful lion' in Spanish and is appropriate given his position on the island. He runs the district of Saint German on this coast for the Viceroy in San Juan."

"Yes, we met one of his officers." Wake muttered.

"Ah, yes, the foolish Velásquez. I always wondered where he got his medals."

Rork pointed to the fields. "Mr. Saunders, is that sugar cane? How are your crops doing?"

"Please, both of you call me Jonathan. Yes, it's sugar cane, and the crop is doing well. We just took over and expanded the farming here and are continuing to do what they have done here for the last hundred years or so. Not that complicated. A few of our people came from Louisiana and have some experience in that area, so we have the skills. We sell to the factors at Mayaguez. They ship it to San Juan and Havana."

"It appears that you have made quite a start here . . . Jonathan." Wake struggled over the use of Saunders' first name, as if he were a friend, but felt the situation demanded it. "Do the local people support you? I don't see any of them around your village."

"We are independent of them for most of our needs. We only use them to ship the product. And I know what your next question will be. No, we don't have any slaves here at Por Fin," Saunders sighed. "It's obvious that slavery will end everywhere, including the Spanish Empire. Any blacks you see are free and came of their own choice."

"Well, I must say you have built a very well-organized settlement here. I wish you luck, sir," Wake said with a sincerity that surprised him.

"Thank you, Captain. We've worked hard to start over here."

Wake was feeling distinctly uncomfortable with the thought that he was beginning to admire this man whom he had fought against for years. "Please call me Peter. It seems only right in the circumstance."

"An' Jonathan, I'll be called Sean, if that's all right with the captain here."

Wake nodded his assent and Saunders shook both their hands on it.

"A new day, my friends. I must go now and see about some last-minute details. We are inviting all of the new settlers in the area—we prefer that term to refugees or ex-Confederates—to the fiesta tonight and the preparations are rather extensive."

Wake became intrigued. "Other settlers? From elsewhere other than Por Fin?"

Saunders' tone changed slightly.

"Yes, there are others. . . . About five hundred Southerners fled the occupation and came here between June and September last year. Fifty went back right away when they found it to be too different from where they were from. Couldn't deal with the tropical weather. The rest have survived reasonably well. We have three hundred here at Por Fin and the rest are scattered in small farms around a landing a mile upriver called Otra Vez. They lease the land like we do, but have a different outlook. More tied to the old ways of agriculture and such."

"Interesting. So the two communities are separate?"

"For most things, yes. The Spanish allow us a certain degree of autonomy. I am the elected mayor, 'alcalde' in Spanish, and am responsible to Don Fidel for what happens here. The people at Otra Vez come under Captain Velásquez's direct control. They and he share common views on slavery and democracy and such."

"But they are coming here tonight?"

"Yes, partly out of curiosity about you and your mission, and partly because they still like to socialize with us. Especially their ladies. It can get lonely out here for a lady."

"Well, I look forward to meeting them."

"Thank you, Peter. I must go now."

After he had made his departure Wake turned to Rork. "I

thought things were a little too perfect around here. Did you feel it too when Saunders talked about the other settlers?"

"Aye, sir. Like a mother talkin' 'bout her son, the sensitive lad that can draw angels, but neglects to say he's been a thief in the jail for the last five years. There's more to this than Saunders, or ol' Jonathan as we should call 'im, has been sayin' to us."

"Let's look around some more."

Wake's first impression of the feast was how similar it was to the ones he attended at Useppa Island. It was even held in the breeze at the top of the hill. Both were a celebration of refugees honoring men who had come from their former world, a connection with the comfortable past, to forget the unpleasantness of the present. The music and food and drink were good, and after the tension of the last few days he felt relaxed. It was as if the feast was a final confirmation that the war was really over.

He was introduced to the settlers from Otra Vez, but had no time to interact with them at length in the evening. As the sun went down, melancholy songs from the North and South were played and the gathering grew quiet as memories took over. Then the dinner was served and more lively music played, stimulating the appetite and increasing the enthusiasm of the people. Even the breeze stayed steady and kept away the insects from the top of the hill. Dancing after dessert involved everyone, and Wake was honor bound to try his best with several of the ladies. It was a gay evening and he was glad to see that his sailors were behaving themselves, under the watchful eye of Rork, while in the unaccustomed company of women.

Saunders came up to where Wake sat watching a dozen couples twirling in an oval of circles while the small string band gave a rendition of a waltz. He lowered himself into a chair beside him with a moan and showed a small bottle in his hand.

"Nothing like a supper of good food to put a mind at ease, eh, Peter? Want some of the sippin' rum? We've got some very good stuff on this island."

Wake agreed and Saunders poured the rum into small brass cups he pulled out of his pocket. Smoke from the bonfires covered them and moved off in the wind, reminding Wake of the gun smoke from his ship during the war. He knew it was time to get the answers he came for.

"Thank you for your very kind reception here, Jonathan. It is greatly appreciated. I'd like to talk to you about your future here, if you'd agree. I am curious."

"Of course, my friend. I suspect your *government* is very curious, and that is why you really came here in the first place."

It was odd to hear of the United States government spoken of as foreign in its own language, but Wake tried not to show any reaction.

"Yes, they are. It's a natural concern, I think. To wonder what your former enemies are doing? Am I being too blunt?"

"No, not at all. I appreciate your speaking candidly. Always did, as a matter of fact, but we'll talk of that later. Let's handle your questions first."

Wake sipped his rum. "Jonathan, the United States wants to know if your settlement is viable and whether your future will be secure here, or if it is uncertain and you may possibly then think of other future endeavors, ones that might be more injurious to our national interests."

Saunders laughed and slapped his knee. "Peter, if that was candid, I'd pay good money to hear you speak subtly! You sounded just like a barrister there for a moment. Now, your question is simple. You want to know if we here at Por Fin will be a problem to your country? The short answer is no. We have freedom here that we would never have under the occupation, or 'Reconstruction' as you call it, back in the former Confederacy. The war is over for us here. It will never be over back there as long as the Yankee troops swagger down the streets of Southern towns and dictate to the populace their every move. The radical

301

Republicans are making everything worse there. We could not possibly stand that and we moved away. We won't be back, Peter."

"I can understand that. What about the economics of your settlement? Will you be viable?"

"Yes. We grow a commodity that is very much wanted, both for sugar and for rum. We help the situation locally with our productivity and we get along with the Spanish authorities. We cause no problems here."

"What citizenship do you claim?"

Saunders shook his head and took a breath. "Confederate States of America. But we are asking for Spanish citizenship in the future. Don Fidel says there will be no problem. They want us here."

"What if the rebels with Betances and Soto win their freedom and the Spanish are kicked out?"

"Well, they have a long way to go for that, and remember Peter, I am very familiar with just how difficult winning your freedom can be." He raised his drink toward Wake. "Especially with a determined enemy."

Saunders poured another round of rum as Wake replied. "I'm glad it's all over."

"I am too. Though we did have some interesting times, didn't we, Peter?"

Wake had wondered since he met Saunders at the dock when they would get around to this conversation. He'd also wondered how he would handle it when it came. He contemplated the former enemy seated next to him as he tried to put into words what he was feeling.

"Yes. I guess we did, Jonathan. Though I didn't think that way at the time. At the time, I was too afraid of the consequences if I failed, to be intellectual about it all."

"Ah yes, the consequences of making a mistake in war. Quite serious indeed. But even with all of that, you did well for yourself in the navy. Managed to get a regular commission too. Very impressive."

"Still, I did make mistakes. Some of them cost lives directly, others indirectly."

Their eyes met.

"Like failing to stop me?"

"You brought munitions in. That kept the war going. And the dying. And yes, I failed to stop you."

"Peter, it certainly wasn't from lack of trying on your part. I did manage to trick you that first time off Sanibel Island, but after that I barely escaped with my life, several times as I recall. You made it personal."

"It was personal. I believed you that first time. You lied."

"A legitimate *ruse de guerre*, Peter. Better than rotting in Fort Warren in Boston harbor."

"And a lesson learned on my part. I never made that mistake again."

"No, you grew far more dangerous after that. Remember in Havana when you tried to have me killed by the Spanish Navy? A particularly nasty intrigue that was, Peter. It took a lot of money to buy my way out of that dungeon. In fact, it took *all* of my money. "

"For a long time I thought they had killed you." Wake shook his head ruefully. "Then I found out you were in the Bahamas."

"Yes, sir, that was a twist of fate. I never dreamed you'd end up in Man-O-War Cay. Thought I was out of the way there—a perfect hiding place that no one would think to look at. You missed me by only a few days, by the way. And that Royal Navy gunboat damn near had you at Abaco. Very risky decision to go over that reef to escape them." Saunders laughed at the surprise on Wake's face. "Oh, I heard all about it later, over rum in Nassau. They couldn't prove it, of course, and there would've been quite the row if they had, but the Brits were beyond angry about the U.S. Navy doing dastardly deeds in their waters.

"And that time in Mexico, after a *two-hundred-fifty-mile* chase! What were the odds that the one captain in the French Navy who knew me was there. Can you believe he wanted to dicker with me? You were closing in and he wants to haggle—had me over a barrel and he knew it. You know, you probably have no idea how much money it's cost me just to stay alive and away from you, Peter Wake."

"We didn't even know it was you until we saw you board the French ship. Too late then. I decided you weren't worth an international incident."

"I am pleased to know my value was not up to that level."

"Well, Jonathan, I must admit that they did outgun me also. Oh, I almost forgot. Thank you for the letter from Canaveral. The *Ramer*'s petty officer was quite confused, but grateful for your assistance. Actually, I was confused too."

"Ah, yes, that last time, by Canaveral. Well, I thought that after all we had been through, you would appreciate a little congratulatory note." Saunders took a long pull of the rum. "All in all, you should have had me—sheer luck saved me each time."

Wake raised his rum in salute. "Two years and I never got you."

Saunders raised his in reply. "Two years of disrupted and failed operations because of your efforts, Peter."

"For some reason I can't exactly explain, I'm happy you survived and are doing well here, Jonathan. The war *is* over, isn't it?"

"For men like us, it is, Peter. Thank God."

A man's shout, down by the docks, rose above the music and got their attention. Wake immediately looked over to where his men were sitting and saw that none of them were involved in an altercation. He saw Rork stand and peer into the darkness beyond the circle of firelight.

Another shout, closer this time, came up the path from the river. Wake could hear other men talking loudly, snatches of angry words between them. The group was heading to the partygoers at the top of hill.

Saunders stood as one of the Por Fin men strode up to him, nearly out of breath from the effort of the run up the hill.

"It's that gang from Otra Vez. Grodin's leadin' them up here.

Says we shouldn't be partying with the Yankees what killed his daddy and brother. Says it's obscene and no real Southern man would do it. He's mad as a bull an' him an' his men got their guns."

"Thank you, Rumbly. Please go rouse the others, now. Have them meet up here." Saunders turned to Wake as the man ran to summon help. "I am extremely sorry for this, Peter, but I didn't tell you something before. The reason some of our people live over at Otra Vez is that they disagree with our vision for the future. We have disavowed slavery and will trade with Americans in the future. They still have some slaves and still hate the Yankees. Hate is what they live on. They hate the fact we've made peace, and they hate the fact we've had a pleasant evening with the Yankee Navy." Saunders glanced over his shoulder. "Here they come. Go to your men and get them down to their boats. Quickly. You're outnumbered here by Grodin's men."

"I'll stay and help you."

"No. This isn't your fight, Peter. You'll just complicate it. Go. Go now"

Wake nodded and walked toward Rork at the far side of the fiesta area on the hilltop, where he was already assembling the men. Rork reported as Wake approached.

"Group of armed ex-rebels came by boat. Didn't touch our guard by our boats at the dock, but threatened to kill him and us as soon as they took care of their own 'traitors' at the party. The sailors are going for their arms at their dwelling now. They will form up there. This is gettin' a bit ugly, Captain. I've seen this kind o' thing in Eire."

Wake knew exactly what he meant. People had been drinking, emotions over dead family were still high. Men were shouting but no one was listening.

"Rork, listen carefully. Get the men armed and formed up at the dwelling, then move them down to the boats. I want them in the boats and ready to leave instantly. Understood?"

Rork cocked an eyebrow. "Aye, sir. And you?"

"I will be along directly. When I get there I want to be departing fast."

Wake walked away without waiting for the reply. He could see the crowd now, forty men led by a stocky older man, eyes glinting in the light of the bonfires as he screamed invectives at Saunders.

As he approached from the periphery, Wake felt horribly exposed in his blue navy coat outlined with brass buttons that flickered in the light. He felt for his pistol and slowed his pace. Seeing the shadow of a tree, he blended into it and watched.

Grodin stood in front of Saunders, who looked frail compared to his opponent's solid physique. Saunders was unarmed and had his hands spread out in front of him in a gesture of conciliation, but Grodin, armed with a double-barreled shotgun that he held across his chest, was continuing to scream. Saunders' calmness clearly infuriated Grodin, but had the opposite effect on the crowd. Wake could see that most of them had become quiet and were starting to listen to Saunders' words, spoken deliberately, with paternal affection.

"We have been driven from our country, yes. But do we stay victims or do we move forward? Do we perpetuate the hatred and death or do we decide to *live* life and make a peaceful future for our children? Aren't we tired of death and hate and fear? We came here to farm, not to fight, and certainly not to fight each other."

Grodin, shotgun held tightly, hands trembling, looked up at Saunders' face. "You coward! While I was marchin' in rags for three long damned years in Virginia with the Ninth, you were playing grandee in the islands. When the blue bellies came into my town an' burned down my brother's house, you were drinking rum with the ladies somewhere's safe. An' while my brother was takin' two days to die from a gut shot, you was countin' the money you made from runnin' fancy goods to Texas. Money you took from Southerners! You make me an' every true son of the South sick to even think of scum like you. . . ."

Wake saw that the crowd was no longer responding to

Grodin's tirade, but it was obvious that he wasn't aware of them anymore, only his hatred. Saunders tried again to placate him.

"Billy, I haven't suffered like you, that's true. But I'm not talking about the past. I'm talking about the future here. A good future. For our children and their children—"

Grodin stepped back and raised the shotgun, the muzzle a foot from Saunders' chest. He cocked the hammers back, screaming an animal-like shriek, and just as he pulled the shotgun's triggers three rapid pistol shots rang out.

The shotgun's blast went over Saunders' head as Grodin spun to the left and fell in a twitching pile on the ground, his eyes locking with Wake's for a split second. The crowd stood in a shocked tableau as Wake advanced out from the shadows with his navy Colt leveled, switching his target from Grodin to the Otra Vez men. Saunders was the first to move, kicking the shotgun away and bending over Grodin, searching his body for the wounds, but saw it was too late. The rounds had entered his chest from the side and it was only a matter of time.

Before Grodin's men recovered from their shock, Rork and four sailors trotted out of the dark on the other side of the gathering, pistols drawn. They spread out in a half circle and covered the men who slowly lowered their weapons, staring at the groaning figure in the dirt. Grodin had stopped moving but was emitting a low moan. Wake knew they had only seconds before the crowd could become dangerous again.

"Men, we came here in peace and were treated as *former* foes, with honor and friendship. We have responded in kind, and will continue to do so, and will help in any way we can. We share the same language, the same faith, and the same attitudes on so many things. All of us on both sides have been through too much in that war to go through it again. It's time to live in peace, as Mr. Saunders said, for our children's future."

The moaning stopped. Grodin's lifeless form was no longer the center of attention as Saunders went into the crowd, touching the men on their shoulders, calling them gently by their first names, looking into their eyes. "Go home everyone. It's over. The hate is over. . . ."

Expecting violence, Wake saw only sad resignation among the men as they listened to Saunders. Moments later, as the Otra Vez men trudged down the path carrying Grodin's body, Rork and the sailors formed a circle around Wake, still wary. Rork reported that the rest of the sailors were waiting at the boats and recommended they leave the settlement now. Saunders walked over to Wake. He had the same exhausted, sad-eyed look on his face that Wake had seen on many men after a battle. Saunders held out his hand.

"Thank you for saving my life, Peter Wake."

Wake shook the offered hand slowly. "I wish it hadn't been necessary, Jonathan. Are there more like him? What about those other men from his village?"

"They aren't as rabid as he is . . . or was. Grodin had the ability to stir them up, to make them boil with a hatred they didn't even understand. The others will be no problem. They might even move back to Por Fin. Otra Vez was Grodin's idea."

"I hope you're right on that. What about the authorities and this . . . this thing . . . tonight?"

"That could get complicated. I suggest you leave downriver now and let me take care of it. There will be enough witnesses to show it was justified, and I will personally take their statements to Don Fidel to make sure there are no repercussions."

"What about Velásquez?"

"He and Grodin were thick and he could be a problem, but I won't let him. I think those two were in cahoots together in some scheme to cut Don Fidel out of some monies due him from the Otra Vez farms. I believe now would be a good time to lay my suspicions before Don Fidel. The Grodin matter will pale, I assure you. Especially if you are gone and it is a *fait accompli*."

Wake suddenly remembered something else. "What about the local anti-Spanish rebels? Will this somehow aggravate them? I met one on the river named Soto. They seem to be against your settlement."

"I know him. He was mainly against Grodin and his farms using slaves, but yes, they are against all foreigners leasing land here. Can't say that I can fault them on that, and of course, I can sympathize with people fighting for their freedom." Saunders paused, then smiled. "But no, Soto will not be a problem on this. And it's my responsibility to try to forge a better future relationship with the local people, not just Don Fidel. I have a feeling that someday they'll be in charge, and we'd better make friends now, don't you agree? They know the difference between Grodin's village and this one. Even the name of his village is ironic."

"How so?"

"*Otra Vez* means 'once again'—as in the Confederacy, once again."

Wake felt a shiver in the tropical night. He started walking down the path, Saunders alongside, Rork and his sailors ahead and behind. Wake eyed Saunders closely, that last answer sparking a question in his mind.

"And what does Por Fin mean?"

Saunders stopped and put a hand on Wake's gold lace shoulder board as he gave his reply.

"It means 'at last,' Peter. As in we finally have peace, *at last. . . .*"

11
Looking Forward

They floated down the river in the darkness, without light or sound. They found the shoals when they smashed against the rocks, and the shoving and hauling through the shallow channels were done with a minimum of commands. Every man understood that they were far from the help of anyone aboard the *Hunt,* and though there was no declared war, each felt as if they were deep in enemy territory. They rowed under the mosquito netting, the drone of the insects occasionally interrupted by the cracking of a bamboo signal reporting their progress west toward the sea.

They moved without stopping for rest or refreshment, and by the following night the boats rounded the final bend of the river before it emptied out into the Caribbean, where their steamer lay at anchor. For the final half-mile they could see the lights of the steamer over the tops of the bushes and marsh grass. She was a beacon keeping up their spirits as they wound through the looping lower stream, taking in deep draughts of the sea air as they bent their backs at the oars in an effort to get home to their ship as fast as they could.

They could hear the crash of the surf as the mouth of the river became faintly visible in the starlight. Wake scanned the beach on either side of the opening and suddenly pounded Rork on the shoulder.

"There. Look over there to starboard."

Several men were standing at the water's edge, their forms black and sinister against the pale sand and starlit sky as they spread out in a skirmish line. Wake looked over at the other side and saw more men. Their boats were an easy shot at point blank range for the shadowy forms on the beach. A voice called out in a commanding tone. Aragón whispered to Wake.

"Sir, it's that Soto man again. He is ordering us to come to the shore. Starboard side, sir. He says they will open fire if we do not comply."

The ebb tide and oars were combining to give the boats four or five knots of speed. That was fast for a launch and dinghy, and Wake knew they could probably make it past the rebel guerrillas, but the cost in blood would be fearsome.

"Rork, steer for the starboard shore. No one goes for their weapons. We'll do this quietly and peaceably. We have no conflict with these people."

As the boats came to a halt in the shallows, Wake told Aragón to go ashore with him and Rork to stay in the boat. The rebels parted as the naval officer, Aragón behind him, sloshed up the beach to where Soto stood, legs apart and arms akimbo.

"Good evening, Señor Soto. We meet again. I wish it was a more pleasant occasion, without your men aiming muskets at us. There is no need for that."

"Good evening, Captain Wake. The need for the muskets arose when we saw boats coming rapidly down the river in the dark. It was very suspicious."

Wake stepped close to Soto, who was a head shorter but had the stocky build of a man with twenty years of lifting heavy loads in the fields.

"Mr. Soto, you knew it was us. You knew it from the bamboo signals and you still aimed guns at us. What do you want?"

Soto was not intimidated and spoke slowly. "Captain Wake, I want to give you and your government a message."

"Which is?"

"Do not come back. This is our island and our home. Not the home of the Spaniards, or the former Confederates, or the Yankees. Go back to your country. Tell the others not to come here. They are not welcome by the people who are the true owners of this land. We will not allow other countries to come here and make our life even more difficult, to rob us of our freedom and destiny."

Even in the other language Wake could feel the intensity of Soto's words. They came slowly, sadly, from the heart. Wake respected this man Soto, a peasant with a poet's passion and a captain's grit, and wondered what his destiny would be.

"I understand your message, Mr. Soto. Hear mine. The American people share your love of liberty. We wish you luck and hope that you will be able to peacefully attain your independence from Spain and the abolition of slavery. We are not like the Spanish, nor the former Confederates. We are not your enemies at all."

Wake knew he was on thin ground with his statement, which could be misinterpreted as an official endorsement of a budding revolution against the Spanish crown in Puerto Rico, but he also knew it was an accurate statement. The Americans were for the independence of the people of Cuba and Puerto Rico, and it was only a matter of time before events bore that out. Perhaps a few kind words now would reap benefits in years to come.

"Those words have a pretty sound, Captain Wake. The people of Puerto Rico will see if the Yankee deeds match them in the future. You may go now to your ship."

"Does your leader, Ramón Betances, share your dislike of us?"

"Doctor Betances has many American friends in New York

and elsewhere. But he has no illusions about the motives of many in your government and commerce. We will not exchange the burden of the Spanish for the burden of the Yankees. My message is simply a warning to those who would walk upon us, as others have done for the last three hundred years. Go on your voyage home."

Wake turned without further comment and waded out past the watching rebels to the launch. After climbing aboard and getting underway, Wake thought about Soto's message, the powerful emotion behind it, and what it might mean for Saunders and the settlers at Aldea Por Fin. Aragón was silent when the other men asked him in whispers about what had happened on the beach. No one in the boat crews spoke after that, and Rork could see Wake was in no mood to converse.

The cruise homeward to Key West was accompanied by easy weather, and a week and two ports later Fort Taylor hove into view. The day was a gorgeous affirmation of the splendor of the tropics in late January. A warm sun sparkled on the harbor waters ruffled by a light easterly breeze as the *Hunt* steamed up the channel to the naval wharf at Key West. The intrigues of the Spanish Empire were far behind them, and the sailors were planning their liberty ashore even before the lines were passed to the men on the dock.

Once secured, Wake made his way to the quarterdeck and descended to the wharf carrying the ship's document pouch full of monthly status reports and requests on such subjects as coal consumption, gunnery, provisions, purser disbursements, deck-log summaries, and engineering. But the most important report was the one addressed to R.S. Stanwell, Senior Deputy to the Assistant Secretary of the Navy. Written over three days, it detailed information about the ex-Confederate settlement at

Aldea Por Fin, on the Anasco River on the western coast of Puerto Rico.

Wake wrote in his report that the settlement posed no danger to the United States and might actually benefit the people of the island. He went on to suggest that a dialogue be opened with the settlers, with the Spanish authorities, and with the islanders along the remote western end of the island so that when the place separated from the Spanish Empire a rapport would have already been established. The incident with Grodin was not in the narrative. Wake covered that in a different report. Ten minutes after leaving the *Hunt* he was standing in front of the admiral and explaining what he had learned on his mission and about the shooting of the ex-Confederate.

Admiral Stroud listened, saying nothing until Wake had finished his story of everything that had happened in Puerto Rico and his opinions of the current situation and the future.

"Captain Wake, you say there was no other alternative to shooting this man?"

"It was a case of stopping a murder, sir. Saunders was defenseless."

Stroud set his jaw and sighed. "I see. Well, this is most unusual. Can't remember when a naval officer last shot a civilian in another country in this type of situation. I will forward the report on to Secretary Welles, of course, but it would appear there needs to be no other legal proceeding if the Spanish don't bring it up. And the Spanish have some other problems to deal with right about now, anyway. There's been a revolution of some sort in Spain and Queen Isabella is fleeing or something. You heard nothing of it in Puerto Rico?"

"No, sir. Communication with San Juan is slow and I saw no indication of disarray in the imperial forces, but then again I only ran into Captain Velásquez, sir. I wouldn't want to be him when freedom does come to the islanders. And it will, Admiral. Soto and Betances and men like them have the passion of liberty."

"Yes, I believe you're right on that. Perhaps you have at least started a rapport, who knows? The entire situation you were in was most unusual, Wake, most unusual. Why is it that it's always *you* that ends up in these kinds of things?"

"Just doing my duty, sir."

"Yes, well, your duty seems to take you along different paths from other captains in my squadron, young man. It appears you are a magnet for trouble, Wake. But somehow you get it turned around." Stroud smiled, shaking his head. "I'm not angry, just perplexed. Now, go and see to your ship and your men. By the way, the squadron is being redesignated as the West Indies Flotilla, a part of the Home Squadron. No longer an admiral's command. I'm retiring. You and your ship may be reassigned to another port soon. Orders will be forthcoming."

Wake had spent the last three years, his entire time in the navy, on ships out of Key West. He wondered about where he would go, and where his family could live. The idea that he even had a family was daunting to him.

"Aye, aye, sir. Do you have an idea where, Admiral?"

"They're putting a few ships at Pensacola, Wake. I think you'll go there. I'll see you again before I leave."

With a wave of his hand, Stroud dismissed Wake and returned his attention to the paperwork on his desk, leaving the lieutenant standing there for a moment trying to understand. Things were changing all over the service, and his return to the bureaucracy of the navy brought back Wake's fears for the future.

He picked up the ship's correspondence from the yeoman in the anteroom as he departed the building. The changes were already obvious at the naval station. There were only three yeoman now, most of the offices had been closed, and the warehouses full of supplies had been sold off. The boiler shops were shut down, the equipment dismantled and shipped to the larger naval yards.

As he walked out into the sunshine he saw that even the town of Key West was changing. Blue was not the predominant color worn by men on the street. The very air was more relaxed. The euphoria of the war's end seven months earlier was still felt—

it was fainter, but there. He wondered about Linda's uncle and what he would do. He wondered about her father and if he had been released from the war prison up north.

Most of all he wondered about Linda herself and his new baby. That the baby must be born by now was certain, and for the last several weeks he had fretted over the health of mother and child. Wake was frightened about the ordeal of childbirth, for he had heard stories of women dying or being so debilitated they never recovered fully. Useppa Island was far from reliable medical assistance, but Wake's fear was eased a bit by the knowledge that Sofira and the other women were there to help. Sofira's Indian ways with herbs sounded strange, but Linda had confidence in them. Wake felt ignorant about the matter, so he resigned himself as best he could to trusting Sofira.

A grinning Hostetler greeted him at the main deck as Wake came back aboard to the sound of the boatswains' pipe calls. The sideboys lined up and came to attention. It was the ceremonial sign of respect for the ship's captain and a warning to all aboard that he was back, but Wake had never put much weight in it. This time he noticed that his reception was grander than ever before and the executive officer saluted him with a formal crispness incongruous with his usual manner.

"Welcome home, sir. Before you become immersed in your many duties, may we impose to ask the captain to honor the ships' officers with his presence at our dinner at the Russell Hotel tonight? Some of the other officers from the squadron, I mean flotilla, will be there also, sir."

He had never received a formal invitation to dinner from his officers. It was not a huge group, for there were only two left—Hostetler and Ginaldi. Rork was still a petty officer, the temporary acting promotion rescinded at the end of the war. A nice dinner ashore with real food was a temptation, though the Russell was the most expensive place on the island.

"Sounds like an excellent idea, Mr. Hostetler. The captain would be delighted."

A discussion on coaling and provisioning the ship ensued and it was an hour before Wake could get into the privacy of his cabin and check the correspondence for news of Linda.

Most of the correspondence was private letters, with only a few official orders. Normally he read the official correspondence first, then savored his personal letters when he had more time, but this was different. He put the official dark blue envelopes aside and went through the letter bundles.

The *Hunt's* mail had arrived over a month earlier, and there were letters waiting for many in the crew, bundled according to officers, petty officers, and non-rated. Wake saw that Rork had one from Ireland, probably from his sister or mother. The officers' bundle included five for Ginaldi, which made Wake laugh. They were from separate women in New York, Philadelphia, and Baltimore. Wake couldn't imagine trying to handle that load of worries. In the same bundle Wake saw two envelopes addressed to him. One was thin, from Massachusetts, and the other was thick, from Useppa Island. His hands trembled as he tore open the flap trying not to rip the pages inside, frustrated that it was taking so long to open.

As usual she had written a little bit each day, page after page, then hurriedly sealed them all in a large envelope when the occasional ship stopped by to collect the mail for Key West. He searched it quickly, casting the pages off as he looked for the crucial information about the birth, his finger following the lines as he mouthed the words. Day after day she wrote of her anticipation, her knowledge that the event was drawing near, making his nervousness mount until he thought he might start to shout with despair.

Then he saw it. December 13th. Six weeks later. Tears flowed from him as he read it.

Sunday, December 13th, 1866

I write this after a very long day. It was not an easy day, in fact it was the hardest day of my life, but now I feel as if everything I have ever done, all that I have endured, and the many twists of fate that brought us together and brought me here to this island, were preparations for this day. Oh Peter, today we were blessed with a little baby girl. She is absolutely beautiful. Healthy and active and smiles all the time. She has your eyes, and definitely your lungs! A quarterdeck shout, I think you'd call it.

Sofira and the other ladies did everything for me while I was in labor. It took eight hours and sixteen minutes, from half past four in the morning until just before one o'clock in the afternoon—I knew you would want the details! I admit I was frightened but Sofira made some herbal tea that calmed me. The others sang chants and held me. Even little Rain helped with wet cloths and gentle words. I have been there when other women had their babies but didn't quite understand. Now I do. It is very hard to explain in a letter.

I am just fine. A little weak but Sofira says that is to be expected. I'll get better. The baby nurses well and I will be up out of bed tomorrow. Peter, we have a baby now, a little miniature person, a helpless life that is in our hands. I want to give her the best future we can. Maybe now that the war is over we can do that.

I know we talked about girls' names and that I wanted to name her after my mother, but I have changed my mind. I know my mother would not object at all, she would be happy. I hope you'll understand and agree. I've named her Useppa, darling, because of the peace and happiness I've found here. That is what I want for her. She is all that we could hope for. I could think of no better name for her.

Useppa is next to me now, sleeping. Her tiny face is so adorable. I think she'll be a daddy's girl, and I will have to watch you carefully, lest you spoil her too much! One look at those eyes and you'll be under her spell. I wish with all my heart you were here too, warm and strong and holding me. I love you so much and need you now more than ever. We have so much to do and to live for now. The days to come will be good, Peter, and the three of us will make it through

anything. I feel better and stronger in my soul than ever before.
  Touching you with love in my dreams,
  Linda

Wake struggled to regain his composure, but he couldn't. He wanted to be there. He could see them both there and wanted to be next to them. He gradually calmed as his New England Yankee core took over and he started to assess the situation. A baby girl, named Useppa. Everyone was healthy. Linda was fine. Useppa. He liked that name. It had so many good memories, so many visions that filled his mind with the beauty of the tropics. It was a perfect name for her. He sat there on the edge of his bed, papers scattered around him, and thought about the most important promotion in his life. Peter Wake was now father to a little girl. It was an incredible responsibility.

He reread every page of her letter, touching the ink, imagining Linda penning the words, as he learned of each day's events, before and after the birth. An hour later he thought of the other letters scattered about and abruptly called for his steward to take them to the various messes that were waiting for them.

He grimly opened the blue envelopes. One was a communication to the admiral, copied to the commanding officer of the *Hunt,* notifying him that the ship was now designated as a fourth-rate gunboat, not an armed tug. Wake knew that it was a political ploy, for as a fourth-rate gunboat she would be considered part of the combatant strength of the navy, even though her twelve-pounders were useless against any modern warship. The next envelope contained his orders as captain. The admiral was correct—Pensacola was to be the *Hunt's* next duty station. She was to report there as soon as possible, refit, and assume duties with the West Indies Flotilla of the Home Squadron of the United States Navy.

He surveyed the documents again. There were no personal orders for him, only to the ship. He had been aboard the *Hunt* for over a year. With the number of officers competing for ship commands, he had expected to be let go after a year so that another could get command time. He searched the pouch one more time, but there were no other official envelopes. His dread of being left on the beach on half-pay was not diminished, and his curiosity was increased. It became obvious to Wake that the orders had gotten lost between Washington and Key West. They would turn up eventually, and in the meantime he had to start thinking about how he would provide for his family.

There was no opportunity in New England for him. The family's lone remaining schooner was in the hands of his brother. Other ships were already manned and officered. Beside that, he didn't want to live there anymore, and he was sure that Linda would not like the bitter cold and harshness. If the navy let him go he would have to find an opportunity somewhere down here in the Gulf of Mexico or the Caribbean.

The loom of the lights from the Russell Hotel shone out along Duval Street, illuminating the comings and goings of the prominent citizenry on a Saturday night in Key West. The sounds of men in the barroom washed over Wake as he entered and shouldered his way through the few blue coats and the many brown, black, and gray. He found Hostetler and Ginaldi sitting at a table in the far corner, with several other officers standing around them, including Lieutenants Walker, Taylor, and Williams. Hostetler's stentorian voice boomed out above the crowd.

"Ah, gentlemen. The man of the hour has arrived! Come over here, sir. Your friends and disciples have gathered."

Wake sat down and accepted hearty congratulations on fatherhood from all around him—evidently the word had spread quickly after he had told Rork and Hostetler. The manager informed them their table was ready in the dining room and the entourage marched through the crowd into the dining room. As he pulled back his chair, Wake heard a feminine voice, sultry and coy.

"My word. The hero who saved me has returned from sea."

Though it came from behind he suspected who it was and frowned. Wake saw Walker attempt to stifle a smile. That confirmed for him whom the voice belonged to.

"Mrs. Williams. How are you this evening?"

"Making do, Peter. Making do."

She looked prettier than ever. Her golden hair was done up in some sort of twist and she was wearing a stylish pink dress with beading. Wake had heard somewhere that beading was expensive. A glittering necklace draped across her chest just above her cleavage. Obviously she had done well in Key West. His mind had a fleeting image of her in a worn and dirty gingham dress on the deck of his ship as they cleaned the decks of blood after the fight aboard the slaver. He felt himself blush as he realized that the other officers were watching intently.

"By appearances you are more than making do, ma'am."

"Ma'am? No need for such formality between us, is there, Peter? I hear you are back from the Spanish islands. Puerto Rico, I believe."

Wake had long ago given up confidence that anything supposedly secret, like their mission to survey the former Confederate settlements, would actually stay that way for very long. Cynda Denaud Williams had a way, not very subtle, of finding out what she wanted. For the tenth time he was amazed at her. The woman had nerve, that was never in doubt.

"Yes, I am back from those islands. And how is your lovely sister, Mary Alice?"

"She's decided to become a shopgirl. Wants to stay here. Her choice. That and tending the blacks occupy her time."

"The former slaves? How are they?"

"Learning. Slowly, but learning. Someday they may even make a positive part of the community. Mary Alice will be very proud."

Wake remembered her begging him to help her, for the sake of her poor victimized slaves. It was chilling how she could change personalities. He wondered which one was the real Cynda. Perhaps there was no real personality, only adjustments to necessity.

"I'm sure she will, as she should be. I hope she does well here. You sound as if you want to leave the island."

"I am. I am going to where you just came from. Por Fin."

Wake's surprise showed clearly. She laughed.

"The word has been out for some time, Peter. Don't look so shocked. There are settlements all over the Caribbean. Por Fin is one of the best. I am headed there to join friends from my earlier years. It's best I go anyway. I am not appreciated here." She glanced at the officers conversing at the table behind him, particularly Walker. "And I know it. The town's people and the navy officers have had their fun at my expense and I am leaving. I have nowhere else to go. At least I'll be among my own there."

"Well, I wish you luck, then. It is a good settlement. I think it has a good future."

She demurely lowered her face and looked up at him. "I hope to see you there someday, Peter. It would be very nice to be with you again. I'll always remember that evening in the little hut."

It made him angry that she thought he would be susceptible to such an obvious ploy. It is time to end this, Wake decided.

"Mrs. Williams, I simply evacuated you and the others during time of war, nothing more." His voice was unmistakably harsh. "I am very proud that we were able to liberate those slaves before they were taken to Cuba, and glad they are making progress in their assimilation. Good-bye, and good luck at Por Fin, ma'am. I cannot imagine that I will see you again."

Wake turned around with a glower and saw that every man at the table was staring. Cynda Williams said nothing in reply and walked quickly away out of the room. Wake sat down and slapped the table.

"The war is over and I am done with the former enemy, gentlemen. All that is in the past. I think I need a drink. Some rum perhaps?"

A roar of laughter came forth from the officers and Hostetler suggested that they order dinner.

The evening progressed, enlivened by stories of past exploits and speculation on future adventures. Wake wished Rork could be there, but his Irish friend was not an officer and could not sit with them. Someday, Wake promised himself, Rork *will be* an officer and sit in the company of men like these. With the war over and promotion rare, especially from the ranks, it would be difficult, but it would be one of his goals if he could stay in.

This brought to his mind the uncertainty of his professional career, of whether he would even be on active duty six months from then. He looked around at the others and wondered if they were as worried about that as he was. Few were married and none had children. It would take some type of influence to maintain his career as a lowly lieutenant, or even maintain employment, let alone to propel him above the surrounding junior officers and make the decision-makers in Washington notice him. There was little chance of that on this station.

Among the men, there was the unspoken realization that this would probably be their last gathering since the squadron was going through its final reassignment. The gaiety near the end of the evening had a tinge of regret and Wake looked closely at each man around the table to remember him and the moment years hence.

As the waiter finished pouring another round of rum, Hostetler suddenly rose holding a newspaper in his right hand. His voice, slightly slurred, rang out across the dining room, which was empty but for the naval officers' table.

"Gentlemen, gentlemen, pipe down and stow. Pipe down now."

Wake chuckled as he noticed his executive officer sway, then recover, standing wide-legged like a sailor in a storm on a tossing deck. Hostetler continued when it grew quiet.

"Tonight, gentlemen, we celebrate several things. Momentous events swirl around our gallant brother officer here," he pointed an unsteady hand at Wake, "like the winds of a hurricane. But our Captain Wake tames those winds and makes 'em fair for all of us. Ne'er seen such as he afore and I won't again with any other man. He's one in a thousand."

Cheers and applause greeted Hostetler's pronouncement. The gaze of his friends started to embarrass Wake and he was about to say something to change the topic, but Ginaldi held up his hand and stood.

"I want to say, as an engineer, that I wish all captains were as decent to their engineers as Captain Wake is to me. A sailor born and bred, he leaves the mechanics to me and doesn't interfere or expect miracles." Ginaldi belched and received cackles of laughter in response. "Oh God, but that others up on deck would do the same!"

Ginaldi was the only engineer officer present and he received good-natured jeers as he fell back down into his seat. Hostetler, still standing with one hand holding on to the shoulder of Lieutenant Taylor seated next to him, resumed his speech.

"As I was attempting to say before I was so hilariously interrupted from the gang below decks," he swung around and leered at the engineer, "our own Captain Wake has been promoted to the rank of father, something none of the rest of us has achieved and a position of unequaled importance to the future of the world. I raise my glass to him in salute."

A chorus of "hear, hear" followed as the waiter flitted around between the men and refilled the glasses again. Hostetler was not done yet, Wake could see.

"And so, it would appear, my friends, that Captain Wake's personal life, with his lovely bride and beautiful little baby girl, has a wonderful future. A future of love and happiness."

Wake laughed and nodded his agreement as more cheers and table pounding ensued until Hostetler held up a wagging finger.

"But what of his professional future, gentlemen? In these

uncertain times for a naval officer, no one knows how long they will be employed." He paused and looked down at his captain. "Captain Wake has no relatives in high places, no political connections, and has never been a sycophant seeking favor. Captain Wake hasn't had time for that—he and his men have been out on the sea getting things done. Getting the work of this navy done. Leading from a deck. Making the decisions at the time, rather than reviewing them in an office a month later," he pounded his glass down on the table so hard Wake thought it would shatter, "and therefore he would probably not stand a chance in this navy anymore!"

The officers grumbled and nodded their heads. The rum had mellowed Wake but he was starting to become uncomfortable. Hostetler was beginning to cross the line of subordination and respect for the senior leaders of the navy. Wake started to rise but Ginaldi grasped his arm, shaking his head as Hostetler went on.

"Except for one apparently little thing, gentlemen. One apparently little thing that a member of our civil society would not quite appreciate, but we navy men know is a huge recognition of our gallant captain's deeds."

Wake suddenly became aware that the others already knew what Hostetler was talking about. Everyone was smiling at him, waiting for Hostetler to release the information. Hostetler held the newspaper up again and spread it out.

"Gentlemen, I have here the only copy in Key West of the December 1865 issue of the *Navy Gazetteer*. Careers are made or broken in the *Navy Gazetteer*. We all hope for the day we will be mentioned, for that day will ensure that our work is recognized at the highest levels. Gentlemen, today one of us has. Our very own, Captain Peter Wake!"

Wake sat there stunned as the men around him went wild with cheers, yelling and pounding the table and coming over to shake his hand. Hostetler shouted above the din and they quieted down.

"Gentlemen, it seems that the powers that be in Washington

have been apprised of the work of Captain Peter Wake, and I quote. 'Lieutenant Peter Wake, commanding officer of the armed tug *Hunt,* attached to the East Gulf Blockading Squadron out of Key West commanded by Rear Admiral Cornelius Stroud, was instrumental in achieving the bloodless victory in Havana harbor over the Confederate oceangoing ironclad raider *Phoenix,* which had threatened a major naval action long after the surrender of the main enemy forces elsewhere. Should that action have taken place, there is no doubt that victory by our brave Navy would have been won eventually, but most certainly at a horrific cost in men and ships, as the *Phoenix* was a most powerful ship and more than a match for any two of ours.'" The room was silent as Hostetler paused for breath before reading on.

"'Lieutenant Wake went ashore at the harbor of Matanzas, proceeded overland to Havana and there, by force of personality and persuasion, made his way through the infamous and intricate intrigue of that port, preempting the impending battle before it began. The means and procedures of his mission are confidential but the results are most certainly not. With the surrender of the enemy ship and crew in the harbor, the lives of hundreds of men on both sides were spared, and a useless battle averted.'"

Hostetler paused again, this time for dramatic effect.

"'Men in our Navy with bravery are common and well known. But men like Lieutenant Wake, with judgment, diplomacy, and verve, as well as bravery, stand out even further and much is expected in the future from this officer.'"

Hostetler handed the newspaper to Wake, who sat there trying to make sense of it all amid the pandemonium of the celebrating officers. It was the hope of all officers to get an honorable mention in the *Navy Gazetteer,* but this mention was a virtual guarantee of a future for his career, even in the tiny peacetime navy. His greatest worry evaporated as he realized that his family's future was financially secure now.

Wake stood as the men around him shook his hand and shouted their congratulations, spilling rum and beer while they draped their arms around his neck. He stood there smiling and laughing and nodding, but his mind was visualizing a different place and time, in the near future.

He had been to that place and could see it clearly—a darkened room in a thatched hut on the side of a hill on a little island called Useppa, where a woman and her baby lay cuddled sleeping together, waiting for their man to come home.

For the first time in a long time, Peter Wake looked forward to the future.

Author's Note

Many of the story lines that unfold in this book are based on actual historical events, as documented in the Official Records. They have been fictionalized to fit into the format of this series. For instance, a U.S. Navy gunboat did disappear in December 1864 and was later found obliterated off Marco Island. The cause of the tragedy was never certain. And there was a powerful Confederate ocean raider that showed up in Havana a month after Lee surrendered in 1865, and brought the East Gulf Blockading Squadron for a short time to the brink of a horrific sea battle—just as everyone else was preparing to go home from the war. The more I study those men, the more in awe of them I become. We should never forget them.

Robert N. Macomber

Acknowledgments

To Dena Macomber who, incredibly, kept the old computer running, even when I just wanted to shoot the damn thing. I still don't know how she did it.

To those unsung men of the Department of the Navy, who a century ago compiled the *Official Records of the Union and Confederate Navies in the War of the Rebellion*. They were, in succession over the years: Professor J. R. Soley, Lt. Commander F. M. Wise, Lt. Commander Richard Rush, Professor Edward K. Rawson, and Mr. Charles W. Stewart. This daunting task took them twenty years, from 1884 to 1904, and resulted in a work that even today, with all of our modern research aids, astounds for its conciseness, completeness, and searchability.

To the best editor I've ever worked alongside, June Cussen. And also to her outstanding production crew, particularly Shé Heaton. Their patience and positive professionalism provide a standard by which I judge all other organizations in the literary business.

To the gifted novelist Randy Wayne White, a fellow islander and subtle mentor in this very odd profession, who let me know where the minefields are.

To the helpful historians, curators, and staff of the many museums and libraries I have sought assistance from, including: the Historical Division of the Department of the Navy; the Cultural Museum of Rincón, Puerto Rico; the Naval Historical Foundation; the National Archives and Records Administration; the National Ocean and Atmospherics Agency, and Cornell University.

And finally, but most especially, to two fine novelists, Roothee Gabay and Dian Werhle, who several years ago made the fateful decision to sign on with Peter Wake and me. Like good shipmates over many cruises, they're always there to share the experience, both at work and on liberty, good times and bad.

Thank you all.

Onward and upward!
Robert N. Macomber
At sea off Sanibel Island, Florida
January 2004

If you enjoyed reading this book, here are some other books from Pineapple Press on related topics. For a complete catalog, write to Pineapple Press, P.O. Box 3889, Sarasota, FL 34230 or call 1-800-PINEAPL (746-3275). Or visit our website at www.pineapplepress.com.

Point of Honor by Robert N. Macomber. Winner of the Florida Historical Society's 2003 Patrick Smith Award for Best Florida Fiction. In this prequel to *Honorable Mention,* it is 1864 and Lt. Peter Wake, United States Navy, assisted by his indomitable Irish bosun, Sean Rork, commands the naval schooner *St. James.* He searches for army deserters in the Dry Tortugas, finds an old nemesis during a standoff with the French Navy on the coast of Mexico, starts a drunken tavern riot in Key West, and confronts incompetent Federal army officers during an invasion of upper Florida. ISBN 1-56164-2740-3 (hb)

At the Edge of Honor by Robert N. Macomber. Winner of the Military Order of the Stars and Bars 2003 Cooke Fiction Award. This Civil War novel, the prequel to *Point of Honor,* takes the reader into the steamy world of Key West and the Caribbean in 1863 and introduces Peter Wake, the reluctant New England volunteer officer who finds himself battling the enemy on the coasts of Florida, sinister intrigue in Spanish Havana and the British Bahamas, and social taboos in Key West when he falls in love with the daughter of a Confederate zealot. ISBN 1-56164-252-5 (hb), 1-56164-272X (pb)

Confederate Money by Paul Varnes. Two young men from Florida set out on an adventure during the Civil War to exchange $25,000 in Confederate dollars for silver that will hold its value if the Union wins. Training to be physicians, they get mixed up in some of the war's bloodiest battles, including the largest battle fought in Florida, at Olustee. Along the way, they meet historical characters like Generals Grant and Lee, tangle with criminals, become heroes, and fall in love. ISBN 1-56164- 271-1 (hb)

A Yankee in a Confederate Town by Calvin L. Robinson. Edited by Anne Robinson Clancy, the author's great-granddaughter, this personal journal follows a loyal Unionist who loses his business and home, his money, and nearly his life in Civil War–era Jacksonville, Florida, when he refuses to join the Secessionist movement. A fascinating, true account of a pivotal time in U.S. history. ISBN 1-56164-267-3 (hb)

Discovering the Civil War in Florida by Paul Taylor. The Civil War in Florida may not have been the scene for decisive battles everyone remembers, but Florida played her part. From Marianna and Tallahassee in northwest Florida to Fort Myers and Key West in the south, this book covers the land and sea skirmishes that made Florida a bloody battleground for four sad years. ISBN 1-56164- 234-7 (hb); ISBN 1-56164- 235-5 (pb)

200 Quick Looks at Florida History by James Clark. Florida has a long and complex history, but few of us have time to read it in depth. So here are 200 quick looks at Florida's 10,000 years of history from the arrival of the first natives to the present, packed with unusual and little-known facts and stories. ISBN 1-56164- 200-2 (pb)

Florida Portrait by Jerrell Shofner. Packed with hundreds of photos, this word-and-picture album traces the history of Florida from the Paleo-Indians to the rampant growth of the late twentieth century. ISBN 1-56164-121-9 (pb)